Writings about John Cage

Writings about John Cage

Edited by

Richard Kostelanetz

Paul Bowles, William Brooks, Joseph Byrd, John Cage, Deborah Campana, Daniel Charles, Henry Cowell, Merce Cunningham, Eric De Visscher, Thomas DeLio, Anne d'Harnoncourt, Peter Dickinson, Henry Flynt, Peggy Glanville-Hicks, Lou Harrison, Hans G. Helms, John Hollander, Jill Johnston, Petr Kotik, Jonathan Scott Lee, Jackson Mac Low, Roger Maren, Heinz-Klaus Metzger, Michael Nyman, Manfredi Piccolonimi, Edward Rothstein, Eric Salzman, Natalie Crohn Schmitt, Stuart Saunders Smith, Ellsworth Snyder, James Tenney, Virgil Thomson, Calvin Tomkins, David Vaughan, Christian Wolff, Peter Yates, Paul Zukofsky, and the editor.

THE UNIVERSITY OF MICHIGAN PRESS

Ann Arbor

Published in the United States of America by
The University of Michigan Press
Manufactured in the United States of America

1996 1995 1994 1993 4 3 2 1

Library of Congress Cataloging-in-Publication Data

Writings about John Cage / edited by Richard Kostelanetz.
p. cm.
Includes bibliographical references and index.
ISBN 0-472-10348-2
1. Cage, John—Criticism and interpretation. I. Kostelanetz, Richard.
ML410.C24W7 1993
780'.92-dc20 92-32218
CIP
MN

Especially for Lars-Gunnar Bodin and the
Electronic Music Studio of Stockholm

The silence we preserve after an experience is a space, created for us as the space of the experience, within which, and on which, we dwell, prolonging the experience, extending it, culminating it, in order to *have* it, progressively, in more significant degree.

Our meta-experiential conversation is like the sound after a sound, in music, which amplifies the silence-resonant aftersound space to extend, to culminate, to cultivate, to—yet further—have the experience our conversation is trying to keep us alive within.

And discourse extends the effort to retain and protract experience to a maximum frontier of time, space, and awareness.

—Benjamin Boretz, *Talk* (1985)

Unfortunately, with the last and highest category of artist—the genius—the test of time comes too late. For when alive he will probably defy recognition by signs. Either he resembles ordinary men too much for our storybook minds, or he gives so few proofs of worldly judgment that it is hard to credit him with any capacity whatever, or again the mixture in him of talent and folly, or talent and turpitude, discourages further inquiry.

It is safer to go to the work than to the man. But the work, the masterpiece, presents difficulties of its own, the chief of which is that it usually does not correspond to any established taste, however sophisticated, and hence is literally of no use. In effect, no one really wants a masterpiece, there is no demand for it, which is why it ultimately signifies an addition to our riches. The only desire for it at first is in the breast of the maker and it is for this that he is called a creator. After a while we see that he belongs to a tradition, that he has forged the next link in a chain, but this hindsight takes a great deal of effort, and often requires the removal of the rubbish that stood between the masterpiece and the world, namely the rubbish of pseudo-art representing as real a world departed.

—Jacques Barzun, "Art Against Society" (1951)

Preface

Though several scholars have finished doctoral theses on John Cage, no one has yet published a full-length critical monograph on work that ranks, by common consent, among the most extraordinary achievements in modern arts. Until such a long-awaited book is published, it seems appropriate to collect an anthology of essays from my fellow Cage critics, writing about various aspects of his activity in a variety of ways. One measure of the weight of an artist is the wealth of critical literature engendered by his or her work. Two rules in selecting Cage criticism were that nothing here should be currently available in a book in print and that reviews of individual concerts would be acceptable only if they appeared before the mid-1950s, when a genuine critical literature begins. (Reviews of Cage's works in other arts could still be reprinted because, even by now, little extended criticism of them exists.) I thought of reprinting Michael Hicks's exhaustive investigation into Cage's early professional history ("John Cage's Studies with Schoenberg," *American Music* [Summer 1990]), but decided it was less criticism than history. James Pritchett's "From Choice to Chance: John Cage's Concerto for Prepared Piano" (1988) would have been here, were it not so long and its author reluctant to make an abridgment. (Besides, Pritchett may well be the first to publish the kind of book described at the beginning of this preface.) I thought of doing a brief history of Cage criticism, to appear as an introduction; but since this manuscript was limited in advance to a certain length, criticism took precedence over criticism-of-criticism. I initially planned to include previously unpublished criticism, especially from those doctoral essays mentioned previously; but since a book could be made from material already in print, it seemed best to leave unpublished Cage criticism to the next editor.

I wish I could have included some of those passing encomia that contribute so much to our understanding of Cage and his influence. Back in 1946, the composer Elliot Carter, in the course of reviewing recent dance concerts for *Modern Music,* identified "one by Merce Cunningham, called *Mysterious Adventure,* to an ingenious fancy of John Cage for prepared piano. The score, a maze of shivery strange and delicate noises, is a play of sound with neutral content and mood which allowed the dancers great latitude." A quarter-century later, in his introduction to *The Collected Poems of Frank O'Hara* (1971), John Ashbery wrote:

> We were both tremendously impressed by David Tudor's performance at a concert on New Year's Day 1952 of John Cage's "Music of Changes," a piano work lasting over an hour and consisting, as I recall, entirely of isolated autonomous tone-clusters seemingly at random all over the keyboard. It was aleatory music, written by throwing coins in a method adapted from the *I Ching.* The actual mechanics of the method escaped me then as it does now; what mattered was that chance elements could combine to produce so beautiful and cogent a work. It was a further, perhaps for us ultimate, proof not so much of "Anything goes" but "Anything can come out."

An ironic appraisal of Cage's presence in the early 1950s appeared in John Gruen's memoir, *The Party's Over Now* (1972), where he quotes the painter Elaine de Kooning.

> [Arts critic] Harold Rosenberg . . . surveyed a full house before a Cage-Cunningham concert and said in his booming voice, "Here it is almost curtain time and [the painter Ibram] Lassaws aren't here yet." Everyone doubled up laughing. We all attended every event, and everyone in the audience knew everyone else.

Buried in the literature about contemporary art are many more like these, perhaps to be collected in yet another book.

My original plan was to include more essays initially published in languages other than English, from writers other than Daniel Charles (whose essays here were originally written in both his native French and his own English) and Heinz-Klaus Metzger, Cage's most persistent European critics; however, the few other examples that came to my attention were not worth reprinting. Perhaps suitable essays in German, Italian, Japanese, and so on will emerge when this anthology is translated, as it should be, into other languages. (The reason I am doing this book, rather than assigning it to someone else, remembering my rule never to do anything professionally that someone else can do better, is that I've done anthologies of *criticism* before.)

I am grateful to Joyce Harrison and her colleagues at the University of Michigan Press for commissioning *Writings about John Cage* as an appropriate sequel to earlier books of mine published elsewhere, then to Don Gillespie for guiding me through the criticism he has collected as Cage's editor at C. F. Peters, to Martin Erdmann for his incomparable bibliography of Cage criticism in several languages, to Deborah Campana for rescuing obscure materials from the John Cage Archive at Northwestern, to Frans van Rossum for sharing his discovery of the 1934 Cage-Cowell colloquy, to Anne Del Castillo for her editorial assistance, and finally to the contributors for granting me permission to reprint their materials.

This book would been dedicated to its subject, had he not already received another book of mine, *Recyclings* (1984); it might have been dedicated to his longtime coconspirator, Merce Cunningham, had he, too, not received yet another book of mine, *American Imaginations* (1983). And so it goes to the composer Lars-Gunnar Bodin, whose invitation to the Electronic Music Studio of Stockholm prompted me to advance my compositional activities far beyond what I had previously imagined. Thanks again, Lars-Gunnar. And thanks again, John, now no longer with us, for letting me do so much with/about your work, both explicitly and implicitly.

Acknowledgments

Paul Bowles, "Percussionists in Concert Led by John Cage," *New York Herald Tribune,* 8 February 1943, reprinted from the public domain by permission of the author.

William Brooks, [*16 Dances*], reprinted from the notes to CP 2 (15) by permission of the author; "*Roaratorio* Appraisiated," reprinted from *ISAM Newsletter* 12, no. 1 (May 1983), by permission of the author and publisher. Copyright © 1983 by the Institute for Studies in American Music, Brooklyn College.

Joseph Byrd, notes on *Variations IV,* reprinted by permission of the author.

John Cage, "Counterpoint," reprinted from *Dune Forum* 1, no. 2 (14 February 1934), by permission of the author.

Deborah Campana, "On Cage's *String Quartet in Four Parts,*" excerpted from *Revue d'Esthetique* 13–15 (1987–88), by permission of the author; English version copyright © 1992 by Deborah Campana.

Daniel Charles, "About John Cage's 'Prepared Piano,'" reprinted from *Ubi Fluxus 1990* (Milan: Mazzotti), by permission of the author; "De-Linearizing Musical Continuity," reprinted from *Discourse* 12, no. 1 (Fall-Winter 1989–90), and *Musicworks* 52 (Spring 1992), by permission of the author and the publishers; "Figuration and Prefiguration," English translation (by Susan Park, Geneva) reprinted from the catalog of the *Video Independents* exhibition (Geneva: Swiss Independent Video, 1991), by permission of the author and Mme. Lysianne Lechot.

Henry Cowell, "Double Counterpoint," reprinted from *Dune Forum* 1, no. 3 (15 March 1934), by permission of Ms. Sidney Cowell.

Merce Cunningham, "Music and Dance," reprinted from *Keynote,* September 1982, by permission of the author and publisher.

Eric De Visscher, "'There's no such thing as silence . . .': John Cage's Poetics of Silence," reprinted from *Interface* 18 (1989) as revised for *Musicworks* 52 (Spring 1992), by permission of the author.

Thomas DeLio, "Structure as Context," reprinted from *Interface* 17 (1988), by permission of the author, who also obtained reprint permissions for the examples.

Anne d'Harnoncourt, "We Have Eyes as Well as Ears . . . ," reprinted from *A Tribute to John Cage* (Solway Gallery, 1987), by permission of the author.

Peter Dickinson, "Cage *String Quartet,*" reprinted from *Music and Musicians* (1972), by permission of the author.

Henry Flynt, "Cage and Fluxus," revised from *Mutations of the Vanguard* (privately published, 1990), by permission of the author. Copyright © 1990 by Henry A. Flynt, Jr.

Peggy Glanville-Hicks, ". . . A Ping, Qualified by a Thud," reprinted from *Musical America,* September 1948, by permission of the publisher and Shane Simpson, Sydney, Australia, for the Estate of Peggy Glanville-Hicks.

Lou Harrison, "Ajemian-Masselos," reprinted from *New York Herald Tribune,* 11 December 1946, by permission of the author.

Hans G. Helms, "John Cage's Lecture 'Indeterminacy,'" reprinted from the English-language edition of *Die Reihe* 5 (1961), by permission of the author.

John Hollander, "Silence," reprinted from *Perspectives of New Music* 1, no. 2 (Spring 1963), by permission of the author and the publisher. Copyright © 1962, 1990 by John Hollander.

Jill Johnston, "Cage and Modern Dance," reprinted from *The New American Arts* (Horizon Press, 1965), by permission of the author.

Richard Kostelanetz, "Beginning with Cage," reprinted from notes to Wergo 60152/55 (1979), by permission of the publisher; "John Cage as a *Hörspielmacher,*" reprinted from *Journal of Musicology* 8, no. 2 (Spring 1990), by permission of the author and University of California Press; "John Cage's Longest and Best Poem," reprinted from *Notes* (June 1991), by permission of the author; "The Development of His Visual Art," reprinted from *Boulevard* (1991), by permission of the author.

Petr Kotik, "On John Cage," reprinted from program note to S.E.M. Ensemble concert, February 1992, by permission of the author. Copyright © 1992 by Petr Kotik.

Jonathan Scott Lee, "Mimêsis and Beyond: Mallarmé, Boulez, and Cage," reprinted from *boundary 2* 15, nos 1–2 (Fall 1986–Winter 1987), by permission of Duke University Press and the author. Copyright © 1986 by *boundary 2.*

Jackson Mac Low, "Something about the Writings of John Cage," revised from a version appearing in *Music Sound Language Theater* (Crown Point, 1980), by permission of the author. Copyright © 1991 by Jackson Mac Low.

Roger Maren, review of *A Year from Monday,* reprinted by *Perspectives of New Music* 6, no. 2 (Spring-Summer 1968), by permission of the author.

Heinz-Klaus Metzger, "Europe's Opera," reprinted from *John Cage Europeras 1 & 2* (Oper Frankfurt, 1987), by permission of the publisher.

Michael Nyman, "Cage and Satie," reprinted from *Musical Times* (1973), by permission of the author. Copyright © 1973 by Michael Nyman.

Manfredi Piccolomini, "*Europeras,*" reprinted from *Contemporanea* 1, no. 4 (November–December 1988), by permission of the author.

Edward Rothstein, "Cage's Cage," *New Republic,* 29 May 1990, by permission of the publisher.

Eric Salzman, "Imaginary Landscaper," reprinted from *Keynote,* September 1982, by permission of the author and the publisher, copyright © 1982 by GAF Broadcasting Company, Inc.; "Cage's Well-Tampered Clavier," reprinted from *Musical Quarterly* (1978), by permission of the author and the publisher. Copyright © 1978 Oxford University Press–*The Musical Quarterly.* Used with permission.

Natalie Crohn Schmitt, "John Cage in a New Key," reprinted from *Perspectives of New Music,* 20, nos. 1 and 2 (Fall-Winter 1981/Spring-Summer 1982), by permission of the author and the publisher.

Stuart Saunders Smith, "The Early Percussion Music of John Cage," reprinted from *Percussionist* 16, no. 1 (Fall 1978), by permission of the author.

Ellsworth Snyder, "Gertrude Stein and John Cage," *Open Letter,* 3d ser., 7 (Summer 1977), by permission of the author.

James Tenney, "John Cage and the Theory of Harmony," revised from *Soundings* 13 (1983) and *Musicworks,* by permission of the author. Copyright © 1983 by James Tenney.

Virgil Thomson, "The Abstract Composers," reprinted from *New York Herald-Tribune,* 5 February 1952; "John Cage Late and Early," reprinted from *Saturday Review,* 30 January 1960, both by permission of Ellis J. Friedman, executor of the Thomson estate.

Calvin Tomkins, "Social Concern," reprinted from *New York Times Book Review,* 21 January 1968, by permission of the author.

David Vaughan, "Merce Cunningham: Origins and Influences," reprinted from *Dance Theatre Journal* 1, no. 1 (Spring 1983), by permission of the author and the publisher.

Christian Wolff, "On Form," reprinted from *Die Reihe* 7 (1960), by permission of the author; "New and Electronic Music," reprinted from *Audience* (1957–58), by permission of the author.

Peter Yates, "Two Albums by John Cage," reprinted from *Arts and Architecture,* March 1960, by permission of Frances Walker Yates.

Paul Zukofsky and John Cage, "*Freeman Etudes,*" reprinted by permission of the publisher from the notes to CP 2, (103) (1991).

Every effort has been made to identify the sources of original publication of these essays and make full acknowledgments of their use. If any error or omission has occurred, it will be rectified in future editions, provided that appropriate notification is submitted in writing to the publisher or editor (P.O. Box 444, Prince St., New York, NY 10012-0008).

Contents

Imaginary Landscaper (1982) 1
Eric Salzman

Beginning with Cage (1979) 8
Richard Kostelanetz

On John Cage (1992) 13
Petr Kotik

Counterpoint (1934) 15
John Cage

Double Counterpoint (1934) 18
Henry Cowell

Percussionists in Concert Led by John Cage (1943) 22
Paul Bowles

Ajemian-Masselos (1946) 24
Lou Harrison

"... A Ping, Qualified by a Thud" (1948) 26
Peggy Glanville-Hicks

The Early Percussion Music of John Cage (1978) 33
Stuart Saunders Smith

About John Cage's "Prepared Piano" (1990) 46
Daniel Charles

Cage's Well-Tampered Clavier (1978) 55
Eric Salzman

On Form (1960) 58
Christian Wolff

Cage and Satie (1973) 66
Michael Nyman

The Abstract Composers (1952) 73
Virgil Thomson

Cage *String Quartet* (1972) 77
Peter Dickinson

On Cage's *String Quartet in Four Parts* (1988) 82
Deborah Campana

New and Electronic Music (1957) 85
Christian Wolff

Two Albums by John Cage (1960) 93
Peter Yates

John Cage Late and Early (1960) 103
Virgil Thomson

De-Linearizing Musical Continuity (1990) 107
Daniel Charles

"There's no such a thing as silence . . .":
John Cage's Poetics of Silence (1991) 117
Eric De Visscher

Variations IV (ca. 1967) 134
Joseph Byrd

John Cage and the Theory of Harmony (1983) 136
James Tenney

John Cage's Lecture "Indeterminacy" (1959) 162
Hans G. Helms

Structure as Context (1988) 163
Thomas DeLio

John Cage in a New Key (1981) 176
Natalie Crohn Schmitt

Mimêsis and Beyond: Mallarmé, Boulez, and Cage (1986–87) 180
Jonathan Scott Lee

John Cage as a *Hörspielmacher* (1989) 213
Richard Kostelanetz

Roaratorio Appraisiated (1983) 222
William Brooks

Freeman Etudes (1991) 225
Paul Zukofsky and John Cage

Europe's Opera:
Notes on John Cage's *Europeras 1 and 2* (1987) 229
Heinz-Klaus Metzger

Europeras (1988) 243
Manfredi Piccolomini

Figuration and Prefiguration:
Notes on Some New Graphic Notions (1991) 248
Daniel Charles

Silence (1962) 264
John Hollander

Social Concern (1968) 270
Calvin Tomkins

A Year from Monday (1968) 274
Roger Maren

Cage and Fluxus (1990) 279
Henry Flynt

Something about the Writings of John Cage (1991) 283
Jackson Mac Low

John Cage's Longest and Best Poem (1990) 297
Richard Kostelanetz

Cage's Cage (1990) 301
Edward Rothstein

Gertrude Stein and John Cage: Three Fragments (1977) 309
Ellsworth Snyder

"We Have Eyes as Well as Ears . . ." (1982) 319
Anne d'Harnoncourt

The Development of His Visual Art (1991) 323
Richard Kostelanetz

Merce Cunningham: Origins and Influences (1983) 327
David Vaughan

Cage and Modern Dance (1965) 334
Jill Johnston

Music and Dance (1982) 338
Merce Cunningham

[*16 Dances*] (1984) 341
William Brooks

Other Sources of Cage Criticism in English 345

Contributors 351

Imaginary Landscaper (1982)

Eric Salzman

When David Tudor sat down at the piano no one laughed. When, after four minutes and thirty-three seconds, he got up from the piano, they laughed and they cried—cried out with rage or admiration. The pianist had played not a single note. John Cage had struck again.

The year was 1952; Cage was 40. This year—September 5, to be exact—he will be 70, and no one is laughing.

What is *4'33"*? A piece of music? A bit of *épater les bourgeois*? Musical dada? Zen Buddhism? The random sounds of the environment revealed by the framework of David Tudor's non-performance? Theater? Conceptual art? A hoax? A mere nothing?

Who is John Cage? A musician? A charlatan? A master of *épater les bourgeois*? A musical dadaist? A Zen Buddhist? The inventor of chance, random, concept, environmental and/or aleatory art? A theatrical entrepreneur and self-aggrandizer? The first performance artist? A hoaxter? A passing fad or a major figure? All of the above? Can one be a Zen master at 40? An *enfant terrible* at 70?

In fact, whatever you think (and anything you say about Cage is probably true), it is impossible to dismiss him anymore. At age 40, the composer (or, if you wish, non-composer) of *4'33"* could be put down by the music world as an eccentric or even a charlatan. At age 70—and John Cage really is 70 this year—he is nothing less than the elder statesman of avant-garde art in America.

Note that I said "art." Cage's influence, like that of his predecessors Thoreau, Whitman, Ives, Frank Lloyd Wright, Henry Cowell, and all the other great American eccentrics, extends far beyond his particular traditional medium. Indeed, more than anyone else, Cage did his part to break down the barriers of those traditional media. Is John Cage a "composer" or "musician" in the traditional sense? He himself has redefined the question so that it no longer means what it used to.

Even the issue of what is traditional and what is radical is no longer obvious. The businessman who pioneers radical changes in technology and society may go home and devote himself entirely to listening to traditional, classical music. Your friendly neighborhood avant-gardist or radical may go live in the country and cultivate guitar-picking. The conservative financier may build an avant-garde house and collect far-out art.

If I said that I thought John Cage was, in many ways, a deeply traditional person—very much in the old-fashioned American vein—a lot of people would think that I had gone off the deep end. But Cage as a pioneer is in a very traditional American mold. We admire pioneers—for breaking ground but also for carrying along the solid, sober, old-fashioned democratic virtues. Deep down, John is just like that: an old-fashioned American democratic humanist who tells us that nothing in human experience is alien to him. He opens his ears, his senses, his heart (and ours, too) to an ever-greater sensibility and an ever-widening circle of possibility. And he invites us to put our critical faculties aside and join in. This is not a small enterprise. Cage has been busy redefining the limits of art and artistic experience out to the limits of perception. And to do this, he has invoked the whole panoply of modern technology and cosmology. He has wrapped up and digested—in an almost casual, good-natured way (and entirely without pompous Germanic, Wagnerian, or Stockhausenish theory)—the entire modernist and avant-garde movements in the arts. Everything and for everybody! Now, in light of this, are we still going to stand around and argue about whether or not he really is a composer or musician?

He is, of course, from California. Cage was born in Los Angeles in 1912. He studied there, in New York (with Henry Cowell, another California eccentric), and again in Los Angeles with, of all people, Arnold Schoenberg. During the 1930s he worked on the West Coast, organizing a percussion ensemble—one of the first anywhere—and accompanying dance classes at the Cornish School in Seattle. After a brief period in Chicago, he came to New York where he wrote for the publication *Modern Music,* organized concerts, studied Zen, helped found the New York Mycological Society (he is an expert on the identification and culinary preparation of wild mushrooms), began his long and famous collaboration with dancer/choreographer Merce Cunningham, infiltrated the New York art scene (with which he became closely identified), and created a great deal of work and controversy.

Cage's earliest composition, somewhat influenced by his studies with Schoenberg, is based on webs of numerical patterns applied to notes and, in particular, rhythms. In the 1930s, the American avant-garde, after a period of experimentation, turned from Europe to the Orient. Composers like Cowell, Lou Harrison, Harry Partch, Cage, and others became deeply involved with qualities of larger rhythmic flow and interweaving, with non-tempered scales, and with percussive timbres. The percussion-ensemble music of that era, far from being loud and noisy, is subtle, deft, delicate, and pleasing. (There are, by the way, many connections between this music and the popular minimalist music of Glass, Reich, and others.)

What is probably Cage's most famous invention, the prepared piano, is a direct outgrowth of this interest in oriental percussion music. In working with dancers, Cage conceived the idea of turning the traditional piano accompaniment into a one-man percussion ensemble by the simple expedient of putting various materials—metal, rubber, wood—in the strings. Once again, the results, far from being noisy and extravagant, are delicate and contemplative. Much of this music is reminiscent of the Javanese gamelan, but even the freer, less oriental-sounding music of some of the later prepared piano sets is subtle and beautifully made.

Cage's interest in unusual and nontraditional instrumentation led him early on to experiment with the new recording technologies. In 1939 he used test-tone recordings on variable-speed turntables to produce a kind of electronic music before its time. This was the first of a series of works called *Imaginary Landscapes*. No. 4 in this series was the infamous piece for 12 radios where the sound was whatever happened by chance to be on the air at the time of performance. At the premiere in New York in 1952, one of the dial twirlers—following Cage's "score" of instructions—happened upon a classical-music station playing Mozart, prompting several scoffers in the audience to shout "Leave it on!"

In the early Fifties, at the very beginning of the tape and electronic-music movement, Cage was right there. He made tape collages, used feedback and the sounds of electronic circuitry. He introduced the notion of live electronic performance, preferring the variability and theatricality of performance to fixed or prepared tape. He opened up the entire external world of sound and noise and brought them into the making of music. He employed the new technologies to transmit and transform these sounds as well as traditional music sounds, and to create new aural possibilities.

This combination of technology and Zen Buddhism led to the creation of some remarkable noise landscapes and some of the loudest and most unpleasant works in the Cage canon. And yet, side by side, there was the *4′33″*—silence or the random sounds of the unplanned environment—to listen to.

Cage's numerical period, his oriental period, and his electronic/environmental period were followed or paralleled by an interest in performance art, multi-media, and chance. He began organizing his talks, lectures, and writings as performance pieces. In 1952—at Black Mountain College, an important center for experimental arts in North Carolina—he produced his *Theater Piece* with Merce Cunningham, in effect the first multi-media/happening/performance art. Not only had Cage opened up the random sounds and happenings of the outside world and brought them into the carefully prescribed world of art but, increasingly, he removed himself from conscious choice in putting these works—or events or performances—together. He rolled dice, he tossed coins according to the ancient Chinese book of *I Ching,* used imperfections on paper or star charts and transcribed them into notes. He had two or more pieces performed simultaneously. He developed complex and beautiful graphic notations—often exhibited as works of art—requiring performers to make choices on every level from small detail to big structure and guaranteeing that no two performances will ever be alike and that each new realization would be unforeseen by the composer himself.

The notion of collaborations—with other musicians as well as with artists in other media—is very important in Cage's work, and the list of his collaborators is long: the dancer/choreographer Merce Cunningham, the filmmaker Stan Vanderbeek, the video artist Nam June Paik, the painters Robert Rauschenberg and Jasper Johns, the musicians David Tudor, Lejaren Hiller, David Behrman, Gordon Mumma are examples. Many artists followed his courses at the New School in New York. Cage, as an artist, as a teacher, as a philosopher, as a guru, came to have the widest influence on the development of new arts in America. Nearly every movement in modern arts—from the late phases of abstract expressionism to pop art to multi-media and happenings, to concrete poetry to experimental audio and visual art to new realism to performance art to conceptual art and minimalism—owes something to Cage.

Composers directly affected by him include La Monte Young, Christian Wolff, Morton Feldman, Earle Brown, Alvin Lucier, Robert Ashley, and, in greater or lesser degree, many others. Nor should this list be confined to the United States. There is the Englishman Cornelius Cardew, the Argentinian Mauricio Kagel, the Japanese Toshi Ichiyanagi, and, yes, the Frenchman Pierre Boulez, the German Karlheinz Stockhausen, and more than one Italian. Cage won the Italian version of "The $64,000 Question" on the subject of mushrooms, made several tape pieces in the electronic-music studios of the Italian radio, and introduced the concepts of indeterminacy and "aleatory"—fancy names for different kinds of chance and random operations—into Europe.

I think I've said enough to prove the statement that Cage was—and to some degree is—the most influential figure in the arts after World War II. In fact, one could say that there is probably no other composer in the history of music whose name and influence is so well known—and whose music is so little heard.

The Ultimate Guru

In a sense, Cage is a superstar of a very special sort. In an age of media—and in spite of the fact that he himself has promoted media as a means of artistic creation and communication—his influence is almost entirely personal. He is, without a doubt, the ultimate guru. In an age and in a field where personal aggrandizement and ego are usually paramount, Cage has actually managed to stay in the public eye while leading an exemplary life that is very much in accordance with his principles. I remember running into him a few years ago after not having seen him for a while and asking him how he was: "It's very difficult," he said, presumably referring to the approach of his seventies. "I find I now get irritated. I don't like to be irritated at people and things." He was truly disturbed by this and determined to deal with it.

The notion of transcending the will, essentially Eastern, was introduced into Western philosophy by Schopenhauer, and it played a role in the thinking of many late-nineteenth-century artists, notably Wagner.

But Wagner, who claimed to be expressing his philosophy in his works, was the supreme willful egoist of all time. And Stockhausen, who sometimes talks the same mystical language and takes similar public stances, is Wagner, Jr. Not Cage. Cage is gentle, Cage is soft-spoken (even when his music is loud), Cage is open-hearted, Cage is all-American, Cage is the ultimate cock-eyed idealist, living a life that is itself a work of art, perhaps his best.

When he was young, he wore his hair in a crew cut and looked at you—at the world—with open eyes and a sense of wonder. Now he has longer hair and a beard (as befits a guru), but the sense of open-eyed wonder has hardly lessened.

The notion, aided by technology and modern sensibility, that everything was possible and available for art and experience was the great discovery of the second half of the century. More even than the randomness and Zen indeterminacy, it changed our thinking and hearing—and in ways that have affected everybody, not just the modern-music devotees. It has sent composers, and artists in general, out to embrace the universe or scurrying for cover in some minimalist monastery or other. It has proved to be the final phase for some kinds of modernist experimentation. When anything is possible, it again becomes important what you do with it. Once you have done *4′33″*—a piece of any length for any number or quality of performers—you cannot really do it again. One man's silence is, after Cage, much like another's. (In fact, all silence, no matter how noisy, is now by Cage.) Conceptual music is either musicless music or it requires the reinvention of music—which is what is happening now. Cage, like Wagner, is the end of an era, but every end is also a new beginning.

In the meantime there is still John Cage himself, living his life simply, modestly like some latter-day Thoreau and yet functioning as an icon. If he were Japanese he would be declared a Living National Treasure or whatever it is that the Japanese designate their great craftsmen. (Perhaps, given the mutual love affair between Japan and Cage, they will do it anyway; it would certainly be fitting.)

We are not likely to do as much, nor is Cage likely to act the part. It is no longer possible for him to play the bad boy—anything he does automatically generates a certain level of acceptance—but he can and will still play the American Zen master, the fellow who makes us hear the sound of one hand clapping.

For the most part, it will be Cage's earlier work—the prepared piano music above all—that will appeal and continue to appeal to a growing public. But I wouldn't want to doubt his ability to amaze us yet with some new and extraordinary concept which, even as it escapes the narrow and traditional idea of a piece of music, redefines and makes us know something more about where we stand and how we hear in a world transformed by technology and transformed, more than a bit, by John Cage.

Beginning with Cage (1979)

Richard Kostelanetz

Although his work is so profoundly audacious that controversies about it will never cease, few can dispute the claim that John Cage ranks among the foremost radical minds of the age. At the core of his originality is a continual penchant for taking positions not only far in advance of established artistic practice, but also beyond both his previous work and much that is currently regarded as avant-garde. For over forty years, Cage has worked on the frontiers of modern music and modern art, and one index of how far he has moved is that, unlike the aging ex-radical, he has never repudiated any of his past works as "too extreme." Indeed, as each phase of his career has attracted greater support, Cage himself has progressed even further into unfamiliar territory—often further than even his most fervent admirers would go. "I like to think," he often says, "that I'm outside the circle of a known universe and dealing with things that I don't know anything about."

Everything about Cage seems a radical departure; his music, his esthetic ideas, his personal behavior, his critical statements are all indubitably inventive. "Oh, yes, I'm devoted to the principle of originality," he once told an interviewer, "not originality in the egotistic sense, but originality in the sense of doing something which is necessary to do. Now, obviously, the things that it is necessary to do are not those that have been done, but the ones that have not yet been done. If I have done something, then I consider it my business not to do that, but to find what must be done next."

Cage's most important compositions of the past three decades have been conceived to deny his intentional desires as completely as possible (although less completely than he sometimes says); and not only is each of them filled with a diversity of disconnected atonal sounds, but their major musical dimensions—amplitude (or volume), duration, timbre, and sometimes pitch—are genuinely as unfixed, or as unspecific, as the overall length of the piece.

This "indeterminate music," as Cage himself prefers to call it, is the result of an artistic evolution that is at once highly logical and faintly absurd. In the history of musical art, Cage descends from that eccentric modern tradition that abandoned nineteenth-century tonal principles, in addition to introducing natural noise as an integral component with instrumentally produced sounds. In this respect, Cage continually acknowledges the French-born American composer, Edgard Varèse, and before him, Charles Ives as the artistic fathers of the radical tendencies that Cage himself later pursued. This tradition could be characterized as the "chaotic" language of contemporary music, as distinct from the tonal language—think of Aaron Copland, Benjamin Britten and Stravinsky of his middle period—and, lastly, the serial language initiated by Arnold Schoenberg and developed by Anton von Webern, Milton Babbitt and by Stravinsky himself in the last decade of his life.

In his earliest extant work, dating from the middle-thirties, Cage displayed a threefold taste for complicated rhythmic constructions, for inventive organizing principles, such as a twenty-five tone system, and finally for distorted instrumental sounds, such as that made by a gong in water. Toward the late thirties, Cage also devised the "prepared piano," the innovation that first won him widespread notice. Here he doctored the piano's strings with screws, bolts, nuts and strips of rubber, endowing the familiar instrument with a range of unfamiliar percussive potentialities. The first famous piece for this invention was *Amores* (1943), now on record—a work which today strikes sophisticated ears as almost euphoniously conventional. Cage's most ambitious score for the prepared piano, the *Sonatas and Interludes* of 1946–48, seemed revolutionary at the time; heard today, as in Joshua Pierce's Tomato recording (1977), it sounds remarkably close to the music for a standard, undoctored piano that Erik Satie did a few decades before.

Cage prepared the piano for several ingenious reasons. In addition to generating unusual sounds, a prepared piano also gives the performer less control over the tones he finally produces—an A string with bolts and nuts is not as precise in pitch or attack as an undoctored A string; and in contrast to the neo-Schoenbergians who wanted a precise rationale for the placement of every note, Cage in the late forties continued to develop methods for minimizing his control over the aural results. For instance, he would sometimes choose his notes by first observing the miscellaneous imperfections such as holes, specks, or discolorations, on a piece of paper and then intensifying them with his pen. A transparent sheet with music staves would then be placed over the marked paper, and Cage would trace the intensified marks onto the staves. *Voilà.* That would be the definitive score.

By the seventies, Cage had consolidated his earlier innovations, producing pieces that, while they were not so radically experimental or outrageously offensive, were still characteristically his. Although they are neither inaccessible nor impossibly difficult, they are original in conception and as listening experiences. Just as it is useful to explain certain things about the work in advance, the listener would be well advised to hear the music not just once but many times.

The title of *Etudes Australes* (1974) comes from *Atlas Australis,* a book of maps of stars as they can be seen from Australia. Cage first placed a transparent grid over these maps. By a complicated process involving decisions made with the aid of his favorite 64-choice Chinese chance manual, *I Ching,* Cage marked the locations of certain stars on the transparent paper. These were transferred to music staves arranged in groups of four—an upper and lower clef for the pianist's right hand, and a second set of upper and lower clefs for the left hand. Since the resulting array of dots might impose impossible demands upon the performer, Cage played the notes himself to make sure that his score could indeed be physically executed. The musical notation is incomplete by conventional standards. Although pitches are precisely scored, there are no rhythmic signatures, such as 4/4 or 6/8, and no vertical bar lines that might indicate a measure. The only index for duration is horizontal visual distance on the score. "Time proportions are given (just as maps give proportional distance)," Cage wrote in the score's preface.

> In a performance, the correspondence should be such that the music "sounds" as it "looks." However, as in traveling through space, circumstances sometimes arise when it is necessary to "shift gears" and go, as the case may be, faster or slower.

In *Etudes Australes,* there are no markings for musical dynamics of attack or decay, no instructions for the pedal and none of these Italian words that tell a musician how the notes should be interpreted. (Decisions about these dimensions are all left to the performer.) The notes themselves are either closed circles or open circles. While the instructions say that the former should be played and released, the open circles must be held as long as possible. One ingenious device is Cage's instruction that for each of the 32 etudes certain keys of the piano must be depressed in advance of playing and held down with a rubber wedge for the entire etude; so that these strings will resonate as sympathetic drones. Indeed, it was Cage's rule for this work that the depressed keys should represent the tones that are *not* played in that etude.

Each of the thirty-two etudes is fit into two pages of score sheets, each set of which has eight blocks of four horizontal staves apiece; so that the pianist may play an entire etude without needing to turn the page. A further structural characteristic is that the etudes get gradually denser in texture. Whereas only one of the 64 *I Ching* options yields an aggregate (or chord) in the first etude, two of 64 produce chords in the second, sixteen of 64 in the sixteenth, and 32 of 64 in the thirty-second, giving the entire piece a roughly accumulative structure.

Musically, these procedures produce great leaps of individual pitches, within a rhythmic frame that turns out to be more regular than erratic; and there are occasional atonal clusters, complex chords, and even triads, in sum, suggesting harmony without being intentionally harmonic. "In my music," Cage explained,

> there is no system of relations any more than there is of tonality. One finds all imaginative chords. There are chords that are completely classical, major or minor; but these are completely unexpected and unforeseeable. When they happen, they have extraordinary freshness, as if one heard them for the first time.

The crowning touch of this work—the characteristic sound that makes it different from other Cage pieces—is the resonating drones. Not only the tones depressed at the beginning of each etude, but the other notes that are held as long as possible, all create overtones that resonate and combine long after the keys are depressed. And when new notes are played, fresh overtones are generated in serendipitous ways. To hear this dimension of *Etudes Australes,* it is best to turn the volume high and place your speakers in a reverberant room. The overtones are more audible, you will find, on your hi-fi system than in a typical large concert hall. Indeed, this may well be the first Cage composition that sounds better and truer on record than in a live performance.

On John Cage (1992)

Petr Kotik

Overcoming romantic and classical concepts in composition has been a major challenge to twentieth-century music. The work of John Cage represents a milestone on this path. It has inspired a new musical consciousness, a new way of listening and music making.

Cage's pioneering work with sound in the 1940s and 1950s is well known. His most lasting contribution, however, is the introduction of his musical ideas and compositional concepts.

In searching for the purpose of composing, Cage, in the late 1940s, discovered an ancient oriental and medieval European statement about music: "To quiet one's own mind, thus making it susceptible to divine influences." To make music which would lead to such a state of mind, it became clear that the romantic idea of self-expression had to be overcome, and that music must align itself with the environment in which it exists. This consequently led Cage to the introduction of chance into composition and performance practice.

Cage abandoned the hierarchy of contrasting parts and dramatic climaxes in composition. Instead of expressing "oneself," he introduced an open musical environment in which the listener, instead of being bombarded by composer's intentions, can find his or her own center. Sounds became themselves, and ceased to illustrate extramusical phenomena. Silences became equally important to sounds, and tones produced on instruments became equally important to noises. In fact, the concept of "noises" was abandoned altogether, and all sounds became an asset to music making.

The mechanics of keeping time in music changed. Instead of measures and beats, Cage introduced a real-time device, the stopwatch, or a conductor, whose function became that of a time-keeping clock.

Along with the new way of time keeping came a new sensibility toward duration and musical form. Formerly unexplored possibilities opened, and enabled the creation of compositions with undetermined beginnings and endings. It became possible, for the first time, to conceive music with undetermined length.

The new concept of time and sound, and the radical departure from the musical thinking of the past, made new demands on performers. The new freedoms required a disciplined approach, one which turns one's attention to "the spirit of the work," and away from the idea of "expressing oneself." In the mid 1970s, in a discussion about performance issues, Cage defined discipline in music as a process in which: "one does not do what one wants, but nevertheless anything goes." This concept is central to understanding Cage's music, not just for the performer, but for the listener as well.

Counterpoint (1934)

John Cage

The preceding article [by a Mr. White] has three parts: (1) Resumé of anecdotal after-the-concert material; (2) "We begin to define music" leading to the conclusion (3) "There is confusion, bewilderment—." It is significantly intelligible as an example of critical unintelligibility. I say this not personally, for I do not know Mr. White at all, nor specifically of his article, but generally as a composer of the body of contemporary music-criticism. This is not the first time I have read an article on "modern music," unfortunately, and I am beginning not to read them at all. I used to read as many as I could find, collecting material for lectures, and, in all that I read, I found only one good collection of articles: *American Composers on American Music* (Stanford University Press, 1933), edited by Henry Cowell. This book should, however, be coming out at least every year, its nature being extremely current. In it, one American composer would write about another one. There was, at least once (let's hope, not once for all), an interest in ideas rather than in words. The only constructive alteration in the scheme of the book that I would suggest would be: one American composer talking about himself and further—not only American composers but composers.

There are, it seems to me, two sides to music as well as to everything else, including life: the side we can know something about (knowledge which is communicable) and the side which we can know nothing about (knowledge which is personal, emotional, etc., uncommunicable). I prefer to communicate those things which are communicable rather than those which are not. Thus: the intellectual experiments of modern music can be communicated in words. This does not mean that modern music is intellectual; if that were true, there would be no necessity for music; the words would be enough. It does mean that any further word-communication is not possible. To make my meaning clearer: When composing, I compose (a matter of relationships, putting-together, arranging) as well as I can intellectually. It seems to others that I just let the emotions, the uncommunicables, take care of themselves, communicate themselves. This is partly true and partly not. I believe that the way in which the composer lives will, like the birth of protoplasm, miraculously and inevitably enter the composition.

How can I further explain this attitude? It is a thing I believe in, and I don't expect to be able to communicate it convincingly.

Music becomes a craft, extending the definition of the word from manual dexterity to mental dexterity. And Life remains Life. Whether it is to be "communicated" as sublime, pathetic, profound, comic or tragic, depends not upon the craftsman with reference to his craft, but with reference to the way he lives. The performers of the *St. Matthew Passion* are not suddenly to become sublime at 8:30 P.M., Shrine Auditorium, L.A. They are merely to sing as well as they can, to exert themselves as vocal and instrumental craftsmen rather than as mystics. A performance should be made with best possible technical mastery. Sincerity and faith should not be summoned for the performance alone but should ideally be the life-attitude of the performer. The Dancer is not to suddenly pose on the stage, but living feeling will make his entrance into the Grocery Store an evidence of the Dance, not, of course, as Art, but as consciousness.

I think of Music not as self-expression, but as Expression.

I think, with reference to contemporary music, that, in view of the relative absence of academic discipline and the presence of total freedom, there is a determining necessity for specific forms given assigned values in order to solve special problems. I am not in sympathy with Tone-Poems, Pictures, nor with the "composer" who is so infected with modern license as to write a "Sonata" which is ¾ Coda (2nd Movement: Free Fantasia).

I have mentioned quite a lot about "the way he lives." The only possible life for me is one of believing. The other brings about the symptom: "I haven't anything to say." A composer, or any other artist, who believes and approaches understanding through belief, will find his music craft expressing increasingly that understanding: e.g. *St. Matthew Passion*.

A more direct reply to Mr. White's article than the above would have included a critical estimate of "Modern Music," that amalgamation of various composers' works. I have, to a certain extent, indicated the impossibility, or at least my disinclination, to do this. How can one discuss in a single article a subject which includes the works of Ives, Hindemith, Harris, Ruggles, Milhaud, Bartok, Poulenc, Toch, Chavez, Cowell, Honegger, Copland, Brant, Stravinsky, Satie, and Schoenberg? I, personally, see, as a "general tendency," an interest away from harmony (verticality: Richard Wagner) and towards counterpoint, or better, linearity (horizontality: Bach, Hindemith, Toch, Honegger, Brant, Riegger), with the resulting interest in fugues, canons and in new allied forms which will, possibly, take the title, invention. Harmony puts an emphasis about a given moment which counterpoint transfers to an emphasis upon movement. This tendency is specifically shown in the development of Schoenberg: from the immense harmonic structure–texture of the *Gurrelieder* to the relatively thin but structurally strong like wire trio of the Minuet, *Suite,* op. 25. Or Stravinsky: from the *Sacre* to the *Symphonie des Psaumes* with its double fugue. Hindemith has shown another, comparatively beside the point, tendency. He has attempted in his pieces for music lovers, amateurs in groups at home, and in his settings for movies, to act as a well-meaning missionary from the intelligentsia to the "others." This move on his part shows a humanity for the now which is not very common in composers who are working so completely abstractly as to be notorious for their lack of interest in economy, politics, or even in the auditory evidence of their "mental dexterity" (Brant). Poulenc, I think everyone agrees, is having a lot of fun in a rather French-folk way. Satie, we're not so sure about. There has been a great effort to endow his *Cold Pieces,* his *Reveries on the Infancy of Pantagruel,* etc., with "profondeur." I sincerely express the hope that all this conglomeration of individuals, names merely for most of us, will disappear; and that a period will approach by way of common belief, selflessness, and technical mastery that will be a period of Music and not of Musicians, just as during the four centuries of Gothic, there was Architecture and not Architects.

Double Counterpoint (1934)

Henry Cowell

I read with interest the two leaflets on modern music in the last issue of *Dune Forum.* Both open material for speculation, and plunge into a maelstrom of swirling currents and mixups of issues being discussed concerning the music of today. But it does not seem to me that either of the combaters (or were they combating?) arrive at any very definite point. To give an answer to the crucial questions that beset present-day musical creators would be too much to expect. But unless the questions are put clearly, the speculations are vague and arrive nowhere.

Mr. White's underlying attitude is subjective. He judges worth in music in the final analysis by its effect on him, and on other auditors. He tried to make so many concessions to the opposite side, however, that his own views remain unclear. The trouble with relying too much on the subjective impression as a basis of criticism is that the goodness or badness may not be in the music, but in the reaction of the person or group of persons. Such reactions are influenced by association, preconception, and even such lesser matters as whim and the mood of the moment. A given musical work may have almost every conceivable effect on human beings, if they are selected over a wide period of time, and from different environments. If we take even such a widespread notion as that that major music is gay, and minor music is sad, we find that it is purely a matter of convention, although one now so strong that it influences a large portion of our subjective reactions. But try major and minor scales and pieces on primitives, or orientals unfamiliar with our music, and it has repeatedly been found that they form no such concepts of the meaning of major versus minor modes.

In the case of the auditors Mr. White describes, it is very doubtful whether those who listened to modern music with "exaggerated attentiveness" or who were "uncontrollably convulsed with laughter" would have a profound appreciation of older music. Their actions had to do with themselves, not with the music. And White's own reaction (although since we do not know the work he heard it is hard to judge) seems bound by convention.

To find life but no "melancholy of reflection," to find exaggeration and unbalance, but never the attempt to attract, seems like an opinion based on a preconceived idea of what is attractive, what is balanced, what is full of life, what is melancholy. White upholds the right of everyone to say that music may be the best in the world, but if it says nothing to the one speaking that he considers of benefit, it is worthless at the present time. This is all very well, but should not be directed as a criticism of the best music in the world! Finally, one might gain the impression that all modern music is alike. It is not, either in aim or consummation of purpose. Some music is the expression, perhaps, of emotional ideas in tone. Other music, equally valuable, is not. There is no reason to limit the field of music to some one of its possibilities. And this is where Cage's statement also is at fault. He thinks of music as Expression (capital E noted). Cage, taking the side of mastery of materials, and very correctly assuming that expression is not something to be striven for, but may come unconsciously in the creation of a perfect structure, nevertheless falls into the conventional attitude of objecting to the intellect in music. Just why anything so magnificent as the intellect should be so ill in musical repute, is a mystery.

The classic Ecclesiastes, who were cognisant of much truth, regarded music as one of the three great intellectual pursuits (the others were astronomy and mathematics). The quintessence of musical ecstasy comes through appreciation of a perfectly coordinated blend of intellectual formulization of what is to be said musically; and this something to say may be either an expression of feeling, personal or impersonal, it may be an attempt to induce certain feelings in others, it may have to do with becoming conscious of eternal truths, not necessarily emotionally, it may be an impression instead of an expression, or it may be a set of sounds which take on definite meaning, like language, through convention. Such music is to be found in China, India, and among all primitives. There are other things that music can say, not all of them strictly emotional. All of these musics are of value. Because some one of them is in greater favor with a certain people at a certain time should not cause the narrow attitude of denying the value of the others. Music which is not emotional nor an expression in the sense meant by either Cage or White is in use by all the peoples of the world except the white race, and in some cases by the white race also. This music is of highest value, and has, also, intellectual coordination.

I find that music without intellectual coordination is so spineless and sentimental as to have the least possible value. Emotion and expression is of decided value, and warmly to be welcomed where it exists; but there are also other values in music. So I feel that of the two, if they were to be separated, (which is not necessary) the intellectual elements are the more universally essential in music. Form and structure with little or no content is often misnamed intellectual. This is utterly stupid. Would a conversation in words be held intellectual if it were in perfect grammar but meaningless? No! Then why apply the term *intellectual,* which should be one of extreme approbation, to anything as valueless as an empty musical shell, or to aimless, wandering experiments of entirely dry nature, or to all modern music which is not understood? Cage made a valuable contribution when he pointed out that after all, Ives, Ruggles, Schoenberg and Stravinsky are different. His diagnosis of tendencies toward counterpoint is probably correct, but this is a very passing matter. Any one element in music is apt to be over-emphasized at some one period, but that does not make it any more or less valuable, nor indicate that all music must follow by not developing some other element.

In spite of my keen appreciation of other than emotional values in music, I find that emotional value and content is very strong in most modern music. The reason that many listeners perceive modern music as though it were an empty intellectual shell without content (to use the word as it is usually used) is that emotion is built up through association. It would be virtually a psychological impossibility to arouse great emotion immediately, and avoid every single known element in music. Modern music makes use of many new elements which have great possibilities of emotional enhancement on acquaintance. Since, however, there is no association with them on initial hearing, it is not surprising that only the form, and not the content, is noted by the casual listener. If, however, a composer be trapped into feeling that he must use known means with already built-up associations in order to immediately move his auditors, then his music will suffer from the fact that what he says as well as how he is saying it will have been composed before him by the masters whose materials he is using; they will have said it better than he, and *they* did not take from former times, but built up their own materials and associations.

The relation of music to society is a problem that neither Cage nor White seemed to consider of import. Yet the ultimate value of music lies in its ultimate value to society. This is a genuine ideal toward which a composer might work, finding materials, structure, and content which work toward that end. And in my opinion it will be found that fresh form and content both will be necessary in carrying out such an aim.

Percussionists in Concert Led by John Cage (1943)

Paul Bowles

The concert was good for the hearing; it was an ear-massage. Fourteen persons, 125 instruments and about fifty sticks to hit them with. When things were not beaten or tapped they were shaken, rubbed, pulled or immersed in water. There was an ominous audio frequency oscillator, recorded sounds went on and off, and both thunder sheet and marimbula were equipped with electric pick-ups.

In percussion music so far there has been very little development other than rhythmical and that pertaining to the general sonorous architecture. Such things as melody and harmony, which involve the use of definite and related pitch, have been largely ignored. Henry Cowell's *Ostinato Pianissimo*, by virtue of the inclusion of a certain amount of both of these, proved to be more immediately enjoyable than some of the other numbers.

In the *Imaginary Landscape No. 3* of John Cage the use of electrical instruments reminded one of Varèse's *Equatorial,* but the sonorous texture seemed better integrated. During the pieces by Roldan and Ardévol one noticed the absence of a sustained sound; one thought of the human voice, perhaps because the music sounded very much like a complicated accompaniment to a "son" and one expected the arrival of a sound with some sort of carrying power.

In most of the music the Oriental and African element dominated. The effects quite clearly, if not consciously, strove to approximate those of the ritual music of the far parts of the world. Even the figures used by Mr. Cage in his delicate *Amores* for piano transformed with screws and clips, were reminiscent of Bali, and often the passages of ensemble work were suggestive of the gamelan music of that same island.

Sometimes the level of excitement reached was below the obviously prodigious amount of energy expended to attain it. The complicated rhythmical juxtapositions then sounded neither complex nor simple, but desultory and accidental. But there were few of these dry spots. The music's principal aim was to achieve a maximum of sonorous effect, and the composers involved were adept at it.

It is not so much in themselves that concentrated manifestations like last night's are important, but rather, being in their very intensity the detonators of ideas, they indicate possible directions for Occidental art music to take.

Ajemian-Masselos (1946)

Lou Harrison

A concert of the works of John Cage was heard at Carnegie Chamber Music Hall last night played by Maro Ajemian and William Masselos, pianists. The program included *Three Dances for Two Pianos, Four Sonatas* for solo piano and *A Book of Music* for two pianos. The stage of the Chamber Hall was attractively spaced and lighted for the occasion by Schuyler Watts.

Since Miss Ajemian and Mr. Masselos will repeat this same concert tonight, those who have not yet become acquainted with John Cage's enchanted and enchanting world of sounds will be enabled to do so, and many who were there might wish to listen more. For this music is so sensuously attractive by reason of the delicacy and color of the sounds its author arranges by muting the piano strings with different materials that it requires much listening for the average ear to find beneath the surface the enormous play of intellect and imagination that is there.

Miss Ajemian and Mr. Masselos performed with precision, spirit and sympathy last night, and succeeded as well in making clear to the ear the larger shapes; the control of which in his special way is Cage's gift to the art of musical form. The present works, three of which were being heard for the first time, are all examples of his basic "square-of-the-phrase" idea, a concept that begins with the distinction of chronological time as separate from psychological time, and establishes in its ramifications what this reporter considers to be the brightest gift to form in our time. In these and other pieces its original inventor has proved that the formulation will work under all needed circumstances, and audibly to the untrained ear.

The final movement of the *Three Dances*, which the pianists took at the fantastic speed called for by Mr. Cage, is a new work, and tends to tighten the stomach muscles as though one were careening off a precipice. Its sonorities and patterns are of a relentless brilliance and make the utmost demands of the pianists.

Miss Ajemian must be especially mentioned for her readings of the solo sonatas in the center of the program. The resonances of the pieces find Cage introducing many unprepared tones which are pleasing and fresh in their context. Miss Ajemian caught well the introspective and ecstatic nature of the ideas in the pieces.

"... A Ping, Qualified by a Thud" (1948)

Peggy Glanville-Hicks

Cyril Connolly once wrote that "a public figure can never be an artist, and no artist should ever become one, unless his work is done and he chooses to retire into public life." This is perhaps putting it a little too strongly, for there are many kinds and degrees of artist, all indispensable to artistic evolution. But to one who is an artist in the highest sense, meditation is an absolute prerequisite; and in the vital pandemonium that is musical America, few have the strength, the inclination, or the awareness of its importance to embark upon a way of life which ensures time for reflection.

John Cage has this strength and this awareness. He is very much a part of America's avant-garde musical progress, and is an important and controversial figure in it. Yet he is in it, and not of it, in a way that a certain type of creative mind can be in his community. He lives on a remote promontory of the lower East River at the top of a tall house. The bare white rooms look out in many directions over the water. There are India matting floors, a few young orange trees in earthenware pots, and a large grand piano, the mechanical "changement" in place for the particular piece on which he is at work. Décor here is a matter of proportions and surfaces, the one concession being an aerial arabesque of delicately constructed wire mobiles which emphatically define space to the eye. These serve as a visual concentration point that frees the ear to receive the unexpected sounds of the "prepared" piano—a disembodied beauty of sound without association, without precedented timbre or form, without aesthetic antecedent.

Mr. Cage was born in Los Angeles and was a thoroughly trained composer in conventional technical systems before he began his transformations of timbre. He was a pupil of Henry Cowell and of Schoenberg, and later was himself a teacher—at the Cornish School in Seattle, at Mills College in California, and at the School of Design in Chicago. It is often said of him that he is an "exotic," an "orientalist" and a "stunt man," but only in the most superficial sense could these categorizations stand. In essence he is exactly the opposite. If there are in his music some parallels to oriental music, it is because there are contemporary musical trends which are evolving structural and spatial procedures similar to those of certain Eastern systems, and the similarities are bound to become increasingly apparent.

Mr. Cage is at once a highly sensitive, curious and mystic creator, and a practical craftsman whose recognition of the limitations, restrictions and possibilities peculiar to the modern composer is most realistic. His practicality has expressed itself amply in an ability to achieve the actual birth in performance of most of his works, in spite of the novel and unlikely ensembles they have often called for. In the past ten years he has organized no less than 14 concerts of music for percussion orchestras (trained by himself) and for "prepared" pianos. Mr. Cage is not the first American to become fascinated with percussion. It is the extroverted aspect of rhythm and rhythm's reincorporation as the vital starting point for construction which is America's outstanding organic contribution to musical history—the germination point for what might be termed the "rhythmic revolution," a phenomenon that has changed form as profoundly as the harmonic revolution of Mussorgsky-Satie-Debussy changed color.

Mr. Cage, like Edgar Varèse, Paul Bowles, Arthur Honegger and others, has also been associated with what has sometimes been called a "dada" movement in music. The incorporation of klaxon horns, milk bottles, telephone bells and factory whistles into scores of quite serious intent was doubly confusing to the listener. In Europe it assumed the aura of a metropolitan folk-lore as part of the proletarian utterance, while here in America it had technical rather than ideological significance, and developed more particularly as an offshoot of the percussion movement. Hilarious results were achieved in this field, finding perhaps more legitimate employment in the documentary film than in the concert hall—though the movement invaded both with equal aplomb. This movement had an entirely serious starting point, however, and sprang from a profound mistrust for the "seriousness" and "classicality" of the academic parade of means as ends. An abuse of the means quickly debunked this ostentation and redirected the emphasis to the esthetic, to the starting point, propounding the theory that anything can be beautiful if the esthetic content is designed and the result expressive. This movement in music has touched everywhere, leaving the terminology widened and uninhibited and audiences more-or-less unprotesting. It was a phase of reaction, and reaction is invariably more vociferous and explosive than action, for its function is to break down old forms, while to action falls the slower and far more arduous task of building a new classicism from renewed elements. It is this responsibility that is in the hands of the composer of today.

The relation between content, form and the terms of expression is a point of consciousness in artistic creation, and is a most delicately adjusted integration. It is with this region that Mr. Cage is preoccupied: he is still an experimentalist. I say "still" because the common ground in contemporary form and idiom is now sufficiently established to allow of two distinct types, classicist and experimentalist. The former finds richly adequate and uses to the full all conventional procedures; the latter continues to push forward the frontiers in the materials of expression and statement. Mr. Cage is definitely an experimentalist, and his relationship to the body of contemporary creative output is rather similar to that of a research scientist to the field of applied science.

This is not to imply that his activities are to be valued purely as contributive discoveries. His musical works exist as integrated utterances of a very high order; but he has abstracted each element with which he works, stripping sound of associations—instrumental, aesthetic, or even, in the associative sense, emotional—until one receives the impression that all legitimate musical elements are present only in their chemically pure state.

With the felt need for this highly individualized research, Mr. Cage has gradually withdrawn from experiments in externalized rhythm, percussive music, to work with its more introverted organic aspect, pulse. He has also become fascinated with the dramatic power of the pause—the intent void as a point of arrival, of climax in a texture of sounds designed to set silence as a jewel. From this need for a one-man laboratory has gradually emerged his prepared piano, which has become to him a miniature orchestra, infinitely varied in its mutations and free of the demands and compromises that are unavoidable in cooperative ventures with percussion and other ensembles. In this laboratory John Cage pursues with the utmost introspection, and with a high sensitivity of intuitive intellect, his brilliant investigations into the nature and origin of inspiration.

It is difficult to describe the sound made by a prepared piano to those who have never actually heard it. Virgil Thomson, in a moment which combined perception and whimsy, wrote that it is "a ping, qualified by a thud." Here and there straight piano tones will be left "unprepared," and these emerge from the thuddy texture like gongs in their shattering limpid elegance, their sound hovering poised in aural space as the less resonant notes pass in scurrying designs. The changement of the piano is differently adjusted for each piece or set of pieces, and is precisely laid out with charts and directions at the front of the book. The changement is achieved by the addition of diverse objects to the strings of the piano at varying distances from the damped point. Screws, bolts, (with careful specifications as to type and size), rubber bands, bamboo slats, weather-stripping, hairpins and a miscellany of strange, small objects of quite humble origin are pressed into service. Their homely nature again evokes to the less thoughtful a reminiscence of the dada days, but a mathematical knowledge of the science of overtones implicit in the "stop" measurements, and exquisite selectivity is manifest in the effects sought and found—above all in the innate strength and craftsmanship evident in the actual composition of pieces within these self-imposed limitations and possibilities. All are wholly convincing, and prove again the contention that the point of departure and the result achieved are far more fundamental to a work of art than are the means selected.

On paper, Mr. Cage's compositional style is basically linear and contrapuntal. But he uses a process of fragmentation of thematic material that is increasingly observed in modern music, a process that seems to incorporate the attributes of both horizontal and perpendicular methods—of fugal and sonata forms—with the added pulverization that intense rhythmic emphasis and subtlety bring, and with a resulting understatement in the harmonic sphere.

Structurally his work is sometimes not unlike Debussy's, if you can discount the harmonic aspect, though perhaps its nearest analogy in form is to be found in the world of science. Cage's aural shapes sound rather as cellular division, subdivision and reunification look under a microscope.

There is another hazard in store for those who would study these works on paper: visually the notes look just as they would if they were written for an ordinary piano, and sequentially the scales rise and fall in the accepted manner. The "prepared" sound, however, may not only bear no relationship in timbre to its unprepared piano counterpart, but its tonality, pitch and whole position in the piano's range territory may be totally unexpected. The sound may jump up three octaves, down one, up a second, down a ninth, all while the fingers are playing notes adjacent to each other in a simple scale passage.

This for instance:

may sound thus:

⅄ sounds resonant and full

O ordinary piano timbre

† woody; a thud with pitch

□ clangy, and split in two

△ woody and split

Similarly, a whole passage which in its written form exists within the range scope of two octaves may in actual sound occupy four or five octaves and include the use of microtones, or pitch differences less than our semi-tones, as well as of timbres that defy description.

From Schoenberg's atonalism Mr. Cage has retained certain elements, such as a non-thematic and non-harmonic basis. But atonalism took over the tones and colors evolved for tonal expression, so that more often than not the method produced a mechanical avoidance of tonal associations rather than a positive statement. Cage, in changing both the timbre and pitch of every note, giving an absolute identity to each, precedes his creative process by a frankly mechanical device, and thus frees the creative and imaginative faculties for a new positive expression.

His affinity with Eastern music is spiritual rather than technical. The Eastern structural concept is one having no beginning or end; its form is its duration, and its aim the making conscious for a space an everlasting phenomenon. Cage retains the Western concept of a beginning and an end, his musical divisions being the breath, the phrase, and its accomplishment—serenity.

It is sometimes said that anything so highly specialized as this music, with all its attendant prerequisites, cannot hope to survive and become important, permanent or widely known. Mr. Cage has given this matter tentative consideration, and has made (with the idea of encouraging reproduction) little boxed sets of all the various pieces used in his changement schemes. All kinds of charming titles for such sets can be imagined—"Pins for Preliminary Practice," and perhaps, "Augmented Outfits for Advanced Pieces." But the problem of a unique creator's reaching his public does not seem to lie in the sphere of creation or production, but in distribution.

Mr. Cage is essentially an artist of his country and time, but his country and time are letting him down. He is creating for a state of affairs in which radio, television and recording facilities would be available to the original creative mind, and not the almost exclusive property of trade and profit campaigns, with production pegged on the basis of retrospective sales statistics. His music is chamber music par excellence, and all chamber music—especially such delicately miniature creations as his—can only reach the wider public awaiting it through the distributive agencies that inhere in the mechanical devices of our time.

The substance of John Cage's music is elusive. It cannot be taught. It is intangible. Such music is highly perishable, and can die with its creator as did the miraculous music of the old courts of Java. But the creative impulse remains and is constantly reborn, guaranteeing a new incarnation of artistic expression in every age. One is reminded here of Mr. Cage's reply to a certain critic's comment, on one of his paper and matchwood mobiles, that it was "so perishable" that it could never be a really serious work of art. "Only a little more perishable than a grand piano, a Rembrandt, or the house," he said. "Given a good-sized bomb, all would be reduced to atoms in the same instant."

It is the impulse and its manifestation that make art, and it is the understanding of the nature of both of these that makes an artist.

Talent, in a creative person, is the ability to incorporate the impulse into a technique, and his main problem is not allowing old techniques to divert new impulses.

John Cage is one of the rarest people working among us. Not only is he endowed with humor, an inordinate sense of beauty and purity, and a brilliant musical brain, but he brings with him, wherever he may be, the happiness and tranquility of an integrated personality and a mind at peace.

The Early Percussion Music of John Cage (1978)

Stuart Saunders Smith

Between the 1930s and 1950s, John Cage devoted much of his considerable energy to the composition of percussion scores (over sixteen) and to inventing compositional procedures and theories especially conceived for percussion music. These composition range from pieces for piano exterior and voice, like *The Wonderful Widow of Eighteen Springs,* to large percussion ensembles, as in *Imaginary Landscape No. 1* through *Imaginary Landscape No. 3* where the instrumentation consists of found objects, "live electronics," and "traditional" percussion instruments.

Cage described percussion music as the "contemporary transition from keyboard-influenced music to the all-sound music of the future. Any sound is acceptable to the composer of percussion music . . . methods of writing percussion music have as their goal rhythmic structure of a composition."[1]

Cage's method of structuring his percussion music, and much of his other music, is based on a simple musical fact. Rhythm is the one musical parameter that measures and defines all the other musical parameters. Rhythm articulates all the parameters of sound. Rhythm is the basic musical parameter. Therefore, a musical structure based on any parameter other than rhythm is a contradiction, because it is the very essence of musical (sound) structure. If sound is shaped by time, then music composition is the temporal organization of sound. Pitch and harmony should not be the primary concerns of a composer of music. Rhythm is the fundamental music parameter. (One does not build a house by first planning the interior decorating.)

Cage's theory concerning the importance of rhythm led him to a radical re-definition of music. This definition is: Music is time passing.

Music is careful attention paid to on-going experience. Music is not an object, but an attitude, a presence of mind. (Music became a verb.) Sound is no longer an issue since we are never without it anyway. One sound is intrinsically no better or worse than another; hence, music is time passing. Sound is time made audible.[2] (A perfect example of this attitude is *4'33".)*

This definition may seem so all-inclusive that it would apply to everyday life. This is true. Cage is out to remove the boundaries separating art and life.

> There is no such thing as an empty space or an empty time. There is always something to see, something to hear. . . . Until I die there will be sounds. And they will continue, following my death. One need not fear about the future of music.[3]

In the article, "For New Sounds" (*Modern Music Magazine,* Volume XIX, p. 245), we can see how interest in composing for percussion instruments led quite logically to Cage's later attitudes concerning musical structure.

> In writing for percussion instruments, the composer is dealing with material that does not fit into orthodox scales and harmonies. It is therefore necessary to find some other organizing means than those in use in the twelve-tone system.
>
> A method analogous to such a case, the "sound row" would contain any number of elements. However, because of the nature of the material involved, and because their duration characteristics can be easily controlled and related, it is more than likely that the unifying means will be rhythmic.

Before we consider Cage's musical structure in more depth, it will be helpful to consider the question: Why include noise as a musical element? It is important to understand why Cage worked with noise, because its use caused him to develop new organizational methods and principles.

> Wherever we are, what we hear is mostly noise. When we ignore it, it disturbs us. When we listen to it, we find it fascinating. The sound of a truck at fifty miles per hour. Static between the stations.

> Rain. We want to capture and control these sounds, to use them not as sound effects, but as musical instruments.[4]

Cage is dealing with a fundamental question: How does one create an art that deals directly with society in terms of the methods for structuring music and of the very sound-elements themselves?

Our culture requires us to deal with multiple layers of highly complex information on a day-to-day basis. Many people react to this barrage of information by "tuning out" much of it, thus being unaware of potentially significant life-experiences. Noise is a constant, integral element in our society, both as a by-product of the culture and as a carrier of information. If we try to ignore the noise, then it becomes a perpetual irritant. Cage's use of noise is a recycling process. He recycles everyday perhaps even hazardous sounds into music, a music that provides the listener with a sensitivity and a usable esthetic for coping with the sounds around us.

> I believe that the use of noise . . . to make music . . . will continue and increase until we reach a music produced through the aid of electrical instruments . . . which will make available for musical purposes any and all sounds that can be heard. . . . In the past, the point of disagreement has been between dissonance and consonance. It will be in the immediate future, between noise and so-called musical sounds, the present methods of writing music, principally those which employ harmony and its reference to particular steps in the field of sound . . . new methods will be discovered bearing a definite relation to Schoenberg's twelve-tone system.[5]

To summarize, Cage wanted to expand the composer's palette to include all sounds so he or she could create a new and relevant art form. New technologies require new modes of perception in order to deal with the life styles created by such technological changes. It should be noted that Cage was not the only composer who called for this timbral expansion. Varèse, Ives, Busoni, composers of the futurist movement, and many others called for a more inclusive rather than exclusive music.

In the 1930s Cage invented what Lou Harrison calls the "square root formula." He used this formula as the structural basis of his music and as a useful procedure to guard against composition being just another culturally conditioned act. For Cage realized that a composer must create a system of obstacles (strictly adhered-to pre-compositional rules) in order to free the composer to be truly creative.

The basic idea behind the "square root formula" is this: "The whole has as many parts as each unit has small parts, and these, large and small, in the same proportion."[6] In other words, the macro-structure is an enlarged image of the micro-structure, or, the micro-structure is a smaller image of the macro-structure.

A good example of how the "square root formula" works can be found in *Imaginary Landscape No. 3,* written, in 1942, for six percussionists performing on an audio frequency oscillator, ten empty tin cans, an electric buzzer, muted Balinese gongs, and a radio aerial coil attached to a phonograph pick-up arm. The rhythmic structure of the work is: 12 × 12 (3, 2, 4, 3). This means that the rhythmic structure of the entire composition is based on twelve repetitions of a twelve-measure phrase structure divided into three, two, four, and three measure phrases. (See fig. 2).

There are four sections in *Imaginary Landscape No. 3.* Each section of the composition is in the same proportion to the entire composition as the small phrases are to the twelve-measure structure. The first section is 3/12 (36m), the second section is 2/12 (24m), the third section is 4/12 (48m), and the fourth section is 3/12 (36m) of the composition. Thus the micro-structure of the twelve-measure phrase-structure, divided into 3, 2, 4, and 3 measure phrases, is in the same proportions employed in the macro-structure of the composition of 144 measures.

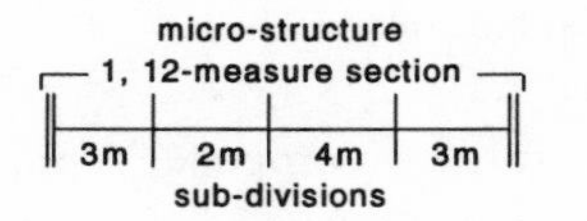

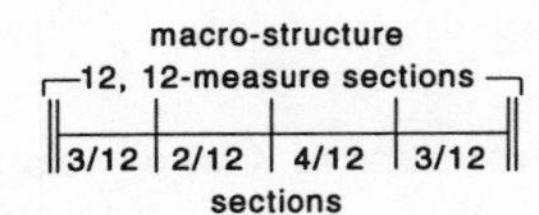

Fig. 1

The beginning of each sub-division of the twelve-measure phrase-structure is often an important point of entry for the performers. The individual parts are constructed of constantly shifting repeating figures. (See fig. 2.)

All of Cage's compositions written between 1939 and 1952 were composed with a similar principle of rhythmic structure, "a rhythmic structure based on duration, not of notes, but of spaces of time."[7] There are three factors that influenced Cage in his approach to rhythmic structure.

Fig. 2

First, Cage met Henry Cowell in 1932 and studied Oriental music with him at the New School for Social Research in New York. Cage studied the cyclic rhythmic structures of the East, like Indian tala, which is very similar to Cage's own later rhythmic concepts. "It [Cage's rhythmic approach] is analgous to Indian tala, but has the Western characteristic of beginning and ending."[8]

Second, in 1937 Cage began his long association with dance. He joined a modern dance company at U.C.L.A. as an accompanist and composer. In that same year he moved to Seattle as the composer-accompanist for Bonnie Bird at the Cornish School. Bird was committed to creating a more subtle relationship between dance and music, so neither one would suffer formalistically.

> In the belief that a too close collaboration between dancer and composer results in a clash of individualities and a series of small compromises destructive to the form of both music and dance, Miss Bird usually gives her composers a written description of her dance idea. . . . She gives them [composers] indications of the *time elements* [emphasis added] involved and they complete the music to their satisfaction away from her.[9]

As this quotation illustrates, Cage's involvement with modern dance surely was an influence that led him to view rhythm as the only viable musical parameter on which to base a composition.

Third, between 1934 and 1937 Cage studied musical analysis and counterpoint with Schoenberg at U.C.L.A. "Since Arnold Schoenberg had impressed upon me the structural function of tonality, I felt the need of finding some structural means adequate to composing for percussion. This led me eventually to a basic re-examination of the physical nature of sound."[10]

To further illustrate Cage's use of rhythm as the primary structural determinate, I will next discuss *Quartet: 12 Tom Toms,* which Cage wrote in 1943. In this piece he utilized an attack-point system as a method of density or textural control. Cage describes it as "a method controlling the number of icti [attacks] within small structural divisions." In other words, this system pre-determines how many sounds will occur in a given period of time. Mr. Cage told me in a phone interview that he was influenced by Lou Harrison's use of a similar method, and furthermore, that Mr. Harrison was influenced by Henry Cowell, who got the idea for an icti-controlled method from Charles Seeger (see *Music Primer,* Lou Harrison, p. 18).

The macro-structure of the *Quartet: 12 Tom Toms* is four thirty-nine-measure sections (hereby referred to as Section I, II, III and IV), each divided into nine smaller sub-divisions.

Cage makes a distinction between structure and method. "By 'structure' is meant the division of a whole into parts; by 'method,' the note-to-note procedure."[11]

The method he devised was cyclic. He drew a circle on which were placed numbers which corresponded to the number of attack-points per measure and/or per sectional sub-division. Mr. Cage informed me that these numbers, used to predetermine the number of attack-points, were derived from the initial idea, which was improvised. No matter where he was on the circle, he would have the option of two choices for the next number (one could go either clockwise or counterclockwise at any point). As Cage said, "What bothered me about serial composition is the unidirectionality of it. Once you begin, you only have one choice."

Cage also said that he is interested in the situation where method and structure have "their own life"; they are not interdependent. The method was often considered improvisation, while the structure was totally pre-determined. "Composition, then, I viewed, ten years ago, as an activity integrating the opposites, the rational and the irrational, bringing about, ideally, a freely moving continuity within strict division of parts, the sounds, their combinations and succession being either logically related or arbitrarily chosen."[12]

The remainder of my article will be an examination of *Quartet: 12 Tom Toms* in detail.

The dimensions of the sound material used in the piece are, one, a timbral scale of twenty-four sounds (the composition is played by the performers using their hands on both the center and the edge of the drums, thus producing two sounds for each instrument; two additional timbres are made when a timpani mallet and brush are used as beaters), and, two, a dynamic scale of *ppp* to *f*.

The nine sub-divisions in the 39-measure sections are grouped into 4, 7, 2, 5, 4, 7, 2, 3, and 5 measures. Each sub-division was assigned a certain number of attack-points (icti) per player. The first four measures of Section I has eight tutti attacks. In the next seven measures, Player A and Player C each have 34 attacks while Player B has 20 and Player D has 14 (the addition of Player B and Player C is 34 attacks; see figs. 3 and 4).

The second section of the piece is a quasi-canonic section; the entry points of the individual performers are 4m, 7m, 2m, 5m, 5m, 5m. These entry points are derived from the sub-divisions in Section I. (See fig. 5.)

Section III is organized in a similar manner to Section I in that each sub-division is assigned a certain number of attack-points. (See fig. 6.)

In Section IV of *Quartet: 12 Tom Toms,* Cage maintains the recurring

Fig. 3

List of the Number of Attack-points per Sub-division in Section 1.

The two-measure phrase:		
Player A	2 attacks	
Player B	2 attacks	
Player C	2 attacks	
Player D	2 attacks	
The five-measure phrase:		
Player A	24 attacks	
Player B	6 attacks	
Player C	7 attacks	6 + 7 + 11 = 24
Player D	11 attacks	
The four-measure phrase:		
6 tutti attacks		
The seven-measure phrase:		
Player A	34 attacks	
Player B	20 attacks	
Player C	34 attacks	20 + 14 = 34
Player D	14 attacks	
The two-measure phrase:		
4 tutti attacks		
The three-measure phrase:		
0 tutti attacks		
The five-measure phrase:		
Player A	24 attacks	
Player B	6 attacks	
Player C	7 attacks	6 + 7 + 11 = 24
Player D	11 attacks	

Fig. 4

durational structure. This section consists of unison rhythms with one contrapuntal interruption. I think of this section as a textural inversion of Sections I and III, as Sections I and III consist of contrapuntal texture and unison interruptions. (See fig. 7.)

Section I consists of combinations of transposed rhythmic values and tonic rhythmic values (tonic rhythmic values are rhythms that occur "naturally" within the meter like 𝄽 ♩♩♫♩ or ♩♩ 𝄼; transposed rhythmic values are values like [musical notation] or [musical notation]). Section II consists of tonic rhythms. Section III consists of a combination of tonic and transposed rhythmic values derived from Section I and II. Section IV consists of tonic rhythms with one contrapuntal interruption of transposed rhythmic values.

Thus the macro-structure reflects the micro-structure of the first seven-measure attack-point design in that Sections I and III are related, and Sections II and IV are different. (See figs. 8 and 9.)

Fig. 5

Cage wished to avoid thematic repetition and variation as a unifying factor in *Quartet: 12 Tom Toms.* The function of the icti method and the rhythmic macro-structure was to provide a new technique to take the place of motivic development as the main unifying factor.

I do feel, however, that there are two rhythmic figures that tend to function as motives throughout the composition. The first figure is ♩. ♪ 𝅗𝅥 ♩ ♩ 𝅗𝅥 which is stated in unison at the beginning. The second figure is 𝄾♫♩ 𝄾♫♩ , a frequently used figure, first stated in measure 6. These figures reappear often, either verbatim or slightly altered.

Example: The first figure as it appears in measure 24 of Section III, played ♩. ♪ 𝄽 ♩ ♩ 𝅗𝅥 with brushes.

Example: The second figure serves as a basic figure in Section II. It appears as:

♫ ♩, ♩ ♫, 𝄾♫♩

In conclusion, Cage uses time as a space to be filled rather than as a by-product of a developmental process. He demonstrates in his early

List of the Number of Attack-points per sub-division in Section III.

The four-measure phrase:

Player	Attacks	
Player A	4 attacks	
Player B	16 attacks	
Player C	4 attacks	4 + 4 = 8
Player D	16 attacks	

The seven-measure phrase:

Player	Attacks	
Player A	34 attacks	
Player B	18 attacks	
Player C	16 attacks	18 + 16 = 34
Player D	34 attacks	

The two-measure phrase:

Player	Attacks	
Player A	1 attack	
Player B	14 attacks	
Player C	0 attacks	1 + 14 + 1 = 16
Player D	1 attack	

The five-measure phrase:

Player	Attacks	
Player A	24 attacks	
Player B	6 attacks	
Player C	7 attacks	6 + 7 + 11 = 24
Player D	11 attacks	

The four-measure phrase:

Player	Attacks	
Player A	4 attacks	
Player B	16 attacks	
Player C	4 attacks	4 + 4 = 8
Player D	16 attacks	

The seven-measure phrase:

Player	Attacks	
Player A	34 attacks	
Player B	22 attacks	
Player C	12 attacks	22 + 12 = 34
Player D	34 attacks	

The two-measure phrase:

Player	Attacks	
Player A	0 attacks	
Player B	14 attacks	
Player C	1 attack	14 + 1 + 1 = 16
Player D	1 attack	

The three-measure phrase:

Player	Attacks
Player A	0 attacks
Player B	14 attacks
Player C	1 attack
Player D	0 attacks

The five-measure phrase:

Player	Attacks	
Player A	24 attacks	
Player B	6 attacks	
Player C	7 attacks	6 + 7 + 11 = 24
Player D	11 attacks	

Fig. 6

Fig. 7

percussion works that any sound, no matter how complex or "unconventional," can be organized into a coherent musical composition. Furthermore, by the very idea that any sound can be utilized in music, given the proper temporal framework, Cage proves that the sound-image (overall timbral icon) of a composition is more transitory in interest and ultimately in value than the rhythmic structure or organizational process of a composition. In the final analysis, Cage, by using any and all sounds, proves that sound is not the primal parameter in music; time is.

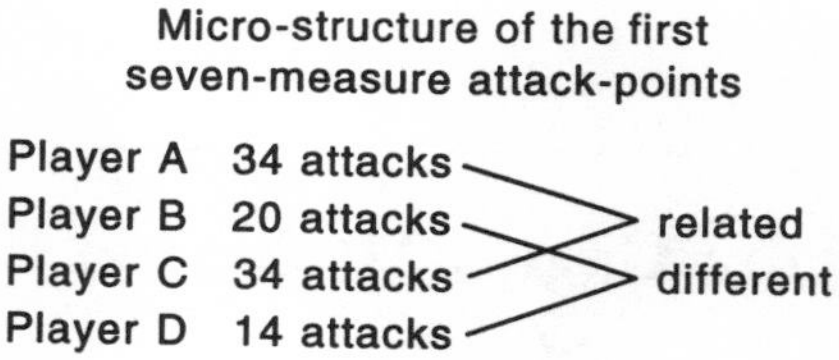

Micro-structure of the first
seven-measure attack-points

Player A 34 attacks
Player B 20 attacks — related
Player C 34 attacks — different
Player D 14 attacks

Fig. 8

Macro-structure of the
entire piece

Section I
Section II — related
Section III — different
Section IV

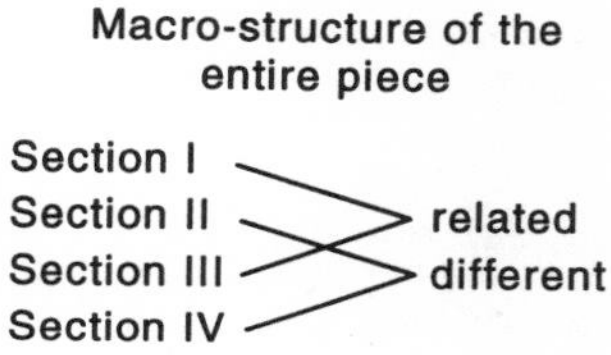

Fig. 9

NOTES

1. John Cage, *Silence,* p. 5.
2. Calvin Tomkins, *The Bride and the Bachelors,* p. 102.
3. John Cage, *Silence,* p. 8.
4. John Cage, *Silence,* p. 3.
5. John Cage, *Silence,* pp. 3, 4, 5.
6. Lou Harrison, *Music Primer,* p. 10.
7. John Cage, *John Cage,* Richard Kostelanetz, editor, p. 127.
8. Ibid.
9. Verna Arvey, *Choreographic Music: Music for Dance,* p. 408.
10. John Cage, *Silence,* p. 127.
11. John Cage, *Silence,* p. 18.
12. John Cage, "Composition as Process," *Silence,* p. 18.

BIBLIOGRAPHY

Arvey, Verna. *Choreographic Music: Music for the Dance.* New York: E. P. Dutton, 1941.

Cage, John. *Silence.* Middletown, Conn.: Wesleyan University Press, 1961.

Cowell, Henry. *New Musical Resources.* New York: Something Else Press, 1969.

Harrison, Lou. *Music Primer.* New York: C. F. Peters, 1971.

Kostelanetz, Richard, ed. *John Cage.* New York: Praeger, 1970.

Snyder, Ellsworth. *John Cage and Music Since World War II: A Study in Applied Aesthetics.* Madison: University of Wisconsin Microfilms, 1970.

Tomkins, Calvin. *The Bride and the Bachelors.* New York: Viking, 1965.

About John Cage's "Prepared Piano" (1990)

Daniel Charles

> I couldn't use percussion instruments for Syvilla's dance, though, suggesting Africa, they would have been suitable; they would have left too little room for her to perform. I was obliged to write a piano piece. I spent a day or so conscientiously trying to find an African 12-tone row. I had no luck. I decided that what was wrong was not me but the piano. I decided to change it.
>
> (John Cage, Foreword to Richard Bunger's *The Well-Prepared Piano,* 1973)

One knows Schoenberg's prophecy about tone colour: if we are able to erect "structures which we call melodies," i.e., "successions whose coherence is similar to that of thought," out of pitch-differentiated sounds, then we will create, out of the dimension of tone colour, successions "whose relationships work with a kind of logic entirely equivalent to that which suffices for a melody of pitches."[1] Even if that could but seem "a Futuristic fantasy" in 1911, Schoenberg firmly believed it would cause "the sensuous, expressive, and spiritual pleasures which art is in a position to offer to grow in unheard-of ways": it would "bring us closer to the bewitchment of dreams."[2] Even without theory or "logic," i.e., without measuring, describing and ordering the variety of tone colours, their succesion would "somehow agree with our feeling for beauty."[3]

In fact Schoenberg himself did not approach the logic of dreams he had been praising in his *Harmonielehre:* having stated that the paradox of tone colours "lies in the contrast between its direct communicative power and the historical inability to grasp it critically or analytically," he never attempted to explain "the principles that interrelate the diverse sounds of a given work."[4] Confining his music to the conventional 12-tone scale, he did not seek to elaborate on the fourteenth-century developments by increasing still further the instrumental techniques or alterations which had led to the wide variety of the orchestral colouring of the full range of discrete chromatic pitches. That perplexed the mind of one of his students and fans, John Cage, for whom the practical problem of how to compose without having at his disposal either the ordinary instrumental resources or the relatively uncommon ones of the percussion ensemble arose. In the late Thirties, Cage was employed as accompanist for the classes in modern dance at the Cornish School in Seattle, Washington; these classes were taught by Bonnie Bird, who had worked with Martha Graham. One of Bonnie's students, Syvilla Fort, asked John Cage to write an accompaniment for a *Bacchanal* she was to perform some days later. Cage had at the time two ways of composing: either 12-tone music for classical instruments, or approximate pitch or noise for little percussion ensembles. Unfortunately, the Cornish Theatre had no space in the wings, and no pit; there was only a piano at one side in front of the stage. Now how was it possible to compose an appropriate, i.e., African, accompaniment, without any percussive device? Having tried in vain to find "an African 12-tone row," Cage "decided that what was wrong was . . . the piano": he decided "to change it."[5]

Cage had studied not only with Schoenberg, but with Henry Cowell: "I had often heard him play a grand piano," he says, "changing its sound by plucking and muting the strings with fingers and hands. I particularly loved to hear him play *The Banshee*. To do this, Henry Cowell first depressed the pedal with a wedge at the back (or asked an assistant, sometimes myself, to sit at the keyboard and hold the pedal down), and then, standing at the back of the piano, he produced the music by lengthwise friction on the bass strings with his fingers or fingernails, and by crosswise sweeping of the bass strings with the palms of his hands. In another piece he used a darning egg, moving it lengthwise along the strings while trilling, as I recall, on the keyboard; this produced a glissando of harmonics."[6] And in parallel with Cowell's experiments in the Twenties, Maurice Ravel's *L'enfant et les sortilèges* (1920–25) had included the weaving of paper into the piano strings.[7] With such examples in mind, Cage didn't hesitate. "I went to the kitchen," he recounts, "got a pie plate, brought it into the living room and placed it on the piano strings. I played a few keys. The piano sounds had been changed, but the pie plate bounced around due to the vibrations, and, after a while, some of the sounds that had been changed no longer were. I tried something smaller, nails between the strings. They slipped down between and lengthwise along the strings. It dawned on me that screws or bolts would stay in position. They did. And I was delighted with the sounds they produced. I noticed the difference obained by use of the *una corda* . . . I wrote the *Bacchanal* quickly and with the excitement continual discovery provided."[8]

As psychophysicist Harvey Fletcher, analyzing the colour of the piano tone in 1962, has shown, the quality of the "colouring" does not only depend, during "normal" piano playing, upon the wave form or spectrum ("Helmholtz's differing partials with differing intensities") of the sound. It also depends "upon the pitch, the loudness, the decay and attack time, the variation with time of the intensity of the partials, the impact noise of the hammer, the noise of the damping pedal, and also the characeristic ending of the tone by the damping felt, etc."[9] It is not "one characteristic, but rather a *bundle of characteristics,* which has come to be called (especially in electronic music) the *sound envelope*."[10] One may very well introduce slight or important changes into the onset, the body or the release of the sound simply by modifying one's minute gesture while playing. Moreover "due to the stiffness of the vibrating string, certain of the partials (particularly of low notes) are sharp; this slight discrepancy of intonation, far from being displeasing, produces an element of 'warmth' in the sound"; and similarly there is a "*necessary slight mistuning* of the two or three 'identical' strings that pianos have for each pitch";[11] so that "a very slight shortening, lengthening, softening, or loudening of the impact noise—as well as narrowing or extending its frequency band—is enough to destroy the sense of piano colour, even if all other characteristics remain unchanged."[12] Conclusion: "To deal adequately with tone-colour phenomena, we must consider the complete vibrational spectra of the sound events, not merely a simplistic reduction of the sound to a fundamental (as in notational conventions and almost all previous theory) or even to instrumentation/orchestration (as in what has until now passed for tone-colour theory)."[13] Such a holistic perspective was already present in 1938, when Cage began to "prepare" his piano for Syvilla Fort's *Bacchanal:* instead of conceiving the transformations of the piano sounds as Schoenberg would probably have conceived them, i.e., as merely rendering the piano tones unidentifiable as such, Cage was opening his ears—and our ears—to a radical expansion of new sonic resources, through a systematically (even if empirically) increased exploration of the available sound materials.

In other terms, he was inventing the new context in which such transformations were to become meaningful.[14]

He himself has explained this specific point.

> When I first placed objects between piano strings, it was with the desire to possess sounds (to be able to repeat them). But, as the music left my home and went from piano to piano and from pianist to pianist, it became clear that not only are two pianists essentially different from one another, but two pianos are not the same either. Instead of the possibility of repetition, we are faced in life with the unique qualities and characteristics of each occasion. The prepared piano, impressions I had from the world of artist friends, studies of Zen Buddhism, ramblings in the fields and forests looking for mushrooms, all led me to the enjoyment of things as they come, as they happen, rather than as they are possessed or kept or forced to be.[15]

First of all, the fact that two pianos are never the same is worth underlining. Let us consider the "scale" (the "entire set of proportions of sounding parts") for any piano design: it is "different," as Richard Bunger explains in his study of *The Well-Prepared Piano,* for every make and model of piano. "Therefore preparations used for one may sound differently or be inapplicable on another piano."[16] For instance, since the string length for any given pitch varies from piano to piano, the location designation (e.g., "four inches behind the damper") must be re-calculated from one instrument to the next, if one wants to obtain some identical sonic result; but if one does *not* wish to repeat the "same" sound, one may very well keep the designation intact. In a similar manner, the second F below Middle C has three strings on some pianos, two on others: since there is, as we have seen, a necessary slight mistuning of these strings, the unisons are to be dramatically controlled; but it is possible as well to leave certain resonances free. Now when the design of a piano includes an "overstringing" ("the design feature whereby the bass strings cross diagonally over the strings of the middle register, at a higher elevation above the soundboard . . . necessary for the efficient use of space inside the piano, for maximum string length in the middle registers, and for added resonance in the middle and lower registers through sympathetic vibrations"), one cannot apply anything to, or remove anything from, the lower strings, without using tweezers, and the objects introduced in the overstrung area may not rattle against one of the set of strings.[17] "The cardinal rule of piano preparation is: *Never force anything between the strings.*"[18] If this rule is observed, preparing a piano will never damage the instrument; the preparations, though they will slightly increase the tension on the strings, will *not* put the piano out of tune, since they will affect it "substantially less than the tension variation caused by normal changes in humidity";[19] and there is no reason why dry hands should corrode the strings. In order to prevent the hammers from striking the preparations, all the objects used will have to be placed over the soundboard area, but in such a way as not to vibrate against the soundboard when the note is played.[20]

Now as concerns the "unique qualities and characteristics of each occasion" which, according to Cage, prevent the live performer from indulging himself with mere repetition, one will easily agree with Richard Bunger: verbal descriptions are too limiting to allow any inventory, even approximate, of the "myriad timbres available by preparation of a piano."[21] Rather, one has to experience and distinguish aurally each nuance. Nevertheless, it is possible to say that "timbres of prepared notes vary from bright to dark as the materials employed vary from hard to soft," and to classify some of the "interdependent variables within each preparation which affect timbre *and* pitch of the resulting prepared sound": the pitch may be lowered if one increases the mass of the preparing object; and it may be raised if one increases the sideways tension on the strings by placing between them objects the diameters of which are gradually enlarged; in both cases, the timbre will be affected. Symmetrically, the relative placement of the object along the string length and the strength and rapidity of the keyboard attack will concern not only timbre, but also pitch. Bolts (including stove bolts, cap screws, carriage bolts, thumb screws, machine bolts and machine screws) and screws (including wood screws, sheet metal screws and lag screws), with all their possible variations of mass, may be used in combination with washers and nuts, which will provide "jangle, buzz, clink or rattle when the note is played";[22] coins (pennies, as specified by Cage, or dimes), wire, L-screws and U-bolts are also to be employed. In his *Suite I for Prepared Piano,* Christian Wolff uses strips from a tin can cover. As concerns wood, every degree of hardness provides its own timbral characteristics: brittle woods such as bamboo offer gong-like sounds and soft woods offer thuds. As concerns cloth mutes, one may use weatherstrips, wool felt, and ribbons; mutes of plastic and rubber of different densities and elasticities will provide drum-like and woodblock-like thuds and thunks: while a wiring insulation may help to imitate Chinese temple blocks, piano tuners' rubber wedges produce, if the notes are played *pp* in the middle piano range, sounds similar to those of the bamboo stamping drums of Polynesia. One is also free to use rubber pencil erasers, like Cage in the *Sonatas and Interludes;* lamp cords; foam rubber; scraps of sheet plastic; etc.[23]

"To thicken the plot," as Sri Ramakrishna—quoted by John Cage[24]—said, it is possible to invent "hybrid preparations, employing "more than a single timbral factor for any one note." For instance on a three-string unison one may place two identical preparations at different distances behind the damper, or prepare a single note with more than one type of preparation material, or combine both procedures.[25] One may also, thanks to the *una corda* pedal, manage transitions from one timbre to another, or from a hybrid preparation to a "pure" one.[26] One may place a preparation at the harmonic node on a piano string in order to emphasize the pitch of that partial.[27] One may also use *surface preparations*—those which "are laid upon the strings rather than being wedged between them"—by damping the strings with one hand, before playing the damped note on the keyboard with the other hand; or by lightly touching a node, thus producing a pure piano harmonics; or by sliding the damping finger or hand along the length of the string in order to vary the timbre; etc. Among the indefinite number of surface preparations available, Richard Bunger has given the following *real* (recently called for by composers during the sixties) selection:

—a book (size specified) laid onto the strings;
—ping-pong balls on the treble-register strings;
—a strip of paper (2″ × 8″) laid onto the strings and slid forward beneath the dampers;
—a chalkboard eraser;
—a metal triangle beater laid on the strings between *a* and *a';*
—metal protractors and 3″ notebook rings linked and laid onto the bass strings;
—a nude woman lying on the piano strings inside the lid.[28]

Another possibility of enhancing the complexity of the preparations has been introduced by the use of electronics. Microphones or relays convert sound vibrations to electrical energy, and amplifiers, filters and modulators are to be employed as modifying devices. "Microphones," Richard Bunger explains, "may be masking-taped to the soundboard, the piano case or the iron plate. They may also be suspended on mike booms underneath or inside the open piano. One should experiment with both air microphones and contact microphones for different effects."[29] And among the innumerable modifying devices currently marketed, one has to mention at least "ring modulator, envelope follower, voltage-controlled amplifier, low-pass filter, 'fuzz box.'"[30]

We may recall here the talk which John Cage delivered at a meeting of a Seattle arts society organized by Bonnie Bird in 1937—one year *before* the invention of the prepared piano—under the title "The Future of Music: Credo."[31] "Given four film phonographs," Cage said, "we can compose and perform a quartet for explosive motor, wind, heartbeat, and landslide." This is certainly not "music" in the ordinary sense. Therefore, "if this word *music* is sacred and reserved for eighteenth- and nineteenth-century instruments, we can substitute a more meaningful term: organization of sound." But unfortunately, "most inventors have attempted to imitate eighteenth- and nineteenth-century instruments, just as early automobile designers copied the carriage."[32] So that "we are shielded from new sound experiences."[33] But, in Cage's perspective of 1937, this rather negative situation was soon to be improved: thanks to electricity, the composer would be "faced with the entire field of sound"; and then, he would not have any more to deal with the old "methods of writing music, principally those which employ harmony and its reference to particular steps in the field of sound."[34] "New methods"—Cage added—"will be discovered, bearing a definite relation to Schoenberg's 12-tone system . . . and present methods of writing percussion music." Why Schoenberg's system? Because while harmony "assigned to each material, in a group of unequal materials, its function with respect to the fundamental or most important material in the group," Schoenberg's method "assigns to each material, in a group of equal materials, its function with respect to the group"; so that it is "analogous to a society in which the emphasis is on the group and the integration of the individual in the group." And why percussion music? Because "percussion music is a contemporary transition from keyboard-influenced music to the all-sound music of the future. Any sound is acceptable to the composer of percussion music; he explores the academically forbidden 'nonmusical' field of sound insofar as it is manually possible."[35]

The invention of the prepared piano is thus to be judged not only in reference to the ancient state of affairs, which involved harmony and hierarchy and unequality, but as a positive step toward the liberation of music and its transformation into the "all-sound music of the future." For the young Cage, Schoenberg is a model inasmuch as he is the herald of *equality* (between the sounds, and between human beings as well); but Cage rejects Schoenberg as a zealot of harmony, i.e., of unequal relationships between sounds as well as between men. In the age of electricity, how could we take it upon ourselves to confront music (and society) in a resolutely feudal and mechanistic manner, as if the arrival of precision technology could only lead to the re-activation of strict determinsm, by right and de facto, as a logical conclusion of the scientific positivism of the twentieth century? By driving to its last extremity the keyboard-influenced music, the prepared piano upsets all allegiance to the inherited pattern of unequality and opens the way to the carrying out of the utopia of *pantonality*:[36] Between 1937 and 1938, between the "Credo" and the *Bacchanal,* it is our entire intellectual equipment which has suddently been modified, as much as—if not more than—our artisan musical practice. . . . Not only has the music of our time ceased to resemble that of yesterday, but, moreover, the category of music itself, the definition of this art-form, has been overthrown. A decisive destabilization: as "organization of sound," music has, in effect, become a *nomad.*

NOTES

1. A. Schoenberg, *Harmonielehre,* Vienna, Universal Edition, 1922, S. 506–507; translated by R. Cogan in R. Cogan and Pozzi Escot, *Sonic Design—The Nature of Sound and Music,* Englewood Cliffs, New Jersey, Prentice Hall, 1976, p. 327.
2. Schoenberg, loc. cit.
3. Ibid.
4. Cogan and Escot, loc. cit., p. 327–328.
5. J. Cage, Foreword to R. Bunger, *The Well-Prepared Piano,* Colorado Springs, The Colorado College Music Press, 1973.
6. Ibid.
7. Cf. W. Brooks, "Instrumental and Vocal Resources," in J. Vinton ed., *Dictionary of Contemporary Music,* New York, Dutton, 1974, p. 348.

8. Cage, loc. cit.

9. H. Fletcher, E. D. Blackham, and R. Stratton, "Quality of Piano Tones," in *Journal of the Acoustical Society of America,* n. 34, 1962, p. 749-61. Quoted in Cogan and Escot, loc. cit., p. 330.

10. Cogan and Escot, loc. cit.

11. Ibid., p. 330.

12. Ibid., p. 332.

13. Fletcher, in Cogan and Escot, loc. cit., p. 333.

14. Ibid.

15. Cage, loc. cit.

16. Bunger, loc. cit., p. 4.

17. Ibid., p. 5.

18. Ibid., p. 6.

19. Ibid., p. 1.

20. Ibid., p. 6.

21. Ibid., p. 9.

22. Ibid., p. 12.

23. Ibid., p. 11-26.

24. Quoted in J. Cage, "Forerunners of Modern Music" (1949), in *Silence,* Middletown, Connecticut, Wesleyan University Press, 1961, p. 63.

25. Bunger, loc. cit., p. 26-27.

26. Ibid., p. 27.

27. Ibid., p. 28.

28. Ibid., p. 29.

29. Ibid., p. 29-30.

30. Ibid., p. 30.

31. Cf. J. Cage, *Silence,* p. 3-6.

32. Ibid., p. 3.

33. Ibid., p. 4.

34. Ibid.

35. Ibid., p. 5.

36. H. K. Metzger, "Abortive Concepts in the Theory and Criticism of Music," in *Die Reihe* 5 *(Reports/Analysis),* Bryn Mawr, Pennsylvania, Theodor Presser, 1961, p. 24.

Cage's Well-Tampered Clavier (1978)

Eric Salzman

Sonatas and Interludes for prepared piano, and *A Book of Music* for two prepared pianos: this is John Cage's Well-Tampered Clavier, his two major sets or cycles of music for the prepared piano.

And if there is still someone in this day and age who does not know about prepared pianos, it should be stated that they are ordinary grand pianos which have pieces of metal, rubber, wood, or plastic inserted between the strings. The effect is that of a percussion ensemble in the hands of a single player, and indeed Cage invented the prepared piano in 1938 in order to be able to provide a percussional music for modern dance without having to employ an army of players and instruments.

Between 1938 and 1951, Cage wrote about sixteen works for prepared piano, including the twenty *Sonatas and Interludes,* written between February, 1946, and March, 1948, and the earlier *Book of Music* for two pianos written in 1944 for Robert Fizdale and Arthur Gold. These are the major works of Cage b.c.—before chance. They represent the confluence of three ideas that came into American music in the Thirties and Forties: numerology, the dominant use of percussion, and influence from the East.

The serial elements in Cage's music are often forgotten since he was later set up as the arch-rival of serialism. But Cage was a pupil of Schoenberg, wrote a kind of twelve-tone music in the Thirties, and was as Pythagorean as any of his contemporaries. Of course, Schoenberg, Babbitt, and even Boulez are still strongly oriented towards the manipulation of pitches, while Cage, almost from the first, demoted pitch as a central organizing element. After his very early pieces, he turned to organizing rhythm and tone color. The fixed, chromatic tuning no longer rules the roost; patterned, rhythmic noise—tuned and untuned percussion—is the essential element, along with the notion adapted from Eastern thought of patterned or affective expressive states.

This fragile synthesis of the ultrarational, the irrational, the emotional and the stylized, the Western and non-Western is characteristic of Cage's earlier work and very different from the aggressive, window-on-the-world randomness that we have come to associate with this composer-philosopher. It is also not a unique contribution of Cage but very much part of a certain period in American music, a period that has really not yet received its due. During the Depression, the mainstream of American art music moved away from avant-gardism toward populism, social realism, and traditionalism. A corollary of this was an interest in folk and ethnic music outside of the Western art music tradition. These crosscurrents are best represented by the figure of Charles Seeger, intellectual guru of the avant-garde in the Twenties, who turned to folk and ethnic music in the following decade. This was not an isolated phenomenon. One need only think of the new and widespread interest in percussion (Varèse, Amadeo Roldán, Henry Cowell, Carlos Chávez) or the orientalizing styles of composers like Colin McPhee (who actually lived in Bali and studied gamelan), Alan Hovhaness, Harry Partch, Lou Harrison and, especially, Cowell, easily the most seminal figure of the time. California—so far West it looks East—was a natural center for this music. A number of major figures of the time lived and worked on the West Coast, and there was actually a new-music percussion ensemble active there for a time.

Cage's two big prepared-piano cycles are then a culmination, not just of his own early interests, but of a whole movement or school of American music. They constitute a kind of musical thought which has roots in Western culture but takes a strong anti-Western position both in technical matters and in the affective content of the music. *Sonatas and Interludes* is an explicit attempt to make a gamut of stylized emotions in the (East) Indian manner—"the heroic, the erotic, the wondrous, the mirthful, sorrow, fear, anger, the odious and their common tendency toward tranquillity." In the plunk, twang, and thump of keyboard percussion we are to hear not so much an expression of emotion but an exorcism of it in the framework of Buddhist quietism.

Of the two works, the earlier, less familiar *Book*—a first recording—is the more intriguing. It was written for a virtuoso duo-piano team, and the introduction of virtuosic elements gives it qualities of concreteness and this-worldliness which I find appealing (the great teachers and masters are rarely "otherworldly," although they mediate between the earthly and the spiritual). This work is less obviously "original" in that it clearly owes something to its Asian and American models, but I do not find that a defect: quite the contrary. By contrast, the *Sonatas and Interludes* are soft, gentle, spacey, never agonized or alienated like expressionistic modern art; in their very gentleness and quietude, they make a very specialized and personal appeal. The expression is ritualized, but the ritual is invented, actually personal to Cage. To get into it, we have to suspend musical belief for an hour—like a Yoga exercise where you must hold your mental breath until you turn blue in order to reach the required states of exaltation and an even keel. This is equivalent to a religious commitment with Cage as our teacher.

It comes as something of a shock to realize that, after all these years, the Cage influence on new music remains notable, but it is early Cage which is now the most relevant. There are many lines of connection between that old, orientalizing avant-garde and those contemporary transcendental musics of long, repeated patterns and slow, pulsating change—the musics of La Monte Young, Terry Riley, Steve Reich, Phil Glass, David Borden, and others. This is also a movement with strong California roots and a vigorous New York transplant, and the historical, spiritual, and musical debt to Cage and Partch, and, through them, Cowell and Harrison is undeniable.

The preparer, mover, and shaker of this album is Joshua Pierce, a twenty-six-year-old pianist and conductor from the Manhattan School of Music. Pierce plays the *Sonatas and Interludes* with great conviction, and is joined in the *Book* by Maro Ajemian, long the outstanding pioneer and exponent of the Cagean prepared piano. The recording is excellent and the attractive production includes the entire (and highly precise) table of preparations for the *Sonatas and Interludes*. Instructions in hand, you could easily make one for yourself and, if you fancy, write your own music for the medium.

On Form (1960)

Christian Wolff

Form in music could be taken as a length of program time.

This is clearest in the work of John Cage of the last four or five years. No distinction is made between the sounds of a work and sounds in general, prior to, simultaneous with, or following the work. Art—music—and nature are not thought of as separated. Music is allowed no privileges over sound. Yet the work is quite distinct. It can be timed and tends to use sounds not always generally heard and in combinations not generally common. But its distinctiveness implies no exclusiveness. The work tends to be at once itself and quite perspicuous (cf. painting on glass and constellations).

A piece as it starts and stops is indicated by the actions of its performers (even when no sounds are scored at all). Form is a theatrical event of a certain length, and the length itself may be unpredictable.

At one remove from the event the form of a piece is reduced to a score, instructions for performers. It is a question of what should go on for how long, a matter of boundaries before an event: boundaries which the event tends to annihilate or obscure.

Take, for example, what John Cage found long ago and called a rhythmic structure: a sequence of proportions which fix time lengths and are expressed both in small for phrases (e.g., 2, 5, $\frac{1}{4}$, 1, 3, 11, $2\frac{1}{2}$ seconds) and in large for the parts of the total structure of a piece (thus seven sections $49\frac{1}{2}$, $123\frac{3}{4}$, $6\frac{3}{16}$, $74\frac{1}{4}$, $272\frac{1}{4}$ and $61\frac{7}{8}$ seconds long, i.e., $2 \times (2 + 5 + \frac{1}{4} + 1 + 3 + 11 + 2\frac{1}{2})$; $5 \times (2 + 5 + \frac{1}{4} + 1 + 3 + 11 + 2\frac{1}{2})$; etc.). The sum of the phrase lengths, $24\frac{3}{4}$, is, then, the square root of the total length of the piece, $612\frac{9}{16}$ seconds. A frame subdivided according to proportions chosen either deliberately or at random, in any case arbitrary as frame, is taken as given. Any criteria for characterizing its subdivisions are possible.

This sequence of lengths may be multiplied through to make a square like the following.

4	10	½	2	6	22	5	(2 x 2, 2 x 5, 2 x ¼, 2 x 1, etc.)
10	25	1¼	5	15	55	12½	
½	1¼	1/16	¼	¾	2¾	⅝	
2	5	¼	1	3	11	2½	
6	15	¾	3	9	33	7½	
22	55	2¾	11	33	121	27½	
5	12½	⅝	2½	7½	27½	6¼	

(The square as it stands has certain properties, for instance, the possibility of a unique series of lengths on the diagonal from the upper left hand corner to lower right, i.e., from beginning through center to end—4, 25, 1/16, 1, 9, 121, 6¼—and the symmetrical spacing of one repetition of each of the remaining lengths—thus the horizontal sequence beginning with 4 = the vertical column beginning with 4; the horizontal sequence beginning with 10 = the vertical column beginning with 10; etc.)

To begin to define the subdivisions of lengths one might next take a second square having a number of elements (subdivisions) equivalent to the first, namely 49. On this second square continuities—in space, discontinuous from a linear point of view—can be indicated by recurrent moves. For example:

				3c		
1a						2b
	4c					3b
	2a					
	3a		4b 1c			
				2c	4a 1b	

There are three continuities here—a, b, c—of four elements each (1–4). Each continuity makes the same move which can be described as: 1 (1a starts anywhere); 2: two spaces down from 1 and one over to the right; 3: one down from 2; 4: two down from 3 and four to the right. The second and third continuities (b, c) repeat the move overlapping at the beginning, that is, 1b starts in the same space as 4a, 1c as 4b. Since the square in its two dimensions can't accommodate all moves thus repeated, its limits at top, bottom and sides are considered continuous, bottom to top and side to side. Thus the first part of the move (two spaces down and one over to the right) in the second continuity (b), from 1b to 2b, must proceed to the top of its vertical column and from there move down two spaces and then over to the right. Similarly, from 3b to 4b one can go down two (as from 3a to 4a), but must then go to the other side of the horizontal line of spaces in order to move four to the right.

The three continuities made on one move can be characterized in any number of ways, i.e., can be used as references to whatever aspects of sound one wishes to compose. And while characterizing them individually, one may also indicate that they all belong to one move by criteria applicable to all of them together. For example, if they are differentiated by having each a particular pitch gamut, they may be related by sharing a common tempo, or timbre or dynamic configuration.

A whole structure would have a number of moves, each in turn separately characterized, perhaps of various numbers of elements (the move described above had four) and repeated for various numbers of times (three above). For instance:

6h	5e	7h		3c	10k	
1a				11k		2b
7g 5h 12k	4c				6g	3b
8j	2a		6f	9j	7f 5g	
	3a		4b 1c		10j	
	6e		7e 5f	11j		
12j 8k				2c 9k	4a 1b	

Now there are three moves (1–4 [as just described], 5–7, 8–12), repeated respectively three times (a,b,c), four times (e,f,g,h) and twice (j,k). Parts of different moves may intersect, as at the beginning of the third line $\left(\begin{smallmatrix}7g\\5h\end{smallmatrix}12k\right)$. And spaces in the square may be left blank, which means they will be silent.

Having thus fixed locations for criteria of sound or its absence, one can fix the extent of these locations, their possible durations, by applying the square of lengths we first described. Superimposing the two squares gives 6h in 4 seconds, 5e in 10, 7h in $\frac{1}{2}$, silence for 2, and so on.

Yet the disposition of the material in a given amount of time can be quite variable. If the element 6h refers one to a given source or gamut of pitches (or timbre or dynamics) and the move in which 6h occurs (5–7) involves a given tempo or configuration of durations, both the move and its particular continuity could still be expressed by just one sound. That sound, to be sure, might come at the beginning of the 4-second length and 5e could start at the beginning of the following 10-second length marking off 4 seconds. Articulating all the structural lengths, then, can indicate a minimal order.

But even this order is not entirely fixed, and the form, originating as a frame or system of frames, is not necessarily closed. Silence, for one, introduces ambiguities. Within the space of 10 seconds, for instance, there may be $3\frac{1}{2}$ seconds of continuous silence. But this theoretically contained, i.e., structurally subordinate, amount of silence cannot be distinguished from the 2 seconds of silence which make up a discrete structural unit.

Further, this order can be elaborated by superimposing different readings of the squares of durations and of elements. Use, say, the square of elements as given (6h, 5e, 7h, etc.) but combine it with the square of lengths beginning with 5, at the end of the first line, and continuing with $12\frac{1}{2}$, $\frac{5}{8}$, $2\frac{1}{2}$, etc., i.e., read this square turned over on one side. Simultaneously, then, in a second "voice," use, conversely, the square of lengths as given (4, 10, $\frac{1}{2}$, 2, etc.) but combine it with the square of elements read as though turned on its side (silence, 2b, 3b, silence, etc.). Superimposing these two sets of readings or "voices" one then gets (time lengths are given first, before the colon, element indications second, after it):

5:6h $12\frac{1}{2}$:5e $\frac{5}{8}$:7h $2\frac{1}{2}$:0   etc.
4:0   10:2b $\frac{1}{2}$:3b 2:0   6:0

The relationship of the voices is, in a general way, like that of the voices of a canon in so far as every reference to an element and every time length is found first in one voice and then in the other, though the repetitions are not continuously from the same to the other, nor at equal distances, and they are variously combined, e.g., 5e is first located in $12\frac{1}{2}$ seconds and then in 22, 4 seconds is first characterized by silence and then by 12j + 8k. Imitation is at geometrical intervals, in space, so to speak, rather than in linear continuities.

Such superpositions make possible a greater degree of internal liveliness, a greater elaboration of particulars. Moves intersecting and voices overlapping can obscure structural outlines and produce meetings or events that are disengaged from them to become simply themselves. Then, a structure that seems closed by a square of time lengths may also be dissolved by including a zero in the sequence of the time lengths' proportions (e.g., $21\frac{1}{4}$, 1, 0, 2 . . .). The zero I take to mean no time at all, that is, no measurable time, that is, any time at all, which the performer takes as he will at each performance. Also, one may take fixed lengths to represent space, leaving the speed of procedure through the space to determinants other than the criteria which gave the lengths (cf. John Cage's *Music of Changes* or the use of a page of score as a structural unit, e.g. in Cage's *Music for Piano* or Earle Brown's *25 Pages*).

So far form, or rather the making of a score, has been taken as a matter of what (this only generally) goes on for how long, and the simultaneity of varying structural lengths having various kinds of material within them. The succession of lengths has been assumed fixed and predictable before a performance. Karlheinz Stockhausen's *Klavierstück XI* introduced the notion of a variable, unpredictable continuity of structural sections, variably characterized according to the sequence in which they happen to appear, and an indeterminacy of the total length of a piece at any particular performance. Beginning with that idea my *Duo for Pianists II* makes a counterpoint of two sequences of structural units each indeterminate before any performance. Each of the two pianists makes his particular continuity of structural units (they total 15 and are from $\frac{1}{16}$ to $42\frac{1}{5}$ seconds long) and is dependent for the successive choice of what units to play not, as in Stockhausen, upon a straying eye, but upon what he has heard. Ten kinds of sounds (e.g., highest octave *ff*, pizzicato in the middle register, 11 seconds of silence) as heard from one piano are cues to the units which the other will play, and vice versa. A given cue may refer to one unit or to a set of alternatives (two or three). A unit may be played any number of times during a performance, depending on how often it is cued. One unit or pair of units needs no cue and so can be used to start the piece and to return to during the piece when one has either not heard or missed a cue. Once the piece has begun there should be no pause between units, that is, one must always be doing something (including the observation of silence) which is indicated by the score: after playing one unit one must play whatever next one is referred to by the cue last heard before the unit one is playing has ended. There is no cue for ending the piece; the performers agree on a total duration.

The material in the various units also can be variably performed. Time is given in seconds, or in one case as zero (see above), and what one is to play in a given length is characterized with varying completeness, allowing the performer varying degrees of free choices. For example: (cue: 5 seconds of silence)

x-
$1\frac{1}{4}$:0 (i.e., silence)/ $\frac{1}{4}$: 3a 2b/ $\frac{1}{5}$:0/ 4:ppp f/ 1:pizz la + $\frac{1}{4}$, 3, $\frac{1}{10}$/ 31: le/
x-

The first number gives seconds. Within $\frac{1}{4}$ second one must first play 3 notes from a pitch source a (in which there are, say, 4 pitches), in any higher or lower octave than the one in which they appear originally (this is indicated by $\substack{x\text{-}\\x\text{-}}$). Any three of the four available pitches can be chosen, or one can be chosen and repeated three times, or two, one of which is played twice. With these one must play two notes from source b (which has, say, 6 pitches in it). How these five pitches are disposed—singly or in chords, their dynamics, and their individual durations—is left to the performer, who must, however, act within $\frac{1}{4}$ second. Where *ppp* and *f* are indicated the specific requirements are two notes and these dynamics; the rest is left to the performer. + $\frac{1}{4}$, 3, $\frac{1}{10}$ means that the notes should have one or more of these durations. One need of course in no repetition of this sequence choose or play the material in the same way.

The idea is to allow for precise actions under variously indeterminate conditions. One may have $\frac{1}{4}$ second to play 9 variously specified notes or 35 seconds in which to play one of one's choosing. Both fluidity and exactness of performance are possible. And no structural whole or totality is calculated either specifically or generally in terms of probabilities or statistics. The score makes no finished object, at best hopelessly fragile or brittle. There are only parts which can be at once transparent and distinct.

Returning, finally, to the notion of form as a matter of what goes on for how long, an inconsistency may have been noticed: the durations of the lengths in the square of durations described earlier bore no particular relation to the durations of individual sounds within those lengths. The form as a sequence of structural lengths bore no precise relation to the material chosen for use in the form. Form and material are taken as separate for the purposes of composition. That form, as a structure indicated on a score, can be derived out of the nature of the sound material is, I think, illusory. So, conversely, a piece is not played to exhibit its composed structure. Form as structure is simply a matter of technique. The tendency to identify form and material, what is intended and what is given (cf. "art" and "nature"), implies the elimination of all expressive intentions: which might be salutary. But it is practically impossible. If one refers form to what is scored then it will never be exactly represented in a given performance. In any case a kind of solipsism is implied. In making a piece initial, completely arbitrary choices are inevitable, e.g., choices of instruments, timing, performers. On the one hand, one is in an automatically open situation. Whatever one does there will be unpredictable interferences (e.g., circumstances of performance, misunderstanding). On the other hand, no matter how open a procedure one adopts, whether "naturally" (in as complete accordance with the nature of one's material as possible) or by chance (in accordance with the nature of events left to themselves), a degree of circumscription, itself characteristic, will still be necessary. So, for example, in John Cage's *Music for Piano* the making of the score seems as free from determination as possible, namely the fixing of pitches and their spacing by marking the imperfections that happen to be on a blank piece of paper. Yet the result is characteristic, less of the material (which is in any case graphic or visual and not acoustic) than of Cage who by inventing or choosing this method and its application to one or more pianos has brought it about that only certain pitches and noises, of certain timbres, will appear, only singly or in flurries, in more or less isolated points. And, recalling the simplest view of form with which we began, namely as a theatrical event, it is by definition not a "natural" event. It might be natural only if it were private. The alternative attending a full acceptance of the equivalence of form and material is, in the end, no longer to write, or perform music: a perfectly valid possibility still leaving much available for the ears to focus attention on.

Cage and Satie (1973)

Michael Nyman

> I rather think that influence doesn't go A–B–C, that is to say, from [Satie] to someone younger than [Satie] to people still younger, but that rather we live in a field situation in which, by our actions, by what we do, we are able to see what other people do in a different light than we do, without our having done anything.
>
> —Cage, 1965

> It is important with Satie not to be put of by his surface (by turns mystical, cabaretish, Kleeish, Mondrianish; full of mirth, the erotic, the wondrous, all the white emotions, even the heroic, and always tranquility, expressed more often than not by cliche and juxtaposition).
>
> —Cage, 1951

Imitation, they say, is the sincerest form of flattery; how much more (or less) flattering and sincere is *cheap* imitation? Cage's *Cheap Imitation* is the most tangible recognition of Satie's indispensability ("It's not a question of Satie's relevance," Cage wrote in 1958. "He's indispensable"), and interestingly provides a direct link with the first available evidence of Cage's musical connection with Satie.

In 1945 Cage made a two-piano arrangement of the first movement of Satie's *Socrate* for Merce Cunningham's ballet *Idyllic Song.* In summer 1969 Cunningham approached the work again with a view to completing it, by adding the remaining two movements. Cage finished the complete two-piano arrangement in October 1969. However, permission for the use of this arrangement was not granted by the copyright holder. So Cage chose to imitate the original, with great care and respect, but cheaply—by his accustomed resort to the *I Ching* (as a mechanical rather than inspirational guide). The *I Ching* was basically used to answer two questions for each phrase of the melodic line of *Socrate:* which of the seven white-note modes was to be used, and beginning on which of the 12 chromatic notes. The original *Cheap Imitation* (1969) is for solo piano and was first used for Cunningham's dance *Second Hand* in 1970. The orchestral imitation of the piano version was made in 1972, using the *I Ching* to decide which of the 24 obligatory instruments capable of playing the melodic line at any point should do so and for how long. (A maximum of 96 instruments may be used.)

To return to the history of Cage-Satie: three years after *Idyllic Song,* Cage organized a mammoth, 25-concert Satie Festival at Black Mountain College, North Carolina, which included a star-studded performance of *Le piège de Méduse* with Buckminster Fuller as the Baron and sets by de Kooning. During the 1950s he continued his publicity for Satie largely on paper: in 1950 and 1951 he indulged in verbal (and conceptual) fisticuffs in the letter columns of *Musical America* with a critic, Abraham Skulsky, while his best-known appreciation of Satie, the "imaginary conversation" in *Silence,* dates from 1958.

When that article first appeared in *Art News Annual* it included (for the first time in the U.S.) the manuscript of Satie's *Vexations* for piano, a piece which proposes 840 repetitions of a 52-beat, unbarred motif, made up of four sections all over the same 13-bar bass theme, in the order: bass alone, bass + two upper parts in rhythmic unison, bass, bass + reversed upper parts. In 1963 Cage organized a posse of pianists to give what must have been the first performance, at the Pocket Theater in New York, and another with students at the University of California, Davis in 1969. Of late Cage has pursued the connection with Satie through *Cheap Imitation* and the gigantic *Song Books, Solos for Voice 3–92* (1970) which is a musical-theatrical exploration of a chance remark he made in the 1969 continuation of his *Diary: How to Improve the World* (*You Will Only Make Matters Worse*): "We connect Satie with Thoreau."

An analysis of the musical evidence for the Satie-Cage connection is crucial for understanding both composers, and goes deeper than that attempted by Peter Dickinson in a *Music Review* article of 1967 (which, incidentally, includes the first English publication of *Vexations*). Dickinson points to both composers' hatred of traditional attitudes which leads them "to the point of declaring anti-art doctrines"; to *Parade, Mercure* and *Relâche* as precursors of "the kind of Dadaist happenings that have interested Cage and the avant-garde"; to Satie's love of incongruities leading him to exploit whatever is to hand "in a deliberate employment of accident" (that is more to the point, if it is true); while he found the combination of music, words and drawings in *Sports et Divertissements* "close to the recent aleatory music where the performer is given a series of indications and diagrams without precise interpretation." (The instructions to *Vexations* provide a more relevant parallel: "Pour se jouer 840 fois de suite ce motif, il sera bon de se préparer au préalable, et dans la plus grand silence, par des immobilités sérieuses.")

The essence of the matter is contained in the lecture "Defence of Satie" which Cage delivered during the Black Mountain Satie Festival in 1948. Here Cage indulged a style of logical and polemical argument that he abandoned in his later aphoristic-mosaic lecture-writings. After giving his most convincing exposition of the distinctions between structure, form, method and material, he concluded that it is only structure (the work's "parts that are clearly separate but that interact in such a way as to make a whole") that today's composers should come to "general agreement" about, the other categories being free.

The music by, and influenced by, Beethoven, defined the structure of a composition by means of harmony. Before Beethoven wrote a piece, Cage maintains, he planned its movement from one key to another; that is, he planned its harmonic structure. The only new structural idea to emerge since Beethoven is to be found in the work of Satie (and early Webern), where structure is defined in terms of time lengths. Before Satie wrote a piece he planned the lengths of its phrases. Whether this is true of all Satie's music, his sketchbooks certainly contain complete pre-compositional rhythmic structures for the ballet *Mercure* and for *Cinéma,* the sound-track for René Clair's film *Entr'acte* included in *Relâche.*

Cage, of course, had based all his music on proportional rhythmic structures since the mid-30s, after having been introduced to oriental rhythmic systems by Henry Cowell and having found no comfort in Schoenberg's pitch manipulation system, which provided only a method and was restricted to musical sounds based on the chromatic scale. The rhythmic structure technique allowed Cage to formulate this revolutionary concept (since it very simply but radically contradicts the traditional attitude towards form and content): "in contrast to a structure based on the frequency aspect of sound, tonality, that is, this rhythmic structure was as hospitable to non-musical sounds, noises, as it was to those of conventional scales and instruments." (These "noises" were for Cage initially the sounds of the percussion orchestra and its "reduction," the prepared piano, but later, notably in the so-called silent piece, *4'33",* were any, including environmental sounds.) Cage found this "hospitality" in Satie too: "Just as Klee was willing to draw people and plants and animals, so into Satie's continuity come folk tunes, musical clichés, and absurdities of all kinds; he is not ashamed to welcome them in the house he builds: its structure is strong."

Since Cage was closely involved with Satie's music in the late 1940s it is not unremarkable that the music he was writing at the time of the Black Mountain lecture should have many features in common with Satie: melody-modality, stasis, flatness of movement (an inevitable consequence of rhythmic pre-planning) and unpretentiousness. (This latter is important: compare the respectful restraint of Cage's handling of *Socrate* with the way Stockhausen imposes himself on Beethoven in *Op. 1970*.) Significantly the very singular melodic line of *Cheap Imitation* is reminiscent of the 1948 monody of *Music for Marcel Duchamp* and *A Dream,* which shares with *Cheap Imitation* even the occasional intrusion of "harmony" in the form of melody notes sounded and then sustained.

Even though *Cheap Imitation* may refer back to the style and purity of Cage's pre-chance music, it is in no way a nostalgic throwback to the earlier, highly attractive modal symmetry. Interestingly, Cage has chosen to randomize that parameter which is freest of the almost palpable rhythmic structure found in the accompaniment to *Socrate,* namely the flowing vocal line (and the instrumental top line when the voice is silent). Cage, around 1960, came "to no longer feel the need for musical structure. Its absence could, in fact, blur the distinction between art and life. An individual can hear sounds as music (enjoy living) whether or not he is at a concert," and has renounced symmetry in favor of "interpenetrating multiplicity," and the multi-modal, multi-transpositional treatment of *Cheap Imitation* is fully in tune with Cage's musical experiences of the last 20 years.

If the rhythmic plotting of Satie's theater and film music is closely related to Cage's own number manipulation, so the static, non-developmental style of Satie's music relates to another important aspect of Cage's musical aesthetic. Roger Shattuck points out that typical bars of *Cinéma* lend themselves to "infinite repetition and do not establish any strong tonal feeling": that is, sounds are treated as separate objects in themselves, not as passing links in a musical continuity. For Cage, Satie's empty time-structures bring about "a time that's just time," which "will let sounds be just sounds and if they are folk tunes, unresolved ninth chords, or knives and forks, just folk tunes, unresolved ninth chords, or knives and forks."

Knives and forks were sounds instanced by Satie in a statement quoted by Cage earlier in his *Silence* article, where he maintains that we should bring about a music "which is like furniture—a music, that is, which will be part of the noises of the environment, will take them into consideration. I think of it as melodious, softening the noises of the knives and forks, not dominating them, not imposing itself." This "working in terms of totality, not just the discretely chosen convention" again brings Satie and Cage close aesthetically. Yet their awareness of the usefulness of environmental noise-sounds leads in opposite directions. For Satie, furniture music would be "part of the noises of the environment," whereas for Cage the noises of the environment are part of his music; for Satie "it would fill up those heavy silences that sometimes fall between friends dining together," while for Cage ambient noise filled those empty silences that regularly fell between the notes of his music until about 1960.

Furniture music was designed to be unassuming, not drawing attention to itself. This may in fact be "anti-art" (depending on how you define art), since the traditional attitude is to be interesting and dominating at all costs. No piece could be more barren, undernourished and monotonous (on the surface) than *Vexations*—a veritable *Ring* cycle totally devoid of any but accidental variation, the complete antithesis of the climax-ridden bleeding-chunk music of the time (Patrick Gowers has dated *Vexations* 1893 on stylistic evidence) where variety would appear to guarantee the impossibility of boredom.

Boredom is a double-edged sword. Satie wrote: "the public venerates boredom. For boredom is mysterious and profound. . . . The listener is defenseless against boredom. Boredom subdues him." Cage raises the question of boredom in a recent *Diary:* "As we were walking along, she smiled and said, 'You're never bored, are you?' (Boredom dropped when we dropped our interest in climaxes. *Socrate.* Even at midnight we can tell the difference between two Chinamen)." Boredom is also a paradox: for most listeners boredom *began* when climaxes disappeared and they lost most of their signposts.

In an essay entitled *Boredom and Danger,* Dick Higgins (a pupil of Cage at the New School for Social Research at the time of the 1958 Satie article) drew attention to the end of Satie's *Vieux sequins et vieilles cuirasses,* where an eight-beat passage evocative of old marches and patriotic songs is to be repeated 380 times. In performance the satirical intent of this repetition comes through very clearly, but at the same time "other very interesting results begin to appear. The music first becomes so familiar that it seems extremely offensive and objectionable. But after that the mind slowly becomes incapable of taking further offence, and a very strange, euphoric acceptance and enjoyment begins to set in." He goes on to say that, if it can be said that Satie's interest in boredom originated as a kind of gesture—there is a certain bravura about asking a pianist to play the same eight beats 380 times—and developed it into a fascinating aesthetic statement, "then it can be said with equal fairness that Cage was the first to try to emphasize in his work and his teaching a dialectic between boredom and intensity."

Cage has never interested himself in such naked repetition, being "averse to all these actions that lead toward placing emphasis on the things that happen in the course of a process"; yet the ethical seriousness of performing *Vexations* is fully in tune with the devotion that his own music demands. Cage set an invariable, ritualistic "rhythmic structure" for the Davis performance, which began at 5:40 one morning and was to go on till 12:40 the next morning. Each player had to play for 20 minutes, and prepare himself for his stint by a 20-minute period of silent contemplation sitting to the left of the currently playing pianist. To fill the allotted 18 hours 40 minutes performers had to play 15 repetitions over 20 minutes, each repetition being timed to last exactly 1′20″.

Although the processes involved in making a version of any of Cage's indeterminate pieces enable the performer to choose any duration, whether two seconds or two days (the performance has to fill the time available, as in the 1969 *Vexations*), it may have been the extremely liberated attitude towards time expressed by *Vexations* that led Cage to have faith in longer durations over the years. Although he maintains a lofty impartiality, he did admit in 1966 that "I very much enjoy our current ability to listen to things for a long time, and I notice this becoming a general practice in society."

Today Cage is concerned with society on a rather more fundamental level, as it is mirrored in microcosm in the symphony orchestra. For in *Cheap Imitation* nothing is left to chance (in performance, that is). A strict rehearsal schedule is prescribed (for the first time in Cage's music): for the first week all players must familiarize themselves with the whole 30-minute melody, while during the second week each player plays his part as specified. A special way of listening is required; if any player is not up to scratch he is asked to leave, and if the quorum of 24 cannot be made up then the performance has to be cancelled (as was the first performance in Amsterdam). But just as Cage claims he wants to improve the world but is convinced that things will only be made worse, so he seems to be aware of the unrealizability of his proposals.

Satie would have been flattered to know that through his music, the most radical, "anarchistic" composer of the century should be exercising his mind with such problems. A wry smile spreads over his face . . .

The Abstract Composers (1952)

Virgil Thomson

When John Cage came to New York some ten years ago out of the Far West (by way of Chicago), he brought with him a sizable baggage of compositions. These were scored for divers groups of what are usually called "percussion instruments," orthodox and unorthodox.

Orthodox instruments, let me explain, are those manufactured with musical intent, such as tom-toms, temple bells, and the like. The unorthodox are those whose adoption by the music profession is not yet general. These include, in Mr. Cage's case, flower pots, automobile brake drums, electric buzzers, tubs of water, and many other sources of interesting and characteristic sounds. Cage's first New York concerts were given with ensembles of players using all these instruments and many more, himself conducting.

A few years later he simplified the execution of his music by devising an instrument on which it could be composed for one man. This instrument, an orthodox one with unorthodox attachments, was none other than the familiar grand pianoforte muted with screws, bits of rubber, copper pennies, and the like to give a large gamut of pings, thuds, and other delicate aural stimuli. As my colleague Arthur Berger has pointed out, the Cage "prepared piano" is a conception not dissimilar to that of the one-man bands common in the jazz world. Nor has the Cage method of composition been radically altered for the solo circumstance.

This method is Cage's most original contribution to music. Designed specifically for making extended and shapely patterns out of non-tonal sounds, it is the most sophisticated method available in the Western world for composing with purely rhythmic elements and without the aid of tonal scales. To quote Lou Harrison, long an associate of Cage in percussive and rhythmic research, Cage has substituted "chronological" for "psychological" time as the continuing element of his music. Any composer who has ever worked with percussion has discovered that all our traditional composing methods deal with the psychological, or "expressive," relations among tones which have among themselves differing, and *unavoidable,* acoustical relations. To make musical forms or constructions without these relations requires a substitute for them. Cage has substituted an arithmetical relation among the durations of sounds for the traditional arithmetical relations among their pitches. He has isolated rhythm as a musical element and given it an independence it did not have before.

In the last year or so he has added a further element to composition, which is chance. So secure does he feel in the solidity of his composition method that he has assayed to prove its worth under conditions the most hazardous. Last year we heard, in a concert of the New Music Society, a piece by Cage for twelve radio receiving sets. The use of fortuitously chosen material in composition has long been familiar to the visual arts. The collage, the spatter, the blot, the accidental texture have been exploited by painters for forty years. From Duchamp and Picasso to the latest American abstractionists the history is continuous. Music itself accepts a high part of hazard in execution; and perhaps it is from this fact that composers have not exploited its possibilities much in actual scoring.

Mozart did play around with composing machines, as well as with performing machines (like the mechanical organ, for which he wrote some very pretty music); but he did not go far with them. How far Cage will go with his Chinese dice-game (for this is the game of chance by which he at present chooses the next sound and its loudness) remains to be seen. One presumes that he will renounce it if and when it ceases to be valuable, as he, the composer, judges value. But let no one think his *Music of Changes* is wholly a matter of hazard. The sounds of it, many of them quite complex, are carefully chosen, invented by him. And their composition in time is no less carefully worked out. Chance is involved only in their succession. And that chance is regulated by a game of such complexity that the laws of probability make continued variation virtually inevitable.

Thus, in Cage's hands, the use of chance in composition gives a result not unlike that of a kaleidoscope. With a large gamut of sounds and a complex system for assembling them into patterns, all the patterns turn out to be interesting, an arabesque is achieved. In the hands of his pupils and protégés the result is not always so distinguished simply because the musical materials employed are less carefully chosen. The method of their assembling, however, remains valid and will remain so until a better approach to rhythmic construction is discovered.

What kaleidoscopes and arabesques lack is urgency. They can hold the attention but they do not do it consistently. The most dependable device for holding attention is a theme or story, the clear attachment of art patterns to such common human bonds as sex and sentiment. How far an artist goes in this direction or in the opposite is up to him. "Abstraction" in art is nothing more than the avoidance of a *clear* and *necessary* attachment to subject matter. It is ever a salutary element in art, because it clears the mind of sex and sentiment. Only briefly, however. Because the human mind can always find ways of getting these things into any picture. And since the civilized mind likes to share its intensities of feeling, and since all the feelings provokable by abstract art are individual, abstract movements invariably end by attaching to themselves an intense feeling about the one thing that is consistent throughout their works, namely, a method of composition. The composition, or the method of composition, becomes the "subject," in the long run, of all abstract art.

This has happened to the music of Cage and his followers. Its admirers, who are many (and include your commentator), tend ever to defend it as a species rather than to attach themselves to any particular piece. This has happened before. Stravinsky's neoclassic production was long a similar cause. Whether it happened just this way in the 1890s to Debussy's impressionistic works I am not sure. We do know that something not dissimilar took place around Beethoven in Vienna, though the attendant polemics were not an attack upon intellectuality in music but rather upon an unusual degree of expressivity.

In any case, Cage and his associates, through their recent concerts at the Cherry Lane Theater, have got the town to quarreling again. Many find the climate of the new downtown group invigorating. Others are bothered by the casual quality of their music. They find it hard to keep the mind on. This has always been one reaction to abstract art. I am sure that Cage's work *is* abstract, in any contemporary meaning of the term. I am also convinced that its workmanship is of the best. The fact that younger men are adopting its methods, as Cage long ago took on the influence of Cowell and Varèse, means that it has become something of a movement. Myself I find it only natural that music, usually, in our time, a good quarter-century behind the visual arts, should have finally acquired its own "abstractionist" pressure group.

Cage *String Quartet* (1972)

Peter Dickinson

It may seem difficult to justify the inclusion of Cage in a series about neglected composers, particularly after discussions of Reger and Suk, but they all have something in common. They have been victimized, in different ways by fashion. In the case of Cage, attention has been focused on the more sensational aspects of his work, on his ideas rather than his music, and the genuine musical tradition from which he comes has been submerged. This has happened before to a composer who wished to deflate the pomposity of establishment fashions—Erik Satie, revered by Cage and the inspiration of some of his best work. Satie, too, is now fashionable, and sometimes for the wrong reasons. He is mercilessly camped by people reading his texts aloud to his music (which he forbade), or making idiotic arrangements using the synthesizer, and the record companies scramble to fill the catalog with mediocre and often carelessly inaccurate performances. The purely musical kernel of his art, which is worthy of Bach or Mozart, is mislaid in the package of presentation. People are not used to satire in music, to finding the same piece witty and sublime. These are responses more familiar in jazz or advanced pop, and only recently entering the enlarged main stream of Western music through the performing traditions associated with the avant-garde.

Cage is widely known for his most extreme gestures: *4′33″* for any number of performers making no intentional sound for that amount of time; his *Variations* pieces for no specific resources, and therefore readily available to any kind of performing group; the prepared piano, regarded as sensational quite apart from its austere music. This is the result of a *Time* magazine interpretation, which Cage, well aware of McLuhan's techniques, has often brought upon himself. Others have suffered this fate. Boulez, for example, makes better copy when rowing with the French musical establishment than when composing.

Of course I have oversimplified Cage's predicament, without the space to elaborate. My long article in *Music and Musicians* (March, 1965) put him into perspective at a time when his aesthetic was less familiar than it is now. Since then Calvin Tomkins in the Penguin *Ahead of the Game* shows what Cage has in common with the avant-garde in general and Richard Kostelanetz in his recent "Documentary Monograph" published by Allen Lane the Penguin Press, offers some valuable material in an uncritical way, isolating Cage from any musical traditions. So it is appropriate to consider the *String Quartet in Four Parts,* a completely notated piece from 1950. The music never approaches the controlled vandalism of Penderecki's Quartet, written some ten years later, but quite naturally accommodates itself to the medium, with important distinctive touches.

The quartet derives from Cage's study of Satie, who composed by measured lengths of time rather than thematic development. It was this aspect of Satie which caused Varèse to describe him as a pre-electronic composer, anticipating methods of tape-cutting. As in the *Sonatas and Interludes* for prepared piano, Cage chooses a series of proportions for the composition. In the quartet this series—$2\frac{1}{2}$ $1\frac{1}{2}$ 2 3 6 5 $\frac{1}{2}$ $1\frac{1}{2}$—applies to the number of bars which make up a larger unit of 22 bars. These larger units are then spread across all four movements so that the first has $2\frac{1}{2} + 1\frac{1}{2}$; the second $2 + 3$; the third $6 + 5$; and the last $\frac{1}{2} + 1\frac{1}{2}$. Thus the proportions of the four movements (referred to in the title as "four parts") reflect those of the smaller units which govern the lengths of phrases. These figures are not much help to the listener, who hears an almost circular flow of similar objects in each of the first three movements, but they do explain why the third movement is almost endlessly long and the last very short. The musical and technical reasons for this are identical.

Players may have been put off by the instruction: "Play without vibrato and with only minimum weight on the bow." A well-known conductor asked me not to insist on senza vibrato in an orchestral work of mine "because the players would sound like amateurs." In the quartet, with some long sustained notes almost necessitating a change of bow, this poses problems. They are not solved in the only performance I have on tape, but Cage has good reason for his demand: a cool, unemotional inevitability can result. Something close to the very soft pieces of Morton Feldman, who asked that the sounds should be as if "sourceless." On the inside page of the score Cage specified how each sound is to be produced and on which string. The strings of the cello are tuned to A, D-flat, G-flat and C, which allows some unusual harmonics not otherwise obtainable. Along with the senza vibrato playing, this accounts for the unique sound of the work.

Cage provides titles on the page before each movement: Quietly flowing along; Slowly rocking; Nearly stationary; and *Quodlibet.* He goes further in relating the work to the cycle of Nature: "The subject of the String Quartet is that of the seasons, but the first two movements are also concerned with place. Thus in the first movement the subject is summer in France whilst that of the second is fall in America. The third and fourth are also concerned with musical subjects, winter being expressed as a canon, spring as a *quodlibet.*" Needless to say, there is nothing programmatic about these movements, which work in an almost automatic way, but it is appropriate that winter should be the slowly oscillating third movement and spring the virile modal tune of the neo-Renaissance *Quodlibet.* In the *Sonatas and Interludes* for prepared piano (1946–48) Cage chose his sounds by trial and error—"as one chooses shells whilst walking along a beach"—and then placed them in a rhythmic structure similar to the proportions given above for the quartet. He noticed that some altered strings on the prepared piano gave chords, or aggregates, rather than single notes, and as a result of this he composed the quartet as "a melody without accompaniment." Chords produced by two or three instruments come round again in the same way: one of these is a first inversion, close position; of F-sharp major with an added C-natural in the middle. At this time Cage was increasingly concerned to remove the element of personal taste from his composing. He was moving towards the happening—the word implies that nobody is responsible. Soon after the *String Quartet* he consulted the ancient Chinese *Book of Changes* to decide the note-to-note procedure, and in some works observed imperfections on manuscript paper, using them to indicate where a note should go. But before Cage finally embarked on this path there came the *Concerto* for prepared piano and chamber orchestra (1951)—available on record. Like the *String Quartet* it uses some major and minor chords in a context completely purged from traditional expectations. Cage says: "The inclusion there of rigidly scored conventional harmonies is a matter of taste, from which a conscious control was absent." Later on Cage did not really abandon his own taste, as he himself decided what machinery to set up in order to bring about a work: he became "the maker of a camera who allows someone else to take the picture." But in the *Quartet* and *Concerto,* both at an important transition, Cage was using instinctive choice for the last time. This gives the music a special kind of atmosphere—like "These fragments I have shored against my ruins," from the end of Eliot's *The Waste Land*. Even fragments have a special kind of eloquence, as Cage learnt from Satie, and this technique is in the foreground of the work of Terry Riley or Steve Reich where a tiny ostinato is unnaturally magnified in a way directly analogous to pop art. Ligeti works like this, in a less impersonal way, in—for example—*Continuum* for harpsichord, or the slow changes of texture in the orchestral *Lontano*.

Technical dissection of the quartet is rewarding because everything fits in neatly. Everything is heard, as the diatonic snippets float past like mobiles (Cage wrote a score to a film about the work of Alexander Calder). The continuity derives from Satie's *Socrate,* which is remarkable for its arioso over unchanging patterns, but Cage goes further as every movement has bar-lengths of four crotchets. The simplicity and compression are a compound of Webern and Satie, and the magic recalls e e cummings, whom Cage has set several times. The repetitions suggest the best in Gertrude Stein rather than her empty garrulousness.

Cage calls the third movement a canon, by which he seems to mean a palindrome within a palindrome. As with the whole work the structure of the movement is reflected in each 22-bar component. These are divided up in various ways, all concerning retrograde, and then from the middle the whole movement reverses on itself. The actual material is heard four times. The final *Quodlibet*—a Renaissance form which brought together snippets from various works, often in an amusing way—offers the maximum contrast. Its antique flavor is reinforced by the playing without vibrato and an arrangement for medieval instruments could easily sound like an obscure contemporary of Machaut. A reduction of part of the *Quodlibet* on to two staves is about the most provocative note upon which to end (see fig. 1). This movement does not sound as simple as it looks, because the notes are unexpectedly shared out between the players rather like Webern's scoring of Bach's *Ricercare à 6. In a landscape* (1948) for harp or piano is another example of Cage's diatonic melody. These works clarify an important strand in twentieth-century music, the line which links Satie, Varèse, Cage, and

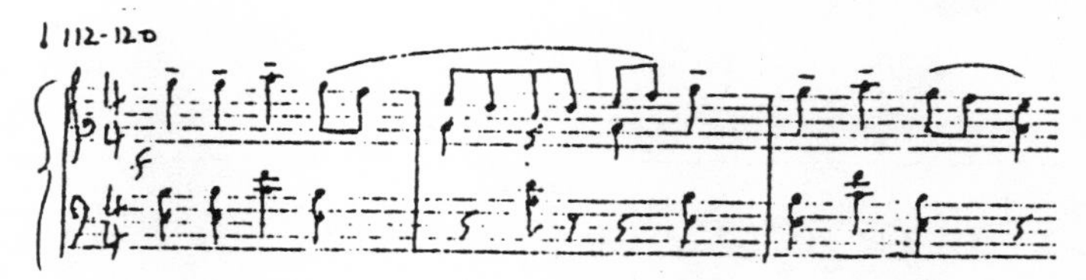

Fig. 1. Opening of the final *Quodlibet,* reduced to two staves

Feldman to today's avant-garde. The music is itself sufficiently remarkable—I have no hesitation in regarding the Cage *String Quartet,* like the best of Satie, as a masterpiece—but its tradition within twentieth-century music of all kinds is still vital and productive.

On Cage's *String Quartet in Four Parts* (1988)

Deborah Campana

There is no counterpoint and no harmony. Only a line in rhythmic space ($2\frac{1}{2} : 1\frac{1}{2}$; $2 : 3$; $6 : 5$; $\frac{1}{2} : 1\frac{1}{2}$).

—John Cage to Pierre Boulez (n.d.), photocopy of holograph letter no. 10, John Cage Archive, Northwestern University Music Library, Evanston, Illinois.

Movement I **Quietly Flowing Along**	**4 units = 2-1/2 units : 1-1/2 units (55 : 33 measures)**
Movement II **Slowly Rocking**	**5 units = 2 units : 3 units (44 : 66 measures)**
Movement III **Nearly Stationary**	**11 units = 6 units : 5 units (132 : 110 measures)**
Movement IV ***Quodlibet***	**2 units = 1/2 unit : 1-1/2 units (11 : 33 measures)**
	22 measures/per unit x 22 units = 484 measures

Fig. 1. Time template unit distribution in *String Quartet in Four Parts*

Fig. 2. *String Quartet in Four Parts:* movement 3, simultaneities

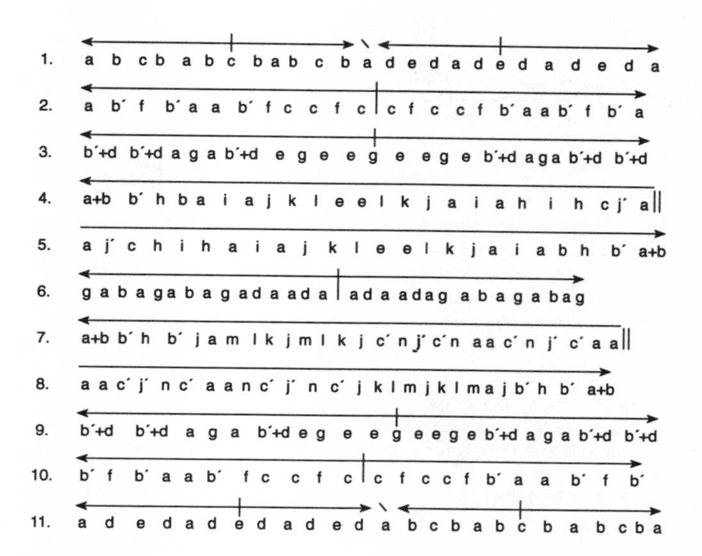

KEY: letters refer to simultaneities listed in fig. 2

- **\ = separation between palindromic patterns within a template unit**
- **| = center point of palindrome within a template unit**
- **|| = end of template unit and center point of palindrome**
- **+ = two simultaneities stated at once**

Fig. 3. *String Quartet in Four Parts:* movement 3, template patterns

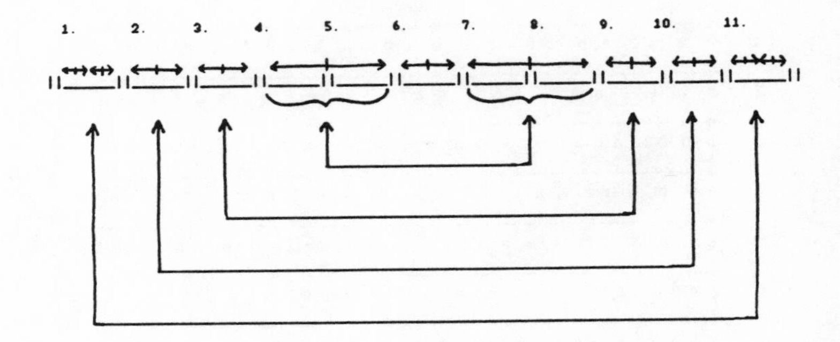

KEY:
numbers refer to template units
| | – denotes division between individual template units
small arrows and brackets refer to palindromes (arrows point away from the mirror center)
large arrows (arch) denote correspondence between palindrome patterns

---

Variations occur within the arch-form as follows:
1. template 2: *a* - at the beginning and end are not present in template 10
2. palindromes occurring in templates 4–5 and templates 7–8 begin and end similarly but continue differently for the most part

Fig. 4. *String Quartet in Four Parts:* movement 3, formal outline

New and Electronic Music (1957)

Christian Wolff

What is, or seems to be, new in this music? Roughly, since 1950, in the works of the Americans John Cage, Morton Feldman, Earle Brown, the German Karlheinz Stockhausen, the French Pierre Boulez, the Swedish Bo Nilsson, the Belgian Henri Pousseur, and the French-American Edgar Varèse, one finds a concern for a kind of objectivity, almost anonymity—sound come into its own. The "music" is a resultant existing simply in the sounds we hear, given no impulse by expressions of self or personality. It is indifferent in motive, originating in no psychology nor in dramatic intentions, nor in literary or pictorial purposes. For at least some of these composers, then, the final intention is to be free of artistry and taste. But this need not make their work "abstract," for nothing, in the end, is denied. It is simply that personal expression, drama, psychology, and the like are not part of the composer's initial calculation: they are at best gratuitous.

The procedure of composing tends to be radical, going directly to the sounds and their characteristics, to the way in which they are produced and how they are notated. John Cage scores amplitude for a stringed instrument, not as "piano" or "mezzo-forte," but by the amount of pressure, graphically represented, with which the bow is to pass over the strings. Stockhausen defines "legato"—continuous sounding—and speed on a wind instrument by requiring a given number of notes to be played on a single, continuous breath, or speed and phrasing on a keyboard by the distances the hand has to travel on it. The composer may take into account the places sounds are heard in, the directions from which they are heard, what one can actually hear (statistically or psychologically), and the nature of performers and their actions.

There are, in fact, elements here which have been called "traditional"—the desire for, or better, the condition, of—objectivity, the indifference to "a worldly matter of 'taste,'" the "treatment of the material used . . . in conformity with the nature of that material" (the phrases are Frithjof Schuon's). The Europeans Boulez and Stockhausen are thoroughly self-conscious about musical history; the first directs a carefully programmed "world" of music; Stockhausen speaks of "the work to be done," the "right way" to be laid down and followed. Both have a constructive and methodical bias.

Among the Americans, on the other hand, there is a greater freedom and intransigence, simplification and disruption, a "cleaning the ears out," as Alan Watts has said.

This music, then, both new and traditional, is often where limits meet and converge. There is great extravagance, in complexity of notation, density of events, exploitation of an instrument's ranges, for example; and extravagances of restraint. Feldman has a series of pieces all dynamically marked "as soft as possible"; I myself have used just three pitches in an entire piece; and Cage has a piece which is only silence. There are moments of the greatest commotion and excitement, as in Stockhausen's *Klavierstück XI,* and of utter stillness and repose, in works of Feldman and Cage. Boulez, Stockhausen, Cage in his *Music of Changes,* and Brown in his *Indices* indicate the greatest detail of specification, the most elaborate instructions to the performer. Pousseur in his *Exercises de piano,* Stockhausen, Cage, Feldman, and Brown have, on the other hand, also left free a gamut of degrees of indeterminacy whose specification is entirely in the performers' hands.

Why is this so? Both control (a more or less high degree of organization) and freedom (a making possible of indeterminacy) may be disinterested means of making music. But there are some differences.

In going to the nature of sound, Stockhausen's procedure is methodical. Only after research on acoustical phenomena and their reception, and the formulation of theory, it seems, is a piece composed, whose tendency is to be organized in accordance with the theoretical nature of the piece's material. But there may be a margin of error between the conception and the realization of a piece (as in the electronic *Studie II*); the theory, no matter how "correct," may not accommodate all eventualities.

For Cage, on the other hand, the only criteria, so to speak, are precisely all eventualities. Though there are the same inevitable stages—ideas at the time of writing, actions at the time of performance, sounds at the time of listening—yet no necessary relationships between these stages are insisted upon. The ideas may have been clear, practical, muddled, complex, the actions of performance accurate, decisive, ineffectual, but there will always be sounds to listen to. While intention or conception may generate sounds, they neither measure nor are measured by them necessarily. The sounds while they last are final and there is no separating from them a score for purposes of comparison. If a score indicates the note *a* to be played and the performer, for one reason or another, hits *b* instead, the existence at that moment of the pitch *b* gives no measure of the score nor is measured by it (though the *b* might not have occurred had there been no score). But the existence of the *b* is, in this view, compellingly real. To call it a "mistake" is beside the point (is meeting someone by chance, is a meteor a mistake?). Nor does this suggest simply a letting-go—that the performer play any pitch he pleases when he is asked to play *a*: a measure of good will is assumed.

So too the absence of dichotomy characterizes Cage's attitude toward the sounds of piece and whatever other sounds happen to be simultaneously going on. No boundary between the two is imposed. The "work of art" is not presented as though it existed in an ideal and privileged isolation but is simply allowed to take its place among other "transient phenomena." This view Cage calls "realistic": eventualities, intended (the work) or not (noises in the street, the rattle of a door, crickets), are all acceptable: can they be denied?

Here the nature of sound as it is actually heard is inseparable from any "composition." While this also generally holds for Stockhausen, his analyses of the nature of sound and its production, and the score which implements them are made separable criteria, measures of the final sound. That sound would be foreseen; and subject to "mistakes" and wrong notes; there is nothing experimental about it. A piece of Stockhausen's is fully self-contained, and at least implicitly in conflict with its acoustical environment—unintended sounds. It is an imposing thing; often dense and involved, deliberately made and complex.

Thus in the views of indeterminacy there are also differences. Stockhausen and Pousseur are concerned with probabilities. They draw circles, so to speak, around a group of elements—for example, those having to do with duration or succession in time—and define by the sizes of the circles a range of possible results; that is, aspects of a piece are given more or less general characterizations statistically defined. The system is, in the end, closed. And marking out probabilities is actually a refinement of organization.

Cage's, Feldman's and Brown's use of chance is concerned rather with the improbable and unpredictable, less with a more generalized control of the musical result than with a more specific generating of incalculability.

Further, the use of chance procedures is not only introduced at the point of a piece's performance, as in Stockhausen, Pousseur, or Feldman, but also at the piece's composition. The fully and precisely detailed score of Cage's *Music of Changes* is the final product of a number of chance operations, and so too Brown's *Indices*.

In the first, for example, charts are made up of sounds—noises, as available on a piano, or pitches and these are taken singly or in conglomerates (chords, tremolos, flourishes); of durations; of dynamics; of tempi; and of superpositions (the number of possible series of events going on simultaneously within a given structural length: from zero to eight). Tossing coins then (according to a procedure described in the *I Ching,* or *Book of Changes*) gives numbers, from 1 to 64, which are indices for the charts, each chart having 64 elements. A number of tosses determines the combinations of the various elements on the various charts: how many superpositions; at what tempo; what particular durations; whether a duration be expressed by a silence or a sound; what sound; at what dynamic. And chance determines whether an element on one of the charts of sounds, durations or dynamics, when once used, will be available for further use or will "change," that is, be crossed off and replaced by a newly made element. The outlines of the piece's structure, however, are planned at the start (like the elements on the charts) and not left to chance (as the configurations of the elements are); though these outlines are space lengths—a number of measures—whose time lengths are in turn dependent on the chance-determined tempi.

In Cage's *Music for Piano,* finally, there are large areas of indeterminacy in respect both to composition and performance. Only pitches or noises and their relative place in space are notated for the performer. One arrives at these by marking the imperfections that happen to be on a blank sheet of paper. Chance determines how many and which markings will be used. Staves drawn on a second, transparent piece of paper are placed over the marked sheet. Each stave is provided with a treble or bass clef, as determined by chance. The pitches are thus located, within the range limits of the staves plus a maximum number of ledger lines (extensions of the staves to cover the piano's range of pitches), and are further specified, randomly, as normal, sharp or flat. The markings that fall outside the ledger line ranges and between the two staves of a system locate noises. And the pitches may have the further notation, by chance, of muting (with the fingers on the pitch's string) or plucking.

How, generally, is the electronic music made? Thus far, in two ways, that may be combined or not.

First, synthetically, that is, all sounds are electronically generated and composed from the start. Any sound, from tone to noise, is analyzable into its simplest measurable components, sine wave frequencies (pure tones). Here the reverse process takes place: a sound is made up by scoring its structure, the configuration of all its measurable components. Composition starts with an absolute minimum of "givens," and can be microcosmic as it has never been before.

Second, electronic music is made reproductively, that is, any existing sounds (violin, conversation, oscillator, glass breaking, frogs) are recorded on magnetic tape and thus made available to any compositional action, which in turn may involve changing and reforming any aspects of the sounds.

Durations and superpositions are, generally, managed in the same way in both cases. The duration of a sound is realized by the measurement of a length of the tape on which the sound has been recorded (though some aspects of duration, such as the speed of impulses or the speed of changing frequencies in a sliding sound—as in glissandi on stringed instruments—would be produced directly by a generating source). For silence or the separation of sounds there is blank tape. The various lengths are successively spliced together. Superpositions are made by the simultaneous recording of two or more tapes.

In either way of making this music there is, thus far, no "performance," as no instruments are involved, other than the various sound generators which produce frequencies, white noise, impulses, or random noise, and the mechanical means which alter the character of given sounds, for example by filtering, distorting, reverberating. The only final realization is a record or tape or series of tapes (in stereophonic presentation).

Some would insist on the use of the first procedure only. The elements of sound being fully measurable and thus, in theory at least, fully controllable, composition could be uniquely extended. Beginning with the most irreducible aspects of sound, one might "rationalize" completely a piece's structure, measuring everything possible according to—perhaps—a single organizational principle (one series of numerical proportions, for example). But there are, in fact, limitations here; for the technical means for realizing sounds, or ideas of sounds, of some complexity are often confined and clumsy or not yet available.

The second procedure, although less "thorough," allows for more immediately available complexities, especially of timbre—"complexities" often when considered only in terms of analytical measurements as we now make them. The sound itself may be quite ordinary (the rustling of paper), but extraordinarily complex in terms of precise acoustical definition and, under present technical conditions, exceedingly difficult to constitute synthetically.

But in either case one is in a thoroughly radical situation, barring concern with analogies to, or imitations of, conventional nonelectronic procedures, such as counterpoint, twelve-tone organization, and so on.

The actual number of electronic pieces is not large. One might mention two, Cage's *Williams Mix* and Stockhausen's *Gesang der Jünglinge.* The first is notable for the great range of its sound sources, including city sounds, country sounds, electronic or synthetic sounds, manual sounds (the snap of fingers, for example), vocal or wind sounds, and "small" sounds—sounds needing amplification to be made audible, such as an ant walking on a piece of paper; and these may be fragmented, a length of the tape of a sound cut into small bits which, scattered and rearranged, are stuck back on another (otherwise blank) tape; and a sound tape may be cut at either end not only vertically but also at all possible angles, which alters in all degrees the character of a sound's attack and decay. Finally, there are up to eight possible superpositions or simultaneous sound events. The sounds, recognizable as their sources may remain (for example, a boat whistle), are not composed with a view to their specific evocative effects. They are presented, long, quick, blatantly clear, all but unrecognizable, ambiguous, fragmented beyond recognition, unheard of, simply as sounds in a number of combinations. *Gesang der Jünglinge* is notable for the range and complexity of its timbres, achieved almost entirely by purely synthetic means, using only electronic sound sources, with the exception of a boy's voice, which itself, once recorded, is subject to many mechanical transformations. The electronic sounds are taken in eleven "elemental" aspects, that is, each aspect is such that it cannot be further subdivided into audibly different kinds of sound. All the material of the piece, including the boy's voice and the letters of the words he sings (they can be permutated, making a continuum from pure vocal sounds to recognizable "sense"), is uniformly rationalized, that is, made available to strictly analogous if not identical means of organization (e.g., permutations of irreduceable elements). Conversely, however, the choice of the material is dictated by considerations of its possible total homogeneity and the fact that all its aspects could be controlled.

Both pieces, then, are intended for performances on, respectively, 8 and 6 variously located loudspeakers. Thus the dimension of spacing, the stereophonic presentation of sound, may provide still another compositional aspect to a piece. A given sound may come from any location in space, from any combination of locations, may move from one location to another, continuously or discretely. Nor is spatial disposition unknown to instrumental music: as in early antiphonal music, Henry Brant, Stockhausen in his piece for three variously placed orchestras, Cage, and others in their pieces for three and four pianos placed in different parts of a concert hall.

As for the electronic music generally, it has brought about, or was coincident with, a self-consciousness about the nature of sound, its production and perception, that has rarely been equaled. The radical way of making this music, and the range of possibilities involved, make it attractive to work with. Yet it is a question of no longer writing instrumental music. There are simply more possibilities available. Boulez speaks primarily of combining electronic and instrumental activity. Varèse has written a work, *Déserts,* which uses both, though only in alternation. Stockhausen transfers many ideas realized in working with electronic means to his instrumental works, and recently seems interested rather in a new instrument of electronic construction, with the attending range of possibilities, but also subjected to the actions of a performer. The evident limitation of electronic music is here focused; its recorded and flat character, the exclusion of the factor of performance with its natural complexities, hazards and loose screws,— for "vulnerability," Simone Weil says, is "a mark of existence."

Notable qualities of this music, whether electronic or not, are monotony and the irritation that accompanies it. The monotony may lie in simplicity or delicacy, strength or complexity. Complexity tends to reach a point of neutralization: continuous change results in a certain sameness. The music has a static character. It goes in no particular direction. There is no necessary concern with time as a measure of distance from a point in the past to a point in the future, with linear continuity alone. It is not a question of getting anywhere, of making progress, or having come from anywhere in particular, of tradition or futurism. There is neither nostalgia nor anticipation. Often the structure of a piece is circular: the succession of its parts is variable, as in Pousseur's *Exercises de piano* and Stockhausen's *Klavierstück XI.* In Cage's recent work the notation itself can be circular, the succession of notes on a stave not necessarily indicating their sequence in time, that is, the order in which they are performed. One may have to read notes on a circle, in two "voices" going in opposite directions simultaneously. An aspect of time dissolves. And the Europeans often view organization as "global," whereby beginnings and ends are not points on a line but limits of a piece's material (for example, pitch ranges or possible combinations of timbres) which may be touched at any time during the piece. The boundaries of the piece are expressed, not at moments of time which mark a succession, but as margins of a spatial projection of the total structure.

As for the quality of irritation, that is a more subjective matter. One might say that it is at least preferable to soothing, edifying, exalting, and similar qualities. Its source is, of course, precisely in monotony, not in any forms of aggression or emphasis. It is the immobility in motion. And it alone, perhaps, is truly moving.

Two Albums by John Cage (1960)

Peter Yates

During the years of this column I have written many times about the music and ideas of John Cage. To write about him has been easier than to offer examples of his work to back up my claims for him. Like most recorded examples of American music, his records have been allowed to go out of circulation before the general public could become aware of their availability, for example the two records of his *Sonatas and Interludes* for prepared piano played by Maro Ajemian for Dial, and his Quartet for prepared string instruments, issued by Columbia.

Now that, temporarily, I have air for broadcasting, I am loosing into space the contents of two recorded albums of work by John Cage which I have received lately, with the conviction that, no matter how many may dislike it, there will be listeners grateful for the chance to learn something of what has been going on along the frontiers of American music all these years. Possibly I should withdraw the word *American* because John Cage has been even more influential in Europe than at home.

What is the good of all this if I don't like what he does?

Your likes contribute nothing. John Cage is one of those creative individuals, like the designer-engineer Buckminster Fuller, or Gertrude Stein or John Jay Chapman in literature, or Ludwig Wittgenstein in philosophy, whose significance is in the full sense of the word, critical. Their fresh-reasoned yet spontaneously unexpected connectives bear upon the fundamental understandings tying together the operative strands of civilization that are continuously growing and decaying within the fluid culture of our time.

Many persons believe that they can be against the culture of their time, or disaffiliated outside of that culture, or aggressively in contradiction of it. These are fallacies. You are in your culture; you grow in it. Culture is where you are, what you are doing. You may dislike it; you may even try to change it; but you cannot live outside it. A cultural convulsion, the seismic spasm at the ending of a time-lag, may throw a man up a revolutionary leader and them break him.

The two albums are: *Indeterminacy* (Folkways Recordings FT 3704), John Cage reading while David Tudor, alternating between piano and electronic equipment, startles the listener by what seem at first encounter fragmentary and non-sequential noises; and *The 25-Year Retrospective Concert of the Music of John Cage,* recorded in performance at Town Hall, New York, May 15, 1958, issued by George Avakian.

The two albums belong together, but to have them together may strain the pocketbook. Certainly they belong in any library, public or university, that wishes to make available to the public the source of much seemingly unrelated experiment which has been going on here and abroad during recent years. Both albums contain useful supplementary reading material, written by John Cage, filling in the background of what is to be heard. The concert album contains in addition printed explanations of the methods of creating and performing the various compositions, with for each an example of the system of notation.

I have said that Cage's work is the source of much seemingly unrelated experiment that has been going on here and abroad during recent years. Here is another of those historic instances where the master keeps running ahead of his disciples, while the disciples exploit the transient awards of fame that result from beginning with a still unknown given and remaining firmly in one place until recognized. From the view down the road behind, the disciples are seen as daring, forward-looking, until eventually you pass them. The seeming leaders are not in fact leading but essentially conservative and their work too easily assimilable.

What's wrong with being assimilable? Any peak is worth climbing, if you enjoy the practice; more climbers are killed falling from the popular than from the less accessible peaks. I can never too often remind my readers that the high-level popular music of Mozart's lifetime was not Mozart's, that the number of persons who heard Beethoven's music during his lifetime would perhaps not fill Hollywood Bowl so completely as a Gershwin program.

In any activity, as we cease being duffers, we enjoy most what most challenges us. The Matterhorn is not less difficult because more people climb or fall from it; Everest and space have set new standards.

Like Gertrude Stein, whom he resembles, though he disowns her influence, John Cage is a master of prose, able to tell about himself exactly what he wishes to be known. A composer-critic said to me recently, "I don't admire Cage's music, but each time I read his prose he reduces me to silence and envy."

I have never discovered for certain, in the midst of Cage's lucidity, what it is about himself, or if there is indeed anything John Cage wishes not to be known. Yet when you have read a good share of all that he has written, even when you have had the privilege of corresponding with him, you may find yourself wondering just what it is, beyond the capacity of anyone to say it, he wishes to accomplish. You are left at the end with the necessity of producing your own supplementary explanation.

Or it may be, and this is likely, that Cage does not wish to explain or to be explained, as one explains Existentialism or the farther developments of the tone-row. He tells you where he is and how he got there, leaving you to examine for yourself what sort of esthetic situation you are in.

Is explanation necessary? Some explanation undoubtedly does help, the technical details for instance, even more the single sentences with which Cage fractures the more obvious objections to his doings. "Everything seems right when he tells about it," a young musician friend who knew Cage for several years said to me the other evening when I had played some of this music. "Afterwards you aren't sure you recall or know what he meant."

I believe we may start by thinking of John Cage as a philosopher, who uses instead of arguments esthetic instances. He is a thinker who will not be confined within esthetics, for whom the doings of music and words and poetry reach out into and affect a larger context than the appreciative. He is concerned with the event, not with its meaning, with the digits and their arrangement, not the total number or the sum. We are accustomed to ask of an esthetic experience: what does it mean or what does it add up to? Cage cares not so much for what the appreciative intelligence is doing as for how the receptor functions. Do you hear this sound? he asks. Now listen to this succession of sounds, as I have thrown it loose across a path of time. Do you hear a melody? Now start again: here are the same sounds differently arranged in relation to each other again tossed out across a different path in time. Do you distinguish the sound patterns? Do you hear a melody?

The fall of the sounds is determinate, the sequence indeterminate. Out of the same selected materials Cage can compose, by "random operations" or by "chance," any number of combinations, annotated by silence, within any given sequences of time. Thus there is no composition but only a continual spontaneous composing. The composer lays down the facts, so to speak, and the random operations set them into sequence. Each time the listener must begin at the beginning and listen again as eagerly. If he doesn't, that's his business. Because the events do not require an audience, the possibility of the events needs no performer, the anticipation of the audience needs no satisfaction, and so on. We are in a world as arbitrarily composed as the mathematics which have succeeded Euclid; our "harmony" has become as problematical as the Theory of Games.

If this is philosophy, what do I mean by philosophy? Cage, who has come by way of Jung and Zen, would perhaps still accept Justice Holmes's statement of the "human condition"—nowadays we don't call it "living": "I look on man as a cosmic ganglion." Which, from another letter by Holmes, may be expanded this way: "I don't see why a man should despair because he doesn't see a beard on his Cosmos. If he believes that he is inside of it, not it inside of him, he knows that consciousness, purpose, significance and ideals are among its possibilities. . . . It is a fallacy, I think, to look to any theory for motives—we get our motives from our spontaneity—and the business of philosophy is to show that we are not fools for doing what we want to do."

As often with Holmes, the negative of the statement is as interesting as the positive—as I like poetry. There Holmes left it to others to start off into the void again.

Philosophy, as I understand it, subsists in a constant questioning of the apprehension and joining of facts. The apprehension has to do with whether or not they are facts; the joining with the manner in which the facts may or may not be connected.

The ethics of this philosophy will appear in accordance with the acceptance or rejection of normative patterns resulting from the tentative answers in practice given to the questions. These tentative answers in practice set up a morality, and actions taken in awareness of these answers will be moral.

An art concerning itself with these questions is therefore philosophical, ethical, and moral in the degree of its relative consistency at each level of apprehension, practice, and awareness of practice.

For most of us, our society, close to, and our civilization, at a distance, establish and maintain or enforce these normative procedures. Our culture is the consistency of apprehension and practice which serves most of us most of the time as the common fluid feeding-ground and atmosphere of our thinking.

All our lives we are being trained to receive impressions and connect them. Too often the connective matter is supplied by habit; we think, we listen, we hear and appreciate as we do, because this is the way we do it. We dislike, we reject, we actively refuse any experience which threatens to break up this easy patterning of habit. The appreciator, the educator wish to pass on as a "killed" virus their once lively appreciation and its data. Within the spontaneous intelligence they wish to generate antibodies against cultural infection.

One of John Cage's purposes is to break up our habitual patterns of receiving esthetic experience and thinking of it as and after we receive it. He promotes that cultural infection the appreciator and the educator would resist. To do so requires a very acute and subtle intelligence, courage, and a deliberate willingness not to be disturbed by any sort of criticism.

Some may doubt, at first thought, the courage required to summon awake the public intelligence, either individual or collective. Try it. No way of bruising the personality can be more painful than playing tackle in the company of the chosen few against the rock-wall solidity of the lined-up public mind. John Cage has won a curious serenity as a result of playing this game for years—the toughness of an old hockey pro—a maddening indifference, one feels sometimes in his presence. Looking back on my several meetings with him, I must say, I wish I had the serenity he has. I don't know whether I would wish the peculiarly self-contained security of his indifference, a telescopic disregard of anything outside his immediate, exclusive line of vision. Sensibility is not easy in our culture; sometimes one feels our entire society a massed enemy. The hardest blows are the denials, the uncourageous withdrawals and discourteous failures of recognition. Our society does not welcome genius, not this side of 80 years of age; it mocks and degrades genius, though it has a right regard for flexible talent; but if the genius is tough, durable, and real, the mocking promotes it. I doubt that the mockery improves it. In our society to accomplish a great amount for little reward is to be self-condemned. Too much, indeed too much, of our esthetic gift is being wasted in pitching rocks at the gleaming windows of respectability, against glass poured so solidly the rocks drop off from it like pebbles, nothing shattered.

Cage's way has been more selective. Knowing that a man who is too vocally against society sounds like a fool, he has confined his questioning to esthetic instances. Sometimes one has trouble separating the stories from the apocrypha; he does have a legend.

I have been told that his "Lecture on Nothing" consisted of standing before the audience and saying nothing; this appears not to be so. The lecture, which has been published, "was written," he tells in the introduction to the *Indeterminacy* album, "in the same rhythmic structure I employed at the time in my musical compositions. . . . One of the structural divisions was a repetition of a single page in which the refrain occurred 'if anyone is sleepy let him go to sleep' some 14 times. . . . Later, during the question period, I gave 5 prepared answers regardless of the questions."

Then he goes on: "When M. C. Richards asked me why I didn't one day give a conventional informative lecture (adding that that would be the most shocking thing I could do), I said, 'I don't give these lectures to surprise people, but out of the need for poetry.' As I see it, poetry is not prose, simply because poetry is one way or another formalized. It is not poetry by reason of its content or ambiguity, but by reason of its allowing musical elements (time, sound) to be introduced into the world of words. Thus, traditionally, information, no matter how stuffy (e.g., the sutras and shastras of India) was conventionally transmitted by poetry. It was easier to 'get' that way."

The lecture "Indeterminacy: new aspect of form in instrumental and electronic music" was delivered first at Brussels and published. Later, for Teachers College, Columbia University the lecture was expanded to 90 stories. When *Folkways* decided to record, the decision was made to accompany the stories with material from Cage's *Concert for Piano and Orchestra* and electronic sound tracks from his *Fontana Mix*. These at first hearing unassimilated and seemingly unassimilable noises were allowed to come between the speaker and the listener like sounds of traffic through an open window. "I explained that a comparable visual experience is that of seeing someone across the street, and then not being able to see him because a truck passes between." Actually the effect is more startling than interfering.

The 90 stories of *Indeterminacy* are formalized by being told in exactly 90 minutes, the speaker timing himself so that each story fills a single minute. The longer stories are told rapidly, the shorter ones more slowly.

> Most of the stories are things that happened that stuck in my mind. Others I read in books and remembered. . . . The continuity of the 90 stories was not planned. I simply made a list of all the stories I could think of and checked them off as I wrote them. . . . Whenever I have given the talk, someone comes up afterwards and insists that the continuity was a planned one, in spite of the ideas that are expressed regarding purposelessness, emptiness, chaos, etc. One lady, at Columbia, asked, during the discussion following the talk, "What, then, is your final goal?" I remarked that her question was that of the John Simon Guggenheim Memorial Foundation, and that it had irritated artists for decades. Then I said that I did not see that we were going to a goal, but that we were living in process, and that that process is eternal. My intention is putting 90 stories together in an unplanned way is to suggest that all things, sounds, stories (and, by extension, beings) *are* related, and that this complexity is more evident when it is not over-simplified by an idea of relationship in one person's mind.

He goes on: "There was no rehearsal beforehand involving both the reading and the music, for in all my recent music . . . there are parts but no score. Each one of us rehearsed alone and employed a stop-watch during the actual recording process. Each did what he had to do, bringing about a situation which neither had foreseen."

Cage then proceeds in his notes, from which I have been quoting, to describe the *Fontana Mix,* which supplies part of the musical accompaniment.

> The manuscript of the *Fontana Mix* is on transparent plastics which may be superimposed in any number of ways. There are ten sheets having points, and ten having differentiated curved lines. There is also a single straight line and a graph having 100 units horizontally

and 20 vertically. By placing one of the sheets with points over one with curves and then superimposing the graph, it is possible to connect a point within the graph with one outside by means of the single straight line, and to make measurements which define the production of the sound in a studio for making tape music, specifically, the choice of the sound source, alterations of frequency, amplitude, timbre, duration, mixtures, loops, and splicing.

Now all of this sounds, as far as the stories are concerned, rather elementary, and, as far as the *Fontana Mix* is concerned, anything but. The stories go along quite pleasantly from record-side to record-side; though I have heard all several times, I have never listened to all 90 at one sitting. Cage writes me that he plans to expand the lecture to three hours and 180 stories; this seems to me rather forcing the point. The effect of the 90 stories is an autobiography, self-satisfied but not defensive. Names are dropped continually, some famous, all of acquaintances or friends, except the anecdotes related to Confucius, Ramakrishna, and some mythical persons. I find the names dropped more distracting than the music. Why? I can hear Cage asking; and I must admit I am not sure. The precise names substantiate an individual landscape. But is it the common flaw by which many of us unwittingly try to place ourselves within a smaller group of assured fame that approves us, among whom we may face the general refusal we expect? And each expects his fame of the other.

In spite of the name-dropping and helped by the recurrent autobiographical reference, the stories run along fresh from incident to incident, an occasional story being spread, with change of pace in the telling, over two minutes; there is no continuous narrative. As is the way of thinkers nowadays, distinguishing them from professional explainers, Cage allows the listener to make his own cross-references. This way of pricking to a graph, which may have to do deeply with our new awareness of the statistical nature of what we had thought to be reality—the chair is there but where is the chair, if it is made of what we know it is made of, by what suspension of other possibilities can we sit in it?—seems to be what is held up by the stories against the formlessness, the emptiness, the chaos. In each an unplanned spontaneity accomplishes or undoes what might have been expected.

The stories report common miracles, that we might see and respond to in a holy gladness, if we could get outside the depressive corridors of interconnecting intelligence we take for our understanding and our knowledge. The automatic pen in the window display is tearing the paper and splashing the ink on the display. When Cage and Tudor play at a girls' college, a student is overheard saying, "Something has happened. One of the music majors is listening for the first time." The miracle is not the fact but "something has happened." When the very young Cage, then as now a natural ascetic, went to the home of the pianist Richard Buhlig to ask to study with him, he waited twelve hours until midnight when Buhlig at last returned home. I know this to be true because Richard Buhlig told me the story. No one who has encountered Cage forgets him. No one is surprised that his feet are not on the ground.

At the first performance of the *Concert for Piano and Orchestra* in New York, the musicians, who had been individually rehearsed, deliberately misplayed their parts, adding a deliberate confusion to a planned order which to them resembled chaos. It was not, but their betrayal made it so. The musicians chose to ensure chaos rather than to obey the prophecy of an order they did not comprehend. At Cologne, where still more care was taken, the same thing happened. The recorded performance, which is only one of an indefinite series of possible performances, miraculously turned out well, because the performers this time were well-intentioned.

The form of the stories resembles that used in the teachings of Zen, a plain exposition and a twist or reversal of what one is to expect. I offer here one of my own.

A poet friend of mine, wishing to experience Zen teaching, went several times to visit the Buddhist Abbott in Los Angeles. At each visit they sat together and conversed, but nothing happened. The last time, as my friend was leaving, resolved not to return, the Abbott, pointing through the open door, said to him, "It is raining." "Oh no," my friend who is a poet answered, "I am sure it isn't." After that teaching my friend was too ashamed to go back for another visit.

Cage did not come by his decisive thinking as a result of studying Zen, though the training may have sharpened the pencil. At the age of 12 he telephoned the supervisor of the Music Section of the Los Angeles Public Library, announced himself by his age and his full triple name which he no longer uses and instructed this devoted lady, who years later told me the story, that he wished her to find him a violinist of his own age with whom he could play sonatas. "And I was so impressed by his authority," she told me, "I agreed to and did."

I have not, as the reader may appreciate, attempted to explain John Cage. I have tried to set him within a context, to ask questions about him, to let him speak in his own words.

John Cage Late and Early (1960)

Virgil Thomson

The 25-year Retrospective Concert of the Music of John Cage, recorded in performance at Town Hall on May 16, 1958 is an album of six LP sides. It contains program notes by the composer and facsimile pages from his manuscript scores. Both the music and Cage's statements about it reveal a powerful personality long preoccupied with both abstraction, as the art world now understands that term, and with naturalistic expression.

Six Short Inventions for Seven Instruments dates from 1934. These are chromatic pieces, canonic in texture, though not serial, deriving tonally from the preoccupations of his subsequent teacher, Arnold Schoenberg. They already have the sweet cheerfulness, humor, liveliness, and refinement that characterize Cage. They also show the beginnings of his preoccupation with arithmetical structure.

Constructions in Metal (1937) employ a layout that Cage was going to use with little change for the next fifteen years. This is a method of structuring a non-tonal piece by organizing a chosen length of playing time into segments interrelated numerically. The sound of *Constructions* is dominated by metal and is utterly resplendent, involving cowbells, a gamelan, automobile brake drums, orchestral bells, thundersheets, anvils, cymbals, gongs of all sizes, and a pianoforte played with a drum beater.

Imaginary Landscape No. 1 (1939) suggests a sorcerer (or his apprentice) in a radio studio, where electronically produced sounds can swoop around and fly through the air with the greatest of ease. The sounds lack charm (as all electronically produced sounds do), and technologically the work is primitive. But for its time, ten years before tape, it is remarkable.

Side no. 2 embodies Cage's chief experiments with vocal music, expertly sung by Arline Carmen. A text from James Joyce, *The Wonderful Widow of Eighteen Springs,* is limited in its vocal line to three notes in the low register and in its accompaniment to a few finger thumps and knuckle knocks on diverse parts of a closed grand piano. The piece does not come off ideally, either as music or as declamation. Much more striking is *Duo,* a vocalise accompanied by prepared piano.

This forms the second part of *She Is Asleep* (1943). The first part is a quartet for 12 Tomtoms (three to a player). The latter has exquisite delicacy and a highly elaborate rhythmic texture. The author describes its effect as hypnotic. This reviewer did not find it so; but the introduction of long silences toward the end clearly illustrates someone falling asleep. The vocalise depicts a state of sleep, its little moans evoking what a watcher might hear. The vowel employed is vague, like humming with the mouth open. Consonants are rare; but grace notes attacked by a glottis stroke and from above, as in the Chinese opera, are present; and sometimes deliberate tremolando is employed, as in Monteverdi. There are glissandi too. The effect is sonorously agreeable and intensely, almost disquietingly, realistic.

Two whole sides are occupied by *Sonatas and Interludes* (1946–48), ten in all, representing one-half of the entire work, which contains twenty. These are admirably played on a prepared piano by Maro Ajemian. Heard separately, they are delightful, varied, sprightly, recalling in both sound and shape the *Esercizi* (or Sonatas) for harpsichord by Domenico Scarlatti. But in spite of the great mastery evident, they do tend to wear down the ear with their repetitions and with the monotony of their pings and thuds.

With *Williams Mix* (1952) we are in full musique concrète and the full expansion of a new structural method—also in full naturalism as to the materials used. This is an assemblage on one tape of eight other tapes, controlled as to the presence and loudness of its musical materials by calculations involving the flipping of coins and the dealing of cards. The Chinese Book of Changes (*I Ching*) is the chief source of these hazard techniques. The length of the tape, four and a quarter minutes, seems to have been chosen arbitrarily.

The materials, according to Cage, are recordings of "city sounds, country sounds, electronic sounds, manually produced sounds, including the literature of music, wind-produced sounds, including songs, and small sounds requiring amplification to be heard with the others."

All these put together ought to make a jolly row, but somehow they do not. I suspect that too many silences, turning up through the games of chance, have left this work a mite below its point of optimum animation.

The summit of the album and its finale is a *Concert for Piano and Orchestra* (1957–58). This is probably Cage's most complex work and certainly his most entertaining. It makes a jolly row and a good show. What with the same man playing two tubas at once, a trombone player using only his instrument's mouthpiece, a violist sawing away across his knees, and the soloist David Tudor crawling around on the floor and thumping his piano from below, for all the world like a 1905 motorist, the Town Hall spectacle, as you can imagine, was one of cartoon comedy.

So, indeed, was the sound of the piece, with every instrument improvising, or seeming to, its most outlandish effects—bleats, burps, bangs, tweaks, squeals, guffaws, and sudden trills. Since all these sounds are produced by musical instruments played by musicians, they are related to those of a classical orchestra, with all the richness and all the variety available from such a highly evolved sound source. They come very high, very low, very loud, very soft, and in an infinite variety of colors. The piano part alone contains eighty-four different kinds of musical event. The result of all this variety, and also of the aristocratic, inherently "musical" character of the instruments and players producing it, is a far cry from the poverty of electronic sound. It is humane, civilized, and sumptuous. And if the general effect is that of an orchestra just having fun, it is doubtful whether any orchestra ever before had so much fun or gave such joyful hilarity to its listeners.

The structural method behind this piece carries chance to its ultimate. Even in performance, the *Concert* could not ever possibly come out twice alike. Nor significantly different either. Its subject is its palette of sounds, nothing else. And if these express through their choice the gaiety and sweetness of Cage's temperament and through their manipulation his high capacity for inventing games, this composer can be said here to have, like many another, expressed himself.

The whole album is like that—pure Cage. His music has from the beginning had a personal sound and a distinctive climate of expression. The music is the man. And the man is a California Western, optimistic, full of laughter and some tenderness, devoted to success and to what he calls "nature." By "nature" he seems to mean a mystical devotion to the casual (in vegetation and in humanity), though he also admits to his music order and number, which have for him all the fascination of the more "natural" phenomena. In any case, like most of our artists from the West Coast, he arranges his "nature," his selected casual materials, according to the best principles of occult symmetry as these have been codified in East Asia.

The present recording, with its excellent notes, gives an ample view of a striking personality who is also our most "far out" composer.

For a more personal acquaintance with Cage, I recommend *Indeterminacy,* subtitled "New Aspect of Form in Instrumental and Electronic Music." In this album (four LP sides) John Cage reads while David Tudor plays intermittent quotations from music by Cage. These do not interfere with the reading; that is to say with its clarity. The text consists of anecdotes—moral, philosophical, and funny—all told deadpan. Their choice gives a picture of the composer's mind, their manner of telling the true sound of his voice. One of the very best personal appearance recordings available anywhere.

De-Linearizing Musical Continuity (1990)

Daniel Charles

Among the main assumptions in which the idea of time in traditional Western music seems to have been firmly rooted, one of the most genuine is *continuity.* Even John Cage, who is automatically considered (at least in Europe) as the pope of discontinuity, has defined musical form as "continuity," and method as "the means of controlling the continuity from note to note."[1] For a composer, Cage explained, two things are indispensable: spontaneity, because it allows form to be itself (that is, unique in its expressive continuity), and structural control over the musical material. But since Cage's own interest in expressivity was likely to impose restrictions and even exclusions among this material, he decided to give up his subjectivity in such a way as to save and even reinforce continuity. Cage describes his *Music of Changes* (1951) as a "composition the continuity of which is free of individual taste and memory (psychology) and also of the literature and 'traditions' of the art. . . . Value judgments are not in the nature of this work as regards either composition, performance, or listening. The idea of relation (the idea: 2) being absent, anything (the idea: 1) may happen. A 'mistake' is beside the point, for once anything happens it authentically is."[2]

Despite its somewhat provocative character, Cage's *rationale* is clear: even if the "continuity" of the *Music of Changes* does not rely on the composer's spontaneity, it has not disappeared and may very well *continue* to be experienced by the listener. Similarly, at least some kind of discontinuity may be experienced as well in the listener's mind without existing in the work itself: "The activity of movement, sound, and light," Cage will write in 1956, "is expressive, but what it expresses is determined by each one of you. . . ."[3] Thus it would be misleading to interpret Cage's refusal of value judgments only in a negative way, as if value judgments were not "often (and habitually) . . . used in ways which are profoundly negative" since they summarize "the old *limitations* imposed on musical imagination";[4] rather one should listen to what Cage himself said in 1957, that "nothing was lost when everything was given away," and that it is only after having practiced such a renunciation that "any sounds may occur in any combination and in any continuity."[5] Now if "the coming into being of something new does not by that fact deprive what was of its proper place,"[6] there can be no doubt that there will be continuity with the past. Therefore, Cage's inclusion of noise in the world of tones, and of silence in the world of sound, can be understood as a development of Busoni's and Varèse's "acceptance of all audible phenomena as material proper to music."[7]

In this respect, Cage's use of the word *field* is meaningful in that it indicates the degree of faithfulness of the composer toward himself. As early as 1937, the young Cage had prophesized that the creator would some day be "FACED WITH THE ENTIRE FIELD OF SOUND."[8] In 1948, he applied the same concept to the temporal dimension: "In the field of structure, the field of the definition of parts and their relation to the whole, there has been only one new idea since Beethoven. . . . There can be no right making of music that does not structure itself from the very roots of sound and silence—lengths of time."[9] In 1955, the notion of field is enlarged to include the reversibility of time, i.e., space: a sound, "*before it has died away,*" "*must have made perfectly exact its frequency, its loudness, its length, its overtone structure, the precise morphology of these and of itself*"; it "*does not exist as one of a series of discrete steps, but as transmission in all directions from the field's center.*"[10] In 1957, the substitution of "transmission in all directions" for "discrete steps" is still more dramatically evoked: "Any sound at any point in this total sound-space can move to become a sound at any other point. . . . [M]usical action or existence can occur at any point or along any line or curve . . . in total sound-space."[11] Finally, in the musical notations themselves the "order of succession" becomes a determinant or a parameter of the sound as such, just as essential as pitch, loudness, timbre, duration, or "morphology" ("how the sound begins, goes on, and dies away").[12]

As strange as it may seem, Cage's emphasis upon the possibility of enlarging the concept of musical continuity has persuaded the composer and theorist James Tenney to base a new theory of "harmonic perception" on the multidimensional character of sound-space. In his essay "John Cage and the Theory of Harmony," Tenney states that "the work of John Cage, while posing the greatest conceivable *challenge* to any such efforts, yet contains many fertile seeds for theoretical developments—some of them not only useful, but *essential.*"[13] For Cage, parameters other than pitch have to be considered, and "each aspect of sound . . . is to be seen as a continuum";[14] therefore Tenney suggests that pitches be represented "by points in a multidimensional space" and labeled according to a specific "frequency ratio" measured with respect to a reference pitch, but within a certain "tolerance range." The distances between the various points will allow the identification of interferences other than "higher" or "lower." And since "tones represented by proximate points in harmonic space tend to be heard as being in a consonant relation to each other, while tones represented by more widely separated points are heard as mutually dissonant,"[15] the "field of force" available in the harmonic space will be taken into account for itself, i.e., without invoking only, as Helmholtz did, the overtone series, or, as Rameau did, the tonic-chord root phenomenon. Moreover, such an enlarged conception of harmony will involve not only the "verticality" of the Western musical writing but all the "pitch-relations manifested in a purely melodic or monophonic situation" as well. It will recognize as its first principle that "there is some (set of) specifically harmonic relation(s) between any two salient and relatively stable pitches."[16]

Now if one of the brightest achievements of the application of the Cagean model in the realm of harmony, i.e., in the treatment of musical spaces, is the conquest of the "horizontal" dimension of melody or monody, one may wonder if a parallel degree of emancipation is not entailed, in the realm of temporality, in what the metaphor of "verticalization" points to, namely the de-linearization of musical continuity. When we draw time, we use a line, and can measure what Hegel called the successive "now-points" of the linearized time. Indeed, as the musicologist F. Joseph Smith has shown, almost the entire history of musical notation "is one of uncritical acceptance of temporality as linear, for we literally follow the notes like now-points across a spatially extended printed page."[17] But this has not always been the case. According to Smith, "the Greeks, even though they made use of a rudimentary tablature, played music 'by ear,' and not by following a visual written notation." The word *tonos,* "which has perdured through medieval *tonus* up to and including both tonality and 'atonality,' has to do exclusively with an audial experience"—that of the tuning of the *kithara* which "had to do with various degrees of tenseness of the strings, as every string player knows in his fingers. Thus the tablature, though mediated through the eye, was really a contact between the fingers and what I would like to call a musical *tensor*. . . . [T]he Greek *tonos,* the building block of western music, was thus a tensor first and foremost. And a tensor, *as a vibrating unit in the primordial experience of music,* is meant for the ear" (154–55). Now what is Cage's purpose when in his scores he blurs the order of succession of musical events, if not to try to get rid of the spatial-visual measuring device of the horizontal line? He thus retrieves the Greek "audial" symbolism of vibration, i.e., of tense, tensility, or tension; and he even speaks Husserl's vocabulary when he describes his own use of Christian Wolff's "zero time" in terms of "going forward" or "backward" through time. Indeed Husserl's "pretentions" or "retentions" are but visual metaphors; yet they allude to musical gestures, so that Husserl's definition of time as "a whole network or tissue of experience that thrusts ahead or pro-tends itself and leaves a trail of aftershadows," or as an experience which "retains itself" so that "each given new point stands not in isolation but in the pattern of thrust and trail, in the manner of a comet"[18] "sounds" Cagean *avant la lettre.* Moreover, Husserl is never reluctant to rely on musical experience as such, as for instance when he describes retention as a musical "tail," or as "a series of after-echoes exemplified in the flight of a bird." "As the forward thrust of time builds a horizon," Smith explains, "it leaves in its wake a whole series of tonal 'shadows' (*Abschattungen*), that spread out in ever-diminishing diagonal 'lines' behind it. . . . This conception of time may be called 'vertical' though it is obvious that the flow is diagonal: and though it is graphed in one dimension, it obviously is a circular flow out and behind the thrusting edge of musical tone as it makes its 'time'" (158).

In spite of the resonance between Husserl's and Cage's conceptions of musical time, Cage never quotes Husserl. His sources and references come from the Orient. In 1945–46 he first became seriously aware of Oriental philosophy through the writings of Ananda K. Coomaraswamy, Aldous Huxley, and Sri Ramakrishna; he devoted his *Sonatas and Interludes* for prepared piano to the expression of the "permanent emotions" of Indian thought. He was the only composer to attend Daisetz Suzuki Teitaro's lectures on Kegon (Chinese: Hua-yen) Buddhist philosophy at Columbia University from 1951 onwards:[19] no wonder the notions central to his aesthetics are deeply rooted in his understanding of Suzuki's explanations of Buddhism and Zen. One may find, for instance, expressed as if in a nutshell, the essence of Cage's doctrine of de-linearized continuity in the well-known formula "interpenetration without obstruction"; as Cage wrote in 1956 to Paul Henry Lang, "'art'" and "'music'" "when anthropocentric (involved in self-expression), seem trivial and lacking in urgency to me. We live in a world where there are things as well as people. Trees, stones, water, everything is expressive. I see this situation in which I impermanently live as a complex interpenetration of centers moving out in all directions without impasse."[20] It would seem that we are not so far from Leibniz's "expressionism." "Every individual substance," Leibniz writes in his *Discourse on Metaphysics,* "expresses the whole universe in its own manner. . . . Each substance is like an entire world and like a living mirror . . . of the whole world which it portrays, each one in its own fashion. . . . Thus the universe is multiplied in some sort as many times as there are substances. . . . It can indeed be said that every substance . . . expresses, although confusedly, all that happens in the universe, past, present, and future."[21] And we may also, as Steve Odin has suggested, describe "such a microcosmic-macrocosmic universe of simultaneous-mutual reflections . . . in terms of the contemporary 'holographic' model, as a three-dimensional multi-coloured laser projection, bright and vivid yet wholly transparent, wherein each part is an image of the whole."[22] However, the most striking of the *similes* through which the doctrine of interpenetration and intercausation has been articulated are doubtlessly to be found in the very Hua-yen texts Suzuki commented upon, namely the Sanskrit *Avataṁsaka Sūtra* (of which he translated the last chapter, the *Gandavyūha Sūtra*),[23] together with the writings of F̈a-tsang.[24] As Odin has written, the *Avataṁsaka Sūtra,* which concerns "the acquisition of astounding spiritual powers throughout an ascending series of fifty-two states . . . describes an infinitely vast and open crystalline universe composed of iridescent and transparent phenomena and all interpenetrated and harmonized together in the non-obstructed *dharmadhātu* of all-merging suchness" (18). The *dharmadhātu,* or field of all the phenomena (*dharma*), as "a cosmic web of interrelationships or universal matrix of intercausation, is analogous to the vast net covering Celestial Lord Indra's Palace, which stretches throughout the entire universe. At each intersection of the latticework is situated a brilliant jewel reflecting all other jewels from its own perspective in the net" (17). Since "each *dharma* is fully present . . . in every other *dharma,* there is a perfect sameness . . . between all things of the universe, negatively expressed as *śūnyatā* or emptiness, and positively expressed as *amalacitta* or purity" (18). As Odin puts it, Cage's renunciation of subjectivity obviously takes into account the fact that, "since everything dissolves into everything else at the ontological level of *śūnyatā,*" "all events are wholly devoid of *svabhava* or unique selfhood" (18).

But does not this "sameness" entail indifferentiation, and this interfusion lead to a confusion? Before trying to answer this question, let us clarify, as Tenney did, the problem of the relationship between Cage the composer and Cage the thinker. According to Tenney, "it is primarily *because of his music*—his very substantial credibility *as a composer*—that we are drawn into a consideration of [Cage's] philosophical and theoretical ideas. To imagine otherwise is to 'put the cart before the horse.'"[25] And one has to agree without reservation to Tenney's suggestion that we apply to Cage what he himself once wrote concerning Satie: "relegating Satie to the position of having been very influential but in his own work finally unimportant is refusing to accept the challenge he so bravely gave us."[26] Now our question about the musical "results" of Cage's denial of *subjectivity* or selfhood may be transformed: far from deciding to "translate" or "express" Hua-yen's "interpenetration without obstruction" into the musical realm, Cage found in such a doctrine the confirmation of his own *musical* quest. As Tenney has shown, the "method" does not cease to allow Cage the composer to control the continuity once he has given up his own spontaneity (that is, after 1951), but it helps him to elaborate a new formal type, the "ergodic" one, in which "any 2- or 3-minute segment of the piece is essentially the same as any other segment of corresponding duration, even though the details are quite different in the two cases."[27] In other terms, the "sameness" which is present in the *dharmadhātu* and may be defined either as "emptiness" (*śūnyatā*) or as "purity," *represents* at a conceptual level the *statistical homogeneity* which is likely to be worked out by the composer since, as Tenney puts it, "certain *statistical properties* are in fact 'the same'—or so nearly identical that no distinction can be made in perception" (9–10).

Tenney's analysis allows us to assess critically the "refutations" of Cage's "orientalism." George Rochberg, for instance, interprets both existentialism and Zen Buddhism as holding that "the present moment is the nodal point of existence." "It is not at all strange therefore," he adds, "that composers of chance music, particularly, are drawn to Zen and imply in their attitude towards music an existential tendency; that is, see music as the occurrence of unpredictable events, each moment of sound or silence freed of formal connection with the moment before or after, audible only as a present sensation." "In this form of existential music," Rochberg adds, "the present erases the past by allowing no recall or return; and promises no future since the present happening is sufficient to itself, requiring no future event for its understanding. . . . All the listener can hope to do is grasp at each occurrence, just as he grasps at life's formless succession of events, hoping to derive some meaningful order. In the case of chance music this is hardly likely; and, from the point of view of the composers of such music, highly undesirable."[28] And nearly as misleading is this statement by Leonard B. Meyer: "When . . . attention is directed only to the uniqueness of things, then each and every attribute of an object or event is equally significant and necessary. There can be no degree of connectedness within or between events."[29] To such arguments, or caricatures of arguments, Cage's music has already answered. But at the theoretical level, it may be fruitful to recall Tenney's analysis: "The relation between the ergodic form and Cage's later methods involving chance and/or indeterminacy is this: an ergodic form will always and inevitably be the result when the range of possibilities (with respect to the sound elements in a piece, and their characteristics) is given at the outset of the compositional process, and remains unchanged during the realization of the work."[30] In this perspective, Thomas DeLio has recently shown in his brilliant analysis of Cage's *Variations II,* how an ergodic piece, though involving both total indeterminacy and total foreseeable procedure, is to be considered as self-generating; and still more clearly, in his study of Morton Feldman's third section of *Durations III,* how "the act of creating the piece, note after note, becomes progressively the piece itself" so that "this is a music born at its conclusion rather than (at) its inception."[31]

As early as 1961, Christian Wolff had described a quasi-ergodic situation where the limits of a piece "are expressed, not at moments of time which mark a succession, but as margins of a spatial projection of the total sound structure."[32] The importance of such a reversal from (linear) time to space is worth being outlined here, since it explains the actual working of "interpenetration without obstruction" in the compositions themselves. Let us note first that if Cage's renunciation of subjectivity meant the "dissolving of everything into everything" at the level of emptiness or *śūnyatā,* it could mean as well access to "purity" or *amalacitta.* In other words, we can agree with Tenney: "Cage's inclusion of 'all audible phenomena as material proper to music' did not mean that distinctions were no longer to be made. On the contrary, it now became possible to distinguish many more varieties of elementary sounds" (10), in particular the "aggregates of pitches and timbres" made available by the use of the prepared piano in Cage's *Sonatas and Interludes,* or the gamut of stringed sounds selected for the *String Quartet.*[33] Wolff's suggestion that we define a piece as resulting from the projection on a specific space of a "total sound structure" actually extended this principle of differentiation. "Moves intersecting and voices overlapping," Wolff will add in 1965, "can obscure structural outlines and produce meetings or events that are disengaged from them to become simply themselves. Then, a structure that seems closed by a square of time-lengths may also be dissolved by including a zero in the sequencing of the time-lengths' proportions (e.g., 2 1/4, 1, 0, 2 . . .). The zero I take to mean no time at all, that is, no measurable time, that is, any time at all."[34] Indeed the introduction of the zero, far from meaning only the creation of a gap in the continuous stream of linear time, questions the basic validity of the entire hourglass concept of time and breaks down Rochberg's and Meyer's misleading metaphor of a unidimensional "present," "freed of formal connection with the moment before or after." Or, more exactly, it undermines its polemical force.

Wolff's conception of "zero time" is in fact deeply akin to Heidegger's idea of a "primordial granting of time," which "keeps open the having-been by denying it its coming as present, just as it keeps open the coming (future) by withholding the present in this coming, that is, by denying it its being present. Thus, the proximity which brings near has the character of a denial and withholding. . . . Furthermore, the present is not at all that which is constant; rather, the authentic comes to pass in each case if and when having-been-ness and future play together and mesh."[35] Hence it seems pertinent to apply here the well-known thesis on the "stillness" of time in Heidegger's *Unterwegs zur Sprache.* "Time times simultaneously the has-been, presence, and the present that is waiting for our encounter and is normally called the future. Time in its timing removes us in its threefold simultaneity. . . . But time itself, in the wholeness of its nature, does not move;

it rests in stillness."[36] It is clear indeed from this definition that "the 'simultaneity' referred to here cannot be thought of as the 'in itself' or time."[37]

Silence or stillness, absence or emptiness, all these Heideggerian-Cagean-Hua-yen notions *prevent* time from being taken as something *already present or already there.* Time *is not*—time *has to spring.* But *in so far as it springs,* it *disappears into its own withdrawal.* And because of this withdrawal, we are prevented from taking into account any feature other than its evanescence, from shoring up our understanding of the signification of music on any notion of "presence" in the sense of a "now moment" separated from the others. So that, by a kind of paradox, Meyer and Rochberg are right: music cannot rely on the isolated dimension of the present. But unfortunately for them, the Cagean—or Heideggerian, or Zen—conception of "interpenetration without obstruction" is *the only one which seriously, radically, supports this idea;* thus it confirms what the musicologist Victor Zuckerkandl had already concluded during the fifties from his analysis of Beethoven and Schubert: "To a great extent the problems posed by the old concept of time arise from the fact that it distinguished three mutually exclusive elements, whereas only the picture of a constant interaction and intertwining of these elements is adequate to the real process."[38]

NOTES

1. John Cage, "Forerunners of Modern Music" (1949), *Silence* (Middletown: Wesleyan University Press, 1961), 62.
2. John Cage, "To Describe the Process of Composition Used in *Music of Changes* and *Imaginary Landscape No. 4*" (1952), *Silence,* 59.
3. John Cage, "In This Day . . ." (1956), *Silence,* 95.
4. James Tenney, "John Cage and the Theory of Harmony," (1983), *Soundings* 13 (1984).
5. John Cage, "Experimental Music" (1957), *Silence,* 8.
6. Cage, "Experimental Music," 11.
7. John Cage, "Edgard Varèse" (1958), *Silence,* 84.
8. John Cage, "The Future of Music: Credo" (1937), *Silence,* 4.
9. John Cage, "Defense of Satie" (1948), *John Cage,* ed. Richard Kostelanetz (New York: Praeger, 1970), 81–82.
10. John Cage, "Experimental Music: Doctrine" (1955), *Silence,* 14.
11. Cage, "Experimental Music," *Silence,* 9.
12. John Cage, see "Composition as Process: I. Changes" (1958), *Silence,* 18–34.

13. Tenney, 3.

14. John Cage, "History of Experimental Music in the United States" (1959), *Silence,* 70–71.

15. Tenney, 22–23.

16. Tenney, 24.

17. F. Joseph Smith, *The Experiencing of Musical Sound* (New York: Gordon, 1979), 154.

18. Smith, 158.

19. Abe Masao, ed., *A Zen Life: D. T. Suzuki Remembered* (New York and Tokyo: Weatherhill, 1986), 223.

20. John Cage, "Letter to Paul Henry Lang" (1956), quoted in Kostelanetz, 116.

21. Gottfried Wilhelm Leibniz, "Discourse on Metaphysics," in *Leibniz: Basic Writings,* trans. G. R. Montgomery (La Salle, IL: Open Court, 1968), 14–15; quoted in Steven Odin, *Process of Metaphysics and Hua-yen Buddhism* (Albany: State University of New York Press, 1982), 16.

22. Odin, 16.

23. H. Idzumi and D. T. Suzuki, eds., *The Gandavyūha Sūtra* (Four Parts) (Kyoto: Sanskrit Buddhist Text Publishing Society, 1934), 6.

24. F̈a-tsang, et al., "Hundred Gates to the Sea of Ideas of the Flowery Splendour Scripture," *A Source Book in Chinese Philosophy,* trans. Wing-tsit Chan (Princeton: Princeton University Press, 1963), 414–20.

25. Tenney, 4.

26. John Cage, "Satie Controversy" (1951), quoted in Kostelanetz, 90.

27. Tenney, 9.

28. George Rochberg, "Duration in Music," in *The Modern Composer and His World,* ed. John Beckwith and Udo Kasemets (Toronto: University of Toronto Press, 1961), 60–62.

29. Leonard B. Meyer, *Music, the Arts, and Ideas* (Chicago: University of Chicago Press, 1967), 164–65.

30. Tenney, 10.

31. Thomas DeLio, *Circumscribing the Open Universe* (Lanham, Md.: University Press of America, 1984), 46.

32. Christian Wolff, quoted in Cage, "Composition as Process: III. Communication" (1958), *Silence,* 54.

33. See Cage, "Composition as Process: I. Changes," *Silence,* 18–34.

34. Christian Wolff, "On Form," *Die Reihe* 7 (1965): 29.

35. Joseph H. Kockelmans, *On the Truth of Being* (Bloomington: Indiana University Press, 1984), 70, 100.

36. Martin Heidegger, *On the Way to Language,* trans. Peter Hatz (New York: Harper, 1971), 106.

37. Kockelmans, 100.

38. Victor Zuckerkandl, *Sound and Symbol,* trans. Willard R. Trask and Nobert Guterman (Princeton: Princeton University Press, 1956), 224.

“There’s no such a thing as silence . . .”: John Cage’s Poetics of Silence (1991)

Eric De Visscher

The concept of silence is more and more to be seen as central in understanding John Cage’s whole work. Cage has, on many occasions, indicated that his silent piece *(4'33")* remained his most important work; and it is not without reason that Cage’s first book was entitled *Silence.*

But Cage’s concept of silence has changed over the years. In fact, a radical evolution of Cage’s thought about silence took place in a relatively short period of time: in 1948, the concept of silence is first developed in Cage’s writings and in 1952, Cage creates his now famous silent piece. Cage’s subsequent music and writings directly stem from this new vision of silence which appeared in *4'33"*.

Silent Prayer

From 1948 on, the question of silence progressively becomes a leading issue for Cage. Although it is first mentioned in the writings of that year, silence was nevertheless already present in Cage’s early music (the music for percussion and prepared—or unprepared—piano): “. . . I had an inclination toward silence that you can discern in very early pieces written in the 1930s. One of my early teachers always complained that I had no sooner started than I stopped” (Kostelanetz 1988, 67).*

But 1948 is also an important date because it is during that same

*See Notes for explanation of citations of John Cage’s writings.

year that Cage first thought of his silent piece. He mentions this idea at the very end of a lecture he gave on February 28, 1948, at Vassar College. The lecture was called "A Composer's Confession" and described Cage's musical itinerary: his first steps in music, his studies with Schoenberg, his ideas about "structural rhythm," his discovery of Indian thought and of C. G. Jung's ideas, etc. Although he confesses a certain embarassment towards the idea of newness (". . . because our culture has its faith not in the peaceful center of the spirit but in an ever-hopeful projection on to the things of our own desire for completion"), Cage acknowledges that he has several new ideas and desires. Among them is the idea of writing a silent piece.

> However, as long as this desire exists in us, for new materials, new forms, new this and new that, we must search to satisfy it. I have, for instance, several new desires (two may seem absurd but I am serious about them):
>
> first, to compose a piece of uninterrupted silence and sell it to Muzak Co. (in manuscript:) It will be 3 or 4½ minutes long, those being the standard lengths of "canned" music (and) its title will be *Silent Prayer.* It will open with a single idea which I will attempt to make as seductive as the color and shape and fragrance of a flower. The ending will approach imperceptibility;
>
> and, second, to compose and have performed a composition using as instruments nothing but twelve radios. It will be my *Imaginary Landscape No. 4.* (1948a, 29)

Silence thus appears here in a somewhat political or polemical context: it is seen as a reaction against the overall presence of music, especially the "music" of Muzak! Besides the intriguing title, one should also notice that the proposed length of the piece already corresponds to the 1952 work, but was given for very specific reasons.

Imagined in 1948, the silent piece was only to be composed in 1952: it thus took Cage four years to be able to realize his ideas about silence in the most direct manner. "Four years to write the silent piece" simply means that it required from Cage several renunciations as well as an openness to certain unknown aspects of music. The importance of these new aspects is manifested in the radical changes which appear in the other pieces written by Cage during that same period: one only needs to compare *Sonatas and Interludes* (1946–48), *String Quartet in Four Parts* (1950), *Music of Changes* (1951), *Imaginary Landscape No. 4* (1951), *Williams Mix* (1952) to realize that at each new piece, some accepted principle of musical form is put into question. These new aspects of Cage's compositional ideas (chance operations, indeterminacy, theater) are all, in some way or another, related to the evolution of the concept of silence.

Structure

During the summer of 1948, Cage organized a Satie Festival at Black Mountain College, during which he presented a speech entitled "Defense of Satie." The speech was given in front of an audience largely made up of German refugees who were apparently all devoted to Beethoven.

During this lecture, Cage presented his theory of the four elements of music (structure, form, method and material), of which structure was the most important element. Cage then literally provoked his audience by saying that Beethoven was wrong, because his structures were based on pitch and harmony, whereas Satie was right to structure his pieces only on "time lengths." Central to the argument is the question of silence.

> If you consider that sound is characterized by its pitch, its loudness, its timbre, and its duration, and that silence, which is the opposite and, therefore, the necessary partner of sound, is characterized only by its duration, you will be drawn to the conclusion that of the four characteristics of the material of music, duration, that is time length, is the most fundamental. Silence cannot be heard in terms of pitch or harmony: It is heard in terms of time length. . . . There can be no right making of music that does not structure itself from the very roots of sound and silence—lengths of time. (1948b, 81)

In March 1949, Cage publishes another famous text, "Forerunners of Modern Music," in which the same ideas are forcefully and convincingly developed. The concept of structure solely based on duration can be found again, as duration is the only element which is common to both sound and silence.

Gradually, structure loses its regulating and organizing aspect to become simply a "measure—nothing more, for example, than the inch of a ruler—thus permitting the existence of any durations, any amplitude relations (meter, accent), any silences" (1949a, 64).

Structure becomes a sort of empty—silent—box, allowing for any kind of sounds to appear. But that very appearance is now conditioned by the presence of silence: sound emerges from silence and goes back to it. In his first texts, Cage showed the necessity of opening musical material to all possible sounds; he now affirms that such opening is only possible when silence is present as a starting-point (and as a point of arrival) for all those sounds.

> Any sounds of any qualities and pitches (known or unknown, definite or indefinite), any contexts of these, simple or multiple, are natural and conceivable within a rhythmic structure which equally embraces silence. (1949a, 65)

This is, in fact, a relatively classical position about silence: silence is considered as absolutely necessary to the existence of sound, but still as an absence of sound. The relation between sound and silence is then seen on a horizontal plane, in which sound and silence are placed one after the other on the axis of time. Structure is based on their succession and their mutual exclusion. Such a conception of silence can be traced back in the music of both Debussy and Webern.

Something and Nothing

Cage's ideas begin to change significantly in his following texts, namely "Lecture on Nothing" and "Lecture on Something." In order to acknowledge the fully positive character of silence, it is not sufficient to recognize its important role in the creation of structure. One should also be able to think of silence without considering it negatively, i.e., as an absence of sounds. This positive aspect of silence appears at the very beginning of "Lecture on Nothing," written in 1949.

> What we require is silence; but what silence requires is that I go on talking. . . . But now there are silences and the words make, help make the silences. . . . We need not fear those silences,—we may love them. (1949b, 109)

The necessary interrelation of sound and silence can now be seen as a bi-directional relation: it is not just silence which allows for sounds to appear, but also sounds which "help make" silence. Silence is no longer a mere absence of sounds, since it is itself nourished by sound and noise. According to the lecture's title, silence can be considered as nothing, but this nothing must be understood in the oriental—and mainly Zen Buddhist—sense: beyond the opposition of Nothing and Something, it is their necessary interpenetration, as well as their constant change of state, which must be considered. Each element contains one part of the opposing element, so that silence may contain sounds, as much as sound must include silence. Each Nothing is a Something and each Something is a Nothing.

In "Lecture on Nothing," Cage indicates a first "musical" or compositional manner of approaching silence. As did Webern before him, he insists on the use of quiet sounds.

> Half intellectually and half sentimentally, when the war came along, I decided to use only quiet sounds. . . . But quiet sounds were like loneliness or love or friendship. Permanent, I thought, values, independent at least from Life, Time and Coca-Cola. (1949b, 117)

Sound then emerges only slightly from silence, without really separating itself from silence and seeking to return to it rapidly. In some of Cage's compositions from that period (like for instance, *Dream* or *In a Landscape,* both dating from 1948), one really perceives the music as a surface, a horizontal line, made of sound and silence. Silence does not disappear when a sound is heard: this is the first step towards a vertical conception of silence, in which sound and silence follow a parallel evolution without excluding each other.

In order to establish a fully positive concept of silence, the composer—and the theorist—has to make a (strictly speaking) radical revolution: he must first turn his attention towards all sounds. He must be able to listen and accept all sounds he is encountering before making any preconceptions, before formulating, in Cage's own words, any "intention." To this new attitude towards sound, Cage briefly alluded at the end of "Lecture on Nothing."

> I begin to hear the old sounds—the ones I had thought worn out, worn out by intellectualization—I begin to hear the old sounds as

> though they are not worn out. Obviously, they are not worn out. They are just as audible as the new sounds. Thinking had worn them out. And if one stops thinking about them, suddenly they are fresh and new. (1949b, 117)

Once again, Cage's position evolves in comparison to his early texts. In those earlier writings Cage pushed towards the constant discovery of new sounds and unheard sonorities. He now also cares for "old sounds": not a return to more traditional music, but on the contrary a move towards integration of all possible sounds, with no exclusion whatsoever, so that each sound, including old ones, can find its place in musical space.

It is precisely that aspect of opening oneself to all sounds which constitutes the main idea of "Lecture on Something," probably written somewhat later, around 1951.

Cage develops those ideas of acceptance and change of attitude towards sound through constant references to Morton Feldman. In itself, this is a curious fact: Cage presents ideas which are in evidence his, by not only demonstrating them through examples taken from Feldman's music (principally the *Intersections*), but also by "leaning" on Feldman's sayings and ideas. The following passage is both revealing of that fact as well as capital in Cage's attitude towards sound and silence.

> Feldman speaks of no sounds, and takes within broad limits the first ones that come along. He has changed the responsibility of the composer from making to accepting. To accept whatever comes regardless of the consequences is to be unafraid or to be full of that love which comes from a sense of at-one-ness with whatever. This goes to explain what Feldman means when he says that he is associated with all of the sounds, and so can foresee what will happen, even though he has not written the particular notes down as other composers do. (1951, 129–30)

That aspect of predictability is probably an important difference between Feldman and Cage. Besides it, the relation between the composer and the surrounding sounds clearly originates in the evolution of Cage's conception of silence.

What is then the relation between accepting all sounds and silence?

Here we are somewhat halfway in that evolution which will lead to the identification of those two terms. Here, they are still different, but clearly influence each other. Again, Cage refers to Feldman.

> I remember now that Feldman spoke of shadows. He said that sounds were not sounds but shadows. They are obviously sounds; that's why they are shadows. Every something is an echo of nothing. (1951, 131)

"The plot thickens" . . . relations between nothing and something, between silence and sound, become more complex. It is not enough to say that something and nothing "need each other to keep on going," not even that sound resonates in silence. Inversely, silence now resonates in sound: sound is the echo of silence.

"All the somethings in the world begin to sense their at-one-ness when something happens that reminds them of nothing" (1951, 133). It is silence which is prominent; in sound, one must be able to find a trace of silence. "Nothing must be taken as a basis," because Nothing is not absence, but life, all surroundings, events taking place in the world, the time in which we permanently and constantly live.

> It is nothing that goes on and on without beginning middle or meaning or ending. Something is always starting and stopping, rising and falling. The nothing that goes on is what Feldman speaks of when he speaks of being submerged in silence. (1951, 135)

The Silent Piece

The co-presence of sound and silence—each one bearing the trace of the other—is now reinforced by the fact that silence—or nothing—equates to life, to the permanence of events constantly changing, without beginning or ending, without any preconception or determination.

The only thing one is allowed to think is "the possibility of nothing." Cage's goal about sounds has always been to let "each thing be what it is" and he has never changed his opinion on that fundamental compositional issue. To do so, one must remind oneself that "each something is a celebration of the nothing that supports it" (1951, 139). Only then, " . . . the prize or sought-for something (that is nothing) is obtained. And that something—generating nothing—that is obtained is that each something is really what it is . . ." (1951, 144).

To let each sound be what it is is thus accepting each sound, provided it emerges from silence. This is only possible if silence is "pregnant with sound" and if "not one sound fears the silence that extinguishes it" (1951, 135).

But even "full," silence does not only extinguish sound, nor does it only allow it to appear. In the "Juilliard Lecture," written—as is the silent piece—in 1952, Cage adds an essential dimension of silence. The relation of sound to silence is not only temporal (in which sound and silence evolve in parallel on the same axis of time, constantly present to each other), but also spatial.

Silence is primarily the space in which sounds can take place; each sound having its proper space, it can really be what it is.

> Silence surrounds many of the sounds so that they exist in space unimpeded by one another and yet interpenetrating one another for the reason that Feldman has done nothing to keep them from being themselves. (1952, 100)

This spatial concept appears very clearly in a work which Cage mentions in a letter to Pierre Boulez, written in the Spring or Summer of 1952.

> After the *Music of Changes* (which I trust you have received) I wrote *Two Pastorales* for prepared piano. The pianist also blows whistles. And in another piece which changes its title according to where it is performed (e.g. *66 W. 12th)* bowls of water, whistles and a radio are used in addition to the piano. Both pieces are composed in the same way as the *Changes* but have fewer superpositions and so the density is slight. The *66 W. 12th* is notated according to actual time and the performer uses a stop watch to determine his entrances. (Nattiez 1990, 194)

About this piece, Deborah Campana writes the following:

> On 2 May 1952, one year after the premiere of *Imaginary Landscape No. 4,* Cage unveiled *66 W. 12th* at the New School for Social Research in New York at 66 W. 12th Street. The work was performed

> at other times, however, under titles for the dates of the particular performances: August 12, 1952 and August 29, 1952. Of the two August performances, the former took place at Black Mountain and the latter in Woodstock, New York, on the same concert that featured the premiere of *4'33"*. The work was later published under the title *Water Music*. (Campana 1989, 247)

In fact, this work could really be called the pre-*4'33"* piece, since the surrounding sounds taking place *hic et nunc* constitute the starting-point of the piece. But although the environment gives its title to the piece, it is not yet the piece itself: "human" actions are still needed in order to constitute the work of art.

Cage is then faced with two propositions about silence: on one hand, silence is the place where sounds appear; on the other hand, it is identified with life, the events permanently taking place.

It remained for Cage to link those two ideas, which became possible thanks to the experience in the anechoïc chamber at Harvard, which Cage undertook in 1951, but the consequences of which were drawn only a year later. Being able to hear, in a soundproof room, sounds from his blood circulation and from his nervous system, Cage proved to himself that silence could not be an absence of sound. Until then, Cage had been somewhat reluctant to identify silence and surrounding sounds, unable to renounce the idea of silence as emptiness.

After the Harvard experience, Cage could bluntly affirm that silence is made up of all the sounds that exist in permanence (life) and which surround us (place). If one adds the attitude of openness and acceptance, with which Cage used to describe Feldman's way of composing, a silent work like *4'33"* becomes possible and constitutes an opening of music to the whole world of sounds, to the non-musical or even non-human environment. Art can then truly "imitate nature in her manner of operation."

4'33" was thus premiered by David Tudor in Woodstock, New York on August 29, 1952. The title of the work has long been considered as some kind of *objet trouvé:* on an AZERTY-type keyboard, 4 shares the same key as ' and 3 as ". The Vassar lecture, mentioned earlier, provides another explanation. And Cage has recently stated that he was then working with time structures and that the silent piece was composed by "pasting" together silent portions of time.

> when i wrote *4'33"* i was in the process of writing *music of changes*

> that was done in an elaborate way there are many tables for pitches for durations for amplitudes all the work was done with chance operations in the case of *4'33"* i actually used the same method of working and built up the silence of each movement and the three movements add up to *4'33"* i built up each movement by means of short silences put together it seems idiotic but that's what i did i didn't have to bother with the pitch tables or the amplitude tables all i had to do was work with the durations . . . i didn't know i was writing *4'33"* i built it up very gradually and it came out to be *4'33"* i just might have made a mistake in addition . . . (1990, 20–21)

After *4'33"*, the whole Cagian perspective is inversed and notably the relation between composing and listening. One listens first, before composing; everyone becomes as much a composer as a listener. The work of art is getting closer to silence and to "real life." Composition becomes, as Daniel Charles has put it, a question of "attaining not life as art, but rather art as life" (Charles 1988, 8).

Therefore, the pieces written after the silent work are, in Cage's own words, "more radical" than those written before. Those works tend to exist "in accordance" with silence, i.e., without contradicting the characteristics of silence, so that sounds keep that "echo of nothing" from which they originate. But we now know what this "nothing" can mean: it can be rich and full, even noisy.

Composing "according to silence" can thus take different shapes: indeterminacy and chance operations, the simultaneous performance of several works, theater pieces, the events and "Musicircus" in the sixties, or more recently, quiet pieces, containing long "empty" moments, where one has to "stretch" one's ears to realize that this emptiness is full of activity.

Intention

After 1952, Cage didn't write any specific text on this new vision of silence. Nevertheless, in almost any text written after this date, the concept of silence and its implications are mentioned and developed.

"45' for a Speaker," for instance, alludes to the experience of Harvard and draws the famous conclusion that "there's no such a thing as silence." Cage particularly insists on the idea of Emptiness or Nothing, which is absolutely needed before any listening experience.

> . . . listening is best in a state of mental emptiness. (1954, 154)

> All that is necessary is an empty space of time and letting it act in its magnetic way. Eventually there will be so much in it that whistles. (1954, 178)

> Keeping one's mind on the emptiness, on the space, one can see anything can be in it, is, as a matter of fact, in it. (1954, 176)

Mental emptiness leads to a perception of nothing, which means that this emptiness is full of "magnetic" activity and movement. Such an experience can take place in all kinds of circumstances, an example of which is given in "Music Lovers' Field Companion."

> I have spent many hours in the woods conducting performances of my silent piece, transcriptions, that is, for an audience of myself, since they were much longer than the popular length which I have had published. (1955, 276)

4'33" is then not a closed work of art, but rather a manner of experimenting with one's relation to the external world—an experience which can take place anyplace and anytime. For any duration as well: a second version of *4'33"* is entitled *0'00"*, a reference to Christian Wolff's "zero time." This last concept indicates a time free from any determination, only guided by the durations of the events themselves.

In fact, time becomes, in Cage's work, more and more related to space and dependent on that space. There is only one kind of time, that of the events taking place in the space where we are and where we can perceive them.

> Time . . . is what we and sounds happen in. Whether early or late: in it. (1954, 151)

Silence, space and time are intertwined in a dense tissue of interrelations, which makes it difficult to distinguish them.

Recently, Cage has indicated that *4'33"* could also be read as "four feet, thirty-three inches."

What about music, then? What distinguishes it from silence? It is, for Cage, a question of intention.

> . . . silence becomes something else—not silence at all, but sounds, the ambient sounds. The nature of these is unpredictable and changing. These sounds (which are called silence only because they do not form part of a musical intention) may be depended upon to exist. The world teems with them, and is, in fact, at no point free of them. (1958a, 22)

Silence becomes a question of non-intention, of "doing nothing," or rather of that "doing without doing" from the Buddhist tradition: because even in the absence of precise and determinate action, there is always movement, activity and noise. When I stop doing things, the world does not stop and activity goes on unchanged. Before doing an action (e.g., before producing any sound), one should ensure that this action will not do any harm to that state of relative "non-activity" and silence. Acting should thus be in accordance with the activity of the external world.

It is in an interview given in 1966 to the BBC that Cage is most explicit on this subject.

> What interests me far more than anything that happens is the fact of how it would be if nothing were happening. Now I want things that happen to not erase the spirit that was already there without anything happening. Now this thing that I mean when I say not anything happening is what I call silence, that is a state of affairs free from intention, because we always have sounds, for instance. Therefore we don't have any silence available in the world. We're in a world of sounds. We call it silence when we don't feel a direct connection with the intentions that produce the sounds. We say that it's quiet, when, due to our nonintention, there don't seem to us to be many sounds. When there seem to us to be many, we say that it's noisy.
>
> But there is no real essential difference between a noisy silence, and a quiet silence. The thing that runs through from the quietness to the noise is the state of nonintention, and it is this state that interests me. (Cage 1966)

Composition thus aims at finding that sound which is "appropriate to silence": a sound which can only be part of an intention (even if each individual sound of a work has been chosen through chance operations, they all proceed from a musical intention), but which does not disturb that "zero state." Zero state, like zero time, is free from any determination, lead by "the absence of likes and dislikes" and allows things to be themselves. Composition becomes "a composing of sounds within a universe predicated upon the sounds themselves rather than upon the mind which can envisage their coming into being" (1958a, 27–28).

Writing about Satie, Cage notes: "It is evidently a question of bringing one's intended actions into relation with the ambient unintended ones. The common denominator is zero, where the heart beats (no one means to circulate his blood)" (1958b, 80).

That is probably why Cage can affirm that *4'33"* is his best and most important piece ("... I would refer to my own past too, which is basically my silent piece ...") (Kostelanetz 1988, 81). It still affects his own work, since *4'33"* is a permanent work, not only on the spatial and temporal level, but also regarding one's intentions. It is a piece with no beginning and no ending and we, as composers or listeners, turn our attention, impermanently, to it.

> ... it leads out of the world of art into the whole of life. When I write a piece, I try to write it in such a way that it won't interrupt this other piece which is already going on. And that's how I mean it affects my work. (Duckworth 1989, 22)

Some Remarks about Cage's Silence

The evolution of Cage's thinking could be represented (chrono)logically in three main steps.

1. A *structural* conception of silence, in which silence is considered to be an absence of sounds—or at least, a lesser degree of sound activity—and helps establish the structure of music. The relation between sound and silence is first seen horizontally (sound and silence following and excluding each other), then vertically (moving in parallel, being always present with each other).
2. A *spatial* concept of silence: silence is made up of all the surrounding sounds which together form a musical space. The limits of such space can be more or less precise and depend on the listener's perception.
3. A *(non)intentional* vision of silence: what links all those sounds is the absence of intention, which means that they do not possess

> any precise direction, determination, or meaning. That zero state starts from Nothing, which is a permanent opening to "whatever happens next."

It is this last aspect which forms, as to Cage, the most important part of his definition of silence. One can listen to any sounds, accept or use any sounds in a composition, only after a tabula rasa of all preconceptions has been made. On this condition only, art rejoins life and the highest form of work—"an art without work" (Duckworth 1989, 21)—is obtained.

One can naturally put such assessment into question, asking whether an art without intention and preconception is feasible. For Cage, it probably remains an ideal, as he has on certain occasions not refrained himself from choosing and taking options. What guides him in such cases is the idea of not placing values on the sounds themselves (i.e., not considering them as good or bad, as ugly or beautiful), but to choose a situation in which any sound is equally appropriate. The composer's choice (and system of values) does not intervene at the level of the individual sounds nor at the macrolevel of the overall structure: it acts before those two levels emerge. Cage's intentions lie in the fact of asking questions, and not in the sounding result. In asking those questions, Cage's intentional action aims at creating a musical state which would be "the most appropriate" to that other state, that of silence and non-intention.

This is how Cage's works (even *4'33"*) remain musical works, even musical works *by* John Cage. But the goal of non-intention (even if considered as an ideal) is certainly what distinguishes Cage's music from that of other composers who have equally been concerned with surrounding sounds: e.g., the French musique concrète school, the acoustical ecology of R. Murray Schafer . . .

The evolution of Cage's thinking about silence must not have been self-evident. This has already been noticed through the fact that it took him four years to conceive his silent piece. Another example of this difficulty is Morton Feldman's role in that process. These ideas were certainly discussed during those crucial years in that small circle of composer-friends, made up of Tudor, Wolff, Feldman, Cage and, somewhat later, Brown. That vision about silence may find its origin in Feldman's early music, especially the graphic pieces. But Feldman did not push the primacy of silence further, as did Cage, and maintained a fairly structural definition of silence.

Two other major influences which helped Cage in this evolution were visual artist Robert Rauschenberg and Oriental philosophy. Rauschenberg had presented, in the early fifties, a series of monochrome paintings entitled the *White Paintings*. Here too, the apparent emptiness reveals an active vitality and presence of light, color and movement. Rauschenberg's radical move towards white paintings certainly drove Cage to present his own "white" work, the silent piece.

> To Whom It May Concern: The white paintings came first; my silent piece came later. (1961, 98)

To study the influence of Oriental philosophy on Cage's vision of silence would require a detailed study of the many Hindu and Zen Buddhist texts read by Cage. Such a perspective clearly exceeds the scope of the present article. But this influence is an important one, as it has been revealed by Cage himself.

> [In 1948,] I was just then in the flush of my early contact with Oriental philosophy. It was out of that that my interest in silence naturally developed: I mean it's almost transparent. If you have, as you do in India, nine permanent emotions and the center one is the one without color—the others are white or black—and tranquility is in the center and freedom of likes and dislikes. It stands to reason, the absence of activity which is also characteristically Buddhist . . . (Kostelanetz 1988, 66)

Finally, how is one to perceive such music which is "appropriate to silence"? When the composer realizes (or seeks to realize) "an art without work," an "art as life," he abolishes the distance between life and the work of art. Such a distance is precisely what Walter Benjamin defined as the "aura" of the work of art. That type of music then perfectly exemplifies a process described by Benjamin, namely "the disintegration of the aura in the experience of shock" (Benjamin 1969, 194).

The experience of shock, characteristic of our modern era, is that which one can feel when facing a crowd of people. The individual movements inside the crowd, Benjamin explains, are perceived as if they were products of "chance."

> Moving through this traffic involves the individual in a series of shocks and collisions. At dangerous intersections, nervous impulses flow through him in rapid succession. (Benjamin 1969, 175)

If one replaces the term *crowd of people* by *crowd of sounds,* one can find a satisfying analogy with Cage's description of "sudden illumination" in face of daily experience. As was Cage's passage in the anechoïc chamber at Harvard, the shock is a physical experience that takes place before speech or thought can interfere: in Husserl's terms, a pre-predicative situation. The experience takes place suddenly: Cage distinguishes northern and southern Buddhism on that very fact. The northern branch stresses progressive illumination through meditation: that aspect is exemplified in the music of Pauline Oliveros or LaMonte Young. For the southern branch, as for Cage, illumination comes suddenly, but only when keeping an open and moving mind, so that the most banal or silent event can be the cause of a new perception: thereby, it is the relation to the surrounding world which is constantly renewed.

that makes It possible
to pay atteNtion
to Daily work or play
as bEing
noT
what wE think it is
but ouR goal
all that's needed is a fraMe
a change of mental attItude
amplificatioN
wAiting for a bus
we're present at a Concert
suddenlY we stand on a work of art the pavement
(1981, 140)

NOTES

References to Cage's writings are as follows: year of writing, page in publication. The chronology of Cage's writings, with slight modifications, is bor-

rowed from James Tenney, "John Cage and the Theory of Harmony," *Soundings* 13 (1984), which is also reprinted in this volume.
Chronological list of quoted texts.

1948a	"A Composer's Confession" (*MW*)
1948b	"Defense of Satie" (*JC*)
1949a	"Forerunners of Modern Music" (*S*)
1949b	"Lecture on Nothing" (*S*)
1951	"Lecture on Something" (*S*)
1952	"Juilliard Lecture" (*AYM*)
1954	"45′ for a Speaker" (*S*)
1955	"Music Lovers' Field Companion" (*S*)
1958a	"Composition as Process: I. Changes" (*S*)
1958b	"Erik Satie" (*S*)
1961	"On Robert Rauschenberg, Artist, and his Work" (*S*)
1981	"Composition in Retrospect" (*X*)
1990	Norton Lectures, Harvard (*I–VI*)

S John Cage, *Silence* (Middletown, Conn.: Wesleyan University Press, 1961).
AYM John Cage, *A Year from Monday* (Middletown, Conn.: Wesleyan University Press, 1967).
JC Richard Kostelanetz, ed., *John Cage* (New York: Praeger, 1970).
X John Cage, *X—Writings '79–'82* (Middletown, Conn.: Wesleyan University Press, 1983).
I-VI John Cage, *I–VI* (Cambridge, Mass.: Harvard University Press, 1990).
MW Eric De Visscher, ed., "John Cage." *Musicworks* 52 (Toronto, 1992).

REFERENCES

Benjamin, W. 1969. "On Some Motifs in Baudelaire" (1939). In *Illuminations*. New York: Schocken Books.
Campana, D. 1989. "A Chance Encounter: The Correspondence between John Cage and Pierre Boulez, 1949–1954." In *John Cage at 75*. Lewisburg, Pa.: Bucknell University Press.
Cage, J. 1966. "Interview with R. Smalley and D. Sylvester." British Broadcasting Corporation, December
Charles, D. 1988. "Eloge de l'Alphabet." In *Revue d'Esthétique*, Special issue on John Cage, no. 13–15. Toulouse: Privat.
Duckworth, W. 1989. "Anything I Say Will Be Misunderstood: An Interview with John Cage." In *John Cage at 75*. Lewisburg, Pa.: Bucknell University Press.
Kostelanetz, R. 1988. *Conversing with Cage*. New York: Limelight.
Nattiez, J.-J., ed. 1990. *Pierre Boulez—John Cage: Correspondance et Documents*. Winterthur: Amadeus Verlag.

Variations IV (ca. 1967)

Joseph Byrd

Some years ago Henry Pleasants, an insensitive but honest critic, wrote a book called *The Agony of Modern Music*. His point is, of course, an ultraconservative one in the last analysis, but he did see that the only music truly representing American culture (that is, the only art music) was jazz. His attack did not really deal with experimental music, since, thanks to the silent conspiracy of those who earn their living in the nineteenth century, he had never had an opportunity to hear any.

But the fact of the matter is that "contemporary music" is dull. It is no longer shocking, nor is anyone writing letters of political or social protest about it; no one is really very much interested in it. It is irrelevant. Not because it is "traditional" but because its tradition—unlike the great musical traditions of the past—has no part of anything living in our culture. The key to this irrelevance may be found in any meaningful definition of the word *contemporary*; that is, that which is in spirit with cybernetics, game theory, the Heisenberg principle, transistorization, genocidal weaponry, the theories of anti-matter, the DNA molecule, the laser, and so on.

Turning toward the discovery of a music that has contemporary relevance, it is enlightening to look at the esthetic outgrowths of existential thought. Morse Peckham, in *Man's Rage for Chaos*, has suggested that a definition of art consistent with other contemporary values is: "any perceptual field which an individual uses as an occasion for performing the role of art perceiver." Dr. Peckham, of course, writes from the vantage point of 1965, but some thirty years previous the young John Cage had implied this definition in suggesting an expansion of music to include the world of the perceived sound. Sound, he said, had "too long been submissive to the restrictions of nineteenth-century music. Today we are fighting for their emancipation. Tomorrow, with electronic music in our ears, we will hear freedom."

A consequence of such a hypothesis is the work John Cage and David Tudor have produced on this record, a work having no real beginning or end, lacking points of expectation and fulfillment, needing no rhetorical dialogue.

This "music-as-experience" may be seen as perception rediscovered. Or perception rescued from its servitude as a mirror of our functional existence. (Functional perception is the level at which sound is translated into signals, symbols, words, notes, and other methods by which the intellectual world is excluded from the sensual.) Cage lives in a world where art is an experiential process, not a thing to be framed out of existence. By making art a dynamic mode rather than a static one, he has provided the basis for a "portable esthetic," a non-exclusive, democratic sense of awareness which can be carried about in one's hip pocket. In the process he has mightily offended tradition, which thrives, in any culture or century, on the initiated esthete, the elite of the sensitive and cultured.

And so the very principle by which the "in" group has always exalted itself—the understanding of an art too intricate for lesser mortals—this is denied them. Cage and Tudor are not propagating some mystical code to be deciphered by the knowing listener; as Cage has said, "We are naive enough to believe that *words* are the most efficient means of communication." What is happening is a synthesis of the music and sound we normally hear in snatches: the elevator ride's worth of Muzak, the passing conversation, and the automobile argument, all mingle freely with Beethoven and the Balinese *Gender Wayong*.

What part, amid all this, does the listener play? According to Cage, the listener has assumed *the creative role.*

> Most people mistakenly think that when they hear a piece of music, that they're not doing anything but that something is being done to them. Now this is not true, and we must arrange our music, we must arrange our Art, we must arrange everything, I believe, so that people realize that they themselves are doing it, and not that something is being done to them.

John Cage and the Theory of Harmony (1983)

James Tenney

Part I

> Many doors are now open (they open according to where we give our attention). Once through, looking back, no wall or doors are seen. Why was anyone for so long closed in? *Sounds one hears are music.* (1967b)

Relations between theory and practice in Western music have always been somewhat strained, but by the early years of this century they had reached a breaking point. Unable to keep up with the radical changes that were occurring in compositional practice, harmonic theory had become little more than an exercise in "historical musicology," and had ceased to be of immediate relevance to contemporary music. This had not always been so. Most of the important theorists of the past—from Guido and Franco through Tinctoris and Zarlino to Rameau (and even Riemann)—had not only been practicing composers, but their theoretical writings had dealt with questions arising in their own music and that of their contemporaries. Arnold Schoenberg (one of the last of the great composer-theorists) was acutely aware of the disparities

A chronological list of Cage's writings referred to in this text may be found at the end. Quotations are identified by date within the text, in order to clarify the evolutionary development of his ideas. Any emphases (italics) are my own. Other sources are referenced in footnotes, indicated by superscripts.

between what could be said about harmony (ca. 1911) and then-current developments in compositional practice. Near the end of his *Harmonielehre* he expresses the belief that "continued evolution of the theory of harmony is not to be expected at present."[1] I choose to interpret this statement of Schoenberg's as announcing a *postponement* of that evolution, however—not the end of it.

One of the reasons for the current disparity between harmonic theory and compositional practice is not hard to identify: the very *meaning* of the word "harmony" has come to be so narrowly defined that it can only be thought of as applying to the materials and procedures of the diatonic/triadic tonal system of the last two or three centuries. The word has a very long and interesting history, however, which suggests that it need not be so narrowly defined, and that the "continued evolution of the theory of harmony" might depend on—among other things—a broadening of our definition of "harmony."

. . . and perhaps, of "theory" as well. By "theory" I mean essentially what any good dictionary tells us it means—for example:

> . . . the analysis of a set of facts in relation to one another . . . the general or abstract principles of a body of fact, a science, or an art . . . a plausible or scientifically acceptable general principle or body of principles offered to explain phenomena . . .[2]

. . . which is to say, something that current textbook versions of "the theory of harmony" are decidedly *not*—any more than a book of etiquette, for example, can be construed as a "theory of human behavior," or a cookbook a "theory of chemistry."

It seems to me that what a true theory of harmony would have to be now is a theory of *harmonic perception* (one component in a more general theory of musical perception)—consistent with the most recent data available from the fields of acoustics and psychoacoustics, but also taking into account the greatly extended range of musical experiences available to us today. I would suggest, in addition, that such a theory ought to satisfy the following conditions.

First, it should be *descriptive*—not pre- (or pro-) scriptive—and thus, *aesthetically neutral*. That is, it would not presume to tell a composer what should or should not be done, but rather what the results might be if a given thing *is* done.

Second, it should be culturally/stylistically *general*—as relevant to music of the twentieth (or twenty-first!) century as it is to that of the eighteenth (or thirteenth) century, and as pertinent to the music of India or Africa or the Brazilian rain forest as it is to that of Western Europe or North America.

Finally—in order that such a theory might qualify as a "theory" at all, in the most pervasive sense in which that word is currently used (outside of music, at least)—it should be (whenever and to the maximum extent possible) *quantitative.* Unless the propositions, deductions, and predictions of the theory are formulated quantitatively, there is no way to verify the theory, and thus no basis for comparison with other theoretical systems.

Is such a theory really needed? Perhaps not—music seems to have done very well without one for a long time now. On the other hand, one might answer this question the way Gandhi is said to have done when asked what he thought of Western civilization: "It would be nice" (1968).

Is such a theory *feasible* now? I think it is, or at least that the time has come for us to make some beginnings in that direction—no matter how tentative. Furthermore, I believe that the work of John Cage, while posing the greatest conceivable *challenge* to any such effort, yet contains many fertile seeds for theoretical development—some of them not only useful, but *essential.*

Such an assertion may come as a surprise to many—no doubt including Cage himself, since he has never shown any inclination to call himself a theorist, nor any interest in what he calls "harmony." The bulk of his writings—taken together—sometimes seems more like that "thick presence all at once of a naked self-obscuring body of history" (to quote his description of a painting by Jasper Johns; 1964) than a "body of principles" constituting a theory. But these writings include some of the most cogent examples of pure but practical theory to be found anywhere in the literature on twentieth-century music. His work encourages us to re-examine all of our old habits of thought, our assumptions, and our definitions (of "theory," of "harmony"—of "music" itself)—even where (as with "harmony") he has not done so himself. His own precise definitions of "material," "method," "structure," "form," etc.—even where needing some revision or extension to be maximally useful today—can serve as suggestive points of departure for our own efforts.

I propose to examine some of Cage's theoretical ideas a little more closely, and then to consider their possible implications for a new theory of harmony. Before proceeding, however, I want to clarify one point. Some of Cage's critics (even friendly ones) seem to think that he is primarily a philosopher, rather than a composer—and my own focusing on his contributions as theorist might be misunderstood to imply a similar notion on my own part. This would be a mistake. I believe, in fact, that it is primarily *because of his music*—his very substantial credibility *as a composer*—that we are drawn into a consideration of his philosophical and theoretical ideas. To imagine otherwise is to "put the cart before the horse." In a letter defending the music of Erik Satie, Cage once wrote:

> More and more it seems to me that relegating Satie to the position of having been very influential but in his own work finally unimportant is refusing to accept the challenge he so bravely gave us . . . (1951)

The same thing can truly be said of John Cage himself.

> Definitions . . . Structure in music is its divisibility into successive parts from phrases to long sections. Form is content, the continuity. Method is the means of controlling the continuity from note to note. *The material of music is sound and silence*. Integrating these is composing. (1949)

Cage's earliest concerns—and his most notorious later innovations—had to do with *method*—"the means of controlling the continuity from note to note." His music includes an astonishing variety of different methods, from one "dealing with the problem of keeping repetitions of individual tones as far apart as possible" (in 1933–34) and "unorthodox twelve-tone" procedures (in 1938) through the "considered improvisation" of the *Sonatas and Interludes* and other works of the '40s to "moves on . . . charts analogous to those used in constructing a magic square" (in 1951), chance operations based on the *I Ching* (from 1951 to the present), the use of transparent "templates made or found" (from 1952 on), the "observation of imperfections in the paper" on which a score was written (from 1952 on), etc. (1958a, 1961). Surely no other composer in the history of music has so thoroughly explored this aspect of composition—but not merely because of some fascination with "method" for its own sake. On the contrary, Cage's frequent changes of method have always resulted from a new and more penetrating analysis of the *material* of music, and of the nature of musical activity in general.

Before 1951, Cage's methods (or rather, his "composing means") were designed to achieve two things traditionally assumed to be indispensable to the making of art: on the one hand, spontaneity and freedom of expression (at the level of "content" or "form"), and on the other, a measure of structural control over the musical material. What was *unique* about his compositional procedures stemmed from his efforts to define these things ("form," "structure," etc.) in a way which would be consistent with the essential nature of the musical material, and with the nature of auditory perception. These concerns have continued undiminished through his later work as well, but in addition he has shown an ever-increasing concern with the larger *context* in which musical activity takes place:

> The novelty of our work derives . . . from our having moved away from simply private human concerns toward the world of nature and society of which all of us are a part. Our intention is to affirm this life, not to bring order out of chaos nor to suggest improvements in creation, but simply to wake up to the very life we're living, which is so excellent once one gets one's mind and one's desires out of its way and lets it act of its own accord. (1956a)

In this spirit, he had begun, as early as 1951, a series of *renunciations* of those very things his earlier methods had been designed to ensure—first, *expressivity,* and soon after that, *structural controls.* The method he chose to effect these renunciations (after some preliminary work with "moves on charts . . .") involved the use of chance operations, and in writing about the *Music of Changes* (1951) he said:

> It is thus possible to make a musical composition the continuity of which is free of individual taste and memory (psychology) and also of the literature and "traditions" of the art . . . Value judgments are not in the nature of this work as regards either composition, performance, or listening. The idea of relation (the idea: 2) being absent,

> anything (the idea: 1) may happen. A "mistake" is beside the point, for once anything happens it authentically is. (1952)

This statement generated a shock-wave which is still reverberating throughout the Western cultural community, because it was interpreted as a negation of many long-cherished assumptions about the creative process in art. But there is an important difference between a "negation" and a "renunciation" which has generally been overlooked: to renounce something is not to deny others their right to have it—though it does throw into question the notion that such a thing is universally *necessary*. On the other hand, such things as taste, tradition, value judgments, etc., not only can be but often (and habitually) *are* used in ways which are profoundly negative. Cage's "renunciations" since 1951 should therefore not be seen as "negations" at all, but rather as efforts to *give up the old habits of negation*—the old *exclusions* of things from the realm of aesthetic validity, the old *limitations* imposed on musical imagination, the old *boundaries* circumscribing the "art of music." And the result? As he has said:

> . . . nothing was lost when everything was given away. In fact, everything was gained. In musical terms, *any sounds may occur in any combination and in any continuity.* (1957)

The fact that his own renunciations need not be taken as negations should have been clearly understood when he said, for example:

> The activity of movement, sound, and light, we believe, is expressive, but what it expresses is determined by each one of you . . . (1956a)

or again:

> . . . the coming into being of something new does not by that fact deprive what was of its proper place. Each thing has its own place . . . and the more things there are, as is said, the merrier. (1957)

but here, it seems, his critics were not listening.

It should go without saying (though I know it won't) that we don't *need* those old "habits of negation" anymore—neither in life (where they are so often used in ways that are very destructive), nor in art.

Still less do we need them in a theory of harmony—and this is one of the reasons I find Cage's work and thought to be essential to new theoretical efforts. His "renunciations" have created an intellectual climate in which it is finally possible to envision a theory of harmony which is both "general" and "aesthetically neutral"—a climate in which a truly *scientific* theory of musical perception might begin to be developed.

> Composing's one thing, performing's another, listening's a third. What can they have to do with one another? (1955)

While the question of method is naturally of interest to a composer—and has been, in Cage's case, the subject of greatest concern to his critics—what is actually *perceived* in a piece of music is not method as such, but *material*, *form*, and *structure*. Cage's most radical earlier innovations had involved extensions of material, and these may one day turn out to have more profound implications for theory than his investigations of method. The pieces for percussion ensemble, for prepared piano, and for electrical devices—composed during the late '30s and '40s—greatly extended the range of musical materials, first to include *noises* as well as tones, and then *silence* as well as sound.

These extensions were not without precedent, of course. As Cage has said, it was "Edgard Varèse who fathered forth noise into twentieth-century music" (1959b) and who

> . . . more clearly and actively than anyone else of his generation . . . established the present nature of music . . . [which] . . . arises from an acceptance of *all audible phenomena as material proper to music.* (1959b)

But Cage was the first to deal with the *theoretical* consequences of this acceptance. Since "harmony" and other kinds of pitch-organization did not seem applicable to noise,

> The present methods of writing music . . . will be inadequate for the composer, who will be faced with *the entire field of sound.* (1937)

More specifically,

> In writing for these [electronically produced] sounds, as in writing for percussion instruments alone, the composer is dealing with material that does not fit into the orthodox scales and harmonies. It is therefore necessary to find some other organizing means than those in use for symphonic instruments . . . A method analogous to the twelve-tone system may prove useful, but . . . *because of the nature of the materials involved,* and because their duration characteristics can be easily controlled and related, *it is more than likely that the unifying means will be rhythmic.* (1942)

This statement, which reads like a prediction, was actually a description of the state of affairs that had already prevailed in Cage's work since the *First Construction (In Metal)* of 1939, but it was not until 1948 that the idea took the form of a general principle—even a rather dogmatic one:

> In the field of structure, the field of the definition of parts and their relation to a whole, there has been only one new idea since Beethoven. And that new idea can be perceived in the work of Anton Webern and Erik Satie. With Beethoven the parts of a composition were defined by means of harmony. With Satie and Webern they are defined by means of time lengths . . . There can be no right making of music that does not structure itself from the very roots of sound and silence—lengths of time . . . (1948)

A year later this principle is repeated, but with a slightly different emphasis:

> Sound has four characteristics: pitch, timbre, loudness, and duration. The opposite and necessary coexistent of sound is silence. Of the four characteristics of sound, only duration involves both sound and silence. Therefore, a structure based on durations . . . is correct (corresponds with the nature of the material), whereas harmonic structure is incorrect (derived from pitch, which has no being in silence). (1949)

Cage was right, of course, in emphasizing the fundamental importance of time and time-structure in music, but—as compelling and persuasive as this argument is—there is a serious flaw in it. On the one hand, *all* music manifests some sort of temporal structure (including harmonically organized music; Beethoven), and on the other hand, neither Webern nor Satie nor Cage himself had ever managed to "define" the successive parts of a composition purely "by means of time lengths." Such time lengths—in order to be perceived as "parts"—must be *articulated* by some other means, and these means may or may not include the specifically "harmonic" devices of cadence, modulation, etc. In the works of Cage intentionally organized according to this concept of time-structure (as in the music of Satie and Webern), the successive parts in the structure are in fact articulated by various kinds of *contrast*—changes of dynamic level, texture, tempo, pitch-register, thematic material, etc.—and such contrast-devices have *always* been used (with or without the benefit of "harmony") to articulate temporal structure.

We needn't be too concerned, however, with the "dogmatic" aspect of these statements, since it was to be only a few years later that Cage would cease to be concerned with determinate structure at all. What is more important is the way in which he was thinking about *the nature of sound:*

> A sound does not view itself as thought, as ought, as needing another sound for its elucidation . . . it is occupied with the performance of its characteristics: before it has died away it must have made perfectly exact its frequency, its loudness, its length, its overtone structure, the precise morphology of these and of itself . . . It does not exist as one of a series of discrete steps, but as transmission in all directions from the field's center. (1955)

This line of thought gradually crystallized into a conception of what Cage calls "sound-space"—that perceptual "space" in which music (*any* music) must exist. His clearest and most complete description of this concept is perhaps the following:

> The situation made available by these [tape-recording] means is essentially a total sound-space, the limits of which are ear-determined only, the position of a particular sound in this space being the result of five determinants: frequency or pitch, amplitude or loudness, overtone structure or timbre, duration, and morphology (how the sound begins, goes on, and dies away). By the alteration of any one of these determinants, the position of the sound in sound-space changes. Any sound at any point in this total sound-space can move

> to become a sound at any other point . . . musical action or existence can occur at any point or along any line or curve . . . in total sound-space; . . . we are . . . technically equipped to transform our contemporary awareness of nature's manner of operation into art. (1957)

Note that the list of "four characteristics" given in 1949 has now been increased to "five determinants," and in a later passage a sixth one is added ("an order of succession"; 1958a). Even so, such a list is by no means exhaustive, and important clues regarding the nature of harmonic perception will emerge from a consideration of the "determinants," parameters, or what I will call *dimensions* of "sound-space" which are missing from all of these lists.

By his own definitions (pre-1951), *form* is "content, the continuity," and *method* is "the means of controlling the continuity"—i.e., of controlling *form*. After 1951, of course, Cage's methods were no longer intended to "control" form in this same sense, and yet a certain necessary causal relationship still holds between method and form—no matter what the intention—and as a result most of Cage's works since 1951 exemplify an important new formal type which I have elsewhere called "ergodic."[3] I use this term (borrowed from thermodynamics) to mean *statistically homogeneous* at some hierarchical level of formal perception. For example, it can be said about many of Cage's post-1951 pieces (and something like this often *is* said, though usually with negative implications not intended here) that any 2- or 3-minute segment of the piece is essentially the same as any other segment of corresponding duration, even though the details are quite different in the two cases. I interpret this to mean that certain *statistical properties* are in fact "the same"—or so nearly identical that no distinction can be made in perception.

The relation between the ergodic form and Cage's later methods involving chance and/or indeterminacy is this: an ergodic form will always and inevitably be the result when a range of possibilities (with respect to the sound-elements in a piece, and their characteristics) is given at the outset of the compositional process, and remains unchanged during the realization of the work. Such a form is quite unlike the dramatic and/or rhetorical forms we are accustomed to in most earlier music, and has been the cause of much of the negative response to Cage's music of the last thirty years. A different attitude is obviously required of the listener to be able to enjoy an ergodic piece—and it is perhaps ironic that it is an attitude which most people are able to adopt quite easily in situations outside the usual realm of "art" (e.g., the sounds of a forest). In this respect, many of Cage's pieces represent an "imitation of nature" in more than just "her manner of operation," but in her "forms" (or, as I'm sure Cage would prefer to say, her "processes") as well.

Cage's inclusion of "all audible phenomena as material proper to music" did not mean that distinctions were no longer to be made. On the contrary, it now became possible to distinguish many more varieties of elementary sounds—some of which Cage called "aggregates." In writing about his *Sonatas and Interludes* for prepared piano (in 1946–48) he says:

> . . . a static gamut of sounds is presented, no two octaves repeating relations. However, one could hear interesting differences between certain of these sounds. On depressing a key, sometimes a single frequency was heard. In other cases . . . an interval [i.e., a dyad]; in still others *an aggregate of pitches and timbres*. Noticing the nature of this gamut led to selecting a comparable one for the *String Quartet* . . . (1958a)

This concept of the aggregate is, I believe, extremely important for any new theory of harmony, since such a theory must deal with the question: under what conditions will a multiplicity of elementary acoustic signals be perceived as a "single sound"? When this question is asked about a compound tone containing several harmonic partials, its relevance to the problems of harmony becomes immediately evident.

Aside from their possible implications for a theory of *harmony,* as such, Cage's extensions of the range of musical materials to include "all audible phenomena" have created a whole new set of problems for the theorist, but his efforts to understand the *nature* of those materials have also indicated ways in which these problems might be solved. One of his statements about composition might also be applied to theory:

> Something more far-reaching is necessary: a composing of sounds *within a universe predicated upon the sounds themselves* rather than upon the mind which can envisage their coming into being. (1958a)

❖ ❖ ❖

> ... when Schoenberg asked me whether I would devote my life to music, I said, "Of course." After I had been studying with him for two years, Schoenberg said, "In order to write music, you must have a feeling for harmony." I explained to him that I had no feeling for harmony. He said that I would always encounter an obstacle, that it would be as though I came to a wall through which I could not pass. I said, "In that case I will devote my life to beating my head against that wall." (1959a)

This metaphor of the wall—and other sorts of boundaries, barriers, or enclosures—is a recurring one in Cage's writings:

> ... once a circle is drawn my necessity is to get outside of it ... No doubt there is a threshold in all matters, but once through the door—no need to stand there as though transfixed—the rules disappear. (1962)

> ... my philosophy in a nutshell. Get out of whatever cage you happen to be in. (1972)

There were many such walls, but "harmony"—in its narrowest sense (the materials and procedures of traditional, tonal, textbook harmony)—was for Cage a particularly obstructive one:

> Harmony, so-called, is a forced abstract vertical relation which blots out the spontaneous transmitting nature of each of the sounds forced into it. It is artificial and unrealistic. (1954)

> Seeking an interpenetration and non-obstruction of sounds ... a composer at this moment ... renounces harmony and its effect of fusing sounds in a fixed relationship. (1963)

> Series equals harmony equals mind of man (unchanged, used as obstacle ...) (1966)

Only once does he suggest the possibility of defining the word differently:

> This music is not concerned with harmoniousness as generally

> understood, where the quality of harmony results from a blending of several elements. Here we are concerned with the coexistence of dissimilars, and the central points where fusion occurs are many: the ears of the listeners wherever they are. *This disharmony*, to paraphrase Bergson's statement about disorder, *is simply a harmony to which many are unaccustomed*. (1957)

Here, Cage was closer than he may have realized to Schoenberg (in the latter's writings, at least, if not in his teaching)—as when he had said:

> What distinguishes dissonances from consonances is not a greater or lesser degree of beauty, but a greater or lesser degree of *comprehensibility* . . . *The term emancipation of the dissonance* refers to [this] comprehensibility . . .[4]

What is it then, in Cage's vision, that lies beyond these "walls"? An *open field*—and this is an image that he evokes again and again in his writings:

> I have never gratuitously done anything for shock, though what I have found necessary to do I have carried out, occasionally and only after struggles of conscience, even if it involved actions apparently outside the "boundaries of art." For "art" and "music" when anthropocentric (involved in self-expression), seem trivial and lacking in urgency to me. We live in a world where there are things as well as people. Trees, stones, water, everything is expressive. I see this situation in which I impermanently live as a complex interpenetration of centers moving out in all directions without impasse. This is in accord with contemporary awareness of the operations of nature. I attempt to let sounds be themselves in a space of time . . . I am more and more realizing . . . that I have ears and can hear. My work is intended as a demonstration of this; you might call it an affirmation of life. (1956b)

This open field is thus life itself, in all its variety and complexity, and an art activity "imitating nature in her manner of operation" only becomes possible when the limitations imposed by "self-expression," "individual taste and memory," the literature and traditions of an "anthropocentric" art—and of course, "harmony"—have all been questioned so deeply and critically that they no longer circumscribe that activity—no longer define "boundaries." Not that these things will cease to exist, but "looking back, no wall or doors are seen . . . *Sounds one hears are music.*" No better definition of "music"—for our time—is likely to be found.

The field—thus understood as life or nature—is much more than just music, but the "sound-space" of musical perception is one part of that total field, and Cage would have us approach it in a similar way. Its limits are *"ear-determined only,"* the position of a sound within this field is a function of *all aspects of sound,* and

> . . . each aspect of sound . . . is to be seen as a *continuum,* not as a series of discrete steps favored by conventions . . . (1959b)

This "total sound-space" has turned out to be more complex than Cage could have known, and within it a place will be found for specifically *harmonic* relations—and thus, for "harmony"—but not until this word has been redefined to free *it* from the walls that have been built around it.

Originally, the word "harmony" simply meant *a fitting together* of things in the most mundane sense—as might be applied to pieces of something put together by a craftsman. It was later adapted by the Pythagoreans to serve a much broader philosophical/religious purpose, describing the order of the cosmos. Its specifically musical uses must have been derived from the earlier sense of it, but for the Pythagoreans, the way the tones of a stretched string "fit together" was seen as an instance—in microcosm—of that cosmic order. Even so, it did not refer to simultaneous sounds, but simply to certain *relations between pitches.*

Similarly for Aristoxenus: the discipline of "harmonics" was the science of melody, considered with respect to pitch (and thus to be distinguished from "rhythmics"—the science of melody with respect to time). These senses of the word "harmony" are carried through in the writings of the medieval theorists. Only after the beginnings of polyphony in about the ninth century did the word begin to carry a different connotation, and since that time its meaning has become more and more restricted. Apel defines it as "the vertical aspect of music"[5]—i.e., chord structure, and (to a limited extent) relationships between successive chords. But in fact the word has come to imply only a certain limited set of such relationships—a certain *type* of vertical structure. Thus, even in the case of some kinds of music in which tones *are* heard simultaneously (e.g., Indonesian gamelan music) it has been said that "harmony" is not involved. But it is absurd to imagine that the Indonesian musician is not concerned with the "vertical" aspect of his music. The word "harmony" obviously needs to be freed from its implied restriction to triadic/tonal music—but this is not enough. Even in a purely "horizontal" or monophonic/melodic situation, the realities of musical perception cannot be described without reference to *harmonic relations* between tones. Clearly, *a new theory of harmony will require a new definition of "harmony,"* of "harmonic relations," etc., and I believe that such definitions will emerge from a more careful analysis of the "total sound-space" of musical perception.

Part II

> This project will seem fearsome to many, but on examination it gives no cause for alarm. Hearing sounds which are just sounds immediately sets the theorizing mind to theorizing, and the emotions of human beings are continually aroused by encounters with nature. (1957)

> Minimum ethic: Do what you said you'd do. Impossible? (1965)

> [More stringent ethic:] . . . make affirmative actions, and not . . . negative . . . critical or polemical actions . . . (1961)

Cage has always emphasized the *multidimensional* character of sound-space, with pitch as just one of its dimensions. This is perfectly consistent with current acoustical definitions of pitch, in which—like its physical correlate, frequency—it is conceived as a *one-dimensional continuum* running from low to high. But our perception of relations between pitches is more complicated than this. The phenomenon of "octave equivalence," for example, cannot be represented on such a one-dimensional continuum, and octave equivalence is just one of several specifically *harmonic relations* between pitches—i.e., relations other than merely "higher" or "lower." This suggests that the single acoustical variable, frequency, must give rise to *more than one dimension* in sound-space—that the "space" of pitch perception is itself multidimensional. This multidimensional space of pitch-perception will be called *harmonic space.*

The metrical and topological properties of harmonic space have only begun to be investigated, but a provisional model of such a space which seems consistent with what we already know about harmonic perception will be outlined here, and may eventually help to clarify aspects of harmonic perception which are not yet very well understood. In this model, pitches are represented by points in a multidimensional space, and each is labeled according to its frequency ratio with respect to some reference pitch (1/1). Thus, the pitch one octave above the reference pitch is labeled 2/1, that a perfect fifth below 1/1 is labeled 2/3, etc. But since our perception of pitch intervals involves some degree of approximation, these frequency ratios must be understood to represent pitches within a certain *tolerance range*—i.e., a range of relative frequencies within which some slight mistuning is possible without altering the harmonic identity of an interval. The actual magnitude of this tolerance range would depend on several factors, and it is not yet possible to specify it precisely, but it seems likely that it would vary inversely with the ratio-complexity of the interval. That is, the smaller the integers needed to designate the frequency ratio for a given interval, the larger its tolerance range would be. What Harry Partch called "the language of ratios"[6] is thus assumed to be the appropriate language for the analysis and description of harmonic relations—but only if it is understood to be qualified and limited by the concept of interval tolerance.

For a given set of pitches, the number of dimensions of the implied harmonic space would correspond to the number of *prime factors* required to specify their frequency ratios with respect to the reference pitch. Thus, the harmonic space implied by a "Pythagorean" scale, based exclusively on fifths (3/2), fourths (4/3), and octaves (2/1), is two-dimensional, since the frequency ratios defining its constituent intervals involve only powers of 2 and 3 (see fig. 1). The harmonic space implied by a "just" scale, which includes natural thirds (5/4, 6/5) and sixths (5/3, 8/5), is three-dimensional, since its frequency ratios include powers of 5, as well as 2 and 3. A scale incorporating the natural minor seventh (7/4) and other "septimal" intervals would imply a harmonic space of four dimensions, and Partch's "11-limit" scale would imply a harmonic space of five dimensions (corresponding to the prime factors 2, 3, 5, 7, and 11)—if (and only if) we assume that all of its constituent intervals are distinguishable. Whether all such intervals among a given set of pitches are in fact distinguishable depends, of course, on the tolerance range, and it is this which prevents an unlimited proliferation of "dimensions" in

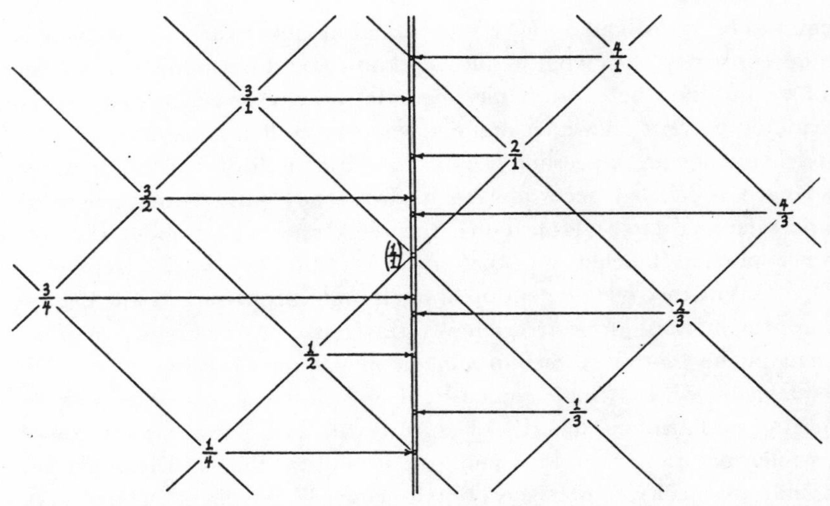

Fig. 1. The 2, 3 plane of harmonic space, showing the pitch-height projection axis

harmonic space. That is, at some level of scale-complexity, intervals whose frequency ratios involve a higher-order prime factor will be indistinguishable from similar intervals characterized by simpler frequency ratios, and the prime factors in these simpler ratios will define the dimensionality of harmonic space in the most general sense.

The one-dimensional continuum of pitch-height (i.e., "pitch" as ordinarily defined) can be conceived as a central *axis of projection* within this harmonic space. The position of a "point" along this pitch-height axis may be specified, as usual, by the logarithm of the fundamental frequency of the corresponding tone, and the distance (or *pitch-distance)* between two such points by the difference between their log-frequency values. That is,

$$PD(f_a, f_b) \propto \log(a) - \log(b) = \log(a/b),$$

where f_a and f_b are the fundamental frequencies of the two tones, $a = f_a / \gcd(f_a, f_b)$, $b = f_b / \gcd(f_a, f_b)$, and $a \geq b$.

Although the pitch-height axis is effectively continuous, harmonic space itself is not. Instead, it consists of a discontinuous network or *lattice* of points. A distance measure which I call *harmonic distance* can be defined between any two points in this space as proportional to the

Fig. 2. The 2, 3 plane of harmonic space, showing the pitch-class projection axis

sum of the distances traversed on a shortest path connecting them (i.e. along the line segments shown in the figures). (The "metric" on harmonic space is thus not a Euclidean one, but rather a "city-block" metric.) This measure of harmonic distance can be expressed algebraically as follows:

$$HD(f_a, f_b) \propto \log(a) + \log(b) = \log(ab).$$

Here again, the tolerance condition must be kept in mind, and it is useful in this connection to formulate it as follows: an interval is represented by *the simplest ratio within the tolerance range* around its actual relative frequencies, and any measure on the interval is the measure on that simplest ratio.

In this model of harmonic space, octave equivalence is represented by another sort of projection—of points in a direction parallel to the "2-vectors" (the right-ascending diagonals in figs. 1 and 2; vertical lines in fig. 3). Alternatively, it can be conceived as a "collapsing" of

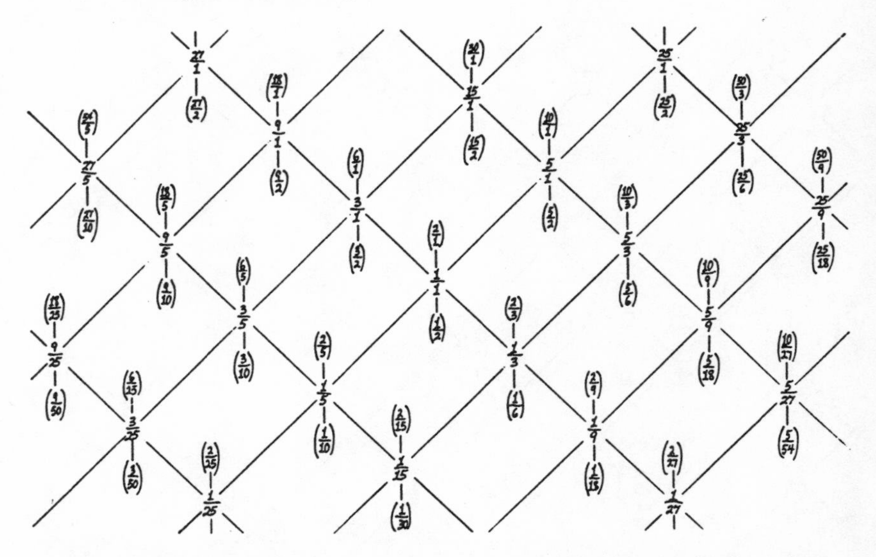

Fig. 3. The 3, 5 plane of harmonic space as a pitch-class projection plane within 2, 3, 5 space

the harmonic space in this same direction, yielding a reduced *pitch-class projection space* with one-fewer dimensions. In a 2-dimensional harmonic space, this will be another projection *axis,* as shown in figure 2. In a 3-dimensional (2, 3, 5) harmonic space, the pitch-class projection space will be a 2-dimensional (3, 5) *plane,* as in figure 3. This pitch-class projection plane can be used to display the primary ("5-limit") harmonic relations of triadic/tonal music. For example, the diatonic major and minor scales appear as shown in figure 4 (using Partch's labeling convention, whereby a given pitch-class is identified by the ratio it has in the first octave above 1/1). With the addition of two scale degrees not included in figure 4 (the minor 2nd and the augmented 4th), these two scales can be combined into a composite structure (similar to what Alexander Ellis called the "harmonic duodene"[7]) which shows many of the primary harmonic relations available within the 12-tone chromatic scale (see fig. 5).

In representing what has become an equally tempered version of this chromatic scale with low-integer ratios in harmonic space we implicitly assume a fairly large tolerance range (on the order of 15 cents or more), but this is precisely what is implied by the use of our tempered scale for triadic/tonal music. Thus it is no wonder that the evolution

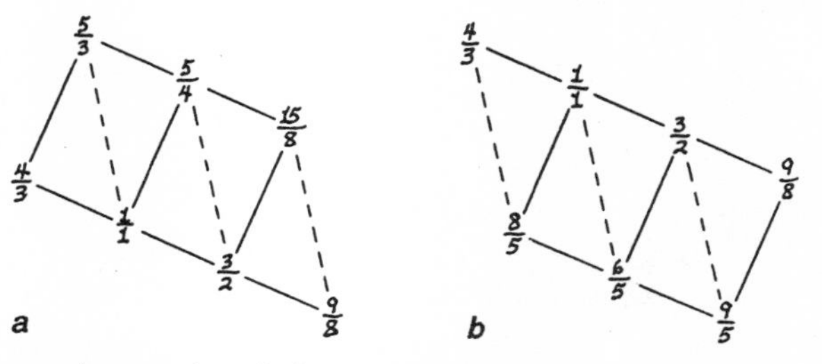

Fig. 4. Primary harmonic relations within the chromatic scales
a. diatonic major
b. diatonic minor

of harmony as a clearly functional force in Western music reached a *cul de sac* around 1910. New compositional approaches to harmony will almost certainly involve new "microtonal" scales and tuning systems, and this model of harmonic space provides a useful tool for the design of such systems, as well as for the analysis of old ones. For example, Ben Johnston has for several years now been using what he calls "ratio lattices"—identical in every respect to those described here—for this very purpose of designing new scales and tuning systems. Although he does not use the term "harmonic space" explicitly, he does refer to "harmonic neighborhoods" demonstrated by the lattice structures, and he distinguishes between what he calls the harmonic and the melodic "modes of perception" in a way which is entirely consistent with the concept of harmonic space presented here.[8]

The physiological correlate of the pitch-height projection axis is surely the *basilar membrane* of the inner ear, while that of the surrounding harmonic space (and of the pitch-class projection space) is assumed to be a set of *pitch-processing centers* in the central nervous system (including some form of "short-term" memory). The functional characteristics of harmonic space will naturally depend on those of its physiological correlate, and a theory of harmonic perception based on this concept requires the elaboration of a viable model of the auditory system. No such model has yet been developed, but preliminary work in that direction suggests the following:

1. Before a point in harmonic space can become activated, the corresponding point on the pitch-height axis must be clearly defined. That is, there must be both pitch-*saliency* and relative

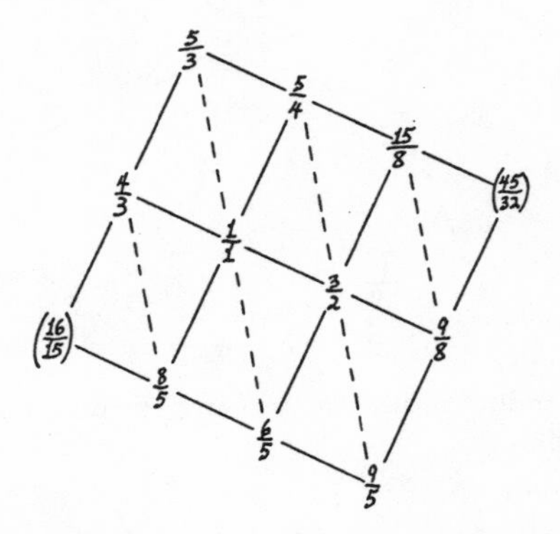

Fig. 5. Primary harmonic relations within the chromatic scale

stability of pitch—and this requires *time*. During the first few hundredths of a second after the onset of a tone, its "image" on the pitch-height axis will not be a well-defined point, but will be spread over some considerable portion of the pitch-height axis, above and below the point representing its nominal pitch. With time, the spread of this image will gradually be reduced to an effective point (i.e., a region confined to the tolerance range), and the corresponding point in harmonic space will then be activated.

2. Once activated, a point in harmonic space will remain active for some considerable amount of time after the tonal stimulus has stopped sounding. That is, points in harmonic space are characterized by a certain *persistence* (due to a sort of neural "resonance" in short-term memory). The extent of this persistence depends primarily on the number and nature of the sounds which follow the first one.

Note that both of these functional characteristics of harmonic space would involve *time*—and they provide some clues to the question that was asked earlier, in regard to Cage's concept of the *aggregate:* "Under what conditions will a multiplicity of elementary acoustic signals be perceived as a 'single sound'?" From a purely physical standpoint, nearly every sound we hear is some sort of "aggregate," made up of a large number of components. But during the first few tens of milliseconds after the onset of a sound it is impossible to distinguish those individual components. As the sound continues, of course, it may gradually become possible to make such distinctions, and these will depend on the separability of these components' "images"—either in harmonic space or on the pitch-height axis alone. There are, however, two common acoustical situations in which a multiplicity of components resists this kind of aural "analysis" almost indefinitely: (1) noise bands, and (2) compound tones with harmonic partials.

In the first case—though there may originally have been a large number of individual frequency components (as in a "tone cluster")—their mutual interferences are such that no one of them remains stable long enough to elicit a tonal percept (i.e., long enough for its image to become a well-defined point on the pitch-height axis). Thus, points in harmonic space will not be activated by a noise band, but its image will appear as a cluster of contiguous points (or regions) along the pitch-height axis.

In the second case, the points in harmonic space activated by the several harmonic partials (assuming them to be stable) also form a "cluster of contiguous points"—but now projected outward (and upward, in the shape of an inverted cone) from the pitch-height axis into the surrounding regions of harmonic space (see fig. 6). What is actually perceived in this case, of course, is a single tone with a pitch corresponding to that of the vertex of the "cone"—whether or not a component of that frequency is actually present in the sound—and a timbre determined by the relative amplitudes of the partials.

On the basis of these examples, the initial question might be answered as follows: a multiplicity of elementary acoustic signals will be perceived as a "single sound"—even long after the initial onset—when their images form *a cluster of contiguous points* either in harmonic space or on the pitch-height projection axis alone.

The two most important problems in earlier harmonic theory—regarding the nature of consonance and dissonance, and the tonic phenomenon (including the whole question of chord roots)—have not yet been mentioned here. I suspect that harmonic theorists in the future will be far less concerned with these problems than earlier theorists were, but I think the concept of harmonic space may shed some light on them, for what it's worth. The problem of consonance and dissonance has been considerably confused by the fact that these terms have been used to mean distinctly different things in different historical periods.[9] And yet there is one simple generalization that can be applied to nearly all of these different conceptions of consonance and dissonance, which

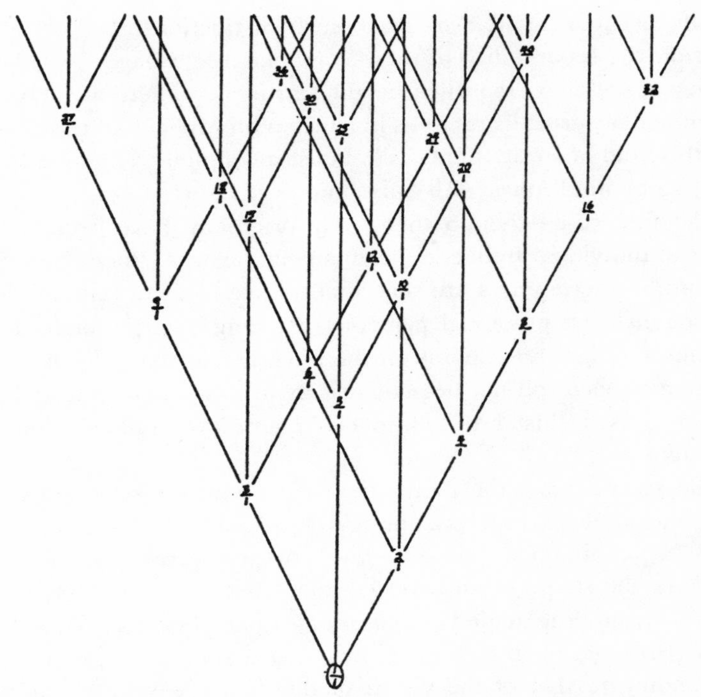

Fig. 6. The harmonic containment "cone" in 2, 3, 5 space

is that tones represented by proximate points in harmonic space tend to be heard as being in a consonant relation to each other, while tones represented by more widely separated points are heard as mutually dissonant. Now this statement serves neither to clarify the distinctions between different senses of consonance and dissonance mentioned above nor to "explain" any one of them. It does, however, indicate an important correlation between consonance and dissonance and what I am calling harmonic space.

Regarding the "tonic phenomenon," our model does not, in itself, suggest either an explanation or a measure of it, but we can incorporate into the model the simple observation that there is a kind of directed "field of force" in harmonic space, such that a tone represented by a given point will tend to "become tonic" with respect to tones/points to the "right" of it (in most of my diagrams—i.e., in the 3/2 or "dominant" direction), and to a lesser extent, "above" it (in the 5/4 direction). Such a tone seems capable of absorbing those other tones into what might be called its "tonic field," and to be absorbed, in its turn, into the tonic field of another tone to the "left" of it (i.e., in the 2/3 or "subdominant" direction), or "below" it. This is analogous to the way in which the harmonic partials in a compound tone seem to be absorbed into the fundamental, but this analogy must not be carried too far, or taken too literally. The harmonic (or "overtone") series has too often been invoked to explain both consonance and dissonance (e.g., Helmholtz[7]) and the tonic/chord-root phenomenon (e.g., Rameau[10]). But the harmonic series cannot truly explain either of these things (any more than this concept of harmonic space can explain them). Although there is one sense of consonance and dissonance which does depend on the harmonic series (and in respect to this one sense of the terms I believe Helmholtz was essentially correct), there are other senses which remain applicable to tones even in the absence of harmonic partials. And it is not—as Rameau postulated—the *son fondamental* which "generates" the triad, but the other way around: when there is a sense that a particular pitch is the root of a chord it is surely the chord itself which creates that sense.

To understand the real relation between the harmonic series and musical perception we must ask the following question: why is it that a compound tone consisting of many harmonic partials is normally and immediately perceived as a *single tone,* rather than as a "chord"? The science of psychoacoustics does not yet provide a satisfactory answer to this question, but I predict that—when it does—it will be seen that it is the nature of harmonic perception in the auditory system which "explains" the unique perceptual character of the harmonic series, not (again) the other way around. The harmonic series is not so much a causal factor in harmonic perception as it is a physical manifestation of a *principle* which is also manifested (though somewhat differently) in harmonic perception. That principle involves the mutual compatibility—as elements in a unitary gestalt or "system" (whether physical-acoustical or psychoacoustical)—of frequencies exhibiting certain rational relations to each other.

We can now define *harmony* as *that aspect of musical perception which depends on harmonic relations between pitches—i.e., relations other than "higher" or "lower."* Thus defined, "harmony" will still include all of those things it now includes—the "vertical aspect of music," chord-structure, etc.—but it is no longer limited to these, and it is certainly not limited to the "materials and procedures of the diatonic/triadic tonal system." It would, for example, also include pitch-relations manifested in a purely melodic or monophonic situation, and—by this definition—nearly *all* music will be found to involve harmony in some way (not just Western "part-music"). In addition, the model of harmonic space outlined here suggests an important "first principle" for a new theory of harmony—that *there is some (set of) specifically harmonic relation(s) between any two salient and relatively stable pitches.*

Yet, by definition, "harmony" does still have some limits in its application, and these are important to recognize. In the case of any music in which no salient and stable pitches occur at all (and there is a great deal of such music in the contemporary literature), harmony—even by this broader definition—would not be relevant. A theory of harmony, therefore, can only be one component in a more general theory of musical perception, and that more general theory must *begin*—as the work of John Cage repeatedly demonstrates—with the primary dimension common to all music: *time.*

REFERENCES FOR "JOHN CAGE AND THE THEORY OF HARMONY"

Writings by John Cage
The titles of books in which these articles are currently to be found (not necessarily where they were first printed) are abbreviated as follows (the page numbers given with these abbreviations are those on which each article begins):

S: *Silence* (Middletown, Conn.: Wesleyan University Press, 1961)
CPC: *Cage/Peters Catalogue,* ed. Robert Dunn (New York: C. F. Peters Corp., 1962)
AYM: *A Year from Monday* (Middletown, Conn.: Wesleyan University Press, 1967)
JC: *John Cage,* ed. Richard Kostelanetz (New York: Praeger, 1971)
M: *M* (Middletown, Conn.: Wesleyan University Press, 1973)
EW: *Empty Words* (Middletown, Conn.: Wesleyan University Press, 1979).
FB: *For the Birds.* In conversation with Daniel Charles (Salem, N.H.: Marion Boyars, 1981)

1937 The Future of Music: Credo (*S* 3)
1942 For More New Sounds (*JC* 64)
1948 Defense of Satie (*JC* 77)
1949 Forerunners of Modern Music (*S* 62)
1951 Satie Controversy (letters; *JC* 89)

1952 To Describe the Process of Composition Used in *Music of Changes* and *Imaginary Landscape No. 4* (*S* 57)
1954 45′ for a Speaker (*S* 146)
1955 Experimental Music: Doctrine (*S* 13)
1956a In This Day (*S* 94)
1956b letter to Paul Henry Lang (*JC* 116)
1957 Experimental Music (*S* 7)
1958a Composition as Process: I. Changes (*S* 18)
1958b Edgard Varèse (*S* 83)
1959a Indeterminacy (*S* 260)
1959b History of Experimental Music in the United States (*S* 67)
1961 Interview with Roger Reynolds (*CPC* 45)
1962 Rhythm Etc. (*AYM* 120)
1963 Happy New Ears! (*AYM* 30)
1964 Jasper Johns: Stories and Ideas (*AYM* 73)
1965 Diary: How to Improve the World (You Will Only Make Matters Worse) (*AYM* 3)
1966 Seriously Comma (*AYM* 26)
1967a Diary: How to Improve the World . . . Continued 1967 (*AYM* 145)
1967b Afterword (to *AYM* 163)
1968 Diary: How to Improve the World . . . Continued 1968 (Revised) (*M* 3)
1972 Diary: How to Improve the World . . . Continued 1971–72 (*M* 195)

NOTES

1. Arnold Schoenberg, *Theory of Harmony,* translated by Roy E. Carter (Berkeley: University of California Press, 1978), 389.

2. *Webster's New Collegiate Dictionary* (Toronto: Thomas Allen & Son, Ltd., 1979).

3. James Tenney, "Form," in *Dictionary of Contemporary Music,* ed. John Vinton (New York: E. P. Dutton, 1971).

4. Arnold Schoenberg, "Composition with Twelve Tones (I)" (1941), in *Style and Idea* (New York: St. Martin's Press, 1975), 216–17.

5. Willi Apel, *Harvard Dictionary of Music* (Cambridge: Harvard University Press, 1953), 322.

6. Harry Partch, *Genesis of a Music* (Madison: University of Wisconsin Press, 1949).

7. Hermann Helmholtz, *On the Sensations of Tone* (1862), translated from the edition of 1877 by Alexander J. Ellis (New York: Dover, 1954).

8. Ben Johnston, "Tonality Regained," in *Proceedings of the American Society of University Composers* 6 (1971).

9. James Tenney, *A History of "Consonance" and "Dissonance"* (New York: Excelsior Music Publishing Co., 1988).

10. Jean-Philippe Rameau, *Treatise on Harmony* (1722), translated by Philip Gosset (New York: Dover, 1971).

John Cage's Lecture "Indeterminacy" (1959)

Hans G. Helms

This lecture by John Cage is temporally organized. Each of the thirty texts of which it consists is to be read in one minute, the time-unit governing this lecture. If optically reproduced, each text is to be printed on one page, the spatial unit, whose shape is not predetermined. The texts vary in length; the maximum, */8'00"-9'00"/*, determines the size and shape of the spatial unit, the page (in this edition the space between the time-indications at top left and bottom right), within whose limits each text is structured. This spatial arrangement—like the temporal one when the lecture is read—was not laid down by the author; all structuring within the spatial or temporal units is interpretation. The original English text is given on pp. 115–20 at *Die Reihe* 5 (1959).

When a spatial interpretation of the German translation of Cage's text was made, its deviser did indeed know of the author's own temporal interpretation (in Brussels), but did not feel in any way bound to it; he consulted only the linguistic material used by the author, and worked with this. Groups of sounds were semantically varied (*/24'00"-25'00"/*). Grammatical complexes fell apart into purely semantic, then purely phonetic units (*/23'00"-24'00"/*). Letters, words, grammatical complexes became blocks, which were then put into a spatial relationship (*/7'00"-8'00"/*). Or else words were "pulverised, fragmented" (cf. */18'00"-19'00"/*). Blocks and similarly destructed material were united to form a macrostructure (as in */3'00"-4'00"/*).

The direction of reading in this interpretation is always left to right and from top to bottom, although this was not predetermined and could equally have been right to left, bottom to top, spiral, or variable within a unit.

Structure as Context (1988)

Thomas DeLio

Despite a plethora of disparate styles and languages, artists of our century seem, consistently, to share at least one common concern—the search for greater understanding of both the human conceptual and perceptual frameworks. As the visual artist Robert Irwin has said:

> To be an artist is not a matter of making paintings at all. What we are really dealing with is the state of our consciousness and the shape of our perceptions.[1]

Such emphasis has served, quite naturally, as catalyst for extensive exploration of the function of context in both the definition of structure and the appropriation of meaning. Such exploration has led, in turn, to the precise definition of those parameters which, in fact, constitute the structure of our consciousness.

The works to be considered in this paper are John Cage's *Variations VI,* Robert Irwin's *Black Line Volume,* Alvin Lucier's *I Am Sitting in a Room,* Dan Graham's *Schema* and Hans Haacke's *Seurat's "Les Poseuses."* Each of these pieces focuses in some way upon the notion of context, articulating its crucial role in all creative and perceptual processes. In addition, the four works, when taken together, seem to spiral outward, progressively expanding the very definition of context itself.

More specifically, what these artists share is their common interest in isolating and exploring the idea of context for its own sake. Rather than using it as ground for meaningful activity, each artist treats the very notion of context as material for exploration and definition. The subject of these works, then, seems, not so much to be the making of a specific form or design, as it is the acquisition of the very construct which enables such making. In each, that which was once considered merely a framework for the shaping of form is elevated to the level of structure itself.

With respect to Cage's *Variations VI,* the structural framework isolated is the very potentiality of raw materials to take on form. Here, a structure is defined solely through the choice of materials and the identification of a range of transformations available as a result of that choice of materials. Expanding upon this more traditional notion of context, Irwin's *Black Line Volume* and Lucier's *I Am Sitting in a Room* each isolate and draw out an actual physical environment located within everyday experience. In both of these pieces the structure defined is the very site of one's perceptions—that crucial place wherein perceiver meets object. Similarly, Dan Graham's poem *Schema* identifies a physical environment within which a literary work typically exists but rarely incorporates into its structure. Finally, Haacke's *Seurat's "Les Poseuses"* alludes to a more conceptual framework. Here the contextual parameters which constitute the artist's subject matter are those unique sociological and historical boundaries within which each perceiver encounters any work. As such, the notion of context is once again expanded, this time to include the complete historical/sociological framework surrounding both the creation of a particular work of art and the creative response to it.

A replica of the score of John Cage's *Variations VI* will be found on the following page. The instructions read, in abridgement, as follows.

Variations VI

For a plurality of sound-systems (any sources, components and loud speakers).

A long straight (vertical) line on a non-transparent sheet, a supply of symbols on transparent material (twelve straight lines, thirty-eight triangles, fifty-seven short lines perpendicularly bisected, one hundred and fourteen half-circles with diameters).

Cut the transparent sheets so that there are two hundred and twenty-one separate sheets, each having one complete symbol.

Reserve as many triangles as there are loud-speakers available, as many half-circles as there are sound sources available, as many bisected short lines as there are components (exclusive of mixers, triggering devices, antennas, etc., inclusive of amplifiers, pre-amplifiers, modulators and filters) available, as many of the straight lines as

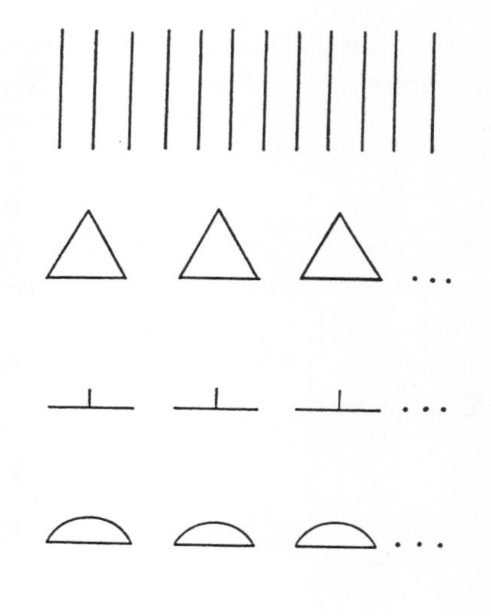

exceed by one the number of sound systems practical to envisage under the circumstances.

Drop each reserved symbol on the non-transparent sheet. Two adjacent straight lines which converge (or would if extended) or cross symbolize a sound system or systems (2, 4). The half-circles, bisected lines and triangles between them symbolize the sources, components and speakers in that system. (When no component or speaker is indicated, consider these either implicit or—an ambient sound—not involved.) The orientation of the converging straight lines with respect to the non-transparent (vertical) line may suggest distribution of sound in space.

The half-circles, bisected lines and triangles have in common a straight line (the longer one in the two last cases). Let this be read as indicating continuously unvaried (or unaltered) operation when it is vertical and the rest of the symbol is to its left, i.e., ◁, ⊣, ◖. Let it be read as indicating continuously varied (or altered) operation when it is vertical and the rest of the symbol is to its right, i.e. ▷, ⊢, ◗. Let other positions, whether up or down, be read relatively to these extremes.

Where there are two or more performers, each will have his own project for the use of the available equipment. If in the course of a performance his project is realized, he may embark on another, etc.

Let the notations refer to what is to be done, not to what is heard or to be heard.[2]

As the instructions state, any configuration of symbols determines, first, a certain number of sound systems and second, the specific constitution of each of those sound systems. For example, one might assume that the following configuration is to be used (in this case the score has been simplified for the sake of discussion).

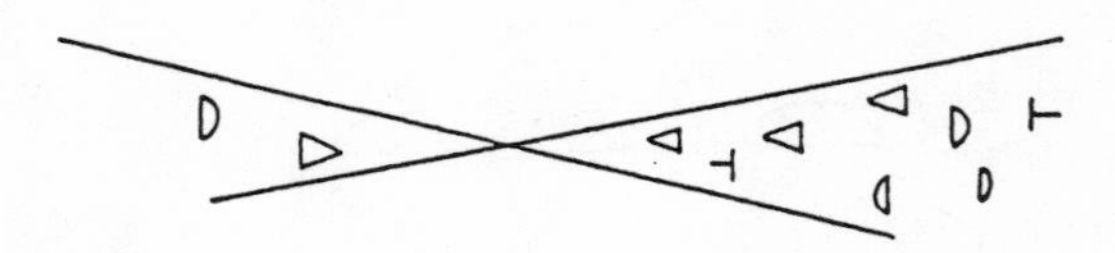

This configuration may be interpreted as:

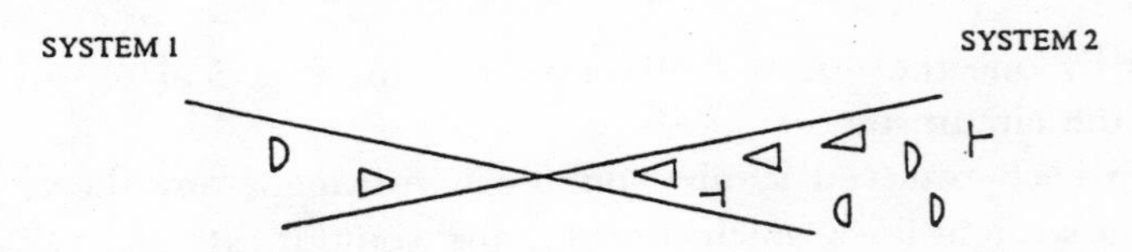

Thus, if the following instruments and electronic equipment were available:

1 clarinet	4 speakers
1 oboe	1 mixer
1 horn	1 filter
1 violin	

they might be assigned to the two systems in the following manner:

System one—one clarinet (unvaried), amplified through one speaker (unvaried);

System two—one oboe, one violin and one horn (two unvaried and one varied) each amplified through several speakers (all varied), mixed together (mixer unvaried) and filtered (filter continuously varied).

Moreover, the designations varied and unvaried may be interpreted as follows:

> For instruments— any change in pitch, timbre, volume, etc.;
> For components— any change in speaker location, filter settings and mixing levels.

At no time, however, does the score determine what is to be played through these sound systems. The score never directs the performer to shape the sonic materials in any way; nor, in fact, does it ever refer to any final sonic result. As the instructions state: "Let the notations refer to what is to be done, not to what is heard or to be heard."[3] Thus, in *Variations VI,* Cage presents the mechanism for creating a musical design but in no way determines the nature of that design itself.

Specifically, each realization (configuration) generates a context consisting of a collection of materials (the sound sources) and the potential for their transformation (the components with their associated indications of varied or unvaried). Within this framework certain acts become possible, and it is this very sense of possibility upon which Cage focuses in *Variations VI.*

As such, the work remains forever within a world of potential forms. It is a structure which is itself a context. The composer never determines or guides the specific evolution of any particular shape or design. Rather, he focuses upon the nature of context, suggesting the infinite multiplicity of forms which each context engenders.

Many of these very same notions of structure are extended simultaneously and in similar directions in the works of both sculptor Robert Irwin and composer Alvin Lucier. In one recent work, *Black Line Volume,* created in 1975 for Chicago's Museum of Contemporary Art, Irwin transformed a large rectangular room by simply bisecting its floor with one black line (see following page).

> By using the existing black baseboards and bisecting the space with another black line, Irwin has made the viewer aware of the volume that was already there as well as of the narrow column which extended to the ceiling in the center of his marked-off area.
>
> The line here is not a circumscribing element in the traditional sense. It functions to break its own limits. *This line has changed, for Irwin, from a mark that exists in a context to an element making a context—*

Robert Irwin, *Black Line Volume,* installation at the Museum of Contemporary Art, Chicago, 1975

> or making it apparent in a Wittgensteinian sense. Where in his early paintings line existed within a boundary, the lines of this piece . . . enlarge the context by extending our awareness of the lines, edges and frames that already existed before the artist made his presence felt in the room. *It is interesting that even after the work is gone, the observer finds his perception of the existing space altered.* A heightened awareness of the light, shape and other phenomena of the space and what occurs within it results in interaction with the work. In other words, it has affected our consciousness *by expanding our sense of the art environment to all immediate surroundings.* We have become aware of the various frames that shape our perception . . .
>
> For Irwin order can only be found within a context. In [this piece] he challenges the underlying orthodoxy that this context must take the form of an object.[4]

That which was for traditional sculpture a context, and for much recent sculpture a very active context has become in Irwin's work the very sculpture itself. The shape of the room, the column in its center, its edging of black and its ceiling grid become the structural elements of the work.

Irwin never directs his activities toward the shaping of form. Rather, he introduces some carefully chosen elements—in this case one simple black line—into an existing structure. As a result he draws to the forefront of our perceptions those materials and constructs already present, albeit not readily apparent, in that location. Thus, the site becomes the artwork itself and the sculptor's traditional activities of making and shaping are replaced by the act of appropriation. In the course of this act, that which is identified is the very substance of our vision. The black line quite literally frames our perceptions. As ground replaces image in the forefront of our consciousness, a new awareness develops with respect to the crucial role of site in the acquisition of meaning.

As with much of Irwin's recent work, this sculpture is a transparency, leading one through its physical presence toward a confrontation with not only the environment, but also those perceptual processes by which one comes to know the environment and all that it contains. As Wittgenstein has written: "One thinks that one is tracing the outline of the thing's nature over and over again, and one is merely tracing round the frame through which we look at it."[5]

Toward similar ends, the composer Alvin Lucier has systematically explored the various acoustical properties inherent to specific places. These properties and, ultimately, the spaces from which they are engendered are, in his pieces, themselves isolated, amplified and projected. As with Irwin's work, a striking transformation takes place, as space, typically a neutral background upon which sounds are projected and manipulated, suddenly becomes an active foreground and is itself projected to the listener.

One of the clearest examples of this procedure may be found in Lucier's *I Am Sitting in a Room,* dating from 1970. In this piece a reader recites a simple text. This is taped as he speaks after which the tape itself is played back in the same space and re-taped on a second recorder. This re-taping process is then repeated many times within that same space until a reading many generations old is produced.

> You know that when you speak in a room certain components of your voice sound strong. That's because those pitches that are in those components reflect off the surface of the room and get amplified.

> The pitches that don't correspond don't get amplified. . . . Now you're unable to perceive that under ordinary circumstances, but if you could amplify that in some way, then you could perceive [it]. The way I amplify it is by recycling the sounds into the room again, again, again, and again, until . . . those pitches that do correspond to the resonances get amplified and those that don't go away.[6]

In the end, those sonic characteristics of the space to which one's attention is not ordinarily drawn are forced out into the open. The acoustical qualities of the performance space are slowly unveiled and become, simultaneously, the mechanism for structuring the piece and the work's structure itself.

> . . . the space acts as a filter; it filters out all of the frequencies except the resonant ones. [This] has to do with the architecture, the physical dimensions and acoustic characteristics of the space.
>
> . . . every musical sound has a particular wavelength: the higher the pitch the shorter the wavelength. [Thus,] as sounds move out into space they can be observed as various sized wavelengths, so you can see how directly the dimensions of a room relate to musical sounds. If the dimensions of a room are in a simple relationship to a sound that is played in it, that sound will be reinforced, that is, it will be amplified by the reflections from the walls. If, however, the sound doesn't "fit" the room, so to speak, it will be reflected out of phase with itself and tend to filter itself out. So, by playing sounds into a room over and over again, you reinforce some of them more and more each time and eliminate others.[7]

That which traditionally, for music, has been the most imperceptible of backdrops has moved into the foreground and become the very subject of the piece. Again in the composer's own words:

> I decided to use the simplest speech I could find . . . because I didn't want the input to be so composed as to take away from the idea of the piece . . . *What the piece does is the content.*[8]

Clearly, as with Irwin's *Black Line Volume,* of importance here are not the materials introduced into the space by the artist but rather those properties of the site itself which are brought to the perceiver's attention.

Developments quite similar to those found in the work of Irwin and

Lucier can also be found in some recent literature. It is clear that any word, for example, can be understood in different ways depending upon its context. One of these ways, rarely acknowledged until recent years is as a mark in a visual field, the page. Traditionally, the page upon which a poem was printed was a very neutral ground against which the poem was perceived. Indeed, words (as well as phrases or sentences) were never perceived as visual marks, but rather as symbols representing ideas, objects, dramatic scenes etc. More recently, poets have recognized that words can and do have meaning as purely visual marks and have become more sensitive to the expressive possibilities of different spatial placements of words on a page and how such placements can affect meaning. As a result, the page itself has been drawn into the realm of poetic structure. This physical context, which until the twentieth century, had little, if any, influence upon one's reading of a poem has, in recent years, taken on a much more dynamic character and, indeed, is now often drawn into the very structure of the poem itself.

It is precisely this context upon which Dan Graham has chosen to focus in his poem *Schema* (1966), reprinted below.[9]

(number of) adjectives
(number of) adverbs
(percentage of) area not occupied by type
(percentage of) area occupied by type
(number of) columns
(number of) conjunctions
(number of) depressions of type into surface of page
(number of) gerunds
(number of) infinitives
(number of) letters of the alphabet
(number of) lines
(number of) mathematical symbols
(number of) nouns
(number of) numbers
(number of) participles
(perimeter of) page
(weight of) paper sheet
(type) paper stock
(thinness of) paper stock
(number of) prepositions
(number of) pronouns

(number of point)	size type
(name of)	typeface
(number of)	words
(number of)	words capitalized
(number of)	words italicized
(number of)	words not capitalized
(number of)	words not italicized

This poem is, quite literally, a scheme to be realized anew each time the work is presented in print. The parenthetical phrases are to be filled in with the appropriate data. For example, with respect to the line "(number of points) size type," the actual size of the type used to print the poem is to be inserted in the left-hand column before the words "size type." Thus, the line, in its final form, might read "14 point size type." The data required to complete the scheme is to be deduced from the page on which the poem is printed. Thus, if two different publications of the poem employ different type sizes, the aforementioned line will read quite differently.

Clearly, this poem can be fully appreciated only when perceived in connection with a specific physical location (a specific page within a specific printed context). It would be meaningless if severed from that context as it might be, for instance, at a poetry reading. Thus, Graham identifies as the subject of his poem, the context within which it is presented and perceived. The work has no subject other than its composition—physical as well as linguistic—and speaks only in terms of concrete measurable units of information.

With regard to this last point, it is interesting to note two particular aspects of the scheme itself. First of all, the poet attempts to be truly exhaustive. The list consists of just about every bit of concrete data one could glean from an analysis of any page and the words printed on it. Secondly, the list has been presented in a formalized manner—alphabetically. These facts lend a rather objective, almost scientific quality to the work. The poem is, quite simply, a catalog of facts about itself. Significantly, however, this catalog contains, not only information about words, but also about the environment within which words are presented and perceived. Indeed, it seems clear, that, in this poem, words, the manner in which they are printed and the page on which they are printed are inseparable, and that all are equally important elements in the poem's structure.

Clearly, with Graham's *Schema* one encounters an artwork the subject of which is context. Moreover, the poet focuses upon a particular level of context which, traditionally, had remained quite neutral, rarely, if ever, influencing the experience of a literary work in any way. This particular context is here drawn to the forefront of the reader's experience. Thus, as with the works of Lucier and Irwin discussed above, that which was traditionally far in the background of one's perceptions is brought to the surface and becomes the very subject of the work.

The recent work of Hans Haacke constitutes an even more remarkable extension of this identification of artwork with context. In contrast with the art and music discussed thus far, Haacke's work focuses more upon the social circumstances of art than any aspect of its physcial composition. As such, the artist seems to espouse the view that, ultimately, "any work of art gets its meaning from the traditions and organized practice of the people among whom it is made and to whom it is presented."[10]

Haacke's *Seurat's "Les Poseuses"* represents a case in point. The work was first exhibited in New York at the John Weber Gallery. It consisted of a full size, color reproduction of Seurat's painting *Les Poseuses* which was displayed on a studio easel in a gallery room. Simultaneously, plaques were hung around the room on which were outlined the social and economic positions of the various persons who had owned the painting over the years and the price that each had paid for it, if known (see following page). Thus, to construct the piece Haacke first borrowed a pre-existing object and then drew attention to certain aspects of that object's history. As is typical of his work, the object chosen is from the art world itself, and the history alluded to is that of the gradual accrual of material value within this particular milieu. It is this very history which is transformed into the structure of the work.

In particular, Haacke focuses upon that identification of artwork as precious object which seems to permeate his culture and its appraisal of art. Such identification is linked, in different ways, to two specific contexts: on the one hand, the private world of the gallery where the merit of a work is determined almost exclusively by its financial value; and, on the other hand, the more public domain of the museum where its value tends to come more from its cultural/historical position. Such differences in social environment may dramatically affect both the status which an object holds within society and, more significantly, the manner in which it and its subject matter are addressed by society.

"Les Poseuses"
(small version)
purchased 1971 for unknown amount (part in art works) by

Heinz Berggruen

Born 1914 in Berlin, Germany.

Studies art history in Berlin and Toulouse, France, graduating there with equivalent of Master of Fine Art degree. In late 1930's moves to California. Postgraduate studies in art history at Berkeley. Assistant Curator of San Francisco Museum of Art. Writes art criticism for *San Francisco Chronicle*. Works at 1939 World Exposition on Treasure Island, San Francisco.

Marries Lilian Zellerbach of prominent San Francisco paper manufacturing family. Birth of son John Berggruen 1943 (now art dealer in San Francisco). Birth of daughter Helen, 1945.

After World War II, service in US Army. Stationed in England and Germany. Works for German language US Army publication in Munich.

Around 1947 move to Paris via Zurich. Employed by cultural division of UNESCO. In late 1940's, starts dealing in art books and prints. Becomes art dealer. Berggruen & Cie, now at 70, rue de l'Université, develops into one of major Parisian art dealers in modern art, particularly Ecole de Paris.

Lives Ile St. Louis, Paris, and on château near Pontoise. Owns large collection.

1974 elected member of the Board of Directors of Artemis S.A., a Luxembourg-based art investment holding company. Chevalier of Legion of Honor.

His purchase of Seurat's *Les Poseuses* at "impressive profit" to Artemis S.A. (annual report). Painting now on anonymous loan in Bavarian State Museum, Munich.

Photo from "Art in America," 1963

Moreover, Haacke identifies these issues by literally transplanting the subject matter of social science into the world of art.

> Speaking to [other] artists, curators, collectors, gallery-goers, critics and museum trustees [he] gets a different effect from the social scientist who [would] speak largely to other social scientists. . . . The same work makes a different statement, is a different act when it appears in the art world rather than the world of social science.[11]

Thus, by shifting the context within which this exploration of power and wealth is presented, the artist is able to dramatically alter its import.

At least one function of the arts of the past few decades has been to serve as a catalyst for the exploration and clarification of the many, as yet, undefined parameters of human perception and cognition. This paper has been concerned with the progressive exploration of just one of these parameters as it has been carried out on various levels by several different artists. The work of these figures reveals the many interrelated levels which, when taken together, constitute the definition of context. In *Variations VI,* John Cage was concerned with the construction of a sonic object "in potentia," thereby identifying the physical contexts which make the creation of a sonic structure possible. Stepping beyond this, Irwin, Lucier and Graham have concerned themselves with all that physically surrounds and colors the perception of the object (sonic or visual) once it is made. Finally, Haacke extends still further, embracing those historical/sociological parameters which, once again, color both our perceptions and conceptualizations. The radical nature of this art, then, seems to have as its purpose the illumination of one of the basic premises which guide all creative and analytical endeavor. Through their penetrating explorations each artist has offered new insight into parameters which govern the creative act.

NOTES

1. Robert Irwin, in an interview with Jan Butterfield in "The State of the Real," *Arts Magazine,* Summer, 1972, 48.
2. John Cage, *Variations VI* (New York: Henmar Press, 1966), 1.
3. Ibid., 1.
4. Edward Levine, "Robert Irwin's Recent Work," *Artforum,* December, 1977, 28–29.
5. Ludwig Wittgenstein, *Philosophical Investigations* (Oxford: Basil Blackwell and Mott, 1958), 48.
6. Alvin Lucier, in an interview with Loren Means, *Composer Magazine,* 1977–78, 9.
7. Alvin Lucier, in an interview with Douglas Simon, in *Chambers* (Middletown, Conn.: Wesleyan University Press, 1980), 35.
8. Lucier, interview with Means, 9.
9. Dan Graham, *Schema,* in *The Old Poetries and The New,* by Richard Kostelanetz (Ann Arbor: University of Michigan Press, 1981), 143–44.
10. Howard S. Becker and John Walton, "Social Science and the Work of Hans Haacke," in *Framing and Being Framed* (New York: New York University Press, 1975), 145.
11. Ibid., 145.

John Cage in a New Key (1981)

Natalie Crohn Schmitt

In 1975, the Canadian Broadcasting Corporation commissioned John Cage to write a piece of music in celebration of the American Bicentennial. To compose it Cage subjected various writings of Thoreau to chance operations. Speaking to Cage about this piece Roger Reynolds remarked, "It struck me as being a far more critical and polemical choice than you might have made fifteen years ago." "It is," Cage acknowledged.[1] Cage's increasingly political concerns have come to be expressed in his music and progressively more in each of his books on music theory: *Silence* (1961), *A Year from Monday* (1967), *M* (1973), and *Empty Words* (1979).[2] In the most recent of these books the political concerns cause a radical and unobserved shift in the basis of Cage's aesthetic.

Cage expresses this shift most directly in an interview conducted with him in 1978: "I think that modern art has turned life into art, and now I think it's time for life (by life I mean such things as government, the social rules and all those things) to turn the environment and everything into art."[3] The function of art now is not to reveal nature in its manner of operation, a position he previously espoused; it is to change society. The shift in function is partly obscured by the fact that heretofore in Cage's writings, nature, through art, has indirectly been the model for society. It is further obscured by Cage's writing, which masks its extremity. The change to an aesthetic based not on nature but on the vision of an ideal society, not surprisingly effects some other changes in the aesthetic. In the future, if Cage elaborates these, they will necessarily become more pronounced despite the parallels Cage may continue to see between nature and the ideal society.

The final essay in *Empty Words* is a theoretical piece which bears the same title as his first essay in his first book, *Silence:* "The Future of Music." The new essay neatly summarizes the changes in modern music which Cage had earlier advocated and which are now so widespread that Anthony Burgess refers to this as the Cage Age. In the essay however, while Cage repeats his old phrases, he craftily turns them to new uses. "Music's ancient purpose—to sober and quiet the mind, thus making it susceptible to divine influences—is now to be practiced in relation to the Mind of which through technological extension we are all part, a Mind, these days, confused, disturbed, and split."[4] The function of music, the repetition of Cage's familiar phrase notwithstanding, is no longer to make us no-minded (accepting) observers but to bring harmony and peace to the world.

The reasons for the shift in function and Cage's accompanying change in tone are stated in the foreword to *Empty Words*. "I am an optimist. That is my raison d'être. But by the news each day I've been in a sense made dumb. In 1973 I began another installment of my *Diary: How to Improve the World (You Will Only Make Matters Worse)*: it remains unfinished. Buckminster Fuller too from prophet of Utopia has changed to Jeremiah. He now gives us eight to ten years to make essential changes in human behaviour."[5] While still believing that "life's more fully lived when we are open to whatever,"[6] he is not willing to accept all the changes brought about by human behavior, changes which in fact imperil life. Art is no longer just something to do. It is an essential means of changing people's perception of their place in the world. Art, now, is not a means of enhancing our appreciation of nature, including its lack of fixity; rather, it is a means of inducing change in society, a means of improving the world. "The usefulness of the useless is good news for artists. For art serves no material purpose. It has to do with changing minds and spirits."[7] The role of the artist in this new view becomes exemplary. But not in the old egoistic sense to which Cage always objected. Humility becomes an essential concern not merely for perception but for existence. Cage dedicates the first essay in *Empty Words* "to the USA that it may become just another part of the world, no more, no less."[8] The artist in his manner of working exemplifies humility and communality.

Cage still hears sounds and silence as music. Presumably he would still view the beach as theater. In the 1978 interview referred to, he reports the following: "I was with De Kooning once in a restaurant and he said, "If I put a frame around these breadcrumbs, that isn't art.' And what I'm saying is that it is."[9] But what most interests Cage now is art as social activity. "It is the social nature of music, the practice in it of using a number of people doing different things to make it that distinguishes it from the visual arts, draws it towards theater, and makes it relevant to society."[10] This social activity, ideally, is communal, non-hierarchical: "We now have many musical examples of the practicality of anarchy. . . . The masterpieces of Western music exemplify monarchies and dictatorships. Composer and conductor: king and prime minister. By making musical situations which are analogies to desirable social circumstances which we do not yet have, we make music suggestive and relevant to the serious questions which face Mankind."[11] Cage is not explicit about the matter, but art, in this changed view, can be evaluated. James Joyce, he puns, uses hierarchical language, i.e., "sintalks." "Due to N. O. Brown's remark that syntax is the arrangement of the army, and Thoreau's that when he heard a sentence he heard feet marching, I became devoted to nonsyntactical 'demilitarized' language."[12] Cage does not discuss the role of technology, the development of which he had celebrated. However, it has now clearly become problematic for him. He believes that its immediate potential is not for providing unlimited abundance, as he had hoped, but unlimited destruction. Hierarchical structures are no longer merely intellectually incompatible with nature; they threaten its continuance.

Cage's view of art as political is not Bertolt Brecht's: art does not constitute an action against existing social structures nor does it urge us to take such action. Art which does so is itself syntactical. Rather, Cage champions an art which, in its structure and in the structure of its making, provides positive models for human activity. Art can provide appropriate models in a variety of ways other than by being non-hierarchical and communal. As process, it can suggest the possibility of change in society. It can make us aware of our human energy resources which can be put intelligently to work: it can exemplify the overcoming of difficulties, the doing of the impossible.

Music is now no longer defined as sounds; it is defined as "work." It is purposeful. "A necessary aspect of the immediate future, not just in the field of environmental recovery, is work, hard work, and no end of it."[13] A serious business which, in part, *Empty Words* serves to exemplify.

In 1959, Cage wrote a "Lecture on Nothing": "I have nothing to say and I am saying it and that is poetry."[14] Now in large portions of *Empty Words* Cage abandons that much meaning. He thinks of much of it as sounds, some of which are words and sentences to sing or dance by: "dance chants." Much of the writing in the book is, as the title suggests, devoid of denotation. The longest section in it, entitled "Empty Words," is "a transition from a language without sentences (having only phrases, words, syllables, and letters) to a 'language' having only letters and silence (music)."[15] His justification for this composition is not, as it was before, that it is like nature in being centerless and meaningless process, but that it models a form for society of which he approves: "Implicit in the use of words (when messages are put across) are training, government, enforcement, and finally the military."[16] Consistent with this political belief, Cage the aesthetician has little place in this book. Cage's prose is, as Jill Johnston once described it, "some of the most crystal-cut prose of contemporary writing."[17] But that prose, which has had so much influence on contemporary art, is here limited to the book's last essay. The rest of the book serves as Cage's most extreme application of his aesthetic theory to his writing and it is, in Cage's way, political.

NOTES

1. "John Cage and Roger Reynolds: A Conversation," *Musical Quarterly* 65, no. 4 (October, 1979): 590.
2. All published by Wesleyan University Press.
3. Interview with Robin White published in *View* 1, no. 1 (April, 1978): 15. For an analysis of Cage's earlier aesthetic, based on nature, see my "John Cage, Nature, and Theatre," *TriQuarterly* 54 (Spring, 1982): 89–109.
4. *Empty Words,* 181.
5. *Empty Words,* ix.
6. *Empty Words,* 179.
7. *Empty Words,* 187.
8. *Empty Words,* 5.
9. *View,* 15.
10. *Empty Words,* 181.
11. *Empty Words,* 183.
12. *Empty Words,* 133.
13. *Empty Words,* 184.
14. *Silence,* 109.
15. *Empty Words,* 133.
16. *Empty Words,* 183.
17. Jill Johnston, "There Is No Silence Now," in *John Cage,* ed. Richard Kostelanetz, (New York: Praeger, 1970), 149.

Mimêsis and Beyond: Mallarmé, Boulez, and Cage (1986–87)

Jonathan Scott Lee

In 1949 John Cage (then thirty-six) went to Paris on a grant from the Guggenheim Foundation, where he met and quickly befriended the young French composer, Pierre Boulez (then twenty-four).[1] This friendship deepened into a relationship of mutual, professional support: Cage arranged for Boulez's work to be published by the leading French music publisher, and Boulez in turn introduced Cage and his most recent music (as well as the prepared piano) to the Parisian musical community. When Cage returned to New York, the two composers carried on an important correspondence, in which Boulez first articulated the rigorous principles of his total serialism and sketched his critique of Cage's gradual turn towards "renunciation of control" in musical composition.[2] In 1952 Boulez came to New York to visit and moved temporarily into Cage's loft. Thanks to Cage's efforts, several concerts of Boulez's music were arranged (featuring such works as the *Second Piano Sonata* [1947–48] and the first book of *Structures* for two pianos [1951–52]), at the last of which music by Cage was programmed as well (the *Music of Changes* [1951]). The reviews of this final concert—which were much more favorable to Cage than to Boulez—seem to have precipitated a break in the composers' friendship, a personal break which was foreshadowed by the theoretical conflict that had been developing between the two men over the previous two years. The break was rendered essentially permanent in 1957, when Boulez attacked Cage for his "chance by inadvertence" in an essay entitled "Aléa" (published in the *Nouvelle Revue Française*). Since that time there has been virtually no contact between Cage and Boulez, although Cage did take Boulez's place at Darmstadt in 1958,[3] and Boulez did extend an invitation to

Cage to work in the electronic music laboratories of IRCAM (Institut de recherche et de coordination Acoustique/Musique) in 1979 (an invitation which led to the realization of *Roaratorio: An Irish Circus on* Finnegans Wake).[4]

In the following pages, I want to suggest that the vicissitudes of the personal relationship between Cage and Boulez turn out to be of great theoretical interest, particularly since the final break between the once close friends appears to have been motivated by Boulez's stinging public attack on Cage's generalized use of chance methods. While the theoretical conflict between the composers (a conflict that Cage seems to have won, if one considers the developments of music in the 1960s and 1970s) may seem of most direct relevance to the practice of musical composition, I will argue that it foreshadows in a striking way thematic conflicts that are only now beginning to come to the attention of philosophers in this country.

"A DICE THROW . . . CHANCE"

I want to begin by suggesting that the opposition between Boulez and Cage over the role of chance methods in musical composition can be seen as one manifestation of a fundamental critical division between two possible and plausible interpretations of the work of Stéphane Mallarmé (and particularly of his later work). Thus Boulez stands as a representative of the reading of the poet which emphasizes a concept of *system,* a concept rooted in Mallarmé's frequent references to "the Idea." In contrast to Boulez, Cage can be seen as a representative of the reading of Mallarmé which emphasizes the notion of *chance* or *indeterminacy,* taking the thematic focus of *Un Coup de Dés* ("Any Thought Utters a Dice Throw") to be a central determinant of Mallarmé's creative preoccupations throughout his life. While it is quite unlikely that Cage's development towards chance compositional methods was influenced in any direct way by Mallarmé, it is noteworthy that Cage himself has on occasion used Mallarméan terms to describe his conflict with Boulez, and it is my hope here to show that such a description is both legitimate and enlightening.[5]

This is hardly the place to open up a full-scale analysis of Mallarmé interpretation (nor am I at all qualified to undertake such a task), but a quick glance at two or three passages from Mallarmé's prose should suffice to show the plausibility of the systematic reading. In a justly famous letter to Henri Cazalis (dated 14 May 1867), the twenty-five-year-old poet writes:

> These last months have been terrifying. My Thought has thought itself through and reached a Pure Idea. What the rest of me has suffered during that long agony, is indescribable. But, fortunately, I am quite dead now, and Eternity Itself is the least pure of all the regions where my Mind can wander—that Mind which is the abiding hermit of its own purity and untouched now even by the reflection of Time. . . . I achieved a supreme synthesis, and now I am slowly recovering my strength. . . . I should add—and you must say nothing of this—that the price of my victory is so high that I still need to see myself in this mirror in order to think; and that if it were not in front of me here on the table as I write you, I would become Nothingness again. Which means that I am impersonal now: not the Stéphane you once knew, but one of the ways the Spiritual Universe has found to see Itself, unfold Itself through what used to be me.[6]

Three characteristically Mallarméan themes are sketched in this extraordinary letter: first, the process of poetic thought is described as a "synthesis" which achieves "a Pure Idea," suggesting that the goal of poetry is to articulate this Idea in the less-than-pure medium of language; second, the reaching of the Pure Idea comes only with the "death" of the author, the "person" of the author apparently constituting a radical source of impurity; and third, the "impersonality" of the author amounts to the (quasi-Hegelian) self-knowledge and self-unfolding of "the Spiritual Universe," suggesting that "that Mind which is the abiding hermit of its own purity" is essentially a process of self-reference and self-reflection which, paradoxically, involves no such thing as a "self." A dense paragraph from the essay, "Crisis in Poetry" (put together over a period of ten years, beginning in 1886), offers a gloss of precisely these themes, adding a fourth (and at first shocking in the light of *Un Coup de Dés*) concern, namely that the book of verse can totally eliminate chance:

> The inner structures of a book of verse must be inborn; in this way, chance will be totally eliminated and the poet will be absent. From each theme, itself predestined, a given harmony will be born

> somewhere in the parts of the total poem and take its proper place within the volume; because, for every sound, there is an echo. Motifs of like pattern will move in balance from point to point. There will be none of the sublime incoherence found in the page-settings of the Romantics, none of the artificial unity that used to be based on the square measurements of the book. Everything will be hesitation, disposition of parts, their alternations and relationships—all this contributing to the rhythmic totality, which will be the very silence of the poem, in its blank spaces, as that silence is translated by each structural element in its own way. (Certain recent publications have heralded this sort of book; and if we may admit their ideals as complements to our own, it must then be granted that young poets have seen what an overwhelming and harmonious totality a poem must be, and have stammered out the magic concept of the Great Work.) Then again, the perfect symmetry of verses within the poem, of poems within the volume, will extend even beyond the volume itself; and this will be the creation of many poets who will inscribe, on spiritual space, the expanded signature of genius—as anonymous and perfect as a work of art. (*SP,* 366–67/41)

Here Mallarmé is remarkably explicit in his insistence that the poem (or work of art generally) must develop from its own resources, that it is simply a set of "inner structures," constituted by "hesitation, disposition of parts, their alternations and relationships," and that it is thus "an overwhelming and harmonious totality" which in its totality and in its "inborn"-ness eliminates the poet and, hence, chance. What we are left with is clearly the poem as a self-constituting and self-enclosing system. This vision of the poem as system is preserved in Mallarmé's "Preface" to *Un Coup de Dés,* where he suggests that the mobile distribution of the poem's text nevertheless is governed by and reflects the unity of the Idea, "the latent conductor wire" of the poem:

> The paper intervenes every time an image, of itself, ceases or withdraws, accepting the succession of others and, since it is not a matter, as always, of regular sound-periods or lines of verse—rather, of prismatic subdivisions of the Idea, the moment they appear and their conjunction in some exact spiritual setting lasts, the text asserts itself in variable positions, close to or far from the latent conductor wire, owing to credibility.[7]

On the basis of these three texts, spanning some thirty years of the poet's creative life, it is clear that it is not at all unreasonable to read Mallarmé's poetry as in some way embodying a notion of the work of art as a complex, self-constituting and self-enclosing system.

It is precisely this Mallarméan notion of the work of art as a system that is carried over into the compositional philosophy and practice of Pierre Boulez. In his early work (up to about 1954) Boulez was primarily concerned with extending the serial technique (invented by Arnold Schoenberg and developed further by Anton Webern) to parameters of musical composition beyond pitch class. In a series of works culminating with the *Second Piano Sonata* (1947–48) and the first book of *Structures* for two pianos (1951–52), he explored the application of serial devices to tempo, rhythm, volume, attack, and global structure, as well as to pitch class.[8] The theoretical basis for these experiments is rather nicely implied in Boulez's very early article, "A Time for Johann Sebastian Bach,"[9] published in 1951, where he suggests first that a "new morphology" in music (in this case, Schoenberg's dodecaphony) demands "a new syntax, a new rhetoric, and a new sensibility" (*N,* 17) and then argues that Bach's music, in its use of canons as "generators of the structure" of larger scale compositions, displays "a technique of form, powerfully unitarian, of uterine relationship between the writing itself and the architecture. The form is essentially variable and is put to the question in each work" (*N,* 17–18). The essay ends with an evocation of Mallarmé (profoundly prophetic in the light of Boulez's later development):

> . . . in the midst of these contemptible activities of the needy in quest of "authenticity" [i.e., those who will eventually write derivative textbooks defining Webern's technique], we shall finally restore its potential to what Mallarmé called the *Hasard.*
>
> We are indebted to the poet for that famous phrase: "One does not make verses with ideas, but with words"—a phrase that, taken literally, has served as a pretext for all compromises. But that is no reason to forget that: *Toute pensée émet un coup de dés. (N, 20)*

What Boulez admires in Bach is, of course, what he himself is trying to do: to generate an entire composition from a single germ (in Boulez's case, the series of pitch classes, which can be transformed quite simply into a series of numbers reflecting the intervallic structure of the series), a germ which is internal to the composition, thereby overcoming the form/content distinction, thus yielding a powerfully unitary work of art. Such a procedure recalls Mallarmé's description of the work of art as a matter of "inborn"[10] inner structures, "hesitation, disposition of parts, their alternations and relationships" (*SP,* 366–/67/41): the Boulezian composition certainly constitutes itself (on the basis of its intervallic series) through a complex process of self-reflection or self-mirroring, and in the extreme case of total serialism the "composer" is effectively eliminated (except for the inherently arbitrary selection of the series), the "Idea" of the series providing the basis for every aspect of the work.

In his more mature work (beginning in about 1954 with the composition of the *Third Piano Sonata* and continuing to the present), Boulez has been concerned to integrate certain chance procedures into his essentially Mallarméan notion of the work of art, recognizing the curious status of *le hasard* in the poet's writings and particularly in Mallarmé's unfinished notes towards *Le Livre* (which were published only in 1957).[11] What is most striking, however, about his use of chance is the extent to which Boulez "controls" or restricts the role of chance procedures in his compositions. This is a feature of Boulez's work often noted by performers: regarding the *Third Sonata* (the composition of Boulez's in which chance techniques are perhaps the most visible), Paul Jacobs remarks that "the piece works only in one particular order, that is the one published and played," while David Tudor (a close friend of and collaborator with John Cage) adds that "the performer is really not involved at all"; regarding Boulez's settings of poems by Mallarmé in *Pli selon pli* (1957–62), Susan Bradshaw points out that Boulez himself restricts tremendously the freedom with which he allows performers to interpret the work: "The second Mallarmé *Improvisation* seemed a beautiful, free piece. In the pauses I did pretty things under another conductor. That was not so when I played it under Boulez. He snaps the whip. Then you do it."[12]

Boulez's interest in controlling chance is clear from his earliest writings on the role of chance in composition (writings no doubt inspired by Cage's radical advocacy of compositional indeterminacy, beginning with the *Music of Changes* of 1951). In an essay of 1954, "Today's Searchings," he offers something of a self-critique, arguing that composition is not simply organization (as it seems to become under total serialism) (*N,* 22–23) and suggesting that " . . . the great effort in the domain proper to us is that of seeking a dialectic that will establish each moment of a composition between a rigorous total structure and a momentary structure submissive to free will" (*N,* 24). The essay ends by maintaining that this "dialectic" can be found by introducing some sort of indeterminacy into the composition:[13]

> I demand for music the right to parentheses and italics . . . ; a notion of discontinuous time, thanks to structures that will be bound together rather than remaining divided and airtight; finally, a sort of development in which the closed circuit will not be the only solution envisaged.
>
> I want the musical work not to be that series of compartments which one must inevitably visit one after the other; I try to think of it as a domain[14] in which, in some manner, one can choose one's own direction. (*N,* 26)

Boulez's most complete theoretical elaboration of this dialectic between rigorous control and indeterminacy comes in two complementary essays: in "Aléa" of 1957 Boulez describes quite abstractly the sort of composition he envisages; in "'Sonate, que me veux-tu?'" of 1960 he elaborates the abstract model by showing how his *Third Piano Sonata* lives up to the demands of "Aléa."

The earlier essay (which was, it will be remembered, the cause of the final break between Boulez and Cage) begins with a scathing attack on those who endorse "chance by inadvertence," thus "masking [their] fundamental weakness in the technique of composition" (*N,* 35); after venting his hostility to Cage, Boulez asks rhetorically: "Nevertheless, will the composer's ultimate ruse be to absorb this chance? Why not tame this potential and force it to an account of itself, an accounting? . . . How, then, reconcile composition and chance?" (*N,* 40). Boulez's method for absorbing/taming chance is to introduce into the musical text "a necessity for chance in the interpretation: a directed chance" (*N,* 42), a chance which theoretically guarantees that there is a many-one relation between interpretations and composition. The "directed" liberty he grants the performer, however, is supposed to grow directly out of the compositional structures themselves:

> On the level of putting the structures themselves into play, I think that at the beginning one could "absorb" chance by establishing a

> certain automatism of relationships among various previously established probabilities. (*N,* 43)

In the place of the total organization of his earlier serialism, Boulez is "loosening" things up so as to allow for rigorous but probabilistic organization. Despite his claims that this really is something qualitatively different from total serialism, Boulez goes on to insist that complicated structuring will be necessary ". . . in order to obviate total loss of the global sense of form as well as to avoid giving away to improvisation with no necessity but that of free will" (*N,* 44–45). This "global sense of form" which is meant to "absorb" chance is perhaps best described in the following (typically abstract) passage:

> Starting from an initial signature, ending at an exhaustive, conclusive sign, the composition comes to put into play what we were seeking at the outset of our search: a problematic "route," a temporal function—a certain number of chance events registered within a mobile duration—always having a developmental logic, a directed over-all sense—caesuras being allowed to interpose themselves there, caesuras of silence or plateaux—sound-forms—routes going from a beginning to an end. We have respected the "finish" of the Occidental work, its closed cycle, but we have introduced the "chance" of the Oriental work, its open unfolding. (*N,* 47)

Boulez betrays the rigorously serialist roots of his aleatorism towards the end of "Aléa," where he re-describes his ideal in the following terms:

> . . . one can adapt to composition the notion of series itself—I mean to say that one can endow structure with the most general notion of permutation, permutation in which the limits are rigorously defined by restriction of powers imposed upon it by autodetermination: there you have a logical evolution fully justified because the same organizing principle simultaneously governs morphology and rhetoric. (*N,* 48)

Boulez's striking emphasis on "the global sense of form," on "a developmental logic, a directed over-all sense," on "routes going from a beginning to an end," and on "autodetermination" (as well as his emphasis on "demonstrating that the divergences are based upon a balanced whole [*N*, 50]) are largely amplified in the later essay on the *Third Piano Sonata.*[15] However, here he explicitly links his move towards indeterminacy to his interest in Mallarmé, both his reading of *Un Coup de Dés* and his discovery of *Le Livre* (Sonate, 35–37), and in effect tries to argue that his techniques for the absorbing or taming of chance are comparable to Mallarmé's controlled aleatoric practice. What the essay does best, perhaps, is to capture Boulez's concerns in two striking metaphors, that of the labyrinth and that of the map. "The modern notion of the labyrinth in works of art," Boulez writes, "is certainly one of the most important leaps accomplished by Western thought—one from which there is no return" (Sonate, 34). Later, describing the *Third Sonata,* he adds: ". . . the five *formants* undoubtedly leave me free to engender other 'developants,' strikingly distinct but nonetheless related by their structure to the initial *formants.* This 'Livre' would then be a labyrinth, a spiral in time" (Sonate, 37). Characterizing the third formant of the sonata, Boulez uses the metaphor of the map:

> Certain directions are obligatory, others optional, but *everything* must be played. In some ways, this *Constellation* is like the map of an unknown city (which plays so large a role in *L'Emploi du Temps,* by Michel Butor). The itinerary is left to the interpreter's initiative; he must direct himself through a tight network of routes. (Sonate, 41)

What the metaphors of the labyrinth and the map share is the notion that there is ultimately a single "Idea" guiding the construction and unfolding of the composition: there is, after all, a single layout of a labyrinth and but one successful route through it; similarly, while there are many ways of getting from point A to point B, a map shows one (at least implicitly) the finite and determinate set of such possibilities. In short, Boulez's favored metaphors for musical compositions reinforce what I have described as the notion of the work of art as *system;* these metaphors offer a definitive confirmation of my basic point about Boulez, namely that he can be seen as a representative of the "systematic" reading of Mallarmé. This point is made crystal clear in yet another text where Boulez uses the metaphors of the labyrinth and the map, in which he concludes that:

> Personally I have never been in favor of chance. I do not think that

> chance has much to contribute on its own account. So my idea is not to change the work at every turn nor to make it look like a complete novelty, but rather to change the viewpoints and perspectives from which it is seen while leaving its basic meaning unaltered.[16]

It is in light of this confession that we must read Boulez's quotation from Mallarmé's *Igitur* at the end of "Aléa:"

> In brief, in any act in which chance is in play, it is always chance that achieves its own Idea by affirming or denying it. Faced with its existence, negation and affirmation run aground. It contains the Absurd—implies it, but in latent state, and prevents its existence: which allows the Infinite to be. (*Oeuvres,* 441; *N,* 51)

It is the systematic reading of Mallarmé which allows Boulez to see in this passage an elimination of chance from the work of art through the transformation of chance into "its own Idea," and it is this reading which justifies Boulez's routine evocations of Mallarmé as the champion of such notions as "developmental logic" and the "absorbing" of chance. For Boulez, Mallarmé's *coup de dés* is the locus of indeterminacy, but crucial to this *coup* is the fact that any *coup* (insofar as it accomplishes something definite, perhaps a definite number) "absorbs" chance.

Having dealt at length with the "systematic" reading of Mallarmé, we may treat the chance-centered reading somewhat more briefly. Throughout his creative career—from the *Igitur* fragment of 1869 to *Un Coup de Dés* of 1897—Mallarmé was clearly obsessed with the notion of chance and, in particular, with the gesture of the dice-throw. While our discussion of Boulez's use of Mallarmé reveals that nothing is as clear as it might seem, it does seem fairly clear that Mallarmé was convinced of the intractable nature of chance. The very title of his final masterpiece—a title which does double duty as "the latent conductor wire" of the poem—is quite straightforward: "A DICE THROW WILL NEVER DO AWAY WITH CHANCE" (*Oeuvres,* 453), and the chance-oriented reading of Mallarmé simply takes this theme of *Un Coup de Dés* to be the central determinant of the poet's preoccupations. Perhaps the simplest way to develop this reading is to move on to the end of the poem—"Any Thought utters a Dice Throw" (*Oeuvres,* 477)—and to argue that every act of thinking (and hence every act of writing) is *itself* a dice throw which engenders an indeterminate variety of consequences (further dice throws). The work of art, then, would be both product of chance and producer of chance(s), and a reading of Mallarmé along these lines would tend to stress equally both of these implications.

While Mallarmé himself has relatively little to say about the origins of the work of art in chance, he certainly does discuss (albeit rather obliquely) the work's indeterminate effects. Judy Kravis, for example, has argued (on the basis of a careful study of a number of Mallarmé's pieces of theater criticism) that the poet is particularly attuned to the nuances and complexities of an audience's reactions to a work on the stage,[17] reactions which in their relative indeterminacy nevertheless constitute a substantive part of the theatrical experience. In his lecture, "Music and Literature" (delivered at Oxford and Cambridge in 1894), Mallarmé attempts to answer the question, "Is there a reason for writing at all?" by appeal again to the (in principle indeterminate) proliferation of effects that writing may have on readers:

> It is not *description* which can unveil the efficacy and beauty of monuments, seas, or the human face in all their maturity and native state, but rather *evocation, allusion, suggestion.* These somewhat arbitrary terms [*cette terminologie quelque peu de hasard*] reveal what may well be a very decisive tendency in modern literature, a tendency which limits literature and yet sets it free. For what is the magic charm of art, if not this: that, beyond the confines of a fistful of dust or of all other reality, beyond the book itself, beyond the very text, it delivers up that volatile scattering which we call the Spirit, Who cares for nothing save universal musicality. (*SP*, 645/45)

In this passage, the chance effects of the work of art's evocation are "that volatile scattering which we call the Spirit" (and it is noteworthy that Mallarmé is here undermining the quasi-Hegelian associations that his earlier use of *l'esprit* seems to carry), while in the very progress of the passage Mallarmé *illustrates* the chance origins of the work of art by commenting that the terminology he is currently using (in the work of art which is the lecture) is itself "somewhat arbitrary."

It is clearly this very open-ended reading of Mallarméan poetics that is presupposed by John Cage's remarks on his relation to Mallarmé. In his conversations with the French philosopher and music critic, Daniel Charles, Cage describes the difference between Boulez and himself in the following terms:

> But he [i.e., Boulez] rejected outright any acceptance of the idea of chance. That wasn't a part of his views. Later came Mallarmé's posthumous *Book,* which could have brought us together again, since in the end Mallarmé too accorded primacy to chance. In fact, Boulez in turn threw himself into chance operations. But for him, chance served as a pretext for inventing the term *aleatory.* I believe he established its present musical definition. Well, he used that word only to describe appropriate and correct chance operations, as opposed to those which seemed to him inappropriate or incorrect—mine! (*FB,* 180–81)

We see here that Cage is quite willing to identify Mallarmé as a precursor of his own ideas about the importance of chance or indeterminacy in art, and (at least in this French context) he suggests that the difference between himself and Boulez is a difference between the true Mallarméan and the false. While we should not put excessive weight on this passage, I want to argue that it is instructive to look at Cage's work in this context and that it is arguably fair to see in his work a genuine flowering of notions first adumbrated by Mallarmé.

In response to a question put by Charles, suggesting in effect that any use of chance in music should be susceptible to a statistical description or explanation, Cage offers a preliminary characterization of the chance in his works:

> . . . the chance of contemporary physics, tables of random numbers, corresponds to an *equal* distribution of events. The chance to which I resort, that of chance operations, is different. It presupposes an *unequal* distribution of elements. That is the contribution of the Chinese *Book of Changes,* the *I Ching,* or the astronomical maps I used for *Atlas Eclipticalis.* I never achieve the physical object that interests the statistician. (*FB,* 79)

This extremely rich response makes at least three crucial points. First, the chance in which Cage is interested (which, in this passage, is at first the variety of chance techniques that lie at the origin of the work of art) is essentially a matter of indeterminacy, because it concerns an "unequal distribution" of events (for example, compositional steps and their resultant sounds), that is, a distribution of events that is—unlike those distributions studied in physics—in principle unpredictable. This unpredictability holds of both the process of composition and the process of receiving the work of art. Second, the inherent unpredictability of the compositional process has the effect of eliminating the ego of the artist (the "ego" being something susceptible at the very least to probabilistic explanation and prediction): as Cage remarks elsewhere in *For the Birds,* "I write by using chance operations to liberate my music from every kind of like and dislike" (*FB,* 202).[18] Third, the unequal distribution of events produced by chance operations constitutes the work of art as something different from a "physical object," precisely because physical objects (as those things that are studied by physics) correspond to equal distributions of events. An implication of this is that works of art are bound to generate a somewhat wider range of responses from their audiences than are ordinary physical objects, and Cage certainly takes this to be a function of the origin of such works in chance operations.[19]

Now, all three of these points can be found highlighted in the chance-centered reading of Mallarmé. Indeed, a paragraph from "Crisis in Poetry" manages almost to mirror Cage's remarks. Just before the long paragraph quoted earlier, Mallarmé writes:

> If the poem is to be pure, the poet's voice must be stilled and the initiative taken by the words themselves, which will be set in motion as they meet unequally in collision. And in an exchange of gleams they will flame out like some glittering swath of fire sweeping over precious stones, and thus replace the audible breathing in lyric poetry of old—replace the poet's own personal and passionate control of verse. (*SP,* 366/40–41)

Here, we see both an insistence upon the inequality (indeterminacy) of the product of artistic creation and an emphasis on the need for the ego of the poet/artist (understood as essentially "passionate") to be eliminated from the "pure" work of art. The third of Cage's points—that concerning the inherently indeterminate reception of the work of art—seems implicit in Mallarmé's evocation of the words of poetry as flaming out "like some glittering swath of fire sweeping over precious stones," an image wildly indeterminate in its force; however, it is perhaps more explicitly put in the passage from "Music and Literature" quoted above where Mallarmé suggests that the effect of writing is "that volatile scattering which we call the Spirit" (*SP,* 645/45).

We have seen that Cage describes his relation to Boulez by reference to Mallarmé, and in the same passage of *For the Birds* he goes on to put his critique of Boulez in terms of the Mallarméan opposition between drama and theater:

> In fact, [Boulez's] chance operations fit into his compositions only as part of a drama. He very strictly distinguishes between determinate passages and "aleatory" passages in the same composition. As a whole, it becomes a drama between opposites: determinate vs. indeterminate. (*FB,* 181)[20]

In contrast to this dramatic conception of the musical work, Cage offers the notion of a "circus" (also "happening")[21] as an inherently "theatrical" form allowing for un-systematized "richness and complexity" (see *FB,* 165 and 181); as early as 1957, Cage had been calling for a theatricalization of music: "Where do we go from here? Towards theatre. That art more than music resembles nature."[22] Features of a Cagean circus include the simultaneous performances of two or more "distinct" works (*FB,* 131–32 and 135), the abandonment of "any pretense of structure" or of measurable temporal correspondences (*FB,* 135), and the acceptance of "non-linearity" (*FB,* 198). In short, Cagean theater abandons the closed structure of dramatic conflict, a structure that is inherently "literary" (*FB,* 181), to celebrate the openness of the theatrical situation, a situation which is essentially sensuous and spatial.

Now, I have described this drama/theater distinction as Mallarméan in large part because Mallarmé in the notes towards *Le Livre* devotes a tremendous amount of space to jottings which explicitly contrast these two terms (usually abbreviated in the notes as 'Dr.' and 'Th.'). What seems clear from these notoriously obscure notes is that Mallarmé favors theater over drama (see, for example, leaves 83 and 84, as well as leaf 169) and that he contrasts the two notions in large part by developing patterns of opposition between related terms: thus, 'Drama' is routinely associated with 'Mystery' and 'Hymn,' while 'Theatre' attracts into its constellation of terms 'Hero' and 'Idea' (see, in particular, leaves 70, 87, and 88, as well as leaf 4). The sense of these cryptic notes seems to be related to ideas developed by Mallarmé in his theater criticism of the 1880s: thus, in his essay on *Hamlet,* Mallarmé articulates a distinction between "the struggle, in man, between his dream and the fates allotted to his life by evil fortune" (*SP,* 300/57), which struggle is the very essence of drama, and "the theatre of the mind alone" (*SP,* 300/58) which dictates that "everything must be carried out *in obedience to a symbolic relationship of characters, either to themselves or to a single figure*" (*SP,* 301/59), the "hero" paradigmatically embodied in Hamlet. In his essay, "Richard Wagner, Revery of a French Poet," Mallarmé seeks a "theatrical miracle" which will serve to eliminate the "decadent" (essentially "dramatic") theater of the past (and of the conservative present) that functions by asking its audience "to believe in the reality of its characters and plot—simply to *believe,* and that is all" (*SP,* 542/73–74). The theatrical miracle called for here is elaborated in a theory of that single figure, the hero (linked now to Myth rather than to the Idea, as in *Le Livre*), who serves as the symbolic center of all the action on stage:

> The Theatre calls not for several established, eternal, or well-known Myths, but for one Myth free of individuality, since it must embrace the many aspects of human life. Art, with a magic befitting the national spirit, must evoke these aspects and mirror them in all of us. The hero must have no name, for there must be a surprise. His gesture will contain, within itself, our dreams of privileged places and of paradise—dreams which were engulfed by the old-time drama, with its foolish desire to contain them or represent them on the stage. It is he that exists, not any particular stage! (Remember the mistake the theatre made, when Music was absent, with its permanent sets and real actors.) Does a gesture of our soul, do symbols in preparation or in blossom need any place for their development, other than the fictitious stage of vision which flashes in the glance of the audience? Myth is the Saint of Saints, but It must live in our imaginations. In a miraculous, supreme flash of lightning giving birth to that Figure which is No One, It embraces each acting pose fitted by the Figure to the symphonic rhythm. And thus It is set free! (*SP,* 545/77)

We see here that Mallarméan theater focuses on the hero as the "Figure which is No One" rather than as a particular character in a particular drama; Mallarmé's central point seems to be that the power of theater on its audience—a power which is indeterminate but striking (note his use of the image of the "flash" to get across the inherent indeterminacy of Myth's translation into "our imaginations")[23]—derives from the basically mysterious and mythic way in which the Hero can occupy the center of the stage while being nothing more than a set of relations to other figures in the play (and hence being "that Figure which is No One").[24] Theater (which in the context of the Wagner essay comes close to being a fusion of drama and music [see *SP*, 543/75]) thus exists only in the precarious and indeterminate relation between the stage and the audience, a relation which renders more-or-less inessential such dramatic necessities as linear plot, relative simplicity of action, and dialectical structure. In short, Mallarmé's "theater" does resemble to some considerable extent Cage's notion of theater as a non-linear, complex, and non-structured "circus."

I have argued that Cage's references to Mallarmé are enlightening in that they allow us to relate quite concretely a number of characteristics of Cage's work to features of Mallarmé's work. At the same time, this analysis should give a relatively specific indication of just what is at stake between the "systematic" reading of Mallarmé favored by Boulez and the "indeterminacy" reading endorsed by Cage (although I am not particularly interested in deciding between these two readings here).

"NOTHING WILL HAVE TAKEN PLACE BUT THE PLACE EXCEPT PERHAPS A CONSTELLATION"

The oppositions between the "systematic" and the "indeterminacy" readings of Mallarmé and between drama and theater and, hence, the opposition between Boulez and Cage can be deepened by reference to two different and non-standard conceptions of *mimêsis* that may be found in Mallarmé's work. In the next few pages, I want to review briefly Jacques Derrida's powerful reading of Mallarmé in terms of *mimêsis* (a reading found in his essay, "The Double Session")[25] and to argue that Derrida's distinction between "polysemy" and "dissemination" provides a useful conceptual tool for distinguishing further between Boulez and Cage. The payoff of this argument will come in the third and final section of this essay, where I examine the possibility that Cage's most recent work might serve as an appropriately post-Derridian model for philosophical writing.

The background of Derrida's reading of Mallarmé is simply that almost all writing, whether literary, philosophical, or scientific, has been taken by the Western (that is, Platonic) tradition to be essentially mimetic. The notion of *mimêsis* involved here implies, among other things, that the truth or falsity of every text is (at least in principle) decidable by reference to some reality external to the text (*D,* 209–13/184–87). Derrida concludes from this that:

> *Logos* must indeed be shaped according to the model of the *eidos;* the book then reproduces the *logos,* and the whole is organized by this relation of repetition, resemblance (*homoiôsis*), doubling, duplication, this sort of specular process and play of reflections where things (*onta*), speech, and writing come to repeat and mirror each other. (*D,* 214/188)

Derrida's interest in Mallarmé is focused in his claim that the poet is one of the first writers to break definitively with this traditional (and Platonic) notion of *mimêsis,* and he argues that this break is made possible by Mallarmé's extraordinary use of syntax.[26] Obliquely describing Mallarmé, Derrida writes:

> The invariable feature of this reference [of *mimêsis* to truth and to external reality] sketches out the closure of metaphysics. . . . Now, this reference is discreetly but absolutely displaced in the workings of a certain syntax, whenever any writing both marks and goes back over its mark with an undecidable stroke. This double mark escapes the pertinence or authority of truth: it does not overturn it but rather inscribes it within its play as one of its functions or parts. (*D,* 220/193)

Derrida's prime example of Mallarméan syntax is the brief prose piece "Mimique" or "The Mime" (*Oeuvres,* 310),[27] ostensibly a critical review/description of a piece or a performance by the celebrated mime, Paul Margueritte. For the purpose of unfolding Derrida's argument here, only one passage from Mallarmé's text is crucial:

> . . . this *Pierrot Murderer of His Wife* composed and set down by himself, a mute soliloquy that the phantom, white as a yet unwritten page, holds in both face and gesture at full length to his soul.

What Derrida first points out about this text is that, since the Mime is to perform a "mute soliloquy" written by himself, he "ought only to write himself on the white page he is" (*D,* 225/198). From this it follows, of course, that "Mimique" is evoking (and, perhaps, illustrating) a *mimêsis* that imitates nothing, and it is precisely this aspect of Mallarmé's text that marks its first break with the Platonic notion of *mimêsis:*

> We are faced then with mimicry imitating nothing: faced, so to speak, with a double that doubles no simple, a double that nothing anticipates, nothing at least that is not itself already double. There is no simple reference. . . . In this speculum with no reality, in this mirror of a mirror, a difference or dyad does exist, since there are mimes and phantoms. But it is a difference without reference, or rather a reference without a referent, without any first or last unit, a ghost that is the phantom of no flesh, wandering about without a past, without any death, birth, or presence.
>
> Mallarmé thus preserves the differential structure of mimicry or *mimêsis,* but without its Platonic or metaphysical interpretation, which implies that somewhere the being of something that *is,* is being imitated. (*D,* 234/206)

In short, Mallarmé's texts substitute (by means of a complex play of syntax) an elaborate form of self-reference—mirrors mirroring mirrors—for the traditional mimetic functions of narrative, description, and expression. His poetry and prose are neither about the world around him nor about any Imaginary synthesis (dependent upon some individual personality) which might be held to confer upon the discrete items of this world some trace of the Idea.

This point is made rather startlingly by Mallarmé himself at the end of "Crisis in Poetry," where he contrasts the language of poetry with the "vulgar" use of language in "narrative, instruction, or description":

> Why should we perform the miracle by which a natural object is almost made to disappear beneath the magic waving wand of the written word, if not to divorce that object from the direct and the palpable, and so conjure up its *essence* [*notion*] in all purity?
>
> When I say: "a flower!" then from that forgetfulness to which my voice consigns all floral form, something different from the usual calyces arises, something all music, essence, and softness: the flower which is absent from all bouquets. (*SP,* 368/42)

That the flower at issue in poetry is "the flower which is absent from all bouquets" marks at once the fact that poetic language is not concerned with the imitation of any reality external to the poem. However, if the point of writing is "to divorce that object from the direct and the palpable," it is also important to note that this divorce is said to "conjure up [the object's] *essence* in all purity." Indeed, the "miracle" of poetic language is precisely this double motion whereby a separation of language from the world can nevertheless yield a grasp of the essence of that world. The key to making sense of this claim lies in the fact that Mallarmé's French reads *notion* where Bradford Cook translates "essence": the essence which poetry conjures up is implicitly an essence *as constituted by the mind,* and—given Mallarmé's equation of mind or spirit (*l'esprit*) with "that volatile scattering" which is generated by "the magic charm of art" (*SP,* 645/45)—it is not so surprising that he maintains that the interplay of mirrors which makes up poetic language can yield some grasp of essence. As Mallarmé indicates at the end of "Crisis in Poetry," poetry (and by extension all "non-journalistic" uses of language [compare *SP,* 368/42]) creates a language that is outside of language precisely insofar as poetic language leaves behind the Platonic notion of *mimêsis:*

> Out of a number of words, poetry fashions a single new word which is total in itself and foreign to the language—a kind of incantation. Thus the desired isolation of language is effected; and chance (which might still have governed these elements, despite their artful and alternating renewal through meaning and sound) is thereby instantly and thoroughly abolished. Then we realize, to our amazement, that we had never truly heard this or that ordinary poetic fragment; and, at the same time, our recollection of the object thus conjured up bathes in a totally new atmosphere. (*SP,* 368/43)

This passage is also of interest, because it sheds new light on the opposition between the "systematic" reading and the "indeterminacy" reading of Mallarmé. While, at first glance, the claim that the "isolation of language" immediately abolishes chance would seem to favor the former reading, a second glance suggests that the elimination of chance comes only in the fashioning of the "single new word which is total in itself." As a product of textual contrivance and syntactic manipulation, this "new word" possesses a specificity lacking to the words of common language (which are indeterminate in their meaning precisely because of the wide range of contexts in which they can be used), and in this sense there is no "vulgar" chance in the poetic word. From this, however, it does not follow that the word neither originates in chance nor generates an indeterminate proliferation of readings.[28]

It should almost go without remarking that this sense of *mimêsis* as self-referentiality, this possibility of a language that is (in some sense) meaningful without presupposing Platonic notions of mimetic closure, mirrors Boulez's ideas (developed in the first section of this essay) about the musical composition as a structure composed of self-mirroring structures. The "double science" marked by Mallarmé's insistently polyvalent and indeterminable syntax (see *D,* 236 n. 19/208 n. 25) can itself be taken to be the very method of systematic serialism (with or without the addition of "controlled chance" elements), precisely to the extent that Boulezian technique rests on what we might call the structural principle of "differential repetition," repetition masked by constant differentiating strategies. Thus, Boulez's compositional theory and his compositions can be seen as involving a rigorous acceptance of the inherent self-referentiality of the claim in *Un Coup de Dés* that "NOTHING WILL HAVE TAKEN PLACE BUT THE PLACE EXCEPT PERHAPS A CONSTELLATION" (*Oeuvres,* 474–77): nothing takes place in Boulezian compositions but the structural mirroring of the basic structures, except (of course) the "guiding idea" around which these basic structures fall into order ("Sonate," 43–44).

While Derrida stresses Mallarmé's replacement of Platonic *mimêsis* with a method of self-referentiality (itself clearly a form of self-*mimêsis*), "The Double Session" goes beyond this to suggest that the ultimate Mallarméan achievement may be the abandoning of *polysemy* (which is inherently finite and closed in character) for *dissemination* (which is infinitely productive of multiple readings and utterly open-ended). Derrida's argument for this controversial claim is rather tortuous, but it begins with his reflections on the passage which ends "Crisis in Poetry" (quoted just above). Noting that the "new word" (fashioned by poetry) "which is total in itself and foreign to the language" clearly works upon language from the outside, Derrida goes on to insist that it

> . . . also *returns* to the language, recomposes with it according to new

> networks of differences, becomes divided up again, etc., in short, does not become a master-word with the finally guaranteed integrity of a meaning or truth. (*D,* 288/256)

All remains dependent upon syntax and its repositioning and "spacing" of words: the poet is essentially a "syntaxer" (in Mallarmé's own self-description) perpetually engaged in distributing the blanks or white spaces between and around words and lines. There are, of course, implications to be drawn from this characterization of the essence of writing:

> The dissemination of the whites (*not* the dissemination of whiteness) produces a tropological structure that circulates infinitely around itself through the incessant supplement of an extra turn: there is *more* metaphor, *more* metonymy. Since everything becomes metaphorical, there is no longer any literal meaning and, hence, no longer any metaphor either. Since everything becomes metonymical, the part being each time greater than the whole and the whole smaller than the part, how could one arrest a metonymy or a synechdoche? How could one fix the *margins* of any rhetoric? (*D,* 290/258)

The break with Platonic *mimêsis* is tantamount to a break with "expression" in the ordinary sense (*D,* 293/261), and this leads inevitably to a breakdown in the ordinary concept of linguistic meaning. With the collapse of meaning there comes—with all the force of logic!—a collapse of such meaning-derivative notions as ambiguity and polysemy:

> If there is thus no thematic unity or overall meaning to reappropriate beyond the textual instances, no total message located in some imaginary order, intentionality, or lived experience, then the text is no longer the expression or representation (felicitous or otherwise) of any *truth* that would come to diffract or assemble itself in the polysemy of literature. It is this hermeneutic concept of *polysemy* that must be replaced by *dissemination.* (*D,* 294/262)

In eliminating the very notion of meaning, Derrida may well seem to be stripping-away the very possibility of *any* sort of *mimêsis* (and not just that Platonic notion of *mimêsis* that has clearly been his target throughout his argument), and yet he goes on to suggest that just as the Mime of "Mimique" "mimes imitation" without thereby being an imitator (*D,* 248/219), so too the disseminating movement of texts like Mallarmé's may in face *mime* the process by which language's self-referentiality gives rise to "meaning." This point is developed in the following extraordinarily difficult passage:

> But is dissemination then the *loss* of that kind of truth, the *negative* prohibition of all access to such a signified? Far from presupposing that a virgin substance thus precedes or oversees it, dispersing or withholding itself in a negative second moment, dissemination *affirms* the always already divided generation of meaning. Dissemination—spills it in advance.
>
> We will therefore not return to dissemination as if it were the center of the web. We return to it, rather, as to the fold of the hymen, to the somber white of the cave or of the womb, to the black-on-white upon the womb, the locus of scattered emissions, of chances taken with no return, of separations. We will not follow up the "arachnoid thread." (*D,* 299–301/268–69)

The deep "truth" according to Derrida, then, is captured with great perspicacity in a line from an early fragment of Mallarmé: "All method is a fiction" (*Oeuvres,* 851).[29] Nevertheless, the fictions set in motion by literary texts (or at least by texts in a Mallarméan "tradition") are such that, by virtue of complexities and games of syntax, they are capable of *enacting,* "affirming," and thus *miming* the mirroring process of self-referentiality which itself constitutes the "generation of meaning." This generation of meaning is itself "always already divided," because of the double character of (Mallarméan) literary syntax—a writing which "both marks and goes back over its mark with an undecidable stroke" (*D,* 220/193)—and it is precisely this process of division (which nevertheless and simultaneously masks itself as undivided)[30] which the Mallarméan text mimes.

This notion of dissemination as a kind of theatrical *mimêsis* is both evoked and theorized in the writings of Mallarmé himself. Thus in the late essay, "Mystery in Literature," he offers the following image of dissemination at work:

> Words rise up unaided and in ecstasy; many a facet reveals its infinite rarity and is precious to our mind. For our mind is the center of

> this hesitancy and oscillation; it sees the words not in their usual order, but in projection (like the walls of a cave), so long as that mobility which is their principle lives on, that part of speech which is not spoken. Then quickly, before they die away, they all exchange their brilliancies from afar; or they may touch, and steal a furtive glance. (*SP,* 386/33).

Here, many of the themes that have come up in our reading(s) of Mallarmé are reprised: the self-constitution of poetic language, the indeterminacy of the effect of such language on its readers, the importance of syntax as the generator of poetic language, and—related to all of these ideas—the emphasis on (indeterminate) mobility as the "principle" of poetic language. All these notions come together in Derrida's unfolding of dissemination. Moreover, Mallarmé himself suggests that even the highly self-conscious syntax and spatial configuration of *Un Coup de Dés* work because they are involved (in some non-standard way) in imitation. In a letter to André Gide, he writes:

> The poem [i.e., *Un Coup de Dés*] is being printed at this very moment, just as I conceived it regarding pagination, in which lies the whole effect. . . . The constellation will inevitably suggest, according to exact laws and to the extent that a printed text can do so, the look of a constellation. The vessel lists, from the top of one page to the bottom of another, . . . for (and this is the whole point of view involved) the rhythm of a sentence about an action, or even about an object, has no meaning and, represented on paper, reproducing in letters the original image, cannot give any account of them at all unless it imitates them. (*Oeuvres,* 1582/"Sonate," 35)

There is a warrant in Mallarmé's texts, then, for Derrida's insistence on the importance of dissemination as a second sort of *mimêsis*, distinct both from the *mimêsis* of the Platonic tradition and from that presupposed in the notion of self-referentiality. While Mallarmé, in his letter to Gide, does not suggest that the imitation operative in *Un Coup de Dés* is *theatrical,* he does suggest that it is a sort of *mimêsis* different from that normally encountered in literature (resembling somewhat more perhaps that to be found in the visual arts).

If Derrida's notion of *mimêsis* as self-reference is relevant to the work of Pierre Boulez, I suspect it is clear that the notion of *mimêsis* as dissemination provides a useful framework for analyzing the work of John Cage. Indeed, this theatrical notion of *mimêsis* is very much in line with Cage's oft-repeated conception of art as "an imitation of nature in her manner of operation" (a conception derived from A. K. Coomaraswamy):[31] rather than a *mimêsis* of the product, art offers a *mimêsis* of the process that produces this product. A key part of the rationale for Cage's emphasis on processes is his claim that the world itself *is* a process. As he remarks in *For the Birds:*

> You say: the real, the world as it is. But it is not, it becomes! It moves, it changes! It doesn't wait for us to change. . . . It is more mobile than you can imagine. You are getting closer to this reality when you say as it "presents itself;" that means that it is not there, existing as an object. The world, the real is not an object. It is a process. (*FB,* 80)

From this, Cage is able to offer a succinct account of the purpose of art:

> The function of art at the present time is to preserve us from all the logical minimizations that we are at each instant tempted to apply to the flux of events. To draw us nearer to the process which is the world we live in. (*FB,* 80–81)

As we have seen, Cage is opposed to the work of art's becoming an object,[32] and part of his strategy for avoiding this is to generate works which demand the active participation of their audiences/readers: such participation in effect destroys the subject/object dualism characteristic of Western thought about the work of art (*FB,* 198–99 and *Silence,* 38). If the audience/reader is really to be an active part of the work of art, the work itself must be "open" enough "so that it may be interpreted in various ways" (*FB,* 59), and this opening of the literary work of art is facilitated in Cage's view by the fact that words themselves are (disseminating) processes as opposed to static things (*FB,* 151).

One implication of this claim (and this is very reminiscent of Mallarmé's distinction between journalistic language and poetic language in "Crisis in Poetry" [*SP,* 368/42]) is that expression or communication need not and perhaps must not be thought of as the essence of language, since notions such as these presuppose a relative stability of linguistic meaning inconsistent with Cage's vision of words as processes. Cage himself puts this point in terms of a distinction between communication and conversation:

> I much prefer this notion of dialogue, of *conversation,* to the notion of communication. Communication presupposes that one has something, an object, to be communicated. The conversation I'm thinking about would not be a conversation which would concentrate on objects. Communicating is always imposing something: a discourse on objects, a truth, a feeling. While in conversation, nothing imposes itself.
>
> Daniel Charles: *But if nothing imposes itself, we could say anything at all . . .*
>
> John Cage: It is that "anything at all" which allows access to what I call the *openness.* To the process. To the circus situation. In that situation, objects surge forth. But the fact that it is conversation, not communication, means that we are deterred from talking *about* them. What is said is not this or that object. It is the circus situation! It is the process. (*FB,* 148)[33]

If the Cagean circus manages to avoid discourse *about* objects, it nevertheless is meant to allow objects to "surge forth" precisely by letting things "be themselves" (*FB,* 232). It accomplishes this, as we have seen, by imitating the *process* of nature rather than its products, and it is in this way that art can and should "resemble nature" without in any ordinary sense involving the (Platonic) *mimêsis* of nature: the disseminating play of the work of art mimes the play of nature without in any way dictating or guaranteeing that the work itself resembles the objects actually found in nature.[34] If we may assume that the "CONSTELLATION" that "PERHAPS WILL HAVE TAKEN PLACE" in addition to "THE PLACE" in *Un Coup de Dés* is a randomly disseminating focus of linguistic (and perhaps non-linguistic) meaning as well as a randomly dispersed scattering of stars, then we may conclude that this Mallarméan image admirably evokes the work of art as theorized by Cage. It is worth adding in conclusion that this image also functions beautifully as a suggestion of the experience of a performance of a piece of Cage's music.

"... a purposeless writing, a pure writing!"

With the distinction between *mimêsis* as self-referentiality and *mimêsis* as dissemination, we are at the threshold of a set of issues that have begun to generate a great deal of interest among philosophers in this country in the past ten years.[35] Derrida's critique of the domination of Western thought by the Platonic conception of *mimêsis* and its inherent decidability and metaphysical closure—a domination reflected in the fact that our models for thinking/writing about everything remain essentially representational—is ultimately a critique of philosophy as a literary genre (although this critique has thus far had a far greater impact on the practice of literary criticism than on the practice of philosophy). To take Derrida seriously is to take seriously the possibility that philosophers should explore alternative literary genres and/or styles (as has Derrida himself). To escape the yoke of decidable *mimêsis,* the post-Derridian philosopher must make some effort to escape the conventions of writing dictated by the Platonic tradition, and (as we have seen) if we are to follow Derrida's own advice we might well look to the writing of Mallarmé for guidance in this direction.

In this light the recent text-compositions of John Cage—works which in fact marvelously illustrate Cage's manner of working with the Mallarméan notions discussed throughout this essay—might serve as models for a new approach to philosophical writing after Derrida. It is only fair to note from the start of this discussion that Cage himself would be bound to be rather ambivalent about this approach to his work. As he notes in the Afterword to *For the Birds,* Cage feels a certain "uneasiness when confronted with any attempt to construct a discourse which [starts] from certain premises in order to draw conclusions from them" (*FB,* 239), and he thus would no doubt disapprove of the argumentative strategy of my attempt to situate his recent work in a Derridian context. On the other hand, Cage leaves open the possibility that philosophy could take a different form from that of logical system-building. Commenting on Daniel Charles's inability to shake off logic, he remarks: "It's simply that I am not a philosopher ... at least, not a Greek one!" (*FB,* 80). However, he goes on immediately to present his conception of the function of art as "to draw us nearer to the process which is the world we live in" (*FB,* 80–81), suggesting that this is something that a non-Greek philosopher might attempt.

In the Introduction to *Themes and Variations,* Cage describes his project in the text-compositions at issue here quite simply:

> This is one text in an ongoing series; to find a way of writing which though coming from ideas is not about them; or is not about ideas but produces them.[36]

In not being *about* ideas, such texts leave behind the traditional notion of texts as means of communication; they no longer embody purposes or meanings which are to be transmitted from author to reader; and in this sense, such a text amounts to ". . . a purposeless writing, a pure writing!" (*FB,* 60).[37] In coming *from* ideas, such texts presuppose the existence of (in general) other texts; they are texts integrally tied to other texts; and as such they are fairly described as disseminations (even "volatile scatterings" [*SP,* 645/45]) of these prior texts. In *producing* ideas, such texts engage in precisely the dissemination—the proliferation of words, texts, and "meanings"—that will give birth to yet more such texts "coming from ideas." In short, Cage's description of his goals in writing remarkably parallels what might naturally be taken to be Derrida's hopes for a post-Platonic genre of "philosophical" writing.

As Cage's own introductions to his various text-works reveal, the methods by which these works are generated are of tremendous importance to him (a further sign of which is the fact that, in his oral performances of these works, Cage goes to the trouble to read to the audience the introductions, which generally elaborate the method used in composing the works, before performing/reading the compositions). In every case, the method employed exploits a variety of forms of indeterminacy, thus assuring that the writing really will be "purposeless." In the extensive series of *Writings through* Finnegans Wake, for example, Cage has employed a number of different chance methods. In the initial *Writing through* Finnegans Wake, Cage writes "mesostics" through the text of *Finnegans Wake,* using the name 'James Joyce' as the guiding thread of his text. In his introduction Cage offers the following explanation of this technique:

> . . . mesostics (not acrostics: row down the middle, not down the edge). What makes a mesostic as far as I'm concerned is that the first letter of a word or name is on the first line and following it on

the first line the second letter of the word or name is *not* to be found. (The second letter is on the second line.)[38]

Using the mesostic technique, Cage constructs a series of 5-line stanzas which take the reader through the entire text of *Finnegans Wake*. While this technique appears rather mechanical, Cage admits that conscious choices need to be made concerning how many words are to be allowed in each line (the mesostic technique merely demanding that the next line's letter cannot appear in the previous line):

> There were choices to be made, decisions as to which words were to be kept, which omitted. It was a discipline similar to that of counterpoint in music with a *cantus firmus*. My tendency was towards more omission rather than less.[39]

Finally, punctuation is scattered over each page in accordance with *I Ching* operations. Thus, necessity combines with choice (both riddled with indeterminacy, of course) to produce the text.[40] Similar methods (with various additional restrictions) govern the generation of *Writing for the Second Time through* Finnegans Wake and *Writing for the Fourth Time through* Finnegans Wake (the third in the series has not, to my knowledge, appeared).[41]

In the case of the most recent of Cage's *Wake* texts, *Muoyce* (*Writing for the Fifth Time through* Finnegans Wake),[42] mesostics have given way to a much more complex set of chance operations involving a variety of *I Ching* decisions and resulting in a text which no longer bears any linear similarity to Joyce's text. A major departure from the earlier texts is that the chance operations are here used to determine (among other things) the spacing of "words," in such a way that the "integrity" of Joyce's words and thus of his syntax is no longer preserved.[43]

In *Themes and Variations* (published in 1982) Cage uses the mesostic technique not on a pre-existent text but on a list of one hundred and ten ideas,[44] derived from his own previous books and related in various ways to fifteen people of importance to Cage's life and work. The product of the interactions (all chance-determined) of the fifteen names (used to construct mesostics) and the one hundred and ten ideas is "a chance-determined renga-like mix" ([xiv]), which seeks to capture the sort of creative indeterminacy of the Japanese group-authored poetry called renga. Cage describes renga in the following passage from the Introduction to *Themes and Variations:*

> Traditionally renga is written by a group of poets finding themselves of an evening together and having nothing better to do. Successive lines are written by different poets. Each poet tries to make his line as distant in possible meanings from the preceding line as he can take it. This is no doubt an attempt to open the minds of the poets and listeners or readers to other relationships than those ordinarily perceived. . . . Thus an intentionally irrational poem can be written with liberating effect. This is called purposeful purposelessness. That renga is written by several poets conduces to its being free of the ego of any single one of them. ([xiii])

This passage is a clear illustration of the way Cage uses his chance operations to generate texts which exemplify the Mallarméan themes discussed earlier in this essay.

In a somewhat earlier text, "Empty Words" (first published in 1974–75), Cage uses the *Journal* of Thoreau as his source-text, and he uses *I Ching* chance operations to select appropriate elements from the *Journal,* but he treats Thoreau's text in radically different ways in each of the four parts of his own text. Thus Part 1 is a mix of phrases, words, syllables, and letters selected from Thoreau; in Part 2 phrases are omitted, while Part 3 omits words; finally, Part 4 omits everything but "letters and silences," offering a text in which "Languages [become] musics, musics [become] theatres; performances; metaphorphoses. . . ."[45] "Empty Words" Part 4 remains without question the most challenging of Cage's text-compositions: in the pursuit of pure writing, Cage has here gone utterly beyond all notions of syntax and meaning, while preserving in his text the materiality (literally, the material building-blocks) of Thoreau's text.[46]

This review of the techniques used by Cage in the construction of his text-compositions should at least suggest the wide variety of possibilities that exist for the generation of disseminating texts. It is Cage's special genius that he is regularly able to write such texts that both "open the minds of . . . readers to other relationships than those ordinarily perceived" and do this while delighting those same readers. In achieving this remarkable synthesis of "liberating effect" and delight,

Cage has much to teach those of us who might wish to write in a post-Mallarméan, post-Derridian age.[47]

NOTES

1. Most of the material concerning the personal relationship of Cage and Boulez is derived from the account given in Joan Peyser, *Boulez: Composer, Conductor, Enigma* (New York: Schirmer Books, 1976); see, in particular, 9–10, 60–62, 69–71, 81–86, and 129.

2. This is Cage's expression; see his description of this correspondence in Richard Kostelanetz, ed., *John Cage* (New York: Praeger Publishers, 1970), 17–18. A long excerpt from Boulez's side of this correspondence is now available in Pierre Boulez, *Orientations,* edited by Jean-Jacques Nattiez, translated by Martin Cooper (Cambridge, Mass.: Harvard University Press, 1986), 129–42.

3. John Cage (in conversation with Daniel Charles), *For the Birds* (Boston: Marion Boyars, 1981), 126; hereafter cited as *FB.*

4. On *Roaratorio,* see the extensive documentation (and cassette tape) included in John Cage, *Roaratorio: An Irish Circus on* Finnegans Wake (Königstein: Athenäum [Ton und Text], 1982); on Boulez's role in the realization of the work, see Cage's remarks on 159.

5. Cage's references to Mallarmé are found largely in his conversations with the French philosopher and critic, Daniel Charles, published as *For the Birds* (see, especially, 44–45, 123, and 180–81). It is also worthy of note that Cage frequently claims to have been influenced by Antonin Artaud (see, for example, *FB,* 165–66 and *John Cage,* 8–9 and 93) and René Char (*FB,* 48 and John Cage, *Silence: Lectures and Writings* [Middletown, Conn.: Wesleyan University Press, 1961], 36).

6. The translation here is that of Bradford Cook in *Mallarmé: Selected Prose Poems, Essays, and Letters,* translated and with an introduction by Bradford Cook (Baltimore: Johns Hopkins University Press, 1956), 93–94; hereafter cited as *SP.* Unless indicated otherwise, all translations from Mallarmé's prose will be those of Cook, usually cited in the text as the second of two page numbers (x/y), the first of which refers to the French version as printed in Stéphane Mallarmé, *Oeuvres complètes,* édition établie et annotée par Henri Mondor et G. Jean-Aubry (Paris: Gallimard [Bibliothèque de la Pléiade], 1945).

7. The translation of *Un Coup de Dés* is that of Keith Bosley in *Mallarmé: The Poems,* a bilingual edition translated with an introduction by Keith Bosley (Harmondsworth: Penguin Books, 1977); for this passage of the "Preface," see 255.

8. For a useful review of Boulez's music, see Paul Griffiths, *Boulez* (Oxford: Oxford University Press, 1978). I am indebted to Griffiths for most of my generalizations about Boulez's technique.

9. This article, as well as most of the others discussed in this paper, is

reprinted in Pierre Boulez, *Notes of an Apprenticeship,* texts collected and presented by Paule Thévenin, translated by Herbert Weinstock (New York: Alfred A. Knopf, 1968); hereafter cited in the text as *N.*

10. Compare Boulez's use of "uterine" (*N,* 18).

11. See Jacques Schérer, *Le "Livre" de Mallarmé (Premières recherches sur des documents inédits)* (Paris: Gallimard, 1957). Schérer's book includes the first transcription of the entirety of Mallarmé's manuscript notes, references to which will be cited in the text by leaf number. For perhaps the most extraordinary attempt to relate these notes to serial technique, see Hans Rudolf Zeller, "Mallarmé and Serialist Thought," translated by Margaret Shenfield, *Die Reihe* 6 (1960/1964): 5–32.

12. For the comments of Jacobs and Tudor, see Peyser, *Boulez,* 128; for Bradshaw, see 162.

13. This demand grows, once again, out of reflections on Mallarmé (and Joyce); see *N,* 25.

14. For a marvelous realization of this concept of a "domain," compare Boulez's composition for clarinet and twenty-one instruments in six groups, *Domaines* (composed between 1961 and 1969).

15. Pierre Boulez, "'Sonate, que me veux-tu?'" translated by David Noakes and Paul Jacobs, *Perspectives of New Music* 1, no. 2 (Spring 1963): 32–44; hereafter cited in the text as "Sonate." See, in particular, Boulez's emphasis on the necessity of "connecting" distinct strophes of the fourth *formant* (42), on the "guiding principle" of the fifth *formant* (43), and on "the general conception governing these five *formants*" (43), emphases which achieve their culmination in the following passage: "Obviously, I did not find this all-encompassing organization all at once; little by little, the ideas fell into order, took their place around the governing idea, which was to conceive the work as a moving, expanding universe" (44).

16. Pierre Boulez, *Par volonté et par hasard,* entretiens avec Célestin Deliège (Paris: Éditions du Seuil, 1975), 107. The translation here is that found in Pierre Boulez, *Conversations with Célestin Deliège,* translated by Robert Wangermee (London: Eulenburg, 1976).

17. Judy Kravis, *The Prose of Mallarmé: The Evolution of a Literary Language* (Cambridge: Cambridge University Press, 1976), 139–47.

18. On this notion of the elimination of the composer's ego, compare also *FB,* 78 and 142. Compare also Cage's description of his *Music of Changes* as "an object more inhuman than human, since chance operations brought it into being" in *Silence,* 36. Boulez too suggests that ". . . a profound motive for the work I have tried to describe . . . would be the search for such *'anonymity'*" ("Sonate," 44).

19. Compare Cage's implicit critique of Boulezian compositional techniques as bringing musical parameters into relationships which dictate that the composition is an object which "must be viewed dualistically," that is, as an object distinct from its auditors; see *Silence,* 38.

20. Later on, Cage insists that the music of Stockhausen is not only drama

but tragedy: "... it's tragedy as there must be determinacy or indeterminacy, one or the other" (*FB,* 199).

21. On Cage's "organization" of the first happening at Black Mountain College in 1952, with much reference to Artaud, see *FB,* 164–66.

22. *Silence,* 12. There is, of course, something of a paradox in Cage's calling for art to "resemble" nature, while denying that the product of chance operations is a "physical object." This paradox will be treated in some detail below, in conjunction with Derrida's treatment of *mimêsis* in Mallarmé.

23. Compare *SP,* 366/40–41, discussed above, on the poem as flaming out "like some glittering swath of fire sweeping over precious stones."

24. Kravis, *The Prose of Mallarmé,* 135–54, offers a particularly rich account of Mallarmé's reflections on the theater.

25. Jacques Derrida, "La double séance," in Derrida, *La dissémination* (Paris: Éditions du Seuil, 1972), 199–317. The version quoted here is that in Jacques Derrida, *Dissemination,* translated with an introduction and additional notes by Barbara Johnson (Chicago: University of Chicago Press, 1981), 173–285. References to this essay hereafter will be cited in the text, preceded by the abbreviation, *"D,"* and will include both the page number of the French version and that of the English version (for example, *D,* 317/285).

26. Derrida puts a great deal of emphasis on Mallarmé's letter to Maurice Guillemot, in which he claims that "... I am profoundly and scrupulously a syntaxer ..." (*D,* 206/180).

27. Barbara Johnson's careful translation of "Mimique" is included in Stéphane Mallarmé, *Selected Poetry and Prose,* edited by Mary Ann Caws (New York: New Directions, 1982), 69.

28. On this attempt to reconcile chance and necessity, see *D,* 309–10/277.

29. Derrida himself notes the importance of this fragment; see *D,* 303/271.

30. Compare Derrida's development of the notion of the *hymen* throughout "The Double Session."

31. For Cage's most recent evocation of this notion, see John Cage, *Themes and Variations* (Barrytown, N.Y.: Station Hill Press, 1982), [viii].

32. See *FB,* 79, discussed in the first section of this essay, as well as *Silence,* 38.

33. Compare also *FB,* 104 and 131.

34. It is in this fashion that the apparent paradox in *Silence,* 12, can be resolved: the work of art can resemble nature ("in her manner of operation") without in any way being itself a determinate physical object.

35. The pioneering philosophical work on Derrida in English is Richard Rorty, *Philosophy and the Mirror of Nature* (Princeton: Princeton University Press, 1979). Important recent works include Irene E. Harvey, *Derrida and the Economy of Difference* (Bloomington: Indiana University Press, 1986), and Rodolphe Gasché, *The Tain of the Mirror: Derrida and the Philosophy of Reflection* (Cambridge, Mass.: Harvard University Press, 1986).

36. *Themes and Variations,* [xii]. This basic characterization of Cage's project is also found in John Cage, *X: Writings '79–'82* (Middletown, Conn.: Wesleyan

University Press, 1983), x and 163. For a useful account of his turn to text composition, see *FB,* 113–15.

37. The Zen Buddhist notion of "purposeful purposelessness" is clearly involved here as well; see *FB,* 168.

38. John Cage, *Writing through* Finnegans Wake (Tulsa: University of Tulsa Monograph Series, 1978), [iv]. This introduction provides much of the text for the introduction to *Writing for the Second Time through* Finnegans Wake, which appears in John Cage, *Empty Words: Writings '73–'78* (Middletown, Conn.: Wesleyan University Press, 1979), 133–36.

39. *Writing through* Finnegans Wake, [v].

40. Similar methods were explored by Jackson Mac Low beginning about 1960 in the poems eventually published in Jackson Mac Low, *Stanzas for Iris Lezak* (Barton, Vermont: Something Else Press, 1972); for Mac Low's account of his methods, see 399–411. Cage himself has high praise for Mac Low's work; see *X,* 53, as well as his dust-jacket comment on Mac Low's *Stanzas.* It is worth adding that Mac Low was for a couple of years (between 1958 and 1960) an invitee in Cage's class at the New School for Social Research in New York; see *John Cage,* 39, 119, and 123.

41. These texts appear, respectively, in *Empty Words,* 133–76, and in *X,* 1–49. For intriguing comments on Cage's performance of one of the *Writings,* see Michel Benamou and Charles Carmello, eds., *Performance in Postmodern Culture* (Madison, Wis.: Coda Press, 1977), 17 n. 5, and 63–65.

42. This text appears in *X,* 173–87.

43. For a revealing account of the technique employed here, see John Cage and Richard Kostelanetz, "Talking about *Writings through* Finnegans Wake," *TriQuarterly* 54 (Spring 1982): 208–16.

44. For this list, see *Themes and Variations,* [viii–xii].

45. *Empty Words,* 33 and 65.

46. It is perhaps not surprising to learn that in Cage's current text project, a variety of the methods used in his earlier work are being combined; nor is it surprising to learn that he is now using a personal computer to help in the construction of mesostics. (We see here a contemporary means by which the Mallarméan death or elimination of the author can be achieved.) In a letter to the author, dated 13 February 1985, Cage writes: "I am currently engaged (as far as texts go) in making a celebration of the life and work of Erik Satie. It is taking the form of 'presents' for him from me and others. I am writing all of them but some are writings through the texts of others and others are 'kus' (from Haiku) in relation to texts in PC memory. I am able with a special program to list and locate all the words in a text that satisfy a mesostic rule (100% or 50%: non-repetition of both letters of a name or permission to use the first one after its mesostic appearance) and then submit these lists to the *I Ching.* The result is a poem that comes from all over a text rather than from it linearly, first beginning then middle then [end]. And others are Renga (like *Themes and Variations*)."

47. This essay owes much to John Cage, Jackson Mac Low, William Matheson, Emma Kafalenos, and Roland Jordan.

John Cage as a *Hörspielmacher* (1989)

Richard Kostelanetz

> Poets should emphatically be brought into the wireless studio, for it is much more conceivable that they should be able to adapt a verbal work of art to the limits of the world of space, sound and music. The film demands the visual artist who has also a feeling for words; the wireless on the other hand needs a master of words who has also a feeling for modes of expression appropriate to the sensuous world.
>
> —Rudolf Arnheim, *Radio: An Art of Sound* (1936)

Few American artists realize the ideal of true polyartistry as completely as John Cage, who has not only changed the progress of music but, by my count, has made substantial contributions to our literature, theater and perhaps visual art, extending in all domains his radical esthetic preference for nonfocused, nonhierarchic, uninflected structuring. Thus, it is scarcely surprising that late in the seventh decade of his productive life he began occupying yet another artistic terrain, a terrain so unfashionable that, its familiarity notwithstanding, it has no critics and few rewards—radio.

Given the low status of Art in American radio, it is no surprise that Cage has done most of this work in Europe, initially for Westdeutscher Rundfunk in Cologne. These radio works are produced not by WDR's music department, which nonetheless airs transcriptions of Cage's music, but by *Hörspiel,* which translates literally as "ear-play" and is, in the German radio bureaucracies, a production department distinct from literature and feature.

In Germany, *Hörspiel* has traditionally meant radio plays, which were customarily not soap operas or comedies (familiar to American radio), but something else—poetic texts, indefinite enough to stimulate the listener's imagination, whose words are read by well-cultivated voices, recorded in a studio, abetted by minimal sound effects. In American radio, the closest analogue was Archibald MacLeish's *Fall of the City*

(1938); perhaps the most famous English-language radio play of this kind is Dylan Thomas's *Under Milk Wood* (1953). Since *Hörspiel* as a word is far more graceful and encompassing than any English equivalent, I will henceforth use it, in an anglicized spelling, to characterize American work.

Two cultural products that Germans value far more than we are opera and horspiel. For the latter, there are annual prizes, the most prestigious being the *Hörspielpreis des Kriegsblinden.* Horspiels are also collected into textbooks that are taught in the universities and gymnasiums. Anthologies and critical books are frequently published; current critical issues are discussed at annual conferences. There is even a prodigious encyclopedia, now outdated, with the unfortunate title of *Hörspielführer.* Twice a year the *Hörspiel* department of Westdeutscher Rundfunk issues a book-length catalog of forthcoming productions, most of which are displayed solo on a full 8″ by 8″ page. In each of these WDR books can be found more first-rank Radio Art, some of it even by native-born Americans, than has ever been produced here. Showing a recent volume to an American radio professional is to watch him faint dead away.

Within the past two decades, a producer on WDR's permanent staff, Klaus Schöning, developed a distinct alternative to traditional German horspiel. Interested in sound as well as in words, he turned first to the great European experimental poets, such as Ernst Jandl and Franz Mon, Gerhard Rühm and Ferdinand Kriwet, as well as the composers Mauricio Kagel and, later, Clarence Barlow—in Rudolph Arnheim's phrases, masters of words with a sensitivity to aural expression. Schöning called this more acoustic work *Neue Hörspiel,* and in his pioneering anthology of that title (1969) all those *Hörspielmachers* (except Barlow, who is younger) are represented. Where radio plays have previously defined an intermedium between literature and theater, Schöning gravitated to points between literature and music. Indicatively, the surest measure of his success, in his colleagues' eyes, is not how many listeners he has but how many *Hörspiel* prizes his artists have won.

Even though Schöning did not enter Cage's life until 1978, the latter had a long creative interest in radio and its principal storage medium (audiotape). His *Imaginary Landscape No. 1* (1939) was written, to quote his publisher's catalog (C. F. Peters, 1962), for "two variable-speed phono-turntables, frequency readings, muted piano and cymbal; to be performed as a recording or broadcast." Two details perhaps unfamiliar to us now are that these "frequency records" had either sustained tones or sliding tones that were, supposedly, scientifically generated and, then, that the speeds of those old-time record turntables could be varied by hand. In Cage's mind, when he wrote this piece, were certain unprecedented capabilities of the new radio studios. A few years later, Cage was commissioned to produce "music" for Kenneth Patchen's radio play, *The City Wears a Slouch Hat*; and what he wanted to do here likewise presaged future work: "Take the sounds out of the play, and make the music out of those sounds." Several years after that, he premiered *Imaginary Landscape No. 4* (1951) for twelve radios and twenty-four performers, one manning the volume control of each machine and another changing the stations, in response to Cage's scored instructions. *WBAI* (1960), named after New York's Pacifica station, extends a principle established two decades before and is described as "a score for the operation of machines [at the radio station]. Durations are graphed in space, their length in time being determined by the performer."

The second strand behind Cage's recent radio art was his early interest in audiotape, which is so familiar to us now that we tend to forget it became commonly available only after World War II. Prior to that, sound was recorded on continuous wire that, while it could be cut, could not be spliced easily. That is, its parts could not be reassembled without making thunderous telltale sounds. Precisely because acoustic tape, by contrast, could be spliced gracefully, sounds separately recorded could be fused without distracting interruptions.

In an interview reprinted in my *Conversing with Cage* (161), Cage remembers that when the French composer Pierre Schaeffer first introduced him to audiotape in 1948, he rejected its possibilities; but within a few years, he was working on *Williams Mix* (1953), which I consider the principal neglected masterpiece in the Cage canon. Here sounds were gathered on tape from a universe of sources, and these tapes were cut into small pieces, some much shorter than audiotape is wide, and then spliced together into an aural pastiche that is continually leaping, with unprecedented shifts, from one kind of sound (and one acoustic space) to another. To complicate the audio experience yet further, Cage required that eight tapes be made, and then that in live concerts any or all of them could be played simultaneously. On the only recorded performance of this work (from the twenty-five-year retrospective concert of 1958), all eight taped "voices" are heard.

Cage's first work for Schöning began with the latter's invitation to read aloud one of his recent *Writings through* Finnegans Wake. These are a series of Cagean texts in which he extracts sequentially certain words from Joyce's classic and then sets them on mesostic axes composed of the name of James Joyce. (If the vertical axis of an acrostic is flush left, a *mesostic* has its axis in the middle.) In *Writing for the Second Time through* Finnegans Wake, which he chose to read for WDR, the opening is:

wroth with twone nathandJoe
A
Malt
jhEm
Shen

pftJschute
sOlid man
that the humptYhillhead of humself
is at the knoCk out
in theE park

Asked to add a "musical background" to this declamation, Cage decided to gather sounds recorded in every geographic place mentioned in Joyce's text. For guidance, he consulted Louis Mink's recent *A* Finnegans Wake *Gazetteer.* By birth a prodigious correspondent, Cage wrote friends around the world and asked Schöning to do likewise; but since most of Joyce's places were in Ireland, he decided to spend a whole month there himself, recording not only places but native musics. This strategy recalls his proposal for the Kenneth Patchen radio play—to extract the acoustic references from the text itself and to compose music from those worldly sounds. All these field recordings were then gathered at IRCAM in Paris, where Cage spent a month (and, by design, only a month) assembling them by chance operations onto sixteen-track tape machines, making dense mixes, at once cacophonous and euphonious, that, while they may vary in detail, are roughly similar in quality (and quantity) for the entire duration.

Whereas some Cage pieces have contained much less sound than music used to have, others have contained much more; for Cage has been at different times a prophet of both minimalism and abundance. This Joycean radio piece, entitled *Roaratorio* (1979), falls securely into the second tradition. The continuous bass is the sound of Cage himself reading. On top of that is an abundant mix of sounds reminiscent of *Williams Mix* (as Cage now realized on multitrack tape the effect of playing several monophonic tapes simultaneously); but whereas nothing in that earlier piece has a sustained presence, in this new one the sounds of Irish music tend to stand out from the mass. In that last respect, *Roaratorio* structurally resembles *HPSCHD* (1969), which has always stood for me as the earlier masterpiece of Cagean abundance. In that earlier work, beneath the continuous microtonal din is heard the sound of seven harpsichords, playing selections from Mozart to the present; and in the single available recording (Nonesuch, 1969), these harpsichords tend to stand out from the mix to the same degree that Irish music does in the newer piece. In one sense, this subtle predominance compromises Cage's aleatory methods; yet in both pieces, it also reveals compositional decisions about components that were made well before the aleatory methods were exercised.

Though Cage produced for WDR a definitive two-track stereophonic mix-down of his gatherings (and then let a cassette of this accompany Schöning's bilingual book about *Roaratorio* [Königstein, Ts: Athenäum, 1982]), he intended from the beginning that this work exist in various forms, in accord with his esthetic biases. "It can be played with all the tracks separately," he told me (for an interview published in *Musical Quarterly* 72, no. 2 [1986]), "or in various combinations." That is to say that the many tracks of *Roaratorio* can be played as the tapes of *Williams Mix* were, with its voices proceeding independently of one another. From the original tape he can also remove his own reading of his Joycean text and the principal Irish musicians and then present those elements live. It is in this last format that *Roaratorio* has accompanied Merce Cunningham's live choreography.

His next major piece for WDR-Horspiel, *Ein Alphabet* (1982), also began with a text that (unlike before) was translated into German. Most of "James Joyce, Erik Satie, Marcel Duchamp: An Alphabet" consists of mesostics that Cage wrote out of his own head on the names of these three heroes, all of whom, in Cage's curious judgment, have made works that "resisted the march of understanding and so are as fresh now as when they first were made." Interspersed among the mesostics are long passages from the writings of each of these men. (The whole original English text appears, along with Cage's spiky preface, in his last collection of writings, *X* [Wesleyan University Press,

1983]). Even though I share Cage's overwhelming admiration for the *Wake,* I have come to prefer, as poetry to be read, those mesostics that are, by contrast, written wholly out of his own head.

The WDR production honors the conventions of traditional radio theater in that certain roles were assigned to various performers—the French musicologist Daniel Charles reading Satie (in inept German), the American artist George Brecht representing Duchamp (in better German), Cage himself reading Joyce (in the original neologistic superEnglish). As the narrative passes through various scenes, their settings are occasionally reinforced with sound effects that tend to be very abrupt, usually sketching a scene suggestively (rather than filling it in). As other figures are included, their voices are represented by yet other performers speaking German—Dick Higgins as Robert Rauschenberg, Christian Wolff as Henry David Thoreau, Buckminster Fuller as himself, and so on.

Ein Alphabet reflects the arrival of audiotape in that it was composed from many parts that were separately recorded (in fact, on two continents, at different times). Insofar as I can understand German, I think the work very good, filled with interesting departures within the tradition of radio plays, as well as suggestive moves that others can adopt (not the least of which is the imaginary conversation among historic figures who did not know one another). On the other hand, Cage himself tends to dislike all the leaps from scene to scene. "All those scenes," he recently told me, "have beginnings and ends. That's what annoys me." In my interpretation, this caveat means that *Ein Alphabet* lacks the pure uninflected, nonclimactic structure that, in all media, has been the signature of Cage's work.

Muoyce (1983) is a more familiar Cagean performance—essentially a solo reading of his *Writing for the Fifth Time through* Finnegans Wake; but to complicate the largely uninflected declamation, Cage decided to use a multitrack audiotape device he had used before (mostly in live performance). The first of the piece's four parts has him whispering the same text simultaneously four times all the way through, in a nonsynchronous chorus; the second part is a self-trio; the third part, a duet; the fourth (and shortest) part, a solo. He interrupts his whispering for full-voiced speaking only when the original text had italics. Here, as well as in the previous work that resembles it, "Empty Words" (1974–75), I have personally come to find this minimalism trivial. Always true to his principles, Cage says, "I find this one easier [than

Ein Alphabet]. What makes this easy for me is that the quiet sober mind is assumed and is not disturbed, even by the lightning imitations which come though the loud interrupting sounds, because they don't really interrupt. Once they are gone, the whispering continues."

HMCIEX (or HCE-mix, with its letters alternating) was commissioned in 1984 by both WDR and International Composers in Los Angeles, which benefited from the Olympics fallout; and even though it is a dense mix, it is also a simple piece (that, contrary to Cage's esthetics, does not resist understanding). In honor of the Olympics, it is an international pastiche of folk songs (and in that respect reminiscent of Karlheinz Stockhausen's similarly ecumenical *Hymnen* [1979]; but whereas Stockhausen favored western sources, Cage draws more upon the Third World. One quality that separates *HMCIEX* from Cage's earlier mixes is that its sources are longer, and thus more often identifiable upon first hearing. Another aspect is problematic in that, given such long excerpts, the sound often falls into a regular beat that is utterly contrary to Cage's esthetics. Compared to *Roaratorio, HMCIEX* is a slighter work, charming nonetheless.

Cage has done several other pieces for WDR. Some have been largely unadorned transcriptions of his recitals of his poetic texts, including *Themes and Variations* and parts of *Diary* (a late-1960s poem that remains a favorite of mine); one of them, *Mirage Verbal* (1989), a writing through the notes of Marcel Duchamp, was in French, which he reads remarkably well. The most distinguished recent radio composition, in my opinion, is *Writing through the Essay "On the Duty of Civil Disobedience" (Thoreau),* which was first broadcast in 1988. This rather abundant work began as a mesostic text based upon the vertical axis of an Erik Satie title—"Messe des Pauvres." Against this constraining structure Cage and his assistant Andrew Culver entered into the computer as source material the text of the classic Thoreau essay. Out came the first available words, horizontally arrayed, whose letters fit into the vertical axis. As Culver wrote in a personal letter, the computer "was allowed to cycle back to the top of the source text until [without duplication] a full search string was no longer findable in a single pass. It ground to a halt at 18 writings through [passes through the text]; the latter ones are, of course, shorter." Read aloud at normal pacing, the initial section ran twenty-one minutes; the last only thirty-six seconds.

Invited to work at the Center for Computer Music at Brooklyn College, with the assistance of Charles Dodge, Frances White, Victor

Frieberg, Paul Zinmann, and Ken Worthy, Cage asked that all eighteen sections be 16′ 47″ long. Whereas an elongated text subjected to pre-computer tape manipulation would drop radically in pitch, the computer technique of linear predictive coding, first developed in Dodge's *Speech Songs* (1973), allows both vocal pitch and duration to be identical. However, since the same voice at a single pitch would be monotonous, Cage decided to make eighteen more readings, each 14′ 04″ in duration, where his vocal pitches would be varied. The last compositional step involved a random mix of all thirty-six sources to determine which ones would enter the final mix.

This tape was initially played continuously, with each track emerging from a different loudspeaker, in a maximal acoustic environment prepared for a church in Kassel, West Germany, on the occasion of the international Documenta exhibition in 1987. For the WDR broadcast, Schöning recorded this installation with the *Kunstkopf* stereo microphone whose configuration resembles human ears. That accounts for why the WDR version is best heard through earphones. What I liked in the original tape is a unique quality that comes from the multiple enrichment of a single voice. By recording the environmental circumstance, rather than merely playing the original Brooklyn tapes, WDR-Horspiel has further enhanced the quality of *Writing through the Essay "On the Duty of Civil Disobedience."*

What Cage has done in his radio art is to define other possibilities for presenting recorded sound, and thus other ways of making records. When Cage has been criticized for releasing records that were "not as good" as live performances of his work, the reply was that, aside from *Williams Mix,* Cage's music has not been written for tape. Now, given the demands of modern radio transmission, he is composing for tape and exploiting its unique capabilities, to make works that are true both to tape and to his esthetics; and, in my opinion, he has produced, at least in *Roaratorio* and the *Writing through Thoreau,* a transcription as good as any of his earlier records.

In this last respect, Cage discovered in radio a truth that another adventurous North American musician also made sometime before him—the Canadian pianist Glenn Gould. Frustrated as a composer, unwilling to do live performances, Gould made in Toronto a series of radio features, scarcely heard here, that represent to my mind the best radio art ever produced in North America; for with multitrack audiotape, Gould could mix speech with speech, speech with music, and music with music, not only in ways that, given his materials, would be impossible in live performance but in fugal arrangements that would also be beautiful. In other words, invitations from radio stations forced both these verbal musicians to compose for tape as they had not composed before, producing valuable work that, if not for these radio invitations, probably would not otherwise have happened. One truth that strikes me from the success of these two artists is that, even in performance arts, it is best to work as writers and painters have traditionally worked—with no more than one assistant.

The principal reason this essay has been so introductory is that it talks about works not commonly available. Whereas *Williams Mix* is included on George Avakian's three-record memento of the 1958 25th Anniversary Concert, *Roaratorio* is found only in a thoroughly bilingual box by the same title, mentioned before, that was published in Germany. In this box are a cassette copy of the work, prefaced by Cage reading part of the text alone, and succeeded by a short interview in English with Schöning; a book about the work (that includes the text of a longer interview with Schöning); and a fold-out score that hides as much as it reveals. Since *HMCIEX* was co-commissioned by a Los Angeles nonprofit outfit, it has been broadcast on our public radio stations. *Ein Alphabet* has never been aired here (and probably won't be, given our bias against broadcasting anything in foreign languages, other than operas); nor at last count has *Writing through the Essay "On Civil Disobedience" (Thoreau).* In truth, most of us can scarcely begin to grasp Cage's achievement as a *hörspielmacher* until all of his radio art is more conveniently available.

Roaratorio Appraisiated (1983)

William Brooks

John Cage's *Roaratorio: An Irish Circus on* Finnegans Wake, a *Hörspiel* commissioned by Westdeutscher Rundfunk, produced at IRCAM, and awarded the Karl-Sczucka-Prize for 1979, is now available in an enticing "sound and text" package from Athenäum containing a 185-page book of commentary, a yard-square poster, and a 90-minute audio cassette. As often happens in Cage's work, the documentation threatens to swamp the music; the cassette seems rather small, plastic, and inconsequential in the context of all those words. But the music is beautiful; though superficially resembling earlier works, its character is its own.

Roaratorio is Cage's most recent venture into what I call his "encyclopedias." Like *Williams Mix, HPSCHD,* and other predecessors, *Roaratorio* was assembled from an immense sound-catalog, in this case one derived from two sources: a list of all the sounds described in *Finnegans Wake,* and a list of the places named in the book (supplied by the late Louis O. Mink). Into *Roaratorio,* then, went 1,210 Joycean sounds, grouped into categories that range from "musical instruments" to "farts," and 1,083 other recordings made in locations Joyce mentions (including the planet Neptune, I believe, courtesy of NASA). This vast array was regulated by and mixed with an hour-long reading by Cage of his own *Writing for the Second Time through* Finnegans Wake, the words of which were extracted from Joyce's book without altering their order, as one might extract landmarks from a journey. Cage used this text as a kind of ruler; each of the sounds he had cataloged was inserted at a time that corresponded approximately to the location in which it was mentioned in the book. A final overlay consisted of 32 pieces of traditional Irish music performed by six musicians and distributed through the work by chance operations.

But, although *Roaratorio* is kin to earlier works, it is a cousin, not a twin. *HPSCHD,* for example, has always struck me as festive, exhilarating, almost giddy; it seems to be a piece about dance, or at least about movement, and encourages conversation and activity. *Roaratorio,* on the other hand, is more contemplative, coupling a special kind of innocent discovery with a reflective, almost nostalgic, awareness of loss. It seems to be concerned, fundamentally, with *narrative* in the broadest, Joycean sense—a tale without beginning or end, whose protagonist is all humanity. Much of *Roaratorio*'s atmosphere is due to Cage's entrancing reading, which trails through the soundscape like a voice borne by wind, not quite intelligible. Cage reads in a kind of *Sprechstimme,* but one which recalls Partch rather than Schoenberg, the voice intoning rather than expressing. Or perhaps the effect is Oriental, like a shadow-puppet play in which a richly textured overlay illustrates and sometimes obscures a half-chanted epic in a foreign tongue. In any case, the voice *is* central, despite the balances; even when only a murmur, it remains the poetry for which all else is a setting.

But the setting, too, contributes to *Roaratorio*'s distinctive atmosphere. Of the 1,210 sound events used, 371 (31 percent) involve the human voice (laughing, crying, singing, shouting). Another 27 percent are of natural origin (animals, birds, water, thunder); 30 percent have to do with music. Six percent involve bells; another 6 percent, guns or explosions. Of the locations from which recordings were collected, a few are urban (Paris, London); most, however, are rural, often Irish (Cage spent a month traveling in Ireland, gathering material). Hence the sounds from the "geographic" catalog harmonize well with the sounds explicitly mentioned by Joyce; in particular, electronically processed sound is wholly absent, and mechanical or technological sources are few.

The soundscape of *Roaratorio,* then, is pastoral, unsullied, spacious. Its inhabitants—its voices—evoke rather than command; freed from syntax, they contribute to what Cage has called the "demilitarization of language." *Roaratorio*'s world is not our own, but Anna Livia's; it is from the nineteenth century, not the present. No, not even that; rather than of the nineteenth century, this soundscape is of what that century might have become. It is a soundscape for Thoreau, for Joyce, for Charles Ives: unreal, dearly loved, joyfully affirmed, but illuminated by the certainty of loss, the recognition that this place cannot be, never was, before us.

Does this mean, then, that Cage himself grows autumnal, has turned toward the past and away from the future? I think not; though Cage shares with Thoreau and Joyce and Ives their visionary idealism, he has always tempered this with an almost ruthless practicality. As he continues to remind us, his father was an inventor; Cage has, above all, a remarkable ability to devise workable schemes for bringing impossible, utopian ideas into reality. *Roaratorio* itself started as such an idea; in this case the compromise (or perhaps insight) entailed the recognition that completeness was impossible: the work was "finished" when the time available to make it ended.

What *Roaratorio*'s evocative soundscape does demonstrate is Cage's continuing sensitivity to text. Cage is, in a very important sense, one of the major song-writers of the twentieth century—not because of early pieces like *The Wonderful Widow of Eighteen Springs,* lovely though they are, nor even because of recent works like the *Song Books* and the *Hymns and Variations,* but rather because his extended "settings" of Thoreau (in *Empty Words*) and Joyce (in *Roaratorio*), as well as his performances of his own texts (like *Mesostics*), serve well the fundamental purpose of song-writing: to marry text and *con*text in such a way that each transforms, rather than enhances, the other.

When Cage named *Roaratorio,* he thought he had invented a Joyce-like title; only later did he find he had subconsciously recalled a fragment from *Finnegans Wake* itself. Miraculously, as always, the fragment not only describes the piece but includes listeners, like ourselves, who "with their priggish mouths all open for the larger appraisiation of this longawaited Messiagh of roaratorios, were only halfpast atsweeeep. . . ." Though "halfpast atsweeeep" we may well be, still trying to "wake up to the very life we're living," and though Cage often seems more leprechaun than "Messiagh," still *my* priggish mouth, for one, will remain all open, longawaiting what next he may serve us.

Freeman Etudes (1991)

Paul Zukofsky and John Cage

When Paul Zukofsky in 1975 asked me to write a work for the violin comparable to the Etudes Australes for piano which I had just finished, a work derived from star maps of the southern sky, using relatively traditional notation, I agreed providing he would answer all my questions. I do not play the violin. And I wanted to subject as many of its possibilities as I could envisage to chance operations to bring about a music suitable for an extraordinary virtuoso, and at the same time a music which I had not heard before. I wanted to move toward the impossible in order to show that the impossible is possible. This is relevant, it seems to me, to the present world situation. In preparation for the Etudes, Zukofsky and I worked closely together to make the violin version of Cheap Imitation. After telling the story of that collaboration in an article entitled "John Cage's Recent Violin Music" (A John Cage Reader, C. F. Peters; originally published in TriQuarterly Magazine, spring 1982), Zukofsky continues with reference to the Etudes named the *Freeman Etudes* in honor of the lovely and generous woman who commissioned them:

Using star maps (as in the *Etudes Australes*) and superimposed transparent paper, John placed each event in a continuum of time after determining the respective density of each etude. I had agreed that a space = time notation would be acceptable although it presented perceptual problems. We solved these by running two time lines under each staff. The lower of these lines supported a series of tactae which divided each line into seven equal segments. Each segment was eventually assigned a nominal value of three seconds—therefore, each line equaled twenty-one seconds. Above this set of "bar-line" tactae was a

Words in italics by John Cage, Roman by Paul Zukofsky.

second line with tactae indicating the exact position of each event. Since the events were placed proportionately on the staff, this may seem redundant; nevertheless, it was quite useful since the perceived spacing between events (as opposed to tactae) is highly dependent upon their nature and procession.

Having decided the temporal occurrences, general classifications of détaché v. legato were specified for each event; single "pitch-classes" were assigned each event, and octave placements were determined. "Stringing" was then decided, and the question of whether these events were to be single notes or the basis of aggregates (intervals or chords of two to four notes each) was answered.

The pitches of all aggregates were determined by successive pitch-range restrictions which depended to a large degree on the order of string-choice. Aggregates were constructed over a series of phone calls in which John might begin by saying: "This is going to be a four-note aggregate. The first note occurs on the third string and it's an 'A-natural' just above four ledger lines above the staff. What can you play on the first string (at the same time)?"

Since any of four fingers could stop the "A" natural on the third string, the possibilities on another string (in this case the first) usually were large and I would give John an available range. There would be as many questions as there were aggregates to solve. Aggregates of more than two notes would require follow-up calls—i.e., John might say, "The four-note aggregate which started with 'A' on the third string, now has (on the first string) a 'D natural' one note above the highest note of the piano (a note chosen from within the range I had given previously). The next note (to be decided) occurs on the fourth string. What can you play?"

Since the hand was now anchored with two pitches, the possibilities on the fourth string were more limited. Once again I would give John a range—sometimes large, sometimes very small and finally (in the case of four-note aggregates only) John would call back again saying that the four-note aggregate now consisted of the following pitches on the third, first, and fourth strings, and asking what I could still play on the second. As the work progressed, a catalog of these aggregates and aggregate-ranges began to exist. We hope to eventually publish the catalog, as it provides a fairly comprehensive guide to chordal possibilities on the violin.

Following aggregates, timbres, note repetitions, and microtones were chance-determined for all events. The timbres category consisted of normal, sul tasto, sul ponticello, harmonics and pizzicato. The note repetitions category consisted of successive marteles, ricochet, spiccato, tremolo, vibrato, and beating. Microtones utilized the standard American notation for quarter tones, i.e. upward or downward pointing arrowheads attached to normal accidentals, but were not to be thought of as quarter tones (although in actuality some of them may be quarter tones). As John says, "When the apple is rotten, cutting it in half does not help." Rather, these microtones are pitches belonging to that large perceptual space where a pitch still maintains its name (i.e. a lowered C natural which is not so low that it will be heard as a sharp B natural).

Once having set this golem in motion *Though the notation is determinate (Tell me, Zukofsky said, exactly what to do; I am like a surgeon; I will make the operation), the use of chance operatons is not as an aid in the making of something I had in mind; rather, a utility to let sounds arise from their own centers freed from my intentions. I just listen. For this reason, also, the use of star maps; to aid in the finding of a music I do not have in mind. Therefore I question the use of the word golem.*[1] We discovered that while every event was in and of itself completely playable, a quick succession of events was something else again, and in many instances was quite unplayable due to the constraints of time. Obviously something had to give, but what? Should time be expanded, and if so, expanded consistently throughout the whole piece, or just for the difficult section? Should stringing be changed, or timbre substitutions be made using harmonics, or should one consider deleting certain pitches? This was quite problematic because in essence we were stating a hierarchy of importance among time, stringing, timbre, and pitch.

John was extremely reluctant to change anything, and I kept insisting that certain things were impossible as they stood. The example of Merce Cunningham finally brought the two of us back together. In his use of chance to create dance, Merce had in many instances derived results that were physically impossible, and, as such, demanded compromise. We had essentially choreographed a ballet of the arms, and chance had given us some results that were physically impossible—therefore, we too had to compromise. The question then became: should the

1. Those readers interested in further discussion of golems may refer to Norbert Wiener's *God and Golem, Inc.* (MIT Press), as that is what I had in mind at the time (PZ).

compromises be rigid and final, or constrained but allowing of evolution? I was most reluctant to create an absolutely final version since, as every violinist is aware, the fingerings and bowings that one uses throughout one's life evolve constantly as the mind and body change.

We finally agreed that the golem would operate, would produce results (some of which, because of the constraints of time, would be manifestly impossible) and that the individual violinist, when it became absolutely necessary, would make such changes as he or she saw fit, preserving the original and its intent to the greatest possible extent.

Since I have only learnt the first eight *Etudes,* I cannot say what the ultimate tempo of all the *Etudes* will be. It would be good to keep the same tempo for all thirty-two, but that may prove impossible. Small tempo deviations or rubati are of course acceptable, but a constant change of the basic tempo to accommodate difficult passages must be avoided at all costs; otherwise, one has the impression of everything happening at the same rate—all very easygoing and without contrast.

The *Etudes* are both fascinating and frustrating for many reasons. They are the most difficult music I have ever played, yet they are also extremely violinistic. They have endless phrasal possibilities, none of which were intentioned in the creation. Some of the *Etudes* are so complex that we may have to synthesize them, but the challenge of playing them live may be too great.

The Freeman Etudes *XVII–XXXII are still in process. They are not only difficult to play; they are difficult to write. Work on them has been interrupted by other projects, works for orchestra, for the theater, radio, etc. One of these was the Etudes Boreales for 'Cello (1978). These are four and they differ from the violin pieces by letting the chance operations also change the range within which the compositional process operates even within a single etude. The "Freeman Etudes," on the other hand, use the full range of the violin at all times.*

Europe's Opera: Notes on John Cage's *Europeras 1 and 2* (1987)

Heinz-Klaus Metzger

> . . . and the acting character as well, who—with purposes, that are themselves arbitrary—therefore enters into a coincidental world with which he does not form an internally congruent whole. The Adventurous is constituted by this, the relative nature of the purposes in a relative environment—an environment the determinateness and intricacies of which do not reside in the Subject, but which rather is determined externally and coincidentally, generating equally coincidental collisions in the form of strangely interlinked ramifications. It is the Adventurous that brings forth the Romantic as a fundamental type for the form of events and actions . . . [1]

Clearly, Cage has not exactly written a Romantic opera, but indeed two "comic" operas—in which the essence of the most European of all traditional forms of theater creates a constellation, namely, the total collage of what comprises the quintessence of those forms and at the same time sublates them critically. As for the quintessence: "It is proper to speak of opera . . . precisely because in more than one respect it posits a prototype of the Theatrical—a prototype specifically of that which today has been cast into doubt. Moments emerge in the process of disintegration that belong to the bedrock of what comprises the stage."[2]And on critical sublation: "The more the opera approximates a parody of itself, the more it at the same time becomes the element most innate in itself."[3] Cage thus foregoes pursuing a purely abstract negation of the essence of opera—as has been expected of all the foremost composers for decades—and resorts instead to new, radical forms of musical theater. Cage was the first person in whose work these forms arose as a logical consequence of matters purely musical: in his *Music Walk* of 1958, written for a random number of pianos and radio receivers used to produce sounds by a random number of players, a theatrical dimension is created as a result of the aisles required between the sources of sound placed at a distance to one another. This dimension prompted me to coin the concept of "instrumental theatre," which then enjoyed great success—in Mauricio Kagel's work. Cage totalized this concept, the specific characteristic of which was the complete abolition of the categorical distinction between music and scene in 1960 in *Theatre Piece,* written for one to eight performers specialized in fields of the widest possible variety and to be recruited at will from among instrumentalists, dancers, singers and other professions. In other words, transposed onto the spatial setting of an opera house the distinction between the orchestra pit and the stage would also be abolished. This highly novel form of musical theater that Cage invented, however, emanated neither from the opera nor from any criticism thereof, but came about independent of these owing to problems inherent in the development of techniques of composition. Their existence thus has nothing to do with a coming to terms with opera, its standards or its legitimation. After careful consideration, however, Cage rejected the possibility of giving this approach another try and making the Frankfurt Opera an instrument for the fusion of each and every acoustic, optical and haptic element within a new concept of theater which, after a quarter of a century, would not be all that new anyway. Rather than negating the operatic abstractly by selecting a different form of musical theater, he chose instead the "determinate negation" of opera in the Hegelian sense; which is to say, that which is to be negated is incorporated in its entirety in the shape the negation takes, constituting the specific substance of negation and sublated concretely within it. Such a process is irreversible, and we can wait with bated breath to see whether the blossoming opera composers of "our time" will immediately comprehend that their hour has come: they are from now on also sublated.

In *Europeras 1 and 2,* as in proper operas, the stage and orchestra are separated from one another

> Everything is separated from everything else—so that the scene is not one in which the various theatrical elements support one another, but each one is in its own state of activity. The lighting is independent of the action, the costumes independent of the songs. . . . It is an experiment, that one could not have foreseen until it happens.[4]

Yet, it is above all the techniques of composition that are separated from the material, and it is this that creates the comicalness of the whole: the materials are all completely and utterly pre-existent as it were, i.e., they are not first generated by the composition, but are given an entirely new function by it. Cage consciously takes up the concept of the *objet trouvé* introduced by Marcel Duchamp. These materials are historical, antiquated in crucial areas, the witnesses of a fragmentary remembrance that, nevertheless, goes to any lengths to remember the relics of a tradition. The procedures by means of which they were fused, in constellation, to form a composition are completely without precedent and their dimensions innumerable. They are the products of most recent history—indeed, following the decline of the idea of the coherently integrated artwork, they are truly the most advanced of all: computer-assisted chance operations.

Compositional Technique

To compose *everything* would usually be too much (Cage himself, however, did it a number of times, for instance in 1958 in *Variations I,* then again in 1961 in *Variations II*); yet to compose *nothing* (and Cage has already done this as well) would be too little, at least for the patron, who expects to receive something substantial for his money. Thus, a compromise seemed advisable: to compose *something*. Under these circumstances the first compositional decisions which had to be made regarded the procedure to be adopted for making selections.

Material

The Orchestra

First of all, the works still under copyright had to be sorted out from among the store of orchestral parts

The material consists of isolated quotations: splintered pieces taken by chance from the orchestral parts

Compositional Technique

from countless European operas housed in the library of the Metropolitan Opera in New York and then eliminated. The first artistic decision in terms of compositional technique was thus based exclusively on a legal criterion—a prerequisite for the project being allowed by law. (Not a few of the most radical artistic projects, particularly those of anarchists, irrespective of the area involved, have failed as existing laws posed an obstacle to them. . . .) The hundreds of operas then left for which the complete parts and scripts had also survived, were then reduced to a manageable number via chance operations. At the same time, they were further divided up and assigned to the respective orchestral instruments—to determine which operas would be the source of the parts to be played by each individual instrument. Which concrete fragments of the orchestral parts selected were to actually be performed was then determined by means of more precise chance operations, as was the earliest point in time when they would have to start and the latest point at which they would have to end ("time brackets"). There is no conductor: time-control is left to each individual musician who monitors it by watching one of the digital time displays.

Material

of the widest variety of old operas. (They represent more than 200 years of opera history.) The extent to which many are greatly similar to one another is amazing, although the original "unique" character of each fragment was faithfully retained—with the original tempo, key, phrasing, dynamics and expression marks. Could it be that the different composers from widely differing epochs always found the same few solutions for the widest variety of problems? Further suspicions are raised if the critical, listening ear, has once descended into the lower levels of the different elements—so masterfully fashioned and concealed by the context of each complete original composition. It is out of these lower levels—especially in the shabby lowlands of the middle and supporting voices—that the whole was structured. And even something that was once a magnificant, dominant melody is unexpectedly left completely naked if it has to dispense with the harmonization that once lent it its glory. This is in any case the price of emancipation: the truth. Confronted by the orchestra parts of so many works—appearing divest of any dressing, left to their own devices—some of which are of the highest quality, all the customary views on the material used in

COMPOSITIONAL TECHNIQUE

MATERIAL

the great European compositions prove to be untenable. I shared the opinion, at least, that we in Europe—to put it bluntly and to simplify things incredibly—once had seven-tone music and then received twelve-tone music. I did not know that we had so much monotone, two-tone, three-tone and four-tone music, and, in contrast, presumably no five-tone, i.e., pentatonic music at all; and that musical figures that drew on six or more tones in any case represented only a statistical minority of what was our tradition . . .

The Voices

Those singers who had agreed to collaborate on the compositions chose the arias in the two operas prior to the work of composition. The singers and their arias are representative of all the different types of voice categories encountered in the European opera tradition. The only thing of consequence for Cage's compositional work was their respective length—in order to be able to determine the "time brackets" necessary by means of chance operations. There is no conductor: time-control is left to each individual musician who monitors it by watching one of the digital time displays.

The material used consists of arias taken from diverse operas of various European composers, whereby it is a matter of chance whether they have been arranged in sequence or simultaneously. Ah-hah effects will in all probability occur more frequently here than in the case of the orchestra parts and above all have a much stronger impact. The standards the traditional form of opera set—and it is the "determinate negation" of these which is the object of the *Europeras*—are thus incorporated into the material. In this manner, the arias are significantly privileged over the orchestral "accompaniment," dissected as it is into

Compositional Technique	Material
	innumerable fragments—indeed they are accorded "undivided" respect: they are never chopped up but are presented in their full integrity—their unmasking exposure becomes total.

Stage Actions

Actions carried out by the players on stage and the props required were chosen according to chance—picked out of a dictionary, namely, the *Webster's Dictionary of the English Language.* The time available for each action was determined by means of chance operations as were the "time brackets" necessitated for their entry and exit. There is no conductor: time-control is left to each individual musician who monitors it by watching one of the digital time displays. Since at times more is demanded of each performer, who are none other than the singers themselves, than can be achieved by a single person alone, and given their constant need of all kinds of help, assistants are available to provide each person with help as required.

I have not listed all the other material item by item either. The materials involved here can, however, not be expressed in the form of categorical or descriptive headings, for they are mutually incommensurable. It is thus absolutely impossible to provide a *summarizing* commentary on them.

Costumes

Cage no longer remembers exactly whether the encyclopedia of historical costumes that Laura Kuhn obtained for him from the library

As the costumes are the only elements of color on the stage and therefore become a focus of attention, they are a sign of a privileged

Compositional Technique

of the New York Fashion Institute and recommended as the sole source for the sartorial parameters of *Europeras 1 and 2* comprised 13 or 14 volumes. By means of chance operations costumes were selected from the overwhelming mass of truly exquisite costume sketches from different ages and countries. Those chosen were then assigned to the individual singers—of course, completely irrespective of what their song numbers were or the actions they had to perform on the stage.

Material

status—equal to that of the arias and the stage action itself—namely, of the central role of star opera singers. It was precisely the composers who were the most radical opponents of this privileged position by justifiably citing the priority of the artwork over all the performers. And yet it is they who have confirmed this role most forcefully by means of a curious—unintentional, and truly objective—dialectic that follows from the very structuring of the work in musico-dramatical terms. One need only think of Schoenberg's monodrama *Erwartung* to find evidence of this confirmation. Costume is assigned a key position among all operatic insignia: ". . . an opera without costumes would, in contrast to theatre production, be a paradox. Just as the gestures of the singers—which they also often somehow bring with them like props from the equipment store—are themselves a piece of costuming; in like manner, it is completely his voice that the normal person in a certain sense dons when he sets foot on stage. The American expression, 'cloak and dagger,' the idea of a scene in which two lovers are singing to each other while murderers lurk behind the pillars on the left and right, is an eccentric way of conveying something of this phe-

COMPOSITIONAL TECHNIQUE

MATERIAL

nomenon—i.e., an aura of dissemblance, of miming, such as that which draws the child to the theatre, not because he wants to see an artwork but because he wishes to have its enjoyment of dissimulation confirmed."[5] It would have been unthinkable for Cage not to have placed the disguises, which have to provide many a libretto with the only strong foundation they have, in the center of the field of vision and thus to have sublated them.

Decors

A selection of pictures for the flats was made from amongst a wealth of pictures that Ursula Markow had hunted out for Cage in the Frankfurt City and University Library. How the images were to be cut was decided next in order to arrive at the excerpts that were to be used; these were then blown up—using either pictorial or photographic techniques—to final size. Lastly, a spatio-temporal plan was drawn up for the movement of the flats, from their appearance through to their disappearance. However, it soon became apparent that there were not enough tracks available on the Frankfurt Opera stage to accommodate the manoeuvres foreseen in the original composition and the facilities for

Cage's *Europeras 1 and 2* do not use a stage set, although numerous "sets" of images appear on stage. These are all culled from former times, and are made up, above all, of portrayals of composers, singers, animals and landscapes. What meets the eye when viewing this material is that it involves quotations from a world of pictures presumed lost, that date from fairly recent times and yet have already become a nightmare, i.e., cited out of the past as emphatically as is possible in aesthetic terms. Everything, incidentally, is done entirely in black and white in order to place the colors of the costumes in the limelight.

COMPOSITIONAL TECHNIQUE

bringing flats on and off the stage from the sides imposed severe limitations on the number of flats which could be used. Consequently, the whole process of chance operations had to be repeated based on a new set of new premises in order to reduce the number of elements to be introduced into the work.

MATERIAL

Lighting

A computer program, compiled by means of chance operations, controls the lighting process. It only makes use of the black-and-white range to avoid any fundamental modification in the chromatic value of the costumes.

The fact that the lighting in the two operas is absolutely independent of what is (or precisely is not!) lit is probably what the audience will at first find disconcerting, for it is a slap in the face of every conventional concept of what theater should be. It is possible that some members of the audience will initially attribute this to a technical failure until they recognize the underlying principle involved.

Forgotten in this Synopsis

The production of alien elements.

The material essence of alien elements.

Notation

The form of the musical score, originally invented to facilitate controlled polyphonic composing, is abandoned in the two operas—in the case of the music. This has

COMPOSITIONAL TECHNIQUE

also been the case in not a few of Cage's works for ensembles since 1957 (when he began conceiving the *Concert for Piano and Orchestra*). On the other hand, a new unprecedentedly rigorous principle is introduced, creating a score for everything that happens on the stage: one can thus hardly speak of a "stage production" in the usual sense. This complete inversion of the relations that normally obtain in opera—and in most of the other, more recent forms of musical theater—has to do with the prevention of physical dangers. If there is a "collision" of tones from the different voices of a chance polyphony then no one is injured or killed: on stage, however, collisions would be real and could cause serious accidents with harm to persons or damage to objects.

> What we thus encounter, particularly in the secular realm, in chivalry and in that formalism of the characters, is more or less the chance nature of both the circumstances under which actions occur and the person's wilful disposition. For such one-sided individual figures can make pure coincidence inform their character, i.e., that which is borne only by the energy of their character and carried out via externally-determined collisions. . . .[6]

Why Cage exclusively chose quotations from the past—from operas, dictionaries, picture books—as the materials for *Europeras 1 and 2* will perhaps be better understood in the future. That is, should humankind ever be blessed with the opportunity to continue existing in the form of a completely new course of history owing to the agency of some chance political-economic-technological-social—put succinctly, "ecological"—device. What is important is that property relations cease to be recognized and the principle of exchange to be abolished—these can for the time being only be violated in the shape of gifts or robbery. However, in anticipation of the overdue Messiah, there is little else that one can do for the time being. Other than bringing back to mind Adorno's theory of the objective historical tendency inherent in musical material—today almost forgotten—in a manner that takes account of the "fury of destruction" in Hegel's *Phenomenology of Spirit.* And then trying to generate a certain vantage point in terms of the philosophy of history, whence one can comment on the phenomenon of Cage's late work. To refresh the reader's memory:

> The assumption of an historical tendency in musical material contradicts the traditional conception of the material of music. This material is traditionally defined—in terms of physics, or possibly in terms of the psychology of sound—as the sum of all sounds at the disposal of the composer. The actual compositional material, however, is as different from this sum as is language from the sounds available to it. It is not simply a matter of the increase and decrease of this supply in the course of history. All its specific characteristics are indications of the historical process. The higher the degree of historical necessity present within these specific characteristics, the less directly legible they become as historical indications. At that very moment when the historical expression of a chord can no longer be aurally perceived, it demands that the sounds which surround it give a conclusive account of its historical implication. These implications have determined the nature of this expression. . . . Music recognizes no natural law; therefore, all psychology of music is questionable. Such psychology—in its efforts to establish an invariant "understanding" of the music of all times—assumes a constancy of musical subject. Such an assumption is more closely related to the constancy of the material of nature than psychological differentiation might indicate. What this psychology inadequately and noncommitally describes is to be sought in the perception [*Erkenntnis*] of the kinetic laws of material. According to these laws, not all things are possible at all times. . . . It is clear, of course, that in the earlier stages of a technique, its later developments cannot be anticipated and, at best, subjectively envisioned. The reverse is also true. All the tonal combinations employed in the past by no means stand

> indiscriminately at the composer's disposal today. Even the more insensitive ear detects the shabby, worn-out quality of the diminished seventh chord and certain chromatic modulatory tones in the salon music of the nineteenth-century. For the technically trained ear, such vague discomfort is transformed into a prohibitive canon. If I am not completely mistaken, today this canon excludes even the medium of tonality—which is to say, the means of all traditional music. It is not simply that these sounds are antiquated and untimely, but that they are false. They no longer fulfill their function.[7]

In the sentence that was in general misinterpreted in 1949—when the book was first published and at least was still read—Adorno states that musical material expanded or contracted itself depending on the course of history. This was read to mean that the material went from contraction to expanion and back again (that being the course of history). Adorno, however, had thought of both as one movement; i.e., he had recognized that contraction and expansion are two simultanously effective dialectical moments of one and the same process and are, in the final instance, identical with one another. The central paradigm taken by the history of music was, at that time, still the Viennese atonal revolution at the beginning of the twentieth century. Here the inherent powers of tonality themselves press for their own sublation, i.e., for their atonal "expansion," which simultaneously means the anti-tonal contraction of the material—the prohibition of tonality. (Ever since then triads have only continued to be written in Hades, and the same holds true for periodic meters.) However, since the 1950s the expansive and the restrictive/selective tendencies of the material—which are opposed and yet identical to one another—have been radicalized in Cage's oeuvre to the point of absolute extremes: the material is "expanded" to embrace everything, and "contracted" to the point of nothingness.

> A. Being
> Being, pure Being, devoid of all determination. In its indeterminate immediacy it is only identical with itself and, at the same time, not non-identical with Others, has no internal or external distinctions. Being would not be retained in its purity by some determination or content that would be differentiated within it or by virtue of which it would be posited as distinct from an Other. It is pure indeter-

minateness and voidness: there is nothing to be contemplated [*anschauen*] within it—that is, if one can speak here of contemplation—or it is only this pure, void contemplation itself. Nothing can be thought of as inherent in pure Being, or, alternatively, it is nothing but this thought, void of all content. Being, indeterminate immediacy, is in fact Nothingness and not more nor less than Nothing.

B. Nothingness
Nothing, pure Nothingness; this is simply a state of identity with itself, perfect void, absence of determination and contents; undifferentiatedness within itself—To the extent that it is possible to speak of contemplation and thought in this context, then whether something or nothing is contemplated or thought can be considered to constitute a difference. In other words, to contemplate nothing or think nothing therefore has a meaning: both are differentiated from one another and thus nothingness is (exists) in our contemplation or thought; or rather it is contemplation or thought void of all content and is the same void contemplation or thought as pure Being.—Nothingness is thus the same determination or rather the same absence of determination and therefore, as such, the same as that which is pure Being.

C. Becoming
a. Unity of Being and Nothingness

Pure Being and Pure Nothingness is thus one and the same. . . .[8]

Thus, it may well be that there is no longer any material, if indeed, there ever was any. Presumably only the belief that material existed existed—and the belief's quotable.

NOTES

Translated from the German by Jeremy Gaines and Doris Jones.

1. Hegel, Georg Willhelm Friedrich: *Vorlesungen über die Aesthetik (Aesthetics)*, Vol. 2, 3d edition, in *Sämtliche Werke [Complete Works]*, Vol. 13, edited by Hermann Glockner based on a facsimile of the original impression by Ludwig Boumann, Friedrich Förster, Eduard Gans, Karl Hegel, Leopold von Henning, Heinrich Gustav Hotho, Philipp Marheinecke, Karl Ludwig Michelet, Karl Rosenkranz, and Johannes Schulze (Stuttgart, 1953), 208–9. All translations, except if otherwise stated, by Jeremy Gaines and Doris Jones.

2. Adorno, Theodor W.: "Bürgerliche Oper" ("Bourgeois Opera"), in: *Gesammelte Schriften, (Collected Works),* Vol. 16, edited by Rolf Tiedemann (Frankfurt am Main, 1978), 24.

3. Ibid.

4. John Cage, in *Die Opernzeitung Frankfurt,* no. 1/2 (October–November, 1987), 11.

5. Adorno, op cit. 24.

6. Hegel, op cit. 213.

7. Adorno, *Philosophy of Modern Music,* translated by Anne G. Mitchell and Wesley V. Blomster with emendations by Jeremy Gaines and Doris Jones. (New York: Seabury Press, 1973), 32–34.

8. Hegel, *Wissenschaft der Logik* 1 (*Science of Logic*) Part 1, *Objective Logic, First Book*, in *Werke,* 5, new edition based on the 1832–1845 *Werke,* revised by Eva Moldenhauer and Karl Markus Michel (Frankfurt am Main, 1986), 82–83.

Europeras (1988)

Manfredi Piccolomini

With life expectancy on the rise in the western world, the age of seventy-five no longer seems to be the crucial finishing line that it once was. It is, therefore, legitimate to wonder whether such an age still commands the reverence and respect that we have traditionally bestowed on the leading figures of our culture. This question is even more relevant when we refer to John Cage, a health buff and sworn macrobiotician who claims that since he has taken control of his body through diet and exercise—and the abandonment of alcohol and cigarettes—his energy and ability to work has increased enormously.

In other words, while there are many reasons why we should honor and celebrate John Cage—the elusive philosopher, the revolutionary musician, the poet of nature and of life, and the permanent enfant terrible of innovation—age is the least important one. Honors such as a featured role at MOMA's Summergarden festival and an invitation by Harvard University to deliver the prestigious Norton Lectures should not be understood as representing the culmination of his career. Furthermore, it should come as no surprise if in the future he produces a body of work that supersedes in strength and novelty the vast amount he has already given us.

This promise for the future is evident in his most recent work, *Europeras 1 and 2,* which was commissioned by the Frankfurt Opera on the occasion of the composer's seventy-fifth birthday. Following its German production last December, *Europeras* had its American premiere at the PepsiCo Summerfare Festival in Purchase, New York, this past July. And since then Cage has been submerged by requests for other productions of this astonishingly innovative work.

Europeras is proof that Cage's stockpile of new and provocative ideas is practically endless. With this work Cage confronted for the first time the most sacred and perhaps most conservative musical genre—opera. Throughout most of the twentieth century, opera relied on its glorious past rather than continuing to evolve. Although in the past few years other avant-garde musicians such as Philip Glass and John Adams have attempted to lead opera into the realm of minimalism, renewing hope for a rebirth of the genre, no one before Cage has tackled this venerable form in such a radical way.

The two artistic directors of the Frankfurt Opera, Heinz-Klaus Metzger and Reiner Riehn, had a specific project in mind when they commissioned *Europeras 1 and 2.* Their goal was to produce a final paean for the leading romantic musical genre. "Rather than abstractly negating opera by selecting another genre," wrote Metzger, "Cage chose instead the 'determinate negation' of opera in the Hegelian sense; that which is to be negated is incorporated in its entirety within the shape the negation takes. . . . Such a process is irreversible, and we can wait with bated breath to see whether the blossoming opera composers of 'our time' will immediately comprehend that their time has come." While future generations may find themselves waiting for opera to disappear, Cage's work is nevertheless an impressive contribution to the current discussion of the genre.

The extreme radicalism of his approach was confirmed when, by the halfway point in the performance I attended, two-thirds of the audience had left the theater. The remainder stayed on in amused bewilderment.

Europeras follows the rules of chance operations: after pulling apart the various components of opera—vocal and instrumental parts, arias, roles, and so forth—and lifting them from their context, Cage recombines them at random. Cage wanted a sample of each of the nineteen different types of operatic voices and asked the individual singers to choose a particular aria that they wanted to perform. The musical parts were selected at random by photocopying parts of different operas in the library of the Metropolitan Opera House. The original instrumentation of these operas, however, was transformed by upsetting the traditional scores and assigning different scores to each instrument; violins may take the role of trombones, cellos that of the oboes. Costumes were also randomly assigned to the singers without reference to their roles or arias. A performer dressed in a costume from the *Marriage of Figaro* might be seen singing the "La donna è mobile" aria from *Rigoletto,* which might be played by the "wrong" instruments; at the same time a *Cenerentola* aria might be sung by a singer in a *Carmen* costume. The harmony and/or disharmony created by this improbabale duet is, for Cage, the highlight of the performance, since it is chance, rather than the imposing personality of the author, composer, or director, that determines the good or bad moments.

The same principle was applied to staging. Large photos and prints showing old opera sets, composers, and singers, all from the past, are arbitrarily dropped on the stage from above and removed without any apparent relation to the action on the stage. Other unlikely elements, such as a jeep and a bathtub (the latter with a singer inside performing an aria), make their surreal appearance. At the end of the opera a dirigible guided by remote control flies from the stage and floats over the audience, signaling the end of this incredible performance.

The lighting cues and the performers' entrances are directed by a computer programmed to follow chance operations based on the *I Ching,* the Chinese *Book of Changes,* which Cage has used for many years in his music composition. While an overall impression of confusion and chaos may result from the viewing of *Europeras,* the idea that with this work Cage captures, in an ironic and self-referential sense, the essence and heart of traditional grand opera should not be discounted too quickly. The final impression, like that in traditional opera, is of things far larger than life. A sense of grandiose impossibility, of incredible richness, and of splendid, dreamlike fantasy pervade *Europeras* just as they do any traditional opera. The only difference is that Cage's work has no story and no drama building to a cathartic end. Viewers can choose to construct stories combining the many elements the show has to offer, or they can choose from among twelve different synopses provided by the program.

Although there is some dispute as to whether John Cage is the greatest contemporary composer, he is perhaps the greatest music critic of our age. Like Oscar Wilde at the turn of the century, the avant-gardes of the early nineteen hundreds, and Marcel Duchamp—an artist he greatly admired and from whom he learned to play chess—Cage derives his strength as an artist from his constant attempt to change our perception of what art is. In an interview he recalled how Willem de Kooning once told him that arbitrarily putting a frame around bread crumbs on a table cannot be considered an artistic act. Cage's response was the opposite: "He [de Kooning] was saying that it wasn't because he connects art with his activity—he connects with himself as an artist [while] I want art to slip out of us into the world in which we live."

In other words, Cage's work is about expansion, about stretching the limits of what is art and abolishing the barriers that for centuries separated art from life. This axiom, while of great importance in itself, also explains his great interest in areas such as the study of mushrooms, or chess, or macrobiotics, which appear to have little relevance to art. As for mushrooms, Cage recalls how his first contact with them came during the Great Depression, when he had nothing else to eat. It was a lucky encounter, however, since it was in an Italian television quiz show that he won the first substantial amount of money he had ever made by answering questions about mushrooms. From a more theoretical point of view mushrooms served as an antidote to infinite possibilities. "I was involved with chance operations in music," Cage recalls, "and I thought it would just be a very good thing if I got involved in something where I could take no chances." Since then mycology became an important part of his life, ranging from courses in mushroom identification at the New School for Social Research to becoming a founding member of the New York Mycological Society and a member of a mushroom society in Czechoslovakia.

Several years ago he said, "When I focus my attention on something, it goes dead; but when I place it in a space that includes things that are not in it, then it comes alive." This is perhaps Cage's most revealing statement about himself. His compositions involve contamination: he mixes things together, changes their context, and confuses life and art in a much more complex and extensive way than any of this century's avant-gardes, including Duchamp, ever did. His radical approach is apparent in all of his creations, from his celebrated collaborations with choreographer Merce Cunningham to his musical pieces.

In a fairly recent collaboration with the Merce Cunningham Dance Company, *Roaratorio: An Irish Circus on* Finnegans Wake, performed at the Brooklyn Academy of Music in the fall of 1986, Cage's music featured noises produced by natural elements such as water and marine shells while the composer himself, sitting in a box, read sections from James Joyce's *Finnegans Wake.* In an older musical piece, *Water Music,* Cage applied his contamination technique, which has since become his trademark, by trying to expose the theatricality of musical performance.

The pianist performing the piece is asked to pour water from one bucket to another and to tune radios by selecting stations at random, while the musical score is blown up on a large panel so that the entire audience can see it and participate in the performance. Cage himself defined this piece as one that tries to contaminate music and theater, transforming a musical performance into a theatrical one.

Cage's relatively early composition entitled *4'33"* remains his most impressive—and certainly most familiar—manifesto. In this piece, a musician (usually a pianist) sits in front of his instrument for exactly four minutes and thirty-three seconds without playing. Thus, the natural noises of the environment and the audience become the "music." Although seemingly ironic, Cage's statement in this piece relates to his beliefs about "disappearing" as an artist and letting art and life become interchangeable. In those four-and-a-half minutes of silence the listeners become aware, at least in the composer's intentions, of the musicality of natural sounds in the environment—they broaden their definition of what music is. And with each new experiment, Cage redefines what music can be.

Figuration and Prefiguration: Notes on Some New Graphic Notions (1991)

Daniel Charles

The role that traditional musicology allocates to the concept of *score* is well known: the main historical facts are mentioned, but on condition that they are kept at a distance and, in any case, care is taken not to go any further. Thus, for example, Arthur Hoérée writes in the *Dictionnaire de la Musique,* published some time ago by Bordas, that a score is a "table which allows separate reading of the various instrumental and vocal lines in a piece of music, or the simultaneous reading of these lines by placing extended bars one above the other so that they can be read together."[1] This is followed by some invaluable remarks on developments in typography and presentation through the years, particularly when Verovia perfected copperplates in 1586, etc. Further information can be garnered, of course, from *Tabula compositoria,*[2] an article which describes how sixteenth-century musicians wrote their compositions on durable materials, such as slate, leather-covered wood, or pieces of parchment, leather, or cloth treated with plaster or varnish, which could be repeatedly erased and engraved by drypoint. This explains the virtual nonexistence of autographic manuscripts. Would you like to learn more about present times? You will learn basically three things: (1) that even in 1786 Philidor was so concerned with having the strings, the basic instruments of the orchestra, before him that he did not allow the timpani and the brass instruments to be put at the top of the score, whereas Cherubini introduced the "present-day order"; (2) that the extreme division of the strings led Xenakis to use pages that were one meter high to accommodate all 85 staves of the *Terrêtekorh* (1966), and that when all is said and done "the improvised passages of aleatory [*sic*] music still require new signs such as arabesques, sine waves suggesting note paths, solid lines to indicate the simultaneous playing of the entire scale, or the 'glissando' over the same notes"; and (3) that "there is a quite recent trend (seen in S. Prokofiev, A. Honegger, A. Berg, E. Varèse) where transposing instruments appear as notes that are really heard, the transposition being carried out by the performer," with the "scoring of electroacoustic works calling for a distinctive notation of its own,"[3] as was to be expected.

In an endeavour not only to present a contrast, but to be better informed about what is happening in our day, I shall now turn toward the most recent—if I'm not mistaken—article on this subject by the author of a fundamental work in this area, the American composer John Cage.[4] In an introduction written on May 7, 1981, to *Sound on Paper: Music Notation in Japan,*[5] a catalog for an exhibition, John Cage, in his typically inimitable, seemingly casual style (although he is really most serious-minded, as we shall find out), expatiates on the whole series of problems which musical notation currently poses (not only in the Land of the Rising Sun . . .). Notation, in his view, is when the composer sends *letters* to musicians, to a particular musician or group of musicians, to whom the work is thus dedicated. Each letter describes the sounds to be created and their sequence, thus acting as a screen between the executor—the *performer*—and the music to be performed. This screen being of paper is only two dimensional, while sound has many more dimensions: pitch, duration, frequency, timbre, spatial origin, and morphological evolution, to name just a few, and technology is presently striving to increase their number, such as when it stipulates the adjunction of diagrams of electronic circuits on a piano part—an example is *Incarnation II* by Somei Satoh, the Japanese "Arvo Pärt."[6] Many new dimensions are, of course, also arising out of the increasing interpenetion of formerly distinct cultures or out of the burgeoning spirit of invention in our times. Hence the current crisis: the *consensus* of the past on choice of instruments and on the definition of musicality of sounds has been replaced by a perfectly explosive fragmentation. Solving the problem could consist simply of sending longer, more cumbersome letters to musicians, peppered with introductory notes explaining the sound alphabet and vocabulary to be used, for example, or charged to excess with supplementary verbal indications. The result would be more a script than a score. One of the most striking impacts of the technological *boom* in the twentieth century is the growth of proportional notation, where, as on a magnetic tape, the duration of a note corresponds to a certain number of centimeters on paper. This time-space notation inevitably furthers the independent stature of graphics; the score begins to be evaluated in its own right, as if it were a drawing, free of any reference to music. In this context, Cage mentions the *Picture Score for Improvisation: Markings—1* by Akio Suzuki, although it is clearly Morton Feldman, Earle Brown and Christian Wolff who should receive first mention. In point of fact, the graphic notations developed in the fifties and the sixties only rarely remained unchanged, i.e., pure, throughout the years. Instead, hybrids evolved, as many composers rejected a complete conversion to the pictorial, preferring either to return to conventional notation or to use it in conjunction with graphemes like Maki Ishii in *Kyoo.* Such hybrids were a response to the increasing complexity of monophonic music with the addition of both vocal (Demetrio Stratos) and instrumental (wind instruments) *multiphonic* sounds, or the simultaneous emission of several sounds. Following the arguments of David Tudor, who felt that the refinement achieved in conceiving and creating new timbres called for a complete renewal of current graphic notation—in particular, the creation of the equivalent of the pictograms and ideograms used by Far Eastern civilizations—the need for a great number of new signs was rapidly felt. This did not, however, end the need for customary notation. So that we have the blossoming of an "action" notation specifying the gesture to be made rather than the result to be obtained, and an "experimental" technique of sign indeterminacy, where the score did not specify how the polyphony was to be generated but simply prescribed its appearance. The performer was left to create it as he could with the means available, that is to the extent of his possibilities when faced with the enigma of the sign. There was thus, on the one side, an apparent return to "prospective" notation, as used in tablatures for the lute and the *vihuela,* which indicated the most advantageous physical posture, just as in the sixteenth century the position of the finger on the string was shown rather than the pitch of the note, and on the other side, a more pronounced, perturbing, and disruptive presence of "foreign" notational elements, which left an exotic impression in a world that had always been governed and encoded by traditional conventions. To illustrate the first trend, Cage mentions Kazuo Fukushima's *Shun-San* for solo flute, in which the composer has depicted above each note the gesture which he thinks is required. As an example of the second trend, Cage quotes *Breeze* by Jo Kondo, who writes out the word in full to indicate a polyphony from the flute or the clarinet, without going into further details. Presumably, anything is possible in such a fluid and open-ended situation, and Cage speaks of a "plethora of possibilities."[7] Confining himself to the Japanese musicians represented, John Cage quotes the "suggestive sketches" by Joji Yuasa in *Time of Orchestral Time,* Takehisa Kosugi's works, which take the form of *koans,* and the librettos by Toru Takemitsu. In all these works, the listener is appealed to as never before, to abandon his traditional passive role and take an active part in creating sound, and also, ultimately, to imitate nature, whether by "listening to the murmurings of the waters" or by "breathing to make a bell tinkle as if wind-swung."[8]

I know much more after having examined Cage's writings than I did after I had read the article by Arthur Hoérée. It is perhaps hardly surprising that a composer, who initially intended to be an artist and who has since made sure that he is never cut off from the spatial arts—his engravings, like his scores, having been exhibited worldwide—who is moreover all the more knowledgable on contemporary musical iconography since it is a subject which he has largely helped to define through his works, should by far outshine a musicologist. In particular a musicologist who has never claimed to be knowledgable on anything but history and who—it must be said—intended only to provide a rough overview of current trends, his main aim having been to chart a detailed synopsis of musical history, and moreover, of Western history alone. Nevertheless, the approach says it all, and Hoérée's preference expressed in his conclusion reveals a great deal about his ideas on the evolution of music, of music *alone,* as if it did not have any real context and did not interact with the other arts and disciplines in a complex, sociocultural environment. Yet, this is an issue which should also be addressed. I shall leave aside the references to Philidor and to "Cherubini's" definition of the score—the reader will undoubtedly be able to savor them. I shall equally leave aside the issue of the transposing instruments, although the question comes to mind, why quote Prokofiev, Honegger, Berg, and Varèse without wondering why Boulez should be immediately placed in the opposite camp, among those who obstinately continue to reject truly audible sound and who, in his opinion, are necessarily nearer to the truth. Following the same line of thought, it would have been interesting to learn why Stockhausen never used flats, only sharps, and why Pousseur indicated flats with white heads and diatonic sounds with black heads, while Kagel used black heads for sharps and white heads for "natural" notes. These are absolutely essential questions, as the reader will agree! On a more serious note, the only composer to receive more detailed mention in Arthur Hoérée's article is Iannis Xenakis, who is approached from the viewpoint of a strictly material, factual definition of the score. Using pages that are one meter high is certainly very strange, but Hoérée does not ask just what were the blueprints that the composer of *Terrêtekorh*—who has moreover gained considerable orchestral experience since *Metastassis*—used as a starting point. Nor does he link the technique of glissando with that of hyperbolic paraboloids, despite Xenakis's explanations of how he had developed it eight years earlier, in 1958, when he was preparing the surfaces to the left of the Philips Pavilion at the Universal Exhibition in Brussels, nor to what extent this technique had dictated his systematic use of sliding sonorities—much to the chagrin, at the time, of Boulez. In short, history, as seen and written by Arthur Hoérée, is neither lofty nor far-reaching, at least as far as our age is concerned. Instead, it is more conspicuous for its preoccupation with a single idea.

Nevertheless, the choice of Xenakis as his only example of the twentieth century's new musical pictography is rather revealing. Clearly, it is not by continuing to question Hoérée about his intentions that we will discover why; they do not carry much weight. But, it is as if the composer of *Achorripsis* and *Eonta* was, in certain respects—even despite himself—if not a lifeline then at least some guarantee of steadfastness and stability in the eyes (and ears) of the advocates of an academic musicology, who could only have been unsettled by the confusion following the invasion of serials, and compounded, so they say, by Cage. Hoérée is certainly not coming round to Xenakis's point of view, at least not in this work, while a certain Jacques Chailley did so in spectacular style, but at least he mentions it. It is just that Xenakis's stance regarding the status of musical scoring has something reassuring about it. Here we have someone who, in the midst of pandemonium, does not hesitate to declare his coolness toward extremisms. Let us say it in Latin, since we cannot do so in Greek as we should, *in medio stat virtus.* This certainly does differ from the view that Schoenberg expresses in the *Three Satires,* which is that, "the *via media* is the only road that does not lead to Rome . . ." In fact, what Xenakis sets out to do is to "restore his dignity to the artist." "When a musician, for example the fourteenth second violin, playing in a symphony orchestra with a classical arrangement, is stuck at his stand waiting for his cue, he is bound to feel like a musical outcast; . . . in my music, I tried to restore his dignity to the artist by making him do different things, . . . by making him try out new forms. Since these forms were new, the musicians were at a loss and had to make an intellectual effort and show greater professionalism and artistic flair than they had done in the past."[9]

Now, what exactly is this "middle road" which I just mentioned in connection with Xenakis? Françoise Escal gives a very good description of it, supported by quotations from the composer, in her book *Espaces sociaux, espaces musicaux.*[10] Xenakis, she says, "takes his distance" as much from the "technocrats" or other "advocates of information theory" as from the "intuitionists." Pure and simple scientism, in its thirst for "objective" criteria, overlooks the fact that "instinct and subjective choice are the only guarantees of the quality of a musical composition. No tablature is based on scientific criteria."[11] Xenakis is very skeptical about Pierre Barbaud, who reduces the score to a mere computer program and never challenges the results obtained. "Pierre Barbaud likens working out a programme to drawing a map of a town from which there is no way out: the composition—or stroll—is one of an exhaustive list of possible strolls in the town. For him, mathematics and musical scoring go hand in hand; his scores are just developed from mathematical premises."[12] All the musician has to do is "to channel random events into a flow chart."[13] Xenakis, on the other hand, does not think twice about rearranging the computer's results. However, he avoids like the plague what he considers to be a dereliction of responsibility on the part of the "intuitionists," who "put graphic symbols on a higher plane than music and sound, and worship the score as if it were a work of art or a source of endless stimulation."[14] "In this group," he says, "it is fashionable not to write down notes but to draw just about any picture."

> The "music" is then judged according to how beautiful the picture looks. They have taken the so-called aleatory music for their own, which, in fact, is just a misuse of the term; the correct term would be grandfather improvised music. This group does not realize that

> graphic notation, whether symbolic, as in the traditional *sol-fa* method, or geometric or numerical, should only be as faithful a reflection as possible of the set of instructions that the composer gives to the orchestra or computer. This group draws the music out of it.[15]

When someone claims to be a centrist, he naturally wishes to see the two extremes in the same light. In the "median" perspective that Xenakis offers, taking up the cudgels for subjectivity only makes sense if the extremes that it opposes are part of the selfsame objectivism. Xenakis makes no distinction between the two and dismisses both the advocates of the final score and the upholders of the "objective computer" view in the same breath. However, the coalition is a formidable one since it brings together musicians who are not concerned by the sounds they produce, which questions the security of the present and the presence of what is present. On the one side, Barbaud lets the computer "dictate" his compositions to him and seem to be quite unconcerned by their unpredictability. However, his programs and other flow charts might well open a Pandora's box at any moment without his knowing. On the other side, the intuitionists so hotly deny the presence of any teleology that it is as if they had lost their memory en route. They had set out to compose and ended up by painting, engraving, or drawing, or vice versa. In short, they are victims of an abortive past which has never been present; or rather they are dependent on the mood of a future *anterior.* Because the "picture" that the score "is supposed to present" does not remain "faithful" to the "instructions" that *should have been followed* (by effects), and goes haywire instead. Thrown off key, it deprives the work (and therefore its composer, who, up to a point, is God the Father, unless he is just another *Zeus Keraunos*) of its identity. This is why Xenakis talks about "improvisation," while this is not, strictly speaking, an established concept for Cage, Feldman, or Christian Wolff. For the centrists, "improvisation" is synonymous with sheer sloppiness and leaving things to chance; since subjectivity no longer has a hand in planning and prefiguring what should be planned and figured out, everything seems lost. As if "instinct" and "subjective choice" were, for Xenakis, in a different vein from the supposedly haphazard and chaotic variety against which the composer is rebelling! Or, if the reader prefers, it is as if life were not the opposite of death or as if music were not a *"meditatio mortis."*[16]

In short, Xenakis's *via media* is like taking out a comprehensive insurance policy, not only against the future, but also against a past which is all the more dangerously rearing its head again since it is immemorial and of unknown origin. Proof of this can be found in chapter 5, *Score, Sketch, and Script* of Nelson Goodman's book *Languages of Art,* in which the distinguished Harvard professor examines, with the most implacable logic, the BB diagram on page 53 of *Solo for Piano* from *Concert for Piano and Orchestra* (1958), written by that other Harvard professor, John Cage.[17] The notational system in question consists essentially of a rectangle, sprinkled with a number of dots, and has five straight lines going across it intersecting at varying angles. This makes it possible—by drawing perpendicular lines linking each dot to the various intersecting ones—to "compose" a score in canon form; the dots are for sounds while the five straight lines refer respectively to the frequency, duration, timbre, amplitude, and succession that may affect each sound proportionally to the distance separating the sound from the line that touches the perpendicular in question. It seems simple enough: the different perpendicular distances just need to be measured for the score to take shape, each sound standing, so to speak, separately and independently without appealing to the judgment and all-powerful subjectivity of a creator, steeped in his own prerogatives. Yet, when Nelson Goodman's eagle eye scrutinizes the situation a little more closely, things get rather more complicated. The author of the graph neglected to specify the minimum unit of measure that should be used to determine the exact distances between dots and lines. The fact that each line could be interpreted as representing a different parameter from the one it did during a previous performance, means that two identical measurements could give rise to two different sonorous products, or that identical results may be consistent with different measurements. The causal link is thus broken: we have no assurance by right that what is being played on a given evening is the *Concert for Piano and Orchestra.* Even reading the score at the same time could be of no use to us, unless we did so through the eyes of a lover of painting or calligraphy. Goodman's critique is concerned less with the inevitable inaccuracy of any measure (how far down the decimal scale need one go to ensure that the small approximations do not produce too glaring an error?) than with the totality of the failure of any written prefiguration of what could well follow. Nothing can be determined to be a copy of an authentic original: what we have is only a copy of a copy. Nor does anything guarantee the fidelity of the performance to the autograph diagram from which it is considered to derive its legitimacy. That diagram is so self-contained, in what should doubtless be called its self-sufficiency, that it sidesteps its notational function. Copy and performance, rather than *modeling themselves after* the score, *come after* it. As effects without causes, they stultify the time signature. They "enervate" its evolution, they deenergize it. No more than a scrap of paper, the score can just as well be discarded and picked up by a gallery owner, who will put it to better use than the professional musician.

Although it is reminiscent of Xenakis's severity with the "intuitionists," Goodman's harshness toward Cage's graphics, for all its purported level-headed impassiveness (do not its arguments display unassailable logic?), betrays just as much his own deference to a temporal doctrine that is quite similar to the impassioned tenets of the composer of *Herma.* In both cases, it is a matter of using the score to protect the work against the risk of loss of identity—or increased entropy—that lurks in acquiescence to the ephemeral, denounced as conveying an absolutely fatal fragility. For Xenakis, salvation lies in escaping into a conversion to *out of time,* which obviously does not dispense with proceeding through time, since all music is played *in time.* It will, however, have the virtue of restraining time and loosening its strictures. This is why Xenakis's own philosophy of timing hinges on the present, which should be given absolute transcendence over the future or the past, since it is the only point of intersection between the out of time and the in time. For how else can one retain the present but by prolonging and immortalizing it in and through the score? Upon reflection, Goodman's strategy is curiously similar. Admittedly, the author of *Languages of Art* scrupulously avoids any bias whatsoever, and in fact displays the most exemplary neutrality right up to the very end of his work. But this caution lends even more force to the fleeting judgment which he allows us to glimpse through the chinks in his arguments and which his irony helps to bring out rather than muffle. The notational system which emerged from the Middle Ages developed over centuries, admittedly not toward a stage of perfection but to the degree of efficiency and authority epitomized by its standardization and attested to by modern-day railings against it. Why should one wish to replace it with another unless he believes he has found a better one? But has this been found? Certainly not in Cage! With one deadly but revealing sentence, Goodman dismisses the Master of Stony Point: Cage's graphic notation system fulfilled the requisites of a true score about as little as the medieval manuscript (eleventh-century) chosen by Goodman as frontispiece to chapter 5 of his book; "sometimes revolution is retrogression."[18]

Was not the sole drawback for Goodman, who, in his irony, does not know how right he is . . . what the ten Cage texts from the 1950s and 1960s have stated and restated in every possible way[19] and which was the focus on one of the first critical interpretations of his thinking, by Leonard Meyer,[20] precisely the urgency, if not of a full-scale revival of eleventh-century customs, at least of a complete repudiation of the Renaissance and its legacy, that is, the period from the fifteenth or sixteenth century to the present day during which the subjectivity of the theme deprived the final work of its objectivity? Why then this rejection? Because Cage's notion of music would throw off the shackles of theme/final work dominance, which secured their grip precisely with the Renaissance. Furthermore, the definition of the musical work as an *opus solidum, perfectum, absolutum,* that is, as an object subordinate to the free will of the theme, seems to Cage extremely confining: it downplays temporality and process, and tends to suffocate the work in gestation and any notion of process, by giving precedence, like Xenakis, to the out of time, casting the flexible model of the transient in the matrix of the present, which is supreme among time spans. However, stated differently, an approach such as that of Goodman seems no less debatable: defending, even in veiled terms, the efficiency of the standard notation system as it gained currency in the West during the nineteenth century, amounts to guarding against any "regression" or "retrogression" that could threaten the hard-earned sovereignty of the theme of composition and, by extension, the social hierarchy itself. On the contrary, questioning the "sense" of history, in other words the primacy of the present or the *status quo,* in short the standard of the score, is tantamount to attacking that very sovereignty and hierarchy. This is why Goodman insists on the *nonaesthetic* nature of his observations: indeed the discussion here is much less aesthetic than political and does not concern art alone.

Let us now turn to the examination and justification of the paradox of Cage's "revolutionary regression," which would be sure to dethrone the ideology of (linear) progression. An initial correction should be made concerning the repudiation of "intuitionism" and of graphic music: contrary to Xenakis's claim, hanging the musical score of a graphic work on a gallery wall neither necessarily nor inevitably sounds its death knell. Furthermore, however relevant Goodman's objections to Cage's graphs may be, they miss what for Cage is the essence: the constraining nature of this graph. Cage in fact compares the score to a camera: composing for him no longer means making a *finite temporal object:* the creative process much sooner sets in motion a whole apparatus meant to make sound recordings which, moreover, are inseparable from photographs, however little we may recall that an ear alone is not a being. The only difference between a score and a camera lies ultimately in the fact that the score is perennial. But in both cases we end up with complex and not necessarily finite processes, rather than with finished self-contained objects. Moreover, the score, like a camera, captures the environment. This does not in any way imply that the score confiscates or imprisons it, but rather glorifies and magnifies it, in other words, molds it to our scale. With this in mind, we better understand why the critical remarks of Goodman fall flat, and why those made by Xenakis ring false; *they continue to lay down the law on the final score when it is the score-process which is involved.* Cage has changed the rules of the game, but our two critics have not yet become aware of this, and this leads to several misunderstandings. In this respect, Goodman's comments on the Cagian BB graph of 1958 must be modified in the light of the masterly analysis of the score of *Variations II* (1961), published by Thomas DeLio in 1981.[21] The 1961 text takes up again and develops the spatial device of the 1958 graph. In this graph, dots and lines are liberally scattered within one performance space, following the superpositioning of numerous transparent elements. Statistical configurations appear in the same performance space and hence produce as many scores as we would like. Thus, the musician actually participates in the writing of a score-process which is the veritable matrix upon which future final scores will be based: *to compose is to prefigure the figurations not yet in existence, not yet available.* Nothing has been decided, *and yet everything is taking shape.* In this sense, Cage is nearer to what Ernst Bloch spoke of under the label of an *ontology of not yet being* (*Noch-nicht-sein*)[22] and, as Dieter Schnebel quite rightly pointed out, he becomes the composer of the "concrete utopia," that is to say, of the *attainable,*[23] in the lines of the "possibility category" [*Kategorie Möglichkeit*].[24] Perhaps, from then on, the formulation of the "revolutionary regression" question should be different from that of Goodman, since he has remained a prisoner of the ideology of linear progression: the anteriority of the *present* henceforth gives way to the *future anterior.* Rather than emphasizing the time dimension of the present (a characteristic of Western metaphysics which has become more predominant in the modern era), we may well emphasize not only Heidegger's idea of "simultaneity" [*Gleichzeitigkeit*], but also Bloch's "nonsimultaneity" [*Ungleichzeitigkeit*]. Herein lies the paradox, and "at the same time" the secret of its formulation. The revolution in which Cage participates, and in which he is one of the most active protagonists, unfolds following trajectories and modes of propagation which are not necessarily "progressive" and not necessarily linear.

Owing to this polysemy and this polyrhythm, it is clear—as I inferred above—that the reference to the *ethos* of such and such a composer, and even to the art of sounds in its purest form, would not suffice to reflect the range of changes in progress. It is not surprising that the general theory of the score-process, developed in 1969 by architect-designer Lawrence Halprin,[25] quoting John Cage throughout, mentions music for the sake of memory alone. Naturally, it is to music that the author refers to support his definition of the score as "the symbol of a temporal process." Yet he immediately adds that "scores exist in all domains," that even a grocery bill can be considered a score. This is a theory which—if one believes Cage—Erik Satie was the first to explore. Since he used his bills, as he might have done with the golden number, to decide on the number of measures to make up the piece which he was to compose. Hence, before the music, there already exists a score, omnipresent. Halprin admits that his interest in scores arose in part from exercising his profession as an environmental architect and *designer,* and in part from the theatrical and choreographic activities in which he had begun to participate with his wife, Anna Halprin. But the countless scores which he lists and discusses—everything from calendars to *I Ching,* from tarot cards to paintings on the sand of the Navajo Indians, from land and astral charts to the map of the Minneapolis subway—all symbolize an experience formed by elements where the elements, however, are not part of the experience. Similarly, music gives life to all which is not part of it, and gradually, we come back to the phrase encountered in Kegon Buddhism "interpenetration without obstruction" which Daisetz Teitaro Suzuki had taught John Cage.[26] The principle involved here is that of *cross-fertilization;* not only notion *polyartistic*[27] in origin, but neither does art cease to encompass (or, in turn, irrigate) all which is not art—beginning with science. This is the very spirit of the "figurational" or iconographic revolution which is currently shaking the foundations of our whole existence. It consists of replacing the final score in all instances by the score-process, or, in the words of Deleuze and Guattari, the *calque* by the *chart.*

The chart/*calque* contrast should be stressed as should the logic of the tree which only reproduces the ready-made in a hierarchical order, and the rhizomatic experimenting of multiple entries and exits, which is constructive because it is neglectful and "effective" because it is "incompetent."[28] Deleuze and Guattari themselves undoubtedly rejected oversimplification. They know that a chart may be transferred and that all multiplicity has its unifications and stratographs. However, when the *calque* is returned to the chart, the dangers which the rhizome faces (such as being constantly interrupted, stratified, structuralized, and, eventually, blocked)[29] are apparent. Similarly, Halprin, in his 1969 text, took certain things into account: taking final scores or transfers arranged as a means of control and repression or simply for effectiveness, he demonstrated that the powerful and yet unfocused score-process had to be removed at all costs. However, it is often difficult to carry out the division successfully: by systematically desystematizing we are simply resystematizing. So we should do well to learn a little modesty and to let the revolution take place *sua sponte,* in its own time, even if this means at a slower pace. Cross-breeds and compromises—not to mention restarts—are a surer advance toward utopia than certain frontal assaults. One need only think of this interlacing of graphic and conventional notation which Cage discovered in several contemporary Japanese composers. He himself approved of it, perhaps following the example of Erik Satie, but certainly to a greater extent following the chiasm between chart and *calque* to which he devoted himself in the numerous readings and rereadings of Satie's *Socrate* which he entitled *Cheap Imitation.*[30]

However, what François Dagognet in *Ecriture et iconographie* calls the "second Gutenbergian revolution" is under way.[31] The invention of printing, which reduced the distance between the producer (God and the Scriptures) and the consumer (who no longer has to pass through the copyist, public declamation, commentary) had contributed to the "division" of the Church: subjectivity and heresy, both a function of the possibility of communing directly with the text, were to undergo spectacular changes. The script, however, remained grafted on phonetics, that is to say based on a restricting linearality. The impact of the methodical clarification, in the encyclopedia of Diderot and Alembert, of the text through a mass of illustrations, diagrams, drawings, and plates should not be underestimated. For the first time, rationality could "suddenly" be explained.[32] It is, therefore, of great significance that the music of our time should be used to commemorate events. Giorgio Battistelli's *Experimentum mundi* takes its title from the last great work of Ernst Bloch. In this piece, forty or so workers are put on stage: masons, bakers, shoemakers, and blacksmiths enter with their tools to perform together, before the public, some of their tasks while a narrator reads the texts from the Encyclopedia. The piece is musically "dressed": there is an orchestral conductor who ponders the entirety of a faultless work, in which there are numerous vocal and percussive punctuations. This performance score, however, is written in such a manner as to leave free rein to the *tableaux vivants* which present the different trades. It becomes a score-process precisely when the images from the Encyclopedia, freed from the framework of the book, come to life as real persons. Each simultaneously acting out the gestures which depict their daily tasks, they incarnate, in a striking vignette, the entire work of a village. The contrast with the voice is even more intensely pronounced: though eloquent, the voice is only able to utter "a string of opaque and nonsensical phrases."[33] *In this respect,* the information conveyed throughout this *in vivo* performance flows fast and well. From here on, the message is undoubtedly conveyed through the use of the redundancies of a written language, but still left to the awkwardness of the spoken word which is "ambiguous, slow, dialectal, capable of obscuring the message and even losing it in the muddle of words running together, subjected to numerous unnecessary constraints."[34] Giorgio Battistelli's *Experimentum mundi* thus clears the way for what Dagognet refers to as a "neo-script," which is immediately intelligible to all since it is "delivered from vocal constraints, directly readable and visible, indeed iconographic and expressive,"[35] in short *transparent.*

NOTES

Translated by Susin Park, Geneva, for Swiss Independent Video.

1. Arthur Hoérée, "Partition," in *Science de la Musique,* by Marc Honeggar (Paris: Bordas, 1976), 2:757.

2. S. Hermelink, "Tabula compositoria," in *Science de la Musique,* by Marc Honegger (Paris: Bordas, 1976), 2:991.

3. Hoérée, "Partition," 758.

4. John Cage with Alison Knowles, *Notations* (New York: Something Else Press, 1969).

5. John Cage, *Sound on Paper: Musical Notations in Japan,* catalog of the exhibition (New York: Japan House Gallery, 1981), 6–8.

6. Somei Satoh, *Incarnation II* (Tokyo: *EX* House, 1978).

7. Cage, *Sound,* 7.

8. Cage, *Sound,* 8.

9. Iannis Xenakis, "Rencontre avec Daniel Durney et Dominque Jameux," *Musique en jeu* 1 (1970): 49.

10. Françoise Escal, *Espaces sociaux, espaces musicaux* (Paris: Payot, 1979).

11. Iannis Xenakis, quoted in Escal, *Espaces,* 162.

12. Escal, *Espaces,* 163.

13. Pierre Barbaud, quoted in Escal, *Espaces,* 163.

14. Escal, *Espaces,* 163.

15. Iannis Xenakis, quoted in Escal, *Espaces,* 163–64.

16. Adam de Fulda (1490), quoted in Carl Dahlhaus, *Esthetics of Music,* trans. William W. Austin (Cambridge: Cambridge University Press, 1982), 11.

17. Cf. Nelson Goodman, *Languages of Art* (Indianapolis: Bobbs-Merrill, 1968), 187–89.

18. Goodman, *Languages,* 190.

19. Cf. John Cage, "In Defense of Satie," in *John Cage,* ed. Richard Kostelanetz (New York: Praeger, 1970), 77–84.

20. Cf. Leonard B. Meyer, "The End of the Renaissance?" in *Music, the Arts, and Ideas* (Chicago: University of Chicago Press, 1967), 68–84.

21. Cf. Thomas DeLio, "The Morphology of a Global Structure," in *Circumscribing the Open Universe* (Lanham, Md.: University Press of America, 1984), 11–26.

22. Cf. Ernst Bloch, *Le Principe Espérance,* trans. Françoise Wuilmart (Paris: Gallimard, 1976), 1:374–75.

23. Bloch, *Le Principe,* 228–35.

24. Bloch, *Le Principe,* 270–300.

25. Lawrence Halprin, *The RSVP Cycles: Creative Processes in the Human Environment* (New York: Braziller, 1969).

26. Cf. Daniel Charles, "De-Linearizing Musical Continuity," in this volume.

27. This term is from composers Francis Schwartz and Costin Miereanu.

28. Cf. Gilles Deleuze and Félix Guattari, *Mille plateaux* (Paris: Edition de Minuit, 1980), 20.

29. Deleuze and Guattari, *Mille plateaux,* 21.

30. Daniel Charles, liner notes to John Cage, *Cheap Imitation,* CRSCD 117 (Nova Musicha no. 17) (Milan: Cramps Records, 1989).

31. François Dagognet, *Ecriture et iconographie* (Paris: Vrin, 1973), 80.

32. Dagognet, *Ecriture,* 80.
33. Dagognet, *Ecriture,* 80.
34. Dagognet, *Ecriture,* 80.
35. Dagognet, *Ecriture,* 85.

Silence (1962)

John Hollander

Even if one is kindly disposed toward John Cage's book, it is hard to decide upon a justly suitable response to it. Perhaps the best thing would be to treat the title, *Silence,* as an imperative which prudence and good humor would give one no cause to violate. But whatever Mr. Cage's intention in publishing this volume of essays, lectures, and personal memoirs, the response of utter silence would seem to be unfair in any case. The typographical peculiarities of a good portion of the material must have cost the book's publishers a tremendous amount of money (this was perhaps not completely incidental to Mr. Cage's intentions), and some serious notice should be taken of such a venture. And yet, again, one feels that a sober discussion of its author's musical theory and practice, followed by an assessment of the relative service or disservice done to Mr. Cage's unique concept of a musical career by the book itself, would be out of the spirit of the thing.

And yet what would be exactly *in* its spirit? Running up to Mr. Cage at a public gathering and firing off a cap pistol? (Wrong: merely a pre-adept's bungled version of a Zen *koan.*) Reading aloud passages from Tovey's analyses of Beethoven sonatas while an amplified tape of an electric typewriter obscures all that is said? (Wrong: right out of Tristan Tzara's performance at a famous dada *Festspiel* in Paris in 1920. And Mr. Cage, as he insists in *Silence,* is not a dadaist.) Other purely musical responses to elements in this book suggest themselves: one would certainly want to include some salon piano music (Ethelbert Nevin, perhaps) played softly in another room, to correspond to the genuinely homely quality of some of the stories that are all to be read aloud in one minute's time, printed in the section called "Indeterminacy." Mr. Cage's writings in the last fifteen years have tended more and more to confuse systematically the musical and the meta-musical; they are as carefully arranged with respect to absolute running-time of aural reception, simultaneity of different messages, and frequent tedium as much of his recent music. It is tempting to break down the conventional barrier between musical composition and critical or theoretical writing, and, in this case, refer to the total corpus of his work as Mr. Cage's *productions.* And so again, perhaps his book calls for some kind of production as a critical approach.

But to appear really sympathetic to the world of these productions puts a great strain on decorum, and I shall conclude this prefatory dance with the following credentials, to be stamped on my passport: I like new music; I have the corniest of sentimental attachments to all avant-gardes; I have read some of the Oriental classics in the same translations as has Mr. Cage; my three-year-old daughter drew a smiling face in the margin of one of the pages of *Silence;* I like mushrooms and know the difference between the edible morel and the fell *gyromitra;* I like fun. But much as I am often truly delighted by Mr. Cage's life works, I shall resist the impulse to have as much fun being a critic as Mr. Cage has being a composer.

For fun he does have. I think that the French writer Valéry Larbaud once remarked that while the symbolist tradition in poetry had involved *la difficulté vaincue,* it was Walt Whitman who had shown the world the importance of *la facilité trouvée.* Perhaps this is not irrelevant here. The spirit of play is at heart of much of Mr. Cage's writings, as it appears to be in his formal productions. But this is not to call him unserious. The trouble with the traditional distinction between frivolity and seriousness (rather than mere *solemnity*) is that the whole self-conscious formal dimension of twentieth-century literature and art makes, among other things, this distinction look far too crude. One cannot even write off Mr. Cage's solemnity about Oriental philosophy, randomness and its sovereign importance in art, the role of noise in modern music, religiously adhered-to analogies between musical and notational space, etc., as simply the underpinning for systematic jokes. Neither, however, can one finally dignify his frequent frivolity by equating it with Nietzsche's celebrated characterization of the *seriousness* of the child at play.

Indeed, what we have is a case of something in unstable equilibrium between the two poles, if it is as poles that we wish to take them. I remember the night of a performance by Mr. Cage at one of the New

Music concerts at McMillin Theater in New York in the spring of 1951. It was his piece for twelve radios that was being unveiled, and, as I was myself playing in a piece of Lou Harrison's that followed it on the program, I was helping to set up the table-model radios to be used in the work, which seemed from the glance I had had at the score to be a fairly strict double-fugue, with broadcast frequency being substituted for pitch. Two players controlled each radio, one "riding gain," the other, the tuning (this required a mastery of such technical problems as the fast *glissando* from WQXR to WMCA in New York). After the apparatus had all been set up, Mr. Cage stepped back and admired the ensemble; he clapped his hands and murmured joyously the half embarrassing trade name of the popular radio set he was using: "Twelve Golden Throats!" he said.

It was lovely and funny and defied criticism. In Christopher Isherwood's *The World in the Evening,* one of the characters discourses about the condition of the sensibility in which one sets about being terribly frivolous about the things he takes most seriously and very solemn about what he thinks is most frivolous. There was something of this in Mr. Cage's response to the preparations for the performance of his piece. The work itself, by the way, invoked another paradox that is crucial for any consideration of Mr. Cage's oeuvre: it was a disaster and a success. The actual performance occurred at the end of a terribly long program, and quite a few stations seemed to have already signed off. The result was an excess of hocketing in all the parts, and of very great duration. There was, in short, a great deal of silence, or static, at entrances and throughout. But the aesthetic behind the work, and the one which has produced so much of Mr. Cage's subsequent composition, contained all this magnificently. Accident had asserted itself magnificently, and does not accident lie at the very heart of universal order?

One might be grumpy about this and say that, for example, as a wonderful kind of musical public parlor-game, the whole thing had been mismanaged. There should have been a quartet, perhaps, or even a duo (for Golden Throat and Capehart), and a better hour should have been chosen; the piece should have been much shorter, too, and then the whole performance might have been delightfully easy for an audience to "read." But even this objection, apparently taking the performance on its own terms and eschewing the covert persuasive definitions in shouting "This is not music," etc., would miss the point.

The point, of course, has been amply elaborated in Mr. Cage's productions since that date, and I am presuming that the reader of this review knows both his compositions and the theories that sanction them. For those who do not, *Silence* will prove illuminating. It consists, in part, of a number of short lectures and essays of a more or less conventional sort, such as "The Future of Music: Credo" from 1937, some musings on Satie, Varèse, and the painter Robert Rauschenberg, and a piece called "History of Experimental Music in the United States." These are all to be read aloud. Then there are a number of productions—"Indeterminacy," "Lecture on Something," "Lecture on Nothing," "45′ for a Speaker" and "Where Are We Going? and What Are We Doing?" among them. They must, I suppose, be considered as scores, for they are mostly designed to be read in an absolute time-span, and, in the case of the last named, with four texts going simultaneously. How often, as has been continually remarked, does the score fail miserably to capture the actuality of the musical event! Alas! Mr. Cage is traditionally conscious of this when he remarks in his prefatory note to this four-track verbal score, "The texts were written to be heard as four simultaneous lectures. But to print four lines of type simultaneously—that is, superimposed on one another—was a project unattractive in the present instance. The presentation here used has the effect of making the words legible—a dubious advantage, for I had wanted to say that our experiences, gotten as they were all at once, pass beyond our understanding." This is a beautiful move, superbly played. The texts themselves vary from a discussion of how to get the lecture started, some remarks on modernity and coming to terms with machines and institutions, to seemingly pointless personal anecdote and general observations on human nature. If one were not aware of the design, one could view samples of these sixty-five pages of widely spaced double columns of roman, italic, bold-face and bold italic type as literary exercises heavily influenced by certain French post-surrealists via the American poet John Ashbery. Mr. Cage's prose throughout the volume ranges from an occasionally wistful anecdotal manner to a frequent, and not ineffective, adaptation of the style of Gertrude Stein in *The Autobiography of Alice B. Toklas* and *Lectures in America*. The rhetorical and dialectical structure of all the productions recorded in this book might also seem to smack of the anti-theater of Antonin Artaud and the verbal mechanics of Eastern teachers.

Mr. Cage comes off throughout much of *Silence* as a kind of jovial *guru.* It is obvious that he is terribly serious about music, nostalgic for the cosmological role of music in the medieval and Renaissance world-pictures, and terribly willing to use any means at hand, preferably modish, to construct both a new model of *musica speculativa* and a new model of music to match it. *Silence* contains within it, in dispersed form, the pattern of this model. (Notice, by the way, in this last sentence, the brilliant effect of the title in transforming almost any statement *about* the book into one that might have come *from* it by the old trick known to logicians as the confusion of use and mention.) And as such, I suppose the book does him justice.

But I hardly feel that it can be read through. There are some amusing personal anecdotes, a lot of amusements for the reader in his notes prefaced to the various sections, some minutely detailed descriptions of the randomizing and organizing processes employed in the construction of several pieces (including the *Imaginary Landscape No. 4* for twelve radios I mentioned earlier). The net effect of *Silence,* however, is peculiarly and appropriately like the characteristic that so many performances of his productions seem to have: one wants to hear about them rather than to hear them. And here, perhaps, is the heart of the matter. One might want to take serious issue with the whole theory of chance upon which Mr. Cage builds his oeuvre, pointing out that it is not so much the *degree* of randomization of musical elements that makes his examples from the music of the past (realization, improvisation, etc.) largely irrelevant, as the *role* of the random process in the compositional one. In one sense, some of his compositions may be taken in part as jokes *about* totally organized music, but in another sense they are part of a largely modish celebration of the Accident in art. The iconography of the drip of paint in abstract expressionist canvases of the past decade involves the growing attempt to make the process of creation stand for more, ultimately, than does the finished work. In painting, music, and literature alike, it is true that the accidental or inspirational moment must always occur at certain points during the composition of a work if that work is to have any life at all. The question is simply one of planning the domain in which the Accident is to operate in the structure of the finished work. The description of one of Mr. Cage's compositional processes is often, it seems to me, more interesting than the performed result.

In short, something seems to be missing. Mr. Cage is devoted, even dedicated to his art; he has no lack of talent, invention, sense of dramaturgy, care for performance, or musical *joie de vivre.* Perhaps what Mr. Cage's career as a composer lacks is a certain kind of hard work. Not the unbelievably elaborate effort, merely, of planning, arranging, constructing, rationalizing (however playfully or dubiously); not the great pains of carrying off a production, but something else. The difference between the most inspired amateur theatricals and the opera, between the conversation that one would like to record and the poem, between the practical joke and the great film, is not one of degree of effort or of conviction. It is that peculiar labor of art itself, the incredible agony of the real artist in his struggles with lethargy and with misplaced zeal, with despair and with the temptations of his recent successes, *to get better.* The dying writer in Henry James's "The Death of the Lion" puts it almost perfectly: "Our doubt is our passion and our passion is our task. The rest is the madness of art." The rest, to be sure; but Mr. Cage's sense of indeterminacy is not this profound doubt, and his métier is not task.

Social Concern (1968)

Calvin Tomkins

For several years now, John Cage's book *Silence* has been what Greenwich Village Booksellers call an "underground best seller." Intense young loyalists of the New York art scene carry it reverently to happenings, thus demonstrating their awareness that Cage, America's reigning musical revolutionary, had initiated the happenings movement at Black Mountain College in 1952. The appearance of a paperback edition of *Silence* last year was followed, curiously enough, by a spectacular increase in sales of the hardcover edition, presumably by those who wished to appear disciples of long and permanent standing.

It has been evident at any rate that Cage's influence extends well beyond the field of contemporary music, where his experiments with "found sound," electronic composition and chance methods have outraged traditionalists for 30 years. To those who have followed Cage's career, it will not be particularly surprising to learn that he now considers music merely "child's play." In this new collection of lectures, essays and other writings completed since *Silence* came out in 1961, he makes plain that he is less and less interested in composing music and more and more interested in improving society—an enterprise to which he devotes himself despite a cheerful premonition that he will only succeed in making matters worse.

"Once one gets interested in world improvement, there is no stopping," Cage notes apologetically. Like Buckminster Fuller and Marshall McLuhan, to whom he gives full and generous credit where credit is due, Cage foresees the electronic transformation of society, the global village, the disappearance of work, money, privacy, individualism, nationalism, war and other linear stigmata. The message is similar; the medium, however, is utterly unique. To read Fuller and McLuhan is to struggle with prose styles that, for all their neologisms and contortions of syntax, are still based on nineteenth-century linear models. Cage, on the other hand, has made it a point to compose most of his writings according to the same methods that he uses in his music, and since 1950 this has meant according to the methods of chance.

Take, for example, his "Diary," three installments of which make up a large portion of the new book. Cage decided in advance that the diary would be a "mosaic of ideas, statements, words, and stories," and before writing in it each day he determined by means of chance operations (a rather elaborate procedure derived from the *I Ching,* the ancient Chinese book of oracles) how many parts of the mosaic he would employ, and how many words there would be in each, the total each day to equal or exceed 100 words.

Using an I.B.M. Selectric typewriter with 12 different type faces, he let chance determine which type face would be used for which idea, statement, word or story, and also where the left-hand margins would fall. The result, which must have caused some typographer untold anguish, is a sort of open-ended prose poem, a verbal collage that proceeds according to its own highly disciplined illogic and whose effect, for this reader, is simultaneously witty, naive, irritating, oddly moving, self-indulgent, evangelistic, and as fresh and surprising as electric flowers in the global village square. It is also stamped at every point with the author's irresistible gaiety and lucid intelligence, a quality of mind that somehow holds together all the fragmentary workings of chance.

What is on Cage's mind at the moment? Global services, for one thing. Hearing that there are now 61 services such as the telephone, electric power and radio that can be described as global in extent, he inquires tirelessly (and unsuccessfully) for a listing of all 61. This is clear proof to Cage that Western technology is indeed leading to a recognition of the Buddhist doctrine of interrelatedness: "The truth is that everything causes everything else. We do not speak, therefore, of one thing causing another." He has a great many thoughts on art and life, and the steady erosion of all traditional barriers between the two. Contemporary art, he tells us, turns spectators into artists; the doors to participation have been opened by artists who no longer place themselves on pedestals, and the goal of the new art is simply "to introduce us to the very life we are living."

Wishing his fellow musician-listener a hearty "Happy New Ears," Cage passes on to more pressing matters. The world can be made to work, not by politicians but by Fuller's comprehensive designers. The breakdown of the old order is at hand: "The burning of draft cards. Haight-Ashbury. Tax evasion. Fourteen thousand Americans renounced citizenship in 1966. Civil disobedience. Nonpayment of taxes. July '67 racial riots in New Jersey ended by removal of police from disturbed areas." As Cage sees it, "Our proper work now if we love mankind and the world we live in is revolution."

Many of the ideas in the present volume will be familiar to students of *Silence.* The difference is mainly one of emphasis: a shifting from esthetic to social concerns, and a reiterated belief that the new art provides us with a key to the new life in tomorrow's electronic universe. The new art, in which great numbers will participate freely and without competitiveness, indicates ways in which "many centers can interpenetrate without obstructing one another." Daily life is what matters, provided one is truly awakened to its wonders. "What's marvelous is that the moon still rises even though we've changed our minds about whether or not we'll ever get there."

None of this, one can say, is especially profound or even strikingly original, and yet I have no doubt that it will be read like Scripture by the young. Read and enjoyed (which is more than can be said for McLuhan), and rightly so, because in Cage's case the medium, which happens to be print, is really the message. Tune into him at any point—statements (outrageous or otherwise), quotations from the books he's been reading (lately, Thoreau and Veblen), sermons (the meeting of East and West; the uses of anarchy), even the seemingly inconsequential, humorous, Zen-like stories that he drops at intervals into the more formal text in order, as he says, to provide "an occasion for changing one's mind"—and you find yourself traveling at high speed along the new electronic wavelength.

What's more, the trip requires no artificial fuels. Cage is an amateur mycologist of considerable note; but he has never tasted the hallucinatory fungi, and he has no use for drug-induced visions. "The visions I hear about don't interest me," he explains. "Dick Higgins ate a little *muscaria* and it made him see some rabbits. Valentina Wasson ate the divine mushrooms in Mexico and imagined she was in eighteenth-century Versailles hearing some Mozart. Without any dope at all other than caffeine and nicotine I'll be in San Francisco tomorrow morning hearing some of my own music and on Sunday, God willing, I'll awake in Hawaii with papayas and pineapple for breakfast. There'll be sweet-smelling flowers, brightly colored birds, people swimming in the surf, and (I'll bet you a nickel) a rainbow at some point during the day in the sky."

A Year from Monday (1968)

Roger Maren

John Cage's new book consists mostly of things he has written since 1961—essays on how to improve the world; statements on Duchamp, Miro, Jasper Johns, Schoenberg's letters, Ives, and other things, including a lot about mushrooms; some diary entries; addresses on various occasions; lots of little stories about his experiences and those of friends, relatives, and colleagues; some jokes and "Zen stories." Most of it was composed by means of one or another of Cage's chance operations. Much of it is either written higgledy-piggledy on the page and/or has unconventional spacing and/or typography. Each piece is preceded by a few paragraphs describing the situation surrounding its composition and the means employed. The intent is didactic. Since Cage would like our activities "to be more social and anarchically so," he tries to show how this might be achieved. There isn't very much about music.

Being didactic and not very interested in music is no novelty for Cage. When he quit composing and began indeterminate production of sound he was very explicit about it: ". . . I said that the purpose of this purposeless music would be achieved if people learned to listen. That when they listened they might discover that they preferred the sounds of everyday life to the ones they would presently hear in the musical program. . . . That that was all right as far as I was concerned."

Many people—especially composers—used to miss the point. At a party once, a composer who had read something I had written about Cage, came up to me very red in the face and shouted, "I sweat blood for every note I write and that s.o.b. . . . " Apparently he thought that Cage and he were competing in the same market and that Cage was managing to hoodwink buyers with a product containing less precious material badly concocted. He seemed not to see that they were producing an entirely different kind of goods. The blood-sweater was composing music for the usual purposes. Cage was making devices intended, in some small way, to help people behave so as to have a better world. Confusion probably resulted—at least partly—because the devices contained more-or-less musical noises, were employed in a more-or-less conventional concert-hall setting, were reviewed by more-or-less music critics, and so on. That does seem an odd and curiously feeble way to improve the world—more like a gag than a noble effort. And the kind of improvement envisaged wouldn't seem like anything much to most people even if they did happen to understand the whole business. Cage is aware of this. In the foreword to *A Year from Monday* he writes, "My ideas certainly started in the field of music. And that field, so to speak, is child's play. . . . Our proper work now if we love mankind and the world we live in is revolution."

I don't know why he stayed in music so long except that it isn't easy to give up something in which you have invested a lot of time and energy. Cage does reveal some stubbornness when recalling a conversation with Schoenberg: ". . . when Schoenberg asked me whether I would devote my life to music, I said, 'Of course.' After I had been studying with him for two years, Schoenberg said, 'In order to write music you must have a feeling for harmony.' I then explained to him that I had no feeling for harmony. He then said I would always encounter an obstacle, that it would be as though I came to a wall through which I could not pass. I said, 'In that case I will devote my life to beating my head against that wall.'" Perhaps he once thought he was good at music. He doesn't think so now. "What was it that made me choose music rather than painting? Just because they said nicer things about my music than about my paintings? But I don't have absolute pitch. I can't keep a tune. In fact, I have no talent for music. The last time I saw her, Aunt Phoebe said, 'You're in the wrong profession.'" (I don't think this is blague or an attempt to get the audience to say "Aw come one, John, you're really brimming with talent." I do get a hint that he feels a little guilty about not being more candid in the past and is now trying to make a clean breast of it even while doing so humorously.) In any event, whatever kept him in music so long has lost a lot of its motive force, and he makes this clear in the present book.

The revolution that Cage wants to make his proper work is libertarian-anarchist in style. To this style he adds the influence of Buckminster Fuller, Marshall McLuhan, Norman O. Brown, and Marcel Duchamp. He isn't thinking of anything very violent. He is still in the field of the arts (or entertainment, if you prefer) and wants to do his bit there. "The reason I am less and less interested in music," he writes, "is not only that I find environmental sounds and noises more useful aesthetically than the sounds produced by the world's musical cultures, but that, when you get right down to it, a composer is simply someone who tells other people what to do. I find this an unattractive way of getting things done. . . ." In looking for an attractive way to get things done he sees a current use for art: "giving instances of society suitable for social imitation—suitable because they show ways many centers can interpenetrate without obstructing one another, ways people can do things without being told or telling others what to do." He quotes Norman O. Brown when he writes that he looks forward to "an environment that works so well that we can run wild in it."

Now I suddenly realize that I am not at all giving the flavor of what Cage is up to or of how the book reads. The previous paragraph doesn't quite sound as though it implies charging admission for entry to the roof of a building in Ann Arbor on which folding chairs are haphazardly placed so that people can sit down while being surrounded not only by the night sky and the sights, sounds, and smells of town, but also by incomprehensible words coming from a six-channel audio system for which the voices of Cage and others are a sound source. (Maybe they didn't charge admission.)[1] Nor does it give the flavor of the book. I have been trying too hard to make the whole business sound rationally connected. This is a great temptation for me not only because I have a yen for explication but because Cage himself is really not so irrational as he makes out. He may be a Zen devotee, but I get the impression that, most characteristically, he is some more-or-less gifted guy from California whose *Amerikanische Kopf* is buzzing with all sorts of real keen notions that are a little fuzzy, unoriginal, and suspiciously full of flaws. He's not very happy with this and so, with Zen, Duchamp, McLuhan, and other such as authorities, he tries to blow his mind without chemicals. He uses devices to fragment and jumble everything, to bring in irrelevancies, to disconcert himself and the reader. To get any ideas such as I have put down, one has to pick them up among the mushrooms and cats and aunts and mothers and Zen patriarchs and pies in Canada and Spider Goddesses and garbage cans in West

Germany and quotes from Buckminster Fuller, and you have to turn the book sideways or peer at squiggles that indicate where John swallowed or coughed when he read the text and so on.

Read the book if that kind of thing sounds appealing. Cage writes quite elegantly, and much of it is straight—especially the anecdotes. I wouldn't go out of my way to place the book in the hands of impressionable youth, however. The flawed reasoning of a lot of it might be a poor influence. Cage is aware that he isn't very good in this line. (He writes about playing chess: "My mind seems in some respect lacking, so that I make obviously stupid moves. I do not for a moment doubt that this lack of intelligence affects my music and thinking generally.") But he persists in trying to make rational statements anyway—just like anyone else you might meet on Main Street. What might be another poor influence is his strong reaction against the situation of many people who listen to music—"off artificially in the distance as they are accustomed to be, trying to figure out what is being said by some artist by means of sounds." This is probably an accurate description of some people, especially of these who give or take mus. app. courses. But that's no reason to come on—and Cage seems to—as though the very act of following the structure of a piece necessitates loss of contact with body, soul, and environment. Such an attitude on the part of a notorious and published man may easily be used by school-corrupted youth as an apology for its rotten relation to the art and as a reason to quit it rather than to experience it in a more healthy manner. What's so bad about understanding the music you hear? It's an experience as much a part of life as digging any silence of Morton Feldman and well worth having. Kids, believe me, it really doesn't have such baneful effects! I do it and it hasn't split me off from everyday life, as any of my friends can attest. I'm even an anarchist. Apparently I've got a good deal of Zen too. (John told me so once before I even knew what Zen was.)

I'm sorry that I can't recommend the book even though the writing is felicitous and the author cites sources of his quotations and influences. It has a certain charm that will please many people, but I wouldn't have finished it had I not been asked to review it. The book does reflect what John claims as a redeeming quality: a sunny disposition; it is serious and jocular all at once; it expresses a desire for community—all things I would find welcome in a neighbor. But what I found particularly appealing about the book was a quality that made me think that, if John were my neighbor, he wouldn't have pestered me about reading it.

NOTE

1. While on the subject of money, I should report the publisher's reply to my inquiry about the book's price. "We did not select this book price entirely at random. Had we done so, the chances are that the book would have been decidedly over or underpriced. But, as we thought of John Cage and the sort of book that this is, we decided that there was no reason to give it a usual book price so we decided—semi-arbitrarily, if you will—on the price of $7.92."

Cage and Fluxus (1990)

Henry Flynt

Toward the end of the Fifties, music acquired an avant-garde role which it had not previously had. Modern classical music had a prestige with the cultural public which it subsequently lost. That very eminence might seem to disqualify it as avant-garde. But the point was that musical composition required an expertise comparable to scientific training. The European notions of laws of music and scientific progress in music were taken seriously. Babbitt, Xenakis, Stockhausen, Cage, and their colleagues were engaged in a frantic race to field the most radical music—rather like the race to the moon. Against this background, scores of Cage's such as *Music Walk* (1958) seemed at the time to be so original—and so artificial—that they might have fallen down from Mars.

Cage initiated a music of calculated randomness with, e.g., *Music of Changes* (1951). He supported his approach with an esthetic of indifference which he ascribed to East Asian thought. (Action painting was not a precedent for him, he has told me.)

At the same time, a quasiscientific analysis of music as nothing but a collection of sounds defined by frequency, amplitude, duration, and overtone spectrum was presupposed by the compositions of Cage and his colleagues (*Silence,* 80). Music, then, was being radically flattened. Cage made a completely flattened use of the Asian sources.

All the same, Cage introduced a process of manipulation which was enigmatic in a new way. Moving to "indeterminacy" in the late Fifties, his music assumed a structural artificiality unlike anything in the past. The score was produced by a process which could not be inferred by the performers unless the composer divulged it. Performers had to carry out a sort of computation, involving free choice, in order to ascertain what sounds they would make. In the course of this process, a single sound's beginning and its length were determined in different and unconnected patterns. What the audience heard, finally, was an extravagant sound-assemblage which could not be re-performed and which gave no clue as to its intentional organization.

Newness emerged here as the ritualized goal of the individual composition. Cage wanted performances of his own compositions to be broadly surprising to him.

Cage was not shy about taking a crusading role. He redefined the leading edge in such a way that the preceding avant-garde was rendered passé.

> This decision alters the view of history [!], so that one is no longer concerned with tonality or atonality . . . (*Silence,* 68–69)

Indeed, the catchword *indeterminacy* understated Cage's originality. Quantum physics is no different from the rest of science in requiring theory to be univocal. Cage exploded wholesale a sort of grimness in the programs whereby humans make order—by designing dissociation, performance choice, coincidence in these programs. The Cagean performer was interactive in a way which has no equivalent in accredited science, including quantum physics.

As Cage pursued his esthetic, music became an attitude of listening, which could just as well be directed to environmental sounds. There had been his silent piece in three movements, *4'33"* (1952)—which was performed as a piano piece, but could have been performed by any ensemble. So *4'33"* prefigured compositions in which the performers' role was indistinguishable from the audience's.

Cage's pronouncements in the period seemed to say that only listening and the environment were necessary for music, that composers and professional instrumentalists were passé. At the time, I took this as encouragement to question the very legitimacy of art.[1] Also, Cage's juniors acknowledged and echoed these dicta. And yet Cage remained a professional composer, he encouraged others to be professional artists, and his students became career professionals. Relative to the issues I am stressing in this survey, seemingly extreme proclamations which are not acted on (and, in hindsight, were not even meant) are troubling.

I am sure that Cage has been, by his lights, a sincere person—an industrious person who bore up under a lot of ridicule. In pursuing an arcane technical endeavor as a bohemian, Cage provided a profound lesson to aspiring innovators.

All the same, what are we to make of the presence of intimations of the end of art in the stances of career artists, intimations which turn out to be nothing of the sort? In Cage's case, it does not appear possible to argue that he was moving toward a breakthrough in 1960 from which he subsequently retreated. But this problem in artists' biographies will appear again in this review.

Some of Cage's students in the Fifties became charter members of Fluxus. Jackson Mac Low began transferring Cage's chance procedures to poetry—yielding a more computational or artificial concrete poetry. In 1958, Cage taught a composition class at the New School for Social Research, whose story has often been told. Participants included Allan Kaprow, Dick Higgins, Jackson Mac Low, Al Hansen, George Brecht, Toshi Ichiyanagi, Scott Hyde, Richard Maxfield.

There were post-Cage developments in New York in 1959. Allan Kaprow's *18 Happenings in Six Parts,* for example, was presented at the Reuben Gallery, 61 Fourth Avenue. Art historians have characterized happenings as plotless theater, and have found a precedent for them in the "concerted action" which Cage presented at Black Mountain College in 1952. (Kaprow has objected that a genuine happening does not consist in a staged performance before an audience.)

Another 1959 event at the Reuben Gallery was George Brecht's show, "Toward Events." At the time, both Happenings and Events were greeted as anti-art manifestations or as non-art: a reaction that has since been forgotten.[2]

Brecht evidently was directly influenced by Cage, but immediately moved beyond Cage's exclusive emphasis on music. I do not find Brecht sympathetic, because his work is deliberately and relentlessly prosaic. Nevertheless, Brecht was a key figure in the post-Cage scene; subsequently he was the pivot in the succession from Cage to Fluxus.

In 1959, musical scores began to appear which consisted of short verbal texts. There is, for example, Brecht's *Time-Table Music* (Summer 1959).[3] This piece is performed in a railway station by separated performers who use the station's timetable to determine when to make sounds—without declaring to passersby that a performance is occurring.

After I became involved in new music, I remember walking through Harvard Yard and seeing a man positioned at the corner of a dormitory, seemingly attentive, but not visibly doing anything. The thought occurred to me that he might be participating in a new music performance whose existence was not announced. Well, Brecht's *Time-Table Music* is such a piece. Cage had pointed out that we are surrounded by invisible electromagnetic broadcasts. But at that time it seemed that we were also surrounded by sounds that might or might not belong to compositions, and by actions that might or might not be controlled by unannounced performance plans.

At what point is it certain that structure or purpose exists?

In 1960, that seemed to dissolve into the nondescript surroundings. That contributed to my sense that we were about to pass beyond all culture that officially existed.

Let me mention that Dick Higgins also has a published one-paragraph text score, *Constellation No. 1,* which is from July 1959.

There is another point in Brecht to which I wish to respond, and I prefer to do so here, even though it means getting ahead of my story. In an interview published in *Art and Artists,* October 1972, Brecht said:

> I pose this as a problem for anybody who thinks they're making art, or anti-art, or non-art: to make a work which cannot possibly be considered art.

Well, here is a cheap solution: "If a contradiction cannot be art, then this sentence is not art or not true." To give a serious solution is beyond the scope of this review.

NOTES

1. Also, Maciunas in 1962 and Ben Vautier in 1965–68 seem to have seen anti-art implications in Cage.

2. Fred McDarrah, *The Artist's World in Pictures* (1961), 176–77; George Brecht, letter to George Maciunas and Henry Flynt, April 18, 1963; Nam June Paik, "The Monthly Review of the University for Avant-Garde Hinduism" (1963).

3. Published in *Kulchur* 3 (1961): 19.

Something about the Writings of John Cage (1991)

Jackson Mac Low

> . . . I myself feel more committed the more diverse and multiplied my interests and actions become.[1]

> Somewhere in Virginia, I lost my hat.[2]

Writing about John Cage is like writing about the ocean. Writing about any aspect involves inevitably writing about most of the others. ("And so we hesitate before crossing the great waters.")[3]

Writing about John as a writer, writing about John's writing, writing about John writing, inevitably demand(s) writing also about his actions and interests as composer, social thinker, mycologist, unorthodox Buddhist . . .

> [V]alue judgment . . . [i]s a decision to eliminate from experience certain things. [Dr. D. T.] Suzuki said Zen wants us to diminish that kind of activity of the ego and to increase the activity that accepts the rest of creation. And rather than taking the path that is prescribed in the formal practice of Zen Buddhism itself, namely sitting cross-legged and breathing and such things, I decided that my proper discipline was the one to which I was already committed, namely the making of music. And that I would do it with a means that was as strict as sitting cross-legged, namely the use of chance operations, and the shifting of my responsibility from that of making choices to that of asking questions.[4]

Cage has often called the use of chance operations and the composition of works indeterminate as to performance "skillful means"

(Skt. *upāya,* a Buddhist term for means employed by Boddhisattvas to help all sentient beings attain enlightenment). I think he views the experiences of composing, performing, and hearing such works as being equally conducive to the arousal of *prājña*—intuitive wisdom/energy, the essence/seed of the enlightened state—by allowing the experience of sounds perceived in themselves, "in their suchness," rather than as means of communication, expression, or emotional arousal or as subordinate elements in a structure.

These considerations are as relevant to his writing as to his music—especially to the poems he has written since about 1970, most of which are alogical and asyntactical collages (i.e., ones "departing from conventional syntax") of language elements: letters, syllables, words, phrases, and/or sentences, freed from "the arrangement of an army" (the original meaning, as Norman O. Brown informed him, of "syntax" [Gk. σύνταξις]), and therefore—like the sounds in the music he wrote after 1950—perceivable in themselves as are objects of perception when one regards them with "bare attention" during *vipaśyana* [Skt., 'contemplation'], the basic form of Buddhist meditation.

(There is some question, of course, whether *any* arrangement of language elements, no matter how different from *normative* syntax, doesn't in itself constitute a new, *nonnormative* syntax. Some theorists would say that Cage and others who eschew normative syntax are "evading the army" by producing their own *new* syntaxes, over which the "generals" have no sway. Nevertheless, such nonnormative syntaxes may well conduce to giving language something approaching "bare attention.")

During the last three decades, Wesleyan University Press (Middletown, Conn.) has published five substantial volumes of Cage's writings: *Silence* (1961), *A Year from Monday* (1967), *M: Writings '67–'72* (1973), *Empty Words: Writings '73–'78* (1979), and *X: Writings '79–'82* (1983, 1986). Moreover, the University of Tulsa published his first *Writing through* Finnegans Wake as a supplement to *James Joyce Quarterly* 15 and as No. 16 in its Monograph Series, and Cage himself, as a member of the now-defunct publishing co-op Printed Editions, published in 1978 a deluxe edition of his first two *Writings through* Finnegans Wake. (He has written five of them, the last two of which "Writing for the Fourth Time through *Finnegans Wake*" and "Muoyce [Writing for the Fifth Time through *Finnegans Wake*]," appear in *X.*)[5] In addition, Station Hill Press published his *Themes and Variations.*[6] While most of his writings have been published in the Wesleyan collections, many have also appeared in magazines, anthologies, record brochures, exhibition catalogs, as forewords to other people's books, and on audiotapes and records.

Cage has written throughout his life, although the earliest work in the Wesleyan volumes, "The Future of Music: Credo,"[7] dates from 1937. His principal subject, of course, has been music, especially modern experimental music, but he has also discussed other music of the past, present, and future. And although he has written extensively on his own music, he has also often discussed other composers, including Earle Brown, Cowell, Feldman, Ives, Satie, Schoenberg, Stockhausen, Christian Wolff, and others. He has also dealt with visual artists: Duchamp, Graves, Jasper Johns, Miró, Rauschenberg, and Mark Tobey; social and religious thinkers: Norman O. Brown, Buckminster Fuller, Marshall McLuhan, D. T. Suzuki, and Thoreau; and dance and dancers, especially Merce Cunningham; and he's written on "something,"[8] "nothing,"[9] and mushrooms.[10]

Much of his writing consists of elegantly composed expository prose and skillfully told stories, most of them drawn from his own and his friends' lives. However, the following discussion will be limited to the writings he has composed by *I Ching* chance operations, by use of materials originally composed to generate realizations of indeterminate musical works, by "writing through" certain texts to produce "mesostics," and by related methods. These fall ostensibly into two categories: lectures and poetry, much of it asyntactical, but, as we shall see, the categories are really "not-two."

In the 1950s and 1960s Cage composed several works for solo speakers, most of which he called "lectures." An early example is "45′ for a Speaker,"[11] for which he adapted the numerical rhythmic structure of his *34′46.776″ for Two Pianists,*[12] in which each piano part's structural units become different in actual duration through the use of a factor obtained by chance operations. When he applied the chance factor to the numerical rhythmic structure of the speech, he obtained 39′16.95″, which proved to be too short a time for him to perform the speech. After experiments he found that forty-five minutes for the whole, two seconds for each line, was the shortest practical duration: "Not all the text can be read comfortably even at this speed," he writes, "but one can still try." He drew the material for this work from previously written lectures as well as new material, and he obtained answers by chance operations to six questions that determined all characteristics of its spoken material and silences.

When the poet, potter, and author[13] Mary Caroline Richards asked him "why he didn't give a conventional informative lecture," which she called "the most shocking thing [he] could do," Cage replied, "'I don't give these lectures to surprise people, but out of a need for poetry.'" And he adds, "[P]oetry is not prose simply because poetry is in one way or another formalized. It is not poetry by reason of its content or ambiguity but by reason of its allowing musical elements (time, sound) to be introduced into the world of words."[14]

In writing "Where Are We Going? And What Are We Doing?"[15] for delivery at Pratt Institute, Brooklyn, in January 1961, Cage used the materials for his *Cartridge Music*[16] to compose four texts that are to be heard simultaneously. They are divided into lines, twenty-five of which may be read in one, one-and-a-quarter, or one-and-a-half minutes, so that the printed relationship between the four texts is only one of many possibilities. Empty lines indicate silences. Much of the lecture (I was there) was unintelligible because of the simultaneity. Two sentences in one of the texts tell us more about Cage's conceptions of poetry:

> We who speak English were so / certain of our language and that / we could use it to communicate / that we have nearly destroyed its potential for poetry. The / thing in it that's going to save / the situation is the high percentage / of consonants and the natural way / in which they produce discontinuity.[17]

So these "lectures"—in which discontinuity in the form of silences longer than punctuational pauses and abrupt shifts in subject-matter, tempo of delivery, and other aspects have been brought about mainly by use of chance operations and materials for realizing musical compositions indeterminate of performance—are really Cage's earliest published poems.

In 1967 he began composing two types of works that are avowedly poems: (1) asyntactical sequences of letters, syllables, words, phrases, and/or sentences drawn from the *Journal* of the American philosopher and naturalist Henry David Thoreau[18] and arranged by *I Ching* chance operations; (2) poems in which the capitalized letters of a name run down the center of each strophe, for which Cage adopted the term *mesostics* (see below).

Many of the latter, e.g., "36 Mesostics Re and Not Re Marcel Duchamp,"[19] are haiku-like poems that are normatively syntactical, if often elliptically so, but most of them are asyntactical, or fragmentarily normative, compilations of phrases, words, and/or word fragments. A large group, "62 Mesostics re Merce Cunningham,"[20] was drawn from Merce Cunningham's *Changes: Notes on Choreography,*[21] and other works on dance, and one group, "Writing through the Cantos,"[22] was drawn from Ezra Pound's magnum opus, but by far the largest number were drawn from James Joyce's *Finnegans Wake.*[23]

Cage's first asyntactical poems are the texts of *Song Books (Solos for Voice 3–92),*[24] which he began in 1967 and of which the irresistibly beautiful No. 30 appears in *M* as "Song."[25] Each solo is either "1) song; 2) song using electronics; 3) theatre; [or] 4) theatre using electronics" and "is relevant or irrelevant to the subject, 'We connect Satie with Thoreau.'"[26] Each exemplifies one of the twenty-five possible combinations or single instances of five language units: letters, syllables, words, phrases, and sentences, all drawn by *I Ching* chance operations from Thoreau's *Journal.*

His first extensive asyntactical text, "Mureau" (1970),[27] includes all the possibilities and was written "by subjecting all the remarks of . . . Thoreau about music, silence, and sounds he heard that are indexed in the Dover edition of the *Journal* to a series of *I Ching* chance operations. The personal pronoun was varied according to such operations and the typing [in a number of different typefaces that often begin or end within a word] was likewise determined. Mureau is the first syllable of the word music followed by the second of the name Thoreau."[28]

"Mureau" differs significantly from the texts in the *Song Books* in that it is a poem to be *read,* aloud or silently, rather than a text to be, in some sense, sung. Hearing Cage read it aloud on the very fine 65-minute S Press tape[29] offers one of his asyntactical poetry's most accessible delights. As he reads it in his calm, precise voice, this sequence of language elements and silences glides through the listener's mind as naturally as the constantly changing configurations of the water in a stream flow between its banks. It is curious how this continuum of discontinuities seems always to be speaking directly to us. Even the separated and recombined letters function as speech—enigmatic interjections in this stream of language and silence about sound and silence.

Subsequently (ca. 1973–75), Cage subjected the whole *Journal,* including eventually Thoreau's sketches, to *I Ching* chance operations to produce the long, four-part poem "Empty Words."[30] In this work a transition takes place, as Cage says, "from language to music."[31] All four parts include silences; however, Part 1 includes no sentences, but mixes phrases, words, syllables, and letters; Part 2 mixes the last three; Part 3, the last two; and Part 4 includes only letters and silences. The language elements in all four parts were not only drawn from the *Journal* by *I Ching* chance operations but were also placed on the page by them. Cage also used such operations to answer the questions: "Of the four columns on two facing pages which two have text?" and, Where, in the remaining spaces, were *which* drawings (as photographed by Babette Mangolte) to be placed?[32]

Cage has often performed one or more parts of "Empty Words," sitting quietly at a small, lamplit table with text, stopwatch, and microphone, emanating an aura of quiet even when he speaks. Mangolte's photographs of Thoreau's sketches are often projected beside him.

Thoreau's writings, not only his *Journal* but also *Walden* and "Civil Disobedience," were the sources of the collage performance text "Lecture on the Weather," composed by means of *I Ching* chance operations to fulfill a 1975 commission from Richard Coulter of the Canadian Broadcasting Company for "a piece of music to celebrate the American Bicentennial." Cage had returned to Thoreau after looking in vain for "an anthology of American aspirational thought," in searching for which he "began to realize that what is called balance between the branches of government is not balance at all: all the branches of our government are occupied by lawyers."[33]

This work's preface is Cage's strongest and most direct political statement, reinforced by his "stating his preference that [the twelve speaker-vocalists and/or speaker-instrumentalists] be American men who had become Canadian citizens," presumably to avoid being forced to fight the Vietnamese.[34]

He writes that although chance operations may seem "counter to the spirit of Thoreau, . . . [who] speaks against blind obedience to a blundering oracle, . . . [they] are not mysterious sources of 'the right answers' . . . [but] a means of locating a single one among a multiplicity of answers, and . . . of freeing the ego from its taste and memory, its concern for profit and power, of silencing the ego so that the rest of the world has a chance to enter into the ego's own experience whether that be outside or inside."

"We would do well," he concludes, "to give up the notion that we alone can keep the world in line, that only we can solve its problems. . . . Our political structures no longer fit the circumstances of our lives. . . . I dedicate this work to the U.S.A. that it may become just another part of the world, no more, no less."[35]

Norman O. Brown suggested to Cage the term *mesostics* to distinguish such poems from acrostics, in which a name or other "index words" run down one side rather than the middle of the verses. The latter's earliest mesostics were poems written for friends on various occasions, somewhat akin to Mallarmé's "Vers de circonstance."[36] His "first mesostic was written as prose to celebrate one of Edwin Denby's birthdays. The following ones, each letter of the name being on its own line, were written as poetry. *A given letter capitalized does not occur between it and the preceding capitalized letter* [Cage's first "Mesostic Rule," see below]." His earliest extensive group, "36 Mesostics Re and Not Re Duchamp," is normatively syntactical, with either one of Duchamp's names running down the middle of each one.[37]

It was only when he began "62 Mesostics re Merce Cunningham"[38] that he began to write *asyntactical* mesostics, employing *I Ching* chance operations and "writing-through" methods: ones which the writer searches through source texts to find, successively, words and/or other language elements that have specific characteristics.

In writing the Cunningham series he "used over seven hundred different type faces and sizes available in Letraset and, of course, subjected them to *I Ching* chance operations. No line has more than one word or syllable. Both syllables and words were obtained from Merce Cunningham's *Changes: Notes on Choreography*[39] and from thirty-two other books most used by Cunningham in relation to his work. The words were subjected to a process that brought about in some cases syllable exchange between two or more of them. This process produced new words not to be found in any dictionary but reminiscent of words everywhere to be found in James Joyce's *Finnegans Wake.*"[40] These poems thus intrinsically anticipated the long series of mesostics constituting Cage's "writings through *Finnegans Wake.*"

The "62 Mesostics re Merce Cunningham" are not only dazzling visual poems that "resemble waterfalls or ideograms,"[41] but have been performed by Cage and others, notably the late Egyptian-born vocalist Demetrios Stratos, who recorded them in 1974.[42]

Of the five writings through *Finnegans Wake,* all except the fifth follow Cage's principal Mesostic Rule: "the first letter of a word or name is on the first line and following it on the first line the second letter of the word or name is not to be found. (The second letter is on the second line.)"[43]

Writing for the Second Time through Finnegans Wake[44] differs from the first "Writing" in that, as Cage writes, "I did not permit the reappearance of a syllable for a given letter of the name. I distinguished between the two *J*'s and the two *E*'s. the syllable 'just' could be used twice, once for the *J* of James and once for the *J* of Joyce, since it has neither *A* nor *O* after the *J*. But it could not be used again. To keep from repeating syllables, I kept a card index of the ones I had already used. . . . [T]his restriction made a text considerably shorter" than the first "Writing."[45]

At N. O. Brown's suggestion, Cage omitted punctuation marks, but kept the omitted marks "not in the mesostics but on the pages where they originally appeared, the marks disposed in the space and those other than periods given an orientation by means of *I Ching* chance operations."[46]

Writing for the Third Time through Finnegans Wake,[47] follows a rule suggested by the late Louis Mink, a professor of philosophy at Wesleyan University. Between any two letters of a name or other index word, it does not let *either* letter appear in any intervening word.

When composing *Writing for the Fourth Time through* Finnegans Wake,[48] Cage not only followed his "Mesostic Rule" and "Mink's Rule" but, as he did when composing the second "Writing," he kept a syllable index and did not permit the reappearance of any syllable for a given letter of the name "James Joyce."

Muoyce (Writing for the Fifth Time through Finnegans Wake)[49] is not a series of mesostics but was composed by means of *I Ching* chance operations, jumping from chapter to chapter, and is made up of four sections that comprise, respectively, eight "stanzas," four, four, and one, having the format of narrow, justified, unpunctuated paragraphs of very different lengths, which reflect, more or less, the proportions of the seventeen parts of *Finnegans Wake.* The stanza/paragraphs are not indented at their beginnings, though they end with indentations from the right, and none begins with a capital letter. "*Muoyce* [Music-

Joyce] is with respect to *Finnegans Wake* what *Mureau* [Music-Thoreau] was with respect to the *Journal* of Henry David Thoreau, though *Muoyce* . . . does not include sentences, just phrases, words, syllables, and letters. . . . [P]unctuation is entirely omitted and space between words is frequently with the aid of chance operations eliminated."[50]

An interesting variant of the writing-through method is found in "Writing through the Cantos" (of Ezra Pound).[51] In writing this poem, Cage followed Mink's Rule, which does not allow the appearance of either letter between two of the name. He also "kept an index of syllables used to present a given letter of the name and . . . did not permit repetition of these syllables,"[52] as he did when composing the third and fourth writings through *Finnegans Wake*. However, this poem does not consist of mesostics but of flush-right lines, each comprising five or more words: in alternate lines the letters of either "EZRA" or "POUND" are capitalized in the words selected through Mink's Rule and the syllable index. A small number of other words that accord with Mink's Rule sometimes appear between successive name-letter words.

The writing-through methods used in composing the first four writings through the *Wake* and "Writing through the Cantos" are not chance operations. For one thing, the inclusion or omission of "wing words" (single words or strings on either side of a "name-letter word") in mesostics and analogous non-name-letter words in the *Cantos* poem, is a matter of choice, as long as the writer obeys the Mesostic Rule, Mink's Rule, and/or the Syllable Rule. (Cage's "tendency was toward more omission rather than less.")[53] Besides, the name-letter words are already there, waiting to be found, even though Cage cannot predict them, and he strives for accuracy: "I read each passage at least three times and once or twice upside down."[54] "It is a discipline similar to that of counterpoint in music with a cantus firmus."[55]

What writing-through methods have in common with chance operations is that both involve a large degree of *nonintentionality*, "diminish[ing the value-judging] activity of the ego and . . . increas[ing] the activity that accepts the rest of creation."[56]

I think Cage assumes the Zen Buddhist psychology that considers all parts of the psyche, including the psychoanalytic "unconscious," to be "parts" of the individual ego. (Those who write about Zen in English, such as Dr. D. T. Suzuki, use the term *Unconscious* as a synonym for the "No-mind," which is not individual but universal.)[57]

Therefore writers and other artists exercise value judgment when any components of their minds make choices, even in the course of "automatic writing," "action painting," or other activities supposedly proceeding from the psychoanalytic unconscious. Procedures operating from *any* level of the ego, in the Zen sense, I call intentional; *nonintentional* refers only to those procedures or components of procedures that do *not* do so. Thus that part of a writing-through method that consists in finding each successive name-letter word is nonintentional, since the poet does not consciously or "unconsciously" *select* the word, but as accurately as possible, *finds* it. Whereas the activity of selecting the wing words in mesostics and the analogous "between-name-letter words" in the *Cantos* poem—deciding which ones to bring into the poems and which to leave out (with the proviso that each "kept" word is contiguous, or part of a string contiguous, to a name-letter word)—is intentional.[58]

Cage has often described his way of working as asking questions and abiding by the answers given to the questions, usually by *I Ching* chance operations. However, it is clear that a certain degree of intentionality is involved willy-nilly in the choosing and framing of questions and of the gamuts of possible answers, as well as in the choosing of source texts. The point is not that he ever entirely evades his individual ego and its predilections, but that he diminishes to some extent the value-judging activity of the ego that excludes possibilities, and thereby he lets in to that extent "the rest of creation."

I cannot attempt in this short essay to describe all of Cage's writings and the methods used in composing them. I want to conclude, however, by discussing two works of the early 1980s: "James Joyce, Marcel Duchamp, Erik Satie: An Alphabet"[59] and *Themes and Variations*.[60]

The title of the former alludes to the fact "that the artists whose work we live with constitute . . . an alphabet by means of which we spell our lives," but it is really "not an alphabet but a fantasy."[61] The three artists of the title, now ghosts, made works that "in different ways have resisted the march of understanding and so are as fresh now as when they were first made." They made the two kinds of art that Cage likes best: "art that is incomprehensible (Joyce and Duchamp) and . . . art that is too nose on your face (Satie). Such artists remain forever useful . . . in each moment of our daily lives."

Though Cage in his introduction first characterizes the "Alphabet" as a "lecture," it is actually a play, divided into thirty-seven scenes, involving, in addition to the three of the title, other "actors . . . mostly people with whose work [he has] become involved." It has been produced as a *Hörspiel*[62] at Westdeutscher Rundfunk (WDR) in Cologne, and on stage at the end of WDR's 2nd Acustica International sound art festival at the Equitable Branch of the Whitney Museum of American Art in New York, on 29 April 1990.

During the scenes, each ghost is either alone, "in which case he reads from his own writings," or "together with another sentient being or beings, ghosts or living, or with a nonsentient being or beings." This schema yields twenty-six possibilities: "the three ghosts alone, each in combination with one to four different beings, the ghosts in pairs with one to three different beings, [and] all three with one or two." Cage "used the twenty-six letters of the alphabet and [*I Ching*] chance operations to locate facing pages of an unabridged dictionary upon which [he] found the nonsentient beings that are the stage properties of the various scenes," which comprise a kind of narrative in "Minkian" mesostics on the names or initials of the three ghosts, among which are interspersed ten prose paragraphs, each drawn from the writings of one of the ghosts. The mesostic "narrative" gives both the "stage directions," introductions of the actors (read in radio and stage productions by a narrator), and together with the prose paragraphs, the speeches of the ghosts and other actors.

Themes and Variations is "one text in an ongoing series; to find a way of writing which though coming from ideas is not about them; or is not about ideas but produces them."[63] It is "a chance-determined renga-like [and asyntactical] mix" drawn from "fifteen themes" and sixty "variations" constituting a "library of mesostics on one hundred and ten different subjects and fifteen different names." (A renga is an extended Japanese poem traditionally written by a group of poets, successive lines being written by different poets.) The subjects are "one hundred and ten different ideas which [Cage] listed in the course of a cursory examination of [his] books" written before 1979. The first and last ideas on his list are: "Nonintention (the acceptance of silence) leading to nature; renunciation of control; let sounds be sounds" and "Goal is not to have a goal." The names are those of fifteen men important to Cage in his life and work, ranging from Norman O. Brown and Marshall McLuhan to Arnold Schoenberg and Daisetz Suzuki (Dr. D. T. Suzuki). Each "theme" and each "variation" (there are four on each name) is a mesostic on one of the names, derived from three, four, or five mesostics of equal length written on the same name and on any of the hundred and ten ideas.

This complexly composed asyntactical text "was written to be spoken aloud. It consists of five sections, each to take twelve minutes. The fourth is the fastest and the last one is the slowest." Tempo of delivery is regulated by numbers in the righthand margins denoting minutes and fractions of minutes up to 60.00, each carried out to as many as four decimal places (e.g., .244, 10.344, 33.4786, 41.5636), which indicate how long the reader should take to read the lines between them, and thus also how quickly or slowly. "The lines that are to be read in a single breath are printed singly or together as a stanza. These divisions or liaisons were not chance-determined, but were arrived at by improvisational means." At the end of the introduction, Cage exemplifies the beginnings of five source mesostics on "DAVID TUDOR DAVID" and the theme and four variations (some truncated) derived from them, which appear at various points throughout the renga.

What these two remarkable texts, "James Joyce, Marcel Duchamp, Erik Satie: An Alphabet" and *Themes and Variations,* have in common—despite the fact that one is normatively syntactical, for the most part, and even narrative, and the other asyntactical and very much fragmented—is their "speakability." Compared to performers of such typographically and performatively difficult poems as "Mureau" and "Empty Words," the actors who perform the "Alphabet" and the soloist who speaks *Themes* aloud are given very clear and easily speakable word strings to enunciate. Not that these texts are "easy" to perform. Making the transitions from character to character and projecting each persona believably when performing the "Alphabet" is no trivial task for actors. And accurately delivering the exactly timed segments of *Themes* while sensitively conveying the meanings of the words demands plenty of practice, despite such helpful directions as "slower" and "faster" at the beginning of each twelve-minute segment after the first. Nevertheless, Cage's relation to the readers, performers, and hearers of these works can credibly be characterized as "genial." As a Zen teacher might put it, they clearly evince the "grandmotherly kindness" that, often less apparently, underlies and motivates all of Cage's work as an artist.

NOTES

1. John Cage, "Lecture on Commitment," in *A Year from Monday,* 116.
2. Ibid.

3. Ibid.

4. John Cage, in an interview conducted by Bill Womack at the Los Angeles County Museum of Art, 27 March 1979, *Zero* 3 (1979): 70.

5. Pp. 1–49 and 173–87, respectively.

6. Barrytown, N.Y., 1982.

7. *Silence,* 3–6.

8. "Lecture on Something," in *Silence,* 128–45.

9. "Lecture on Nothing," in *Silence,* 108–15.

10. "Mushroom Book," *M,* 117–83.

11. *Silence,* 146–92.

12. For prepared pianos; commissioned by the Donaueschinger Musiktage in 1954; also known as *34'46.776" for a Pianist.*

13. Mary Caroline Richards, *Centering: In Poetry, Pottery, and the Person* (Middletown, Conn.: Wesleyan University Press, 1964), *The Crossing Point: Selected Talks and Writings* (Middletown, Conn.: Wesleyan University Press, 1973). Most recently, *Imagine Inventing Yellow: New and Selected Poems of M. C. Richards* (Barrytown, N.Y.: Station Hill Press, 1991).

14. *Silence,* x.

15. Ibid., 194–259.

16. Composed in 1960. "*(A cartridge is an ordinary phonograph pick-up in which customarily a playing needle is inserted.) This is a composition indeterminate of its performance, and the performance is of actions which are often indeterminate of themselves. Material is supplied, much of it on transparent plastics, which enables a performer to determine a program of actions* [causing amplification and modification of small sounds by insertion, use, and removal of various objects from a cartridge and production of auxiliary electronic sounds].)" From Cage's note, in the catalog of his works organized by Robert Dunn (New York: C. F. Peters, 1962), 34.

17. *Silence,* 224.

18. Edited by B. Torrey and F. H. Allen (New York: Dover, 1962).

19. *M,* 26–34.

20. Ibid., 4–211, passim.

21. New York: Something Else Press, 1968.

22. *X,* 109–15.

23. New York: Viking Press, 1939.

24. New York: C. F. Peters, 1970.

25. *M,* 86–91.

26. *Empty Words,* 11.

27. *M,* 35–56.

28. Ibid., ix.

29. S Press Tonband/Tape No. 14 (Hattingen, [West] Germany: Edition S Press, 1972).

30. *Empty Words,* 11–27.

31. Ibid., 65.

32. Ibid., 33.

33. "Preface to 'Lecture on the Weather,'" in *Empty Words,* 3–4.

34. Introduction to the preface, in *Empty Words,* 1.

35. "Preface," in *Empty Words,* 5.

36. *Oeuvres complètes* (Paris: Gallimard, 1945), 81–186.
37. *M,* ix.
38. See n. 17.
39. See n. 18.
40. *M,* x.
41. Ibid.
42. *Gli anni di Demetrio,* [a memoir of Stratos] ed. G. Sassi, Milano-poesia 1989 (Milan: Cooperativa Nuova Intrapresa/Fondazione Mudima, 1989), 8.
43. *Empty Words,* 134.
44. Ibid., 133–76.
45. Ibid., 135–36.
46. Ibid., 135.
47. This poem has never been published in a book.
48. *X,* 1–49.
49. Ibid., 173–87.
50. Ibid., 173.
51. Ibid., 109–15.
52. Ibid., 109.
53. *Empty Words,* 135.
54. Ibid., 136.
55. Ibid., 135.
56. See n. 4.
57. D. T. Suzuki: *The Zen Doctrine of No-Mind* (London: Rider and Co., 1949), 60, 140–43; also see 56–63, 101, 115.
58. These are not Cage's terms or formulations but my own, except possibly for "wing words": some people call the words and strings to the right and left of name-letter words in mesostics "wings."
59. *X,* 53–101.
60. Barrytown, N.Y.: Station Hill Press, 1982.
61. This and the following quotations concerning "An Alphabet" come from its introduction in *X,* 53–55.
62. *Hörspiel:* "radio play"; this term now has an extended meaning, "sound-art work," mainly because of the so-called *Neue Hörspiel* developed and encouraged at Westdeutscher Rundfunk Köln by the producer Klaus Schöning.
63. This and the following quotations concerning *Themes and Variations* come from its twelve-page introduction.

John Cage's Longest and Best Poem (1990)

Richard Kostelanetz

When those powers-that-be behind selecting the Charles Eliot Norton Professor at Harvard chose John Cage, they knew in advance that he would not pontificate in the manner of previous holders of that revolving chair (Ben Shahn for *The Shape of Content,* Igor Stravinsky for *Poetics of Music,* etc.). They also knew that Cage, unlike certain previous Nortons, would write his own stuff, which, furthermore, would not resemble traditional exposition but be a kind of poetry. Thankfully, there was enough respect for Cage to produce a handsome book twelve inches high, well over one inch thick, with two audiocassette tapes on an accompanying card, all moderately priced by current standards.

I–VI, as the package is modestly called, actually has two texts. The first is Cage's six lectern-based recitations. This dominates most of 420 pages. The second part is a transcript of his informal seminars, given in response to his generous assumption that, since the main presentations were difficult, he should respond to questions. This prose runs continuously along the bottom of each page, as a kind of smaller-type counterpoint that is four lines high and 6½" wide, with the unidentified questioners speaking in an italic typeface and Cage answering in roman. Further to create the illusion of a continuous conversation, the transcripts are printed wholly without commas, periods, capitalizations, or breaks for new paragraphs.

As the author of *Conversing with Cage* (1988), an Ur-interview composed of passages from interviews that Cage has given for over three decades, I can testify that, even in his late seventies, he is still capable of new revelations, even, say, about his much-discussed silence piece, *4'33"* (1952). "i was in the process of writing the *music of changes* that was done in an elaborate way there are many tables for pitches for durations for amplitudes all the work was done with chance operations in the case of *4′33″* i actually used the same method of working and i built up the silence of each movement and the three movements add up to *4′33″* i built up each movement by means of short silences put together." Otherwise, Cage is prompted to speak about his favoring Henry David Thoreau over Ralph Waldo Emerson (for good reasons), he recalls Morton Feldman's discovery of graph music. He is as comfortable talking about visual art and poetry as music, demonstrating that it was not inappropriate for Cal Arts to award this college dropout a unique honorary Doctor of All the Arts.

One quality I find in this part of *I–VI,* as nowhere else in print, is Cage's rare ability to respond intelligently to questions that most of us would find unintelligible. I remember being on a panel with him in 1977, one Saturday afternoon in a SoHo art gallery. From the audience came questions that made Merce Cunningham, Nam June Paik, Dore Ashton, and myself look at one another in puzzlement. Without hesitation, Cage took the microphone, looked directly at the questioner, and delivered a coherent reply that made those beside him collapse in awe. Some moments in this counterpoint reminded me of that exquisite performance.

For the past quarter-century, Cage has been producing poetic texts that, by operations mixing choice and chance, draw selectively upon prior texts. (He speaks of his results as "poetry," as do I, because they cannot be classified anywhere else.) For *Empty Words* he chose Thoreau's remarks about acoustic experience (including music). Cage's next poetic sequence went through James Joyce's *Finnegans Wake,* producing five different texts composed entirely of Joyce's words. For these last poems he developed the form he still favors, the *mesostic.* Whereas an acrostic is composed horizontally from a key word extending down the left margin, a mesostic situates the axis word in the middle.

For his first departure from Joyce, the chapbook *Composition in Retrospect* (Westdeutscher Rundfunk, 1982), Cage selected ten words important to his esthetic experience: method, structure, intention, discipline, notation, indeterminacy, interpenetration, imitation, devotion, circumstances; but instead of drawing upon texts written by others, he chose, or wrote horizontally, words out of his own mind (much as he did with *Diary,* his major poem of the late 1960s, that was written within other constrains). *Composition in Retrospect,* his most satisfactory middle-length poetic text, is also the closest semblance of an intellectual autobiography that has written so far.

For his Norton lectures, Cage continued writing mesostics; but to the earlier collection of ten key words, he has added five more: variable structure, nonunderstanding, contingency, inconsistency, performance. Instead of writing out of his own head (or drawing upon a single literary source), he now selects words from several disparate sources: Ludwig Wittgenstein, Marshall McLuhan, Buckminster Fuller's followers, daily newspapers during the summer of 1988, his own *Composition in Retrospect* (curiously) among others. The result is a more expansive text that not only befits Cage's taste for heady ideas (see *Conversing with Cage* for more evidence of this) but it encompasses the whole world, in part because it draws upon writings with global range, its theme becoming meditations on a scale at once personal and sociopolitical. Because its effects are so drawn out, a short quotation might be less sufficient than usual; nonetheless, consider this:

space vehIcle earth
to work with it in the Most long term humanly advantageous ways
whIch as
copper and aluminum and sTeel
chose to keep efficiency levels And
developmenT how can we accelerate
earth's present economIc and industrial
prOblems of thermal
uNdeveloped nature
as those used In
costuMes
In
The
All
in The
sIdes
Of
aNd

By opening out and encompassing all at a considerable length, *I–VI* comes to resemble, more than any other American poem, Walt Whitman's *Song of Myself!* Need I say that, very much like *Finnegans Wake,*

Cage's *I–VI* is at once unreadable and *re*readable. The tape of the fourth lecture helps, especially if heard with the text in hand; listen to it as you would a piece of music, for among its themes is the possibilities of less-syntactic verbal communication.

To my mind, the most amazing quality of Cage is that even in his late seventies he has moved ahead. He has never doubled back, dismissing earlier work as too radical. He is always modern, never postmodern; always avant-garde, never retrograde; always libertarian, never conservative. That is why he continues to do major work that, in my opinion, makes decisive contributions to his chosen arts. Just as his *Europeras* (1987) ranks among his best music theater—indeed, among the most innovative music theater anyone has done in the past few decades—so *I–VI* is his finest poem, a major poem in a unique style, surely among the best American epic poems of the post–World War II period, although powers-that-be in the poetry business would be the last to acknowledge it.

Cage's Cage (1990)

Edward Rothstein

I'm not sure what made me finally grasp the importance of fungi for the career of John Cage. It may have been the retrospective performances I heard, nearly a decade ago, of some of the composer's most memorable works—the one for twelve radios tuned to different stations (*Imaginary Landscape No. 4*), or his famed *4′33″* of musical silence, or his scrambling of the phonemes and syllables of James Joyce's *Finnegans Wake* to create about three hours of melodically chanted gibberish. (It was a "form of poetry which I devised that enables me to read all the way through a book that otherwise I would not read through.") Like mushrooms that grow wild in the forest, such works lack chlorophyll; they cannot support themselves on light, they seem to grow or thrive in shadowy regions. In fact, too much illumination and scrutiny would probably cause them to shrivel. These works cannot even be said to exist as "works" without feeding off other, decaying objects, which often happen to be the rituals and the art works that make up our frayed and fragile musical tradition. Cage's dadaist fungoids have fastened on that tradition for the duration, pushing composition toward compost.

Sporophores keep surfacing in his life and his writing as well. Cage won a mushroom quiz contest in 1958 on Italian television, which is how he made his first substantial sum of money. He has haunted forests and rotting tree stumps in all regions of the world. He is a founder of the New York Mycological Society and a member of a Czechoslovakian mushroom society. He has even had his stomach pumped after mistaking one species for another.

This interest may be no accident. As Cage once pointed out, "music" and "mushroom" often appear next to each other in dictionaries. "A mushroom grows for such a short time," he also once said, "and if you happen to come across it when it's fresh it's like coming upon a sound which also lives a short time." His music is preeminently mushroomlike in this respect: its sounds are explicitly designed to pass quickly by and never be duplicated. They deliberately defy memory and pattern. "I am not interested in the relationships between sounds and mushrooms," the composer has quipped, "any more than I am in those between sounds and other sounds."

And now Cage has done it again: in the midst of the humid academic overgrowth another of his sporophores has taken root. That ground—provided by the prestigious Norton lectures at Harvard University—was once cultivated, architectonic, severe. Cage's distinguished musical predecessors in these lectures included Igor Stravinsky, Roger Sessions, and Charles Rosen. But for the 1988–89 season at Harvard the heritage of theoretical and critical rigor was put aside. After all, modernism has fallen on hard times, contemporary musical culture has long since subsided into sullen regularity, and many universities have become weary of disinterested scholarship. So Harvard turned its attention to the only remaining sign of life—the sometime avant-garde.

Hence the book: *I–VI* (1990). The title is a shorthand abbreviation of the lectures' real title: *MethodStructureIntentionDisciplineNotationIndeterminacyInterpenetrationImitationDevotionCircumstances VariableStructureNonunderstandingContingencyInconsistencyPerformance.* The volume is well made, expensively produced, and extravagantly set. It is even packaged with two tapes, one of which contains the entire performance of one of the six lectures that Cage delivered, and the other a session of questions and answers with the Norton lecturer that followed the talks. "Instead of looking for mushrooms in a forest," the composer tells one interrogator when describing his lectures, "I'm looking for ideas in a brushing of source material." Cage doesn't develop ideas, or create them. They just happen to appear as he strolls through his "source material," mushroom basket in hand.

Here, for example, is one specimen that the casual hiker in these pages might come across:

> Is/the Number of pages of your next composition this/calleD for an/ is no play in thEm for/is noT a blank loss of/Employing the same technique to/what aRe called/their own hands and provided food for theMselves and/have dIscovered legal ties to/burN wooden/points in

time when there Are not points but/rejeCted israel and the united states face to/a new job and even a totallY new

The capital letters should align themselves vertically on the page to spell INDETERMINACY. Each set of lines in the lectures, in fact, has one of the words from the lecture's titles—Method, Structure, Intention, etc.—running down its center. Cage refers to these constructions as "mesostics," a term invented by Norman O. Brown to describe Cage's peculiar variation on the acrostic. Printed underneath this poesy are three lines of small print, without punctuation or capitalization, that contain the running text of Cage's discussions with questioners and challengers—as if forming a layer of mulch out of which the text seems to sprout. Cage is asked about the time he played poker with Jacqueline Susann (he doesn't remember it), or for his views on politics and performance (he is an "anarchist"), or to respond to observations about how difficult it is to concentrate on the lectures.

The source of the difficulty is simple enough. Each line in the lecture had its central word selected by what Cage calls "chance operations." There is no particular reason why one line should follow another; they are randomly put together. "This frees me," Cage gleefully explains, "from memory, tastes, likes and dislikes." Cage once used the *I Ching* as his instrument of liberation—thus giving the choices of tones and phrases a semimystical aura as he tossed sticks according to the ancient Chinese oracle. But the aura evidently became less convenient the more exotic Cage's techniques became. Now he depends on a computer program for assistance, its spit-out numbers determining the locations of words and ideas and sounds.

The most surprising thing about this technique—which Cage has used for nearly four decades—is how influential it has been. Our century has been notable for continuing attempts to create musical systems to replace conventional tonality. One system, popularized by the European avant-garde during the 1950s, involved increasing the territory governed by law, to systematize everything from pitch to timbre. Cage's system—which affected generations of self-inspired American avant-gardists—abdicated law and control nearly completely by submitting to the vagaries of dice or the *I Ching*. (At the Phillips Gallery in Washington, there is currently a show of watercolors by Cage painted in consultation with the *I Ching*.) Schoenberg, with whom Cage once studied counterpoint (and who was himself preoccupied with creating a compositional system), called him an "inventor of genius," but declined to use the word "composer."

For Cage was not primarily looking for a way to create art music. In the midst of the discussions that accompany these lectures, Cage tells a story he has told before, of a dinner with Willem de Kooning in which they discussed the aesthetic qualities of bread crumbs falling on the table. The painter argued that haphazardly dropped crumbs were hardly deserving of much aesthetic notice. But Cage argued that the crumbs, as they landed, were art enough. The point was simply to come upon them and to point to them.

It is an idea that Cage has turned into his own distinctive aesthetic religion, mixing it with allusions to Zen. All sounds, all words, all crumbs, are worthy of equal attention. All life is art. All art is beyond judgment. For Cage, the object is almost to become innocent of all choice and rules and distinction, and then to remain ignorant of why one thing is being heard over another. "What is the advantage of not knowing what you are doing?" John Ashbery once asked Cage. "It cheers up the knowing," the composer answered. "Otherwise, knowing will be very self-conscious and frequently guilty." Cage's choice is to avoid choice.

But of course Cage doesn't treat all events equally. He makes guilty choices; he just hides behind the dice. One such choice is to give "chance" events more value over anything chosen, to value chaos more than regulation. Cage's art is not just "found" art. It is created as found. It's as if mushrooms were planted in the woods and harvested as wild.

Cage makes sure to plant them in very particular places—wherever they will hasten the disintegration of ordinary language and meaning, which Cage calls "militarized." His mushrooms feed off these meanings, destroying them. "During the period of harmony and counterpoint," Cage once said, "there was good and bad, and rules to support the good against the bad. Today we must identify ourselves with noises instead." One of music's purposes, he told one interviewer, is "to undermine the making of value judgments," and his works take this as their project. Cage once said he would agree to conduct the Beethoven symphonies only if he could assemble enough players to perform every symphony at the same time. He has also suggested the founding of a university in which all lectures would be given in the same room simultaneously.

So the point is not really some Zen-like appreciation of bread crumbs; it is the dadaist mess they make. But it is not even fully dadaist, this mess. Cage has claimed, for example, he wanted his music to "be free of my own likes and dislikes," and he claims the same for these lectures. Yet the "point" of most of these lectures, the exercise of likes and dislikes in their composition, is unmistakable. Every random word in the lectures is chosen from a long text reprinted at the book's conclusion—a set of quotations Cage has put together from newspapers and pet philosophers. Thoreau is quoted, as are Buckminster Fuller and Wittgenstein. ("I have long been attracted to his work," Cage says, "reading it with enjoyment but rarely with understanding.")

These quotes are organized into fifteen sections, each labeled with one of the fifteen concepts making up the title of these lectures—though, Cage hastens to add, they may have nothing to do with those concepts. He quotes himself as well ("People often ask me what music I prefer to hear. I enjoy the absence of music more than any other"). He quotes McLuhan on the power of the media ("A cliché is an act of consciousness: total consciousness is the sum of all the clichés of all media or technologies we probe with"). He quotes libertarian sentiments ("Maximize human free time, minimize human coerced time"). He cites Wittgenstein's questionings of ordinary language and Thoreau's dissent from ordinary society.

Cage also went through the *New York Times,* the *Wall Street Journal,* and the *Christian Science Monitor,* putting together quotations on foreign affairs, mixing phrases from different articles into one sentence, creating a sort of news-style gibberish that manages to invoke nearly all the "military" evils Cage finds across the globe. Such oracular collages include: "Israel said Sunday it might nullify opposition parties in a brief ceremony that would most likely help Panama solve its problems."

Cage speaks solemnly in the question-and-answer sessions about his attempts to deliberately "fox" any meanings that might arise out of his texts. But intentions are revealed everywhere. "Why not read a phone book?" one questioner asks. Because if the lectures turn out to make a suggestion, Cage points out, "I want that suggestion to be in a spirit that I agree with"—specifically with the program of "anarchism." That anarchism is playfully antinomian. ("I'm looking forward to the time when no one votes," he once said, "Because then we wouldn't have to have a president. . . . We can get along perfectly well without the government.")

Fragments of the source text serve as ideological atoms, full of allusions to pastoralism and dadaism and anarchism and simple sentiments. These fragments protrude because they are the only elements of ordinary meaning provided by Cage. We hear scattered phrases in the midst of random words: "demonstrators and bystanders were Charged and attacked," or "wrecks The wilderness with its," or "we chose to keep efficiency levels And." The result is a random collection of atoms bumping into each other, creating a Brownian motion of clichés. Cage tries to have it all, hovering above his text like some dadaist clown, while he drops his pointed allusions for the listening faithful.

What is the direction of this much discussed career? Mainly a traditional, almost conservative avant-gardism—a trajectory unchanged by chance or the *I Ching.* Much of Cage's more traditionally composed works of the 1940s, for example, are little more than antibourgeois jest. In *Credo in Us* (1942), nineteenth-century orchestral music is interrupted by percussive strikes and buzzings; *Living Room Music* (1940) uses ordinary middle-class objects for percussion. Cage's most intriguingly musical compositions—the haunting works from the later 1940s for which Cage stuck foreign objects into the hammers and strings of a piano (creating a "prepared piano")—have a discreet charm and playfulness, echoing Satie. But recently released Wergo recordings show that these pieces are also inherently polemical, the archetypal instrument of the tradition turned into a toy, and Western musical phrases overturned by something resembling Balinese gamelan music. The *String Quartet in Four Parts* of 1950, soon to be released in a recording by the Arditti Quartet, is an active rejection of counterpoint and intellectual intricacy, anticipating the similar turns in taste that created the now defunct movement of minimalism.

Cage is, of course, a sweet and coy and charming avant-gardist. So sweet and coy and charming that it is tempting to tolerate the obvious polemics, the platitudes and unsophisticated politics, the pseudo-Zen aesthetic. After all, when he is not deathly tedious, he can be quite funny. And, as Cage himself said of his compositional method, "It neither wounds nor wrongs anyone in the end."

But how harmless are his views? His vision of human life is strangely skewed for one who claims a Whitmanesque embrace of nature and the world. Even his seemingly apolitical anarchism is full of ideological turns. He speaks, for example, of a family of starving "naked human beings" he saw in Bombay, searching for some water as they trudged through mud. His point is not to evoke their suffering, but to add another log to an anti-Western fire he keeps burning in his anarchist heart. "They were dignified," he says proudly of these Indians; but when he turns in contrast to "our poor," he simply asserts, with third worldist energy, that "our poor" have been stripped of dignity as well as water.

Cage's ostensible love of anarchism and chance is also shadowed by an attraction to the most extraordinary systems of control and order and regulation. Even in constructing these lectures, all sorts of fetishistic restrictions are made. Between any two consecutive capital letters in the randomly chosen words, for example, Cage insists that neither letter may appear in lower case. This rule is purely lexicographical: it means nothing, particularly since the words with the capitalized letters are arbitrarily chosen. But this method is typical of Cage: mixing the random with the rigid.

Yes, all language is arbitrary and all art involves disciplines of arbitrary technique. The rules of the sonnet are even more intricate than those of Cage's mesostics. But such rules also bear some relation to the meanings or the sensibilities created; and if they don't, they are soon enough invested with such meaning. Here "militarized syntax" is rejected only to be replaced by even more confoundingly intricate rules that are deliberately meaningless. Cage's compositional procedures—using star charts or clocks or tossed sticks—become authoritarian in their own way. Cage has the same attitudes in his political commentary. Anarchism may be his credo, but he also seems to welcome authoritarian control when it suits him. In 1972 he wrote: "The Maoist model managed to free a quarter of humanity; that gives cause for thought. Today, without hesitation, I would say that, for the moment, Maoism is our greatest reason for optimism."

Even his strictly musical notions can have disturbing effects. In the Norton lectures Cage recalls a class he was hired to teach by the WPA, which turned out to be a bit of a fiasco because the parents objected to his technique of letting the children just make sounds without teaching them counterpoint. We are now paying the cultural price of musical and intellectual illiteracy for such experiments. Yet it appears that Harvard, in inviting Cage to deliver the Norton lectures, is intent on carrying the experiments even further.

Still, one can't get too solemn about Cage. His career—and these lectures—are best seen as symptoms of our era's poverty, rather than as causes of it. It is best to grin at Cage's caginess, because he will never be pinned down. "You won't find me consistent," he has boasted.

One of the stories that Cage tells seems particularly appropriate as a sort of *koan* on his career. A woman from Philadelphia once asked Cage, "Have you an explanation of the symbolism involved in the death of the Buddha by eating a mushroom?" Cage explained: "Mushrooms grow most vigorously in the fall, the period of destruction, and the function of many of them is to bring about the final decay of rotting material. In fact, as I read somewhere, the world would be an impassible heap of old rubbish were it not for mushrooms and their capacity to get rid of it. So I wrote to the lady in Philadelphia. I said, 'The function of mushrooms is to rid the world of old rubbish. The Buddha died a natural death.'"

Gertrude Stein and John Cage: Three Fragments (1977)

Ellsworth Snyder

Introduction

Gertrude Stein's importance is as a writer. But since her writing is often also an example of process as writing, even her theories are stated as poetry. The more important of these theories have to do with what content can be, and how time passes.

And then there is John Cage who has from another direction completed some of Stein's ideas, and allowed us the quality of mind to better understand her.

Both writers write examples of process, and this process makes a new content, not just a twentieth century complication of content, but a new content which contains entity suspended in time and not identity remembered.

Let us begin.

I

Gertrude Stein was the first writer to free words systematically from hidden meanings and to keep them from being suffocated by content. Because of her interest in the difference between internal and external reality, she found new ways to use language by the re-adaptation of existing words. Her belief that already existing external reality was not necessary as a determinant for art made it possible for her to derive new forms strictly from the internal considerations of her material. It was internal reality which brought about entity and not identity thus opening up, in her view, the possibility of creating masterpieces. As she stated in *What Are Masterpieces and Why There Are So Few of Them:*

> I once wrote in writing *The Making of Americans* I write for myself and strangers but that was merely a literary formalism for if I did write for myself and strangers if I did I would not really be writing because already then identity would take the place of entity. It is awfully difficult, action is direct and effective but after all action is necessary and anything that is necessary has to do with human nature and not with the human mind. Therefore a master-piece has essentially not to be necessary, it has to be that is it has to exist but it does not have to be necessary it is not in response to necessity as action is because the minute it is necessary it has in it no possibility of going on. . . . The manner and habits of Bible times or Greek or Chinese have nothing to do with ours today but the masterpieces exist just the same and they do not exist because of their identity, that is what any one remembering then remembered then, they do not exist by human nature because everybody always knows everything there is to know about human nature, they exist because they came to be as something that is an end in itself and in that respect it is opposed to the business of living which is relation and necessity. That is what a master-piece is not although it may easily be what a master-piece talks about. . . . It is not extremely difficult not to have identity but it is extremely difficult the knowing not having identity.

She put it less poetically, but very plainly, in an interview with John Hyde Preston. When Preston asked, "Do you really think American writers are obsessed by sex? And if they are, isn't it legitimate?" Gertrude answered:

> It is legitimate, of course. Literature—creative literature—unconcerned with sex is inconceivable. But not literary sex, because sex is part of something of which the other parts are not sex at all. No, Preston, it is really a matter of tone. You can tell, if you can tell anything, by the way a man talks about sex whether he is impotent or not, and if he talks about nothing else you can be quite sure that he is impotent—physically and as an artist too.
>
> One thing which I have tried to tell Americans [she went on] is that there can be no truly great creation without passion, but I'm

not sure that I have been able to tell them at all. If they have not understood it is because they have had to think of sex first, and they can think of sex as passion more easily than they can think of passion as the whole force of man. Always they try to label it, and that is a mistake. Now Byron had a passion. It had nothing to do with his women. It was a quality of Byron's mind and everything he wrote came out of it, and perhaps that is why his work is so uneven, because a man's passion is uneven if it is real; and sometimes, if he can write it, it is only passion and has no meaning outside of himself. Swinburne wrote all his life about passion, but you can read all of him and you will not know what passions he had. I am not sure that it is necessary to know or that Swinburne would have been better if he had known. A man's passion can be wonderful when it has an object which may be a woman or an idea or wrath at an injustice, but after it happens, as it usually does, that the object is lost or worn after a time, the passion does not survive it. It survives only if it was there before, only if the woman or the idea or the wrath was an incident in the passion and not the cause of it—and that is what makes the writer.

Often the men who really have it are not able to recognize it in themselves because they do not know what it is to feel differently or not to feel at all. And it won't answer to its name. Probably Goethe thought that *Young Werther* was a more passionate book than *Wilhelm Meister,* but in *Werther* he was only describing passion and in *Wilhelm Meister* he was transferring it. And I don't think he knew what he had done. He did not have to. Emerson might have been surprised if he had been told that he was passionate. But Emerson really had passion; he wrote it; but he could not have written *about* it because he did not know about it. Now Hemingway knows all about it and can sometimes write very surely about it, but he hasn't any at all. Not really any. He merely has passions. And Faulkner and Caldwell . . . They are good craftsmen and they are honest men, but they do not have it.

This concept of content as a quality of the mind in which entity is established over identity, i.e., entity is that which is within the content, is brought about by process. A process which seeks to maintain the "continuous present," that is to presently hold the present, even as that present is in continuing flux. Repetition might be one way to initiate such a process. Repetition is an amoebic sense of cells dividing. Or words might be used just as words not as symbols, thus cutting off remembering and making the experience with words direct as in a landscape.

More recently John Cage, because of Zen influences, has been eager to remove taste and identity from music, allowing sounds to be fact not symbols. His idea is that art should imitate nature in her manner of operation. This operation, or movement of the universe, is one of process, and that process is a random one, hence the use of chance operations in his works.

In 1946, the year she died, Gertrude Stein said in an interview:

> I have done [the] narration because in narration your great problem is the problem of time in telling a story of anybody. And that is why newspaper people never become writers, because they have a false sense of time. . . . You have as a person writing, and all the really great narration has it, you have to denude yourself of time so that writing time does not exist. If time exists your writing is ephemeral. You can have historical time but for you the time does not exist and if you are writing about the present the time element must cease to exist. I did it unconsciously in the *Autobiography of Alice B. Toklas* but I did it consciously in *Everybody's Autobiography* and in the last thing, *Wars I Have Seen.* In it I described something momentous happening under my eyes and I was able to do it without a great sense of time. There should not be a sense of time but an existence suspended in time. That is really where I am at the present moment. I am still largely meditating about this sense of time.

II

The celebrated fourteenth-century European mystic and scholastic Meister Eckhart said, ". . . all time is contained in the present Now-moment." Cage has written:

> By music we mean sound; but what's time? Certainly not that something begins and ends. . . . Music without measurements, sounds passing through circumstances . . . Time is what we and sound exist in.

In the twentieth century there has been a renewed interest in time in art. Early in the century Gertrude Stein wrote:

> Then at the same time is the question of time. The assembling of a thing to make a whole thing and each one of these whole things is one of a series, but besides this there is the important thing and the very American thing that everybody knows who is an American just how many seconds minutes or hours it is going to take to do a whole thing. It is singularly a sense for combination within a conception of the existence of a given space of time that makes the American thing the American thing, and the sense of this space of time must be within the whole thing as well as in the completed whole thing.

Later Cage was to say that if structure in music is its divisibility into successive parts from phrases to long sections, and if there is any structure involving sounds and silences, then it must be based on durations, i.e., time lengths, since of all the aspects of sound (frequency, amplitude, and timbre) duration alone is also a characteristic of silence. In other words, since the activities of the sounds result in time lengths, these time lengths become structural. Hence Cage was to write:

> With Beethoven the parts of a composition were defined by means of harmony, with Satie and Webern they were defined by means of time lengths. The question of structure is so basic, and it is so important to be in agreement about it that we must now ask: Was Beethoven right, or are Webern and Satie right? I answer immediately and unequivocally, Beethoven was in error, and his influence, which has been as extensive as it is lamentable, has been deadening to the art of music.

Early in Cage's history, then, duration became structural. But more than that, duration objectified as clock-time became the frame which separated his music from the total universe. Though for Cage there was no real difference between the sounds of a "piece of music" and the usual sounds of nature, i.e., sounds before, at the same time as, or after the piece of music, the piece of music was distinguished from nature in that it happened within a determined duration. By mid-century this interest in time had shifted from objective, clock-time, to subjective, lived-through time. Robbe-Grillet has written:

> . . . if passing time is indeed the essential character of many works of the early part of this century, and of those which follow them, as it had been, moreover, of works of the last century, present investigations seem on the contrary to be concerned, most often, with private mental structures of "time." *Last Year at Marienbad,* because of its title . . . has from the start been interpreted as one of those psychological variations on lost love, on forgetting, on memory. The questions most often asked were: Have this man and this woman really met before? Did they love each other last year at Marienbad? . . . Matters must be put clearly: such questions have no meaning. The universe in which the entire film occurs is, characteristically, that of a perpetual present which makes all recourse to memory impossible. This is a world without a past, a world which is self-sufficient at every moment and which obliterates itself as it proceeds. . . . But, it will be asked, what do the scenes we have watched represent? . . . It can here be a question only of a subjective, mental personal occurrence. These things must be happening in someone's mind. But whose? . . . [J]ust as the only time which matters is that of the film itself the only important "character" is the spectator; *in his mind* unfolds the whole story, which is precisely *imagined* by him . . . in the modern narrative time seems to be cut off from its temporality. It no longer passes. It no longer completes anything. Here space destroys time, and time sabotages space.

In the 1970s it would appear that music for Cage is the experience of subjective, lived-through time which is present when it is the object of a perception of which the perceiver is self-consciously aware, there is no question of beginning or ending. If the perceiver is conscious, time *is.* It is the perpetual present. We and sound exist in time.

Stein had long before Cage and Robbe-Grillet created subjective, lived-through time, i.e., private mental structure of time, in order to establish a continuous present.

In his book *Twentieth Century Music* Peter Yates says of Cage:

> His concentrated attention to what the work of art is doing at any

moment, disregarding tradition, formalistic convention, precedent, links him with Gertrude Stein and Ludwig Wittgenstein.

By the time Cage was attending Pomona College, he was already attracted to the works of Gertrude Stein. Indeed the similarities between Cage and Stein are considerable. First of all, they are both Americans, and as Cage has said: "Actually America has an intellectual climate suitable for radical experimentation. We are, as Gertrude Stein said, the oldest country of the twentieth century. And I like to add: In our air way of knowing nowness." Stein had said earlier:

> After all anybody is as their land and air is. Anybody is as the sky is low or high, the air heavy or clear and anybody is as there is wind or no wind there. It is that which makes them and the arts they make and the work they do and the way they eat and the way they drink and the way they learn and everything.

Both Cage and Stein have realized to what extent we live in a visual age and both have had painters as close friends. Stein was influenced by Cézanne and Picasso and, in addition to Picasso, knew Gris, Matisse, and Braque among others. Cage has been close to Robert Rauschenberg and Jasper Johns, and it would seem fair to assume that there has been a mutual influence since Cage has written about both Rauschenberg and Johns and has acknowledged that Rauschenberg's all-white paintings came before his *4′33″*. Although Cage never met Stein they had one friend in common, Virgil Thomson, and Stein did know Erik Satie who has so influenced Cage. Cage did, however, meet Alice Toklas. Strangely, they did not "hit it off," and Cage has explained: "Before going to see A. Toklas (as had been arranged) I had dinner with the 'Baron' Mollet and so it occurred to me to take him with me. I called A. T. and asked whether I might bring him. She agreed but later wrote to V. Thomson to say that since I took liberties in social situations, she suspected I was also taking them in music." Furthermore, both have written essays (supposedly for information) in which the writing itself illustrates a manner of creating. Stein called her essay *Composition as Explanation* and, although it is difficult to know whether it is a similarity or a consequence, Cage called his *Composition as Process*. Their writing (and composing) style has ranged from a simple informative one to a very hermetic one. It is in

Stein's hermetic works that words are just words, that is, words are fact, not symbol. Thus Stein antedates the concept of many creative minds in the mid-twentieth century, including Cage. Moreover, particularly early in his career, Cage has been interested in clock time, repetition, and the artistic use of the materials of daily living, all ideas that occupied Stein at one time or another.

Stein often used the term *landscape* when speaking of her plays, and Cage has named a number of his works *Imaginary Landscape,* while one work is called *In a Landscape.* In the Stein plays, and in certain of the Cage works, there is a static quality that invites comparison.

There is also a similarity between Stein's view of the creative act, and Cage's view. Stein writes: "At any moment when you are you you are you without the memory of yourself because if you remember yourself while you are you you are not for purposes of creating you." Cage has said that at the moment of the creative act "the head should be empty, but alert."

Stein's concepts, of repetition as everything being always the same only different, with no beginning, middle or end, and that out of this sameness comes variety, have a follower in Cage, though not for the same reason. In "Portraits and Repetitions," from her *Lectures in America,* Stein explained that the essence of repetition is insistence, and if you insist, even though you are repeating, you use emphasis, and this nuance in emphasis means that no repetition can be like any other repetition. Stein's use of repetition comes from her interest in Western psychology and human nature, while Cage's interest in static effect comes from Eastern philosophy and self-realization.

Furthermore ". . . in Gertrude Stein's method anything that comes to one in a moment of concentrated working, is properly a part of the poem." This naturally ties up with Cage's concept of unintentional sound's always being present and therefore a part of the music. In addition, like Cage who admits noise or "unmusical" sound into music, Stein was willing to admit commonplace words as well as "poetic," words into poetry. Sherwood Anderson in his introduction to Stein's book *Geography and Plays* writes that Stein was willing ". . . to go living among the little housekeeping words, the swaggering bullying street-corner words the honest working, money saving words. . . ."

There also appears to be a certain similarity in personality between Stein and Cage. In a letter of condolence to Alice Toklas after Gertrude's death, the French historian Bernard Faÿ spoke of Stein's marvelous laugh which dispelled all the dull objections, and in the preface to his book, *A Year from Monday,* Cage speaks of his fortune in being born with a sunny disposition. There seems to be no evidence that Cage has intentionally imitated Stein. The similarities exist because Cage and Stein come from a common mental milieu, and he has found her ideas to be very stimulating.

Finally, both could say, as Stein did: "I was a martyr all my life not to what I won but to what was done."

Ending

History is curious. There are facts and that is veracity; there are interpretations and that is fantasy. Stein once wrote that she thought a creator was not someone ahead of his time, but simply someone who recognized what was happening to his generation as it was happening. Her idea was, that while others are going about the business of daily living, the creative mind is occupied with seeing. What the creator sees are those things that are happening which make his generation different from any other generation. Gertrude Stein and Alice Toklas were unusual, creative, innovative women quite content with the formalities of nineteenth-century society. And in that society manners were of the uppermost importance. Stein simply cannot be made into a 1970s feminist. In the same manner, Cage was not demonstrating and being arrested in the 1960s. Not because his ideas were not attuned to revolution. Far from it, but because he felt it a negative action which would keep him from his work, i.e., creating, which is a constructive action.

Stein said:

> I write with my eyes not with my ears or mouth. I hate lecturing because you begin to hear yourself talk, because sooner or later you hear your voice and you do not hear what you say. You just hear what they hear you say. As a matter of fact as a writer I write entirely with my eyes. The words as seen by my eyes are the important words and the ears and mouth do not count. I said to Picasso, the other day, "When you were a kid you never looked at things." He seemed to swallow the things he saw but he never looked, and I said, "In recent years you have been looking, you see too much, it is a mistake for you." He said "You are quite right." A writer should

write with his eyes and a painter paint with his ears. You should always paint knowledge which you have acquired not by looking but by swallowing. I have always noticed that in portraits of really great writers the mouth is always firmly closed.

I like a thing simple but it must be simple through complication. Everything must come into your scheme, otherwise you cannot achieve real simplicity. A great deal of this I owe to a great teacher, William James. He said, "Never reject anything. Nothing has been proved. If you reject anything, that is the beginning of the end as an intellectual." He was my big influence when I was at college. He was a man who always said, "complicate your life as much as you please, it has got to simplify."

What a splendid story. Thank you very much.

"We Have Eyes as Well as Ears . . ." (1982)

Anne d'Harnoncourt

John Cage has been using his eyes as well as his ears for forty-five years of work, and it is his audience—alternately delighted, outraged, bewildered—which now finds itself able to see and hear more clearly. Always interested in the visual arts, Cage wavered between devotion to music and painting, chose the former, but kept a weather eye on the latter. The rigorous purity of Mondrian's abstraction attracted his admiration in the 1930s, and in 1948 we find him quoting the fresh and pithy statements of Paul Klee.[1] The erratic, floating shapes of Calder's mobiles and the crystalline structure of Richard Lippold's gold and silver wire sculptures have found in him a rapt observer. Among the litany of names which appear and reappear in his writings and interviews, Mark Tobey, Morris Graves, Robert Rauschenberg, Jasper Johns recur, and he has written thoughtfully about each of these friends and colleagues. Tobey's *White Writings,* Graves's magic circles, Rauschenberg's myriad silkscreened images, Johns's serried or superimposed numbers, could constitute notations for possible worlds of sound as Cage's extraordinary varieties of notation pull his music into the visual field.

Scores have exerted a fascination over non-musical viewers for centuries. We are grateful to Cage and the collection of scores by modern composers he assembled for the Foundation for Contemporary Performance Arts (currently housed at Northwestern University and published in part of his *Notations* of 1969) for revealing the profusion of graphic invention in experimental music. The increasing interest on the part of present-day observers in notations of all sorts (dance as well as music) may have to do with our passion for the working drawing.

Thomas Eakins's analyses of the angles at which ripples of water catch the light now attract as many admirers as do his finished paintings of scullers on the Schuylkill River. Marcel Duchamp's scribbled notes and his fastidious plans and elevations for the *Large Glass* share its status as major work. The *Glass* itself operates as a giant blueprint or mechanical model, activated by its changing environment and the viewers who could be said to be "performing" it as they look. Interested in making a work which was not a work of "art," Duchamp resorted to any method at hand, including musical composition.[2] Cage, in his turn, borrows images and methods from the visual arts and employs any material at hand to write much of his music.

As his compositions grew increasingly complex and (after 1950) were generally based on chance operations, Cage's notation changed as a matter of course: "Everything came from a musical demand, or rather from a notational necessity."[3] From the earliest pieces for prepared piano, his scores have often included handwritten pages of intricate instructions, which in later works such as *Water Music* fuse with the score to become a kind of visual poetry. Another cluster of scores derives from astronomical maps, still another from chance determinations as to whether flaws in the paper are to be read as notes or silences. In one group of pieces, many of them for magnetic tape, Cage employed transparent sheets of plastic printed with lines, dots, or small symbols. By superimposing these materials, or in some cases by cutting out each symbol in a little square and letting them fall at random on a sheet of paper, each would-be performer arrives at his own score. Cage introduced color into his notations in *Aria* of 1958, and it runs delicately riot in several works of the 1970s.

But the visual abundance of scores is customarily reserved for performers, and Cage has always sought to give his listeners something to look at. During his long and fruitful collaboration with Merce Cunningham, audiences have needed to be "omniattentive":[4] watching the dancers, listening to sounds and silences, and enjoying the costumes, sets, and lighting designed by a distinguished succession of artists. After 1958, Cage himself moved with increasing alacrity toward his own version of "theater," which he saw as providing greater richness and flexibility than music alone, coming closer to his goal of resembling "Nature in her manner of operations."[5] Resisting recordings of his music as frozen history. Cage stressed the spatial properties unique to live performance. He has given increasing attention to the visual components of his compositions, using projected slides and films, and encouraging his audiences to make use of all their faculties.

Neglecting no faculty of his own, Cage made his first decisive venture into printmaking in 1969, producing two lithographs and eight plexigrams in celebration of his friend Duchamp, who had died in October of the previous year. Since that time, and with growing intensity since 1978, he has devoted himself to making prints as he continues to write music and a range of poetry and prose. In fact, the three activities are sometimes inseparable from one another in his work, which seems to please him. One field for the intersection of creative energies has been provided by Cage's admiration for Henry David Thoreau, neither artist nor musician, but a passionate observer of nature. Thoreau's thinking and writing often surface in Cage's music (the *Song Books* of 1970, for example, in which "we connect Satie with Thoreau") and in his lectures. Cage discovered Thoreau's *Journal* through a poet friend, Wendell Berry, in 1967, and was delighted by the tiny drawings they included: "When I first saw them [as slides, no longer illustrating the text], I realized I was starved for them."[6] These minute records of trees and leaves, hills and waterfalls, feathers and rabbit tracks, interrupt the flowing lines of brown ink in Thoreau's handwritten journals as a stone or twig diverts a stream.[7] Joyfully adopting printed versions of the drawings as a ready-made shorthand for the natural world. Cage found that they could be played as music—*Score (40 drawings by Thoreau) and 23 Parts*—projected on a screen as part of a performance—*Empty Words*—or transformed through color and enlargement into an abundant vocabulary of images for an ongoing sequence of print editions. Determinedly unconcerned with self-expression, Cage finds it interesting to see what will happen as he combines straight lines and curves (the latter always obtained by dropping pieces of string on the plate, in memory of Duchamp) with the Thoreau drawings through chance operations, just as he accepts and enjoys unforeseeable variations in the performance of indeterminate music. Yet his most non-intentional works are undeniably his own: "Your chance is not the same as my chance," as Duchamp remarked in another context.[8]

The question of skill arises. Whether using star charts or observing imperfections in a sheet of paper to devise a piece of music, Cage performs often painstaking and extended labor with patience and discipline, a quality he prizes. New freedoms do not imply less work. His recent prints are similarly feats of careful observation and precise execution:

although chance operations may dictate that an entire image falls outside of the printed sheet (*Changes and Disappearances*), its absence is as specific as its presence would have been. Above all, Cage pays attention. The first to sight a mushroom, he also knows its scientific name. Never having attempted etching or engraving prior to his first visit to Crown Point Press, he deliberately explored his lack of knowledge in *Seven Day Diary (Not Knowing)* as he gained in skill.

Cage has always been interested in the interpenetration of fields: music, technology, poetry, mycology, theater, dance, and the visual arts come alive in their encounters in his work (itself often taking the form of collaboration with others). He seeks to make us more aware of life itself, in its multiplicity of detail and infinite possibilities, by letting things be themselves and operate freely and simultaneously on our astonished sensibilities.

NOTES

The title is taken from Cage's 1955 article, "Experimental Music," published in *Silence* (Middletown, Conn.: Wesleyan University Press, 1961), 12.

1. In "Defense of Satie," a lecture delivered at Black Mountain College in 1948, printed for the first time in Richard Kostelanetz, ed., *John Cage* (New York: Praeger, 1970), 82.

2. Duchamp note published in *A l'infinitif* (New York: Cordier and Ekstrom, 1966). Duchamp's two known scores are *Musical Erratum* of 1913 (Collection of Mme Duchamp) and *La Mariee Mise a nu par ces celibataires, meme* of 1913 (Foundation for Contemporary Performance Arts; gift of John Cage).

3. Quoted in *For the Birds: John Cage in Conversation with Daniel Charles* (Boston: Marion Boyars, 1981), 159.

4. A word used by Cage in a letter to Michael Zwerin, 1966, reprinted in Kostelanetz, *John Cage,* 167.

5. From a statement by Ananda K. Coomaraswamy, often referred to by Cage; see "Happy New Ears," in Cage's *A Year From Monday* (Middletown, Conn.: Wesleyan University Press, 1967), 31.

6. Quoted by Jane Bell in "John Cage: 'You can have art without even doing it. All you have to do is change you mind,'" *Art News* 78, no. 3 (March 1979): 64. The bracketed phrase in the text is Cage's clarification to the author.

7. Thoreau's handwritten journals, which Cage has not yet seen, are in the collection of the Pierpont Morgan Library, New York. They were published in printed form (with drawings copied by hand and then introduced into the text) in 1962: *The Journal of Henry D. Thoreau,* ed. Bradford Torrey and Francis H. Allen, 2 vols. (New York: Dover Publications).

8. Quoted by Calvin Tomkins, *The Bride and the Bachelors* (New York: Viking Press, 1965), 33.

The Development of His Visual Art (1991)

Richard Kostelanetz

> A mind that is interested in changing . . . is interested precisely in the things that are at extremes. I'm certainly like that. Unless we go to extremes, we won't get anywhere.
>
> —John Cage

By the 1990s, it is clear that John Cage is not just a composer or a "composer-writer" but a true *polyartist,* which is to say someone who has produced distinguished work in more than one nonadjacent art—the principal qualifier being *nonadjacent.* In contrast, sculpture and painting are adjacent visual arts, just as poetry and fiction are adjacent literary arts. However, music and writing are nonadjacent; likewise, painting and poetry. We can distinguish the polyartist from the master of one art who dabbles in another, such as Pablo Picasso, who, we remember, wrote modest poetry and plays; we can distinguish the polyartist from the dilettante who excels at nothing. Moholy-Nagy was a polyartist, and so, in different ways, were William Blake, Kurt Schwitters, Theo van Doesberg, and Wyndham Lewis.

It could be said that of the arts in which Cage has excelled he was slowest to come to visual art. In my 1970 documentary monograph on Cage is reproduced *Chess Pieces,* done around 1944 for the Julian Levy exhibition of works related to Marcel Duchamp's interest in chess. What we see is a square chess-checkerboard in which half of the sixty-four squares have bars of musical notes in black while those squares adjacent to them have notes in white, all against a continuous gray background. Because there is no notational continuity from square to square in any direction, or even from one black square to the next black square (likewise in any direction), Cage is suggesting that the boxes can be read (or played) in any order—from top to bottom or the reverse, from inside out or outside in, or whatever. That is another way of saying that *Chess Pieces* has noncentered activity that is evenly distributed "all-over" to the very edges of the work.

Elsewhere in my documentary monograph is reproduced an untitled drawing that Cage made in 1954 while cleaning his pen during a certain music composition. Rescued at the time by his colleague, the composer Earle Brown, this piece of unintentional art resembles a Jackson Pollock, who was likewise concerned with all-over nonhierarchical distribution; the drawing additionally looks forward to the cross-hatching that Jasper Johns introduced in the 1970s. Finally, the visual arts world was always predisposed to appreciate the exquisite calligraphy of Cage's musical scores, many of which were exhibited at the Stable Gallery in New York in 1958. As Dore Ashton wrote in the *New York Times* at the time, "Each page has a calligraphic beauty quite apart from its function as a musical composition."

In 1969, the year after Marcel Duchamp's death at seventy-nine, Cage was a composer in residence at the University of Cincinnati. Alice Weston, a local art patron, "got the idea that though I had not done any lithographs, I could do some. Marcel had just died, and I had been asked by one of the magazines here to do something for Marcel. I had just before heard Jap [Jasper Johns] say, 'I don't want to say anything about Marcel,' because they had asked him to say something about Marcel in the magazine too. So I called them, both the Plexigrams and the lithographs, *Not Wanting to Say Anything About Marcel,* quoting Jap without saying so."

Not wanting to say anything particular with language, Cage decided to use chance operations to discover words in the dictionary. At the time, he was favoring the use of three coins that, when flipped, could yield Head-Head-Tail, HHH, HTT, THT, HTH, THH, TTH, TTT, which is to say eight different combinations. So he made squares with sixty-four options (8 × 8), flipping one sequence of three coins to get the vertical location of a chance-derived square and then another sequence to get its horizontal location. Therefore, any collection of possible artistic choices had to be divided into sixty-four alternatives. Taking the 1,428 pages of the *American Dictionary* (1955), Cage defined twenty groups of 23 pages apiece and forty-four groups of 22 pages apiece. Once the coin flips forced him to isolate one group of pages, he flipped again to find out which page. After counting the number of entries on that page, he did another set of flips to locate an individual word. Since some of these words had different forms (plural, past tense, gerund), he often flipped again to find out which one to use. Then he had other charts dividing 1,041 typefaces available in a standard catalog of press-on (Letraset) type. Once this was determined, he flipped again to discover whether to use uppercase letters or lowercase. And then another time to discover where in the available 14″ × 20″ space to locate the chosen word/typeface. And then again to discover in what direction the word should face. And finally yet another flip to discover whether the word should be perceived intact or have missing parts or "whether it is in a state of nonstructural disintegration." And so forth.

The effect of such chance operations, as always in Cage, is to divorce the details from any personal taste and then to give all the elements, whether whole words or just parts of letters, equal status in the work. Since he had nothing particular to say about Duchamp, it is scarcely surprising that the words behind the first plexigram, say, should be "agglutination, voltaic, wild rubber, trichoid, agrological, exstipulate, suc-, undershrub, shawl, advanced, moccasin flowers," and so forth. He used similar aleatory methods to collect images from a picture encyclopedia.

Regardless of what individual words, letters, parts of letters, or images appear, if you put such randomly chosen and randomly deconstructed images on Plexiglas, you're likely to get an evenly distributed, all-over field of linguistic/visual materials devoid of syntactic connection or semantic connotations. If you distribute different collections of such materials on a succession of eight Plexiglas sheets, stacked vertically on a single base, the chaotic effect is multipled. What you see is a three-dimensional field that can be viewed variously, both horizontally and vertically, with the possibility of discovering continuously varying relationships between elements on the front Plexigrams and those in the back. As the Plexigrams can be removed from their slots, you are also free to reorder them. It is not for nothing, I've always assumed, that in its verticality and its inscriptional style the entire work resembles a gravestone. (Cage also derived from this research two lithographs on black paper, lesser works in my judgment; and they too have a dense, all-over field reminiscent of Pollock.)

Cage's principal collaborator on this project was graphic designer Calvin Sumsion. "I composed it. I wrote it," Cage told an interviewer. "First we worked together, then I was able to tell him to do something, and then he would send back the work completed. Albers has used such methods—hasn't he with his own work?—or he gives it to some craftsman to do. Many artists now, when they don't know a particular craft, learn how to tell a craftsman what to do." Cage's other associates on this project included lithographic printers Irwin Hollander and Fred Genis.

Cage insists Duchamp would have appreciated the fragmentation of language. "I found a remark of his after I had done the work, that he often enjoyed looking at signs that were weathered because, where letters were missing, it was fun to figure out what the words were before they had weathered. The reason, in my work, that they are weathered is because he had died. So every word is in a state of disintegration." Like the truest Cagean work, *Not Wanting to Say Anything* is extreme, not only in its refusal to say but in the use of three-dimensional verbal-visual materials. As Barbara Rose put it, "The result of Cage's investigation surely proves that the artists asserts himself even in negation."

Some of Cage's works are minimal, having much less content than art previously had (beginning with his so-called silent piece, initially for solo pianist), while others are maximal, having a spectacular abundance of artistic activity. In my appreciation of his individual works, I've tended to favor the maximal over the minimal and thus prefer, among his strictly musical works, *Sonatas and Interludes* (1946–48) and *Williams Mix* (1953); among his theatrical works, *HPSCHD* (1969) and *Europeras 1 and 2* (1987); among his writings, the Diary poems of twenty years ago and *I–VI* (1990). Especially in comparison to the visual art following it, *Not Wanting to Say Anything About Marcel* represents his maximal imagination at its visual best.

Merce Cunningham: Origins and Influences (1983)

David Vaughan

Merce Cunningham was born in Centralia, a small town in the state of Washington, in the American Northwest, in 1919. Although no one in his family had any connection with the theater (his father was a lawyer, and both of Cunningham's brothers followed him into that profession), he early developed what he has described as an "appetite for movement," and began to study dancing at the age of ten. From a local teacher, Mrs. Maude M. Barrett, he learned tap and ballroom dancing—she even taught him a Russian character dance—and began to perform in school recitals as the partner of Mrs. Barrett's daughter Marjorie. In about 1935 Cunningham went with the Barretts on what he has called "a short and intoxicating vaudeville tour," dancing wherever they could pick up engagements and driving as far south as Los Angeles. Mrs. Barrett's "devotion to dancing as an instantaneous and agreeable act of life," her "feeling that dance is most deeply concerned with each single instant as it comes along," had a profound effect on Cunningham. Years later, he used a soft-shoe step he had seen her perform in his solo "A Single" in *Antic Meet.*

After leaving school Cunningham went to the Cornish School in Seattle, Washington (now Cornish College), originally with the intention of studying theater. Dance classes were a requirement for drama students, and he began to attend those taught by Bonnie Bird, a former member of the Martha Graham Dance Company. He soon realized that he wanted to be a dancer, not an actor, and changed his course of studies accordingly. In Cunningham's second year at Cornish, 1938–1939, Bonnie Bird engaged a young composer, John Cage, as dance accompanist and composer. Occasionally, in her absence, Cage would teach classes in dance composition, through which Cunningham became aware of a more experimental approach to choreography and its relation to music—Cage encouraged the students to write music themselves, using percussion instruments. (He also organized a percussion orchestra, in which Cunningham played.)

Nancy Wilson Ross, the authority on Zen Buddhism, who was living in Seattle in the late thirties, has written of the similarity of the landscape of the Northwest to that of Japan—the two regions had also a long-standing commercial link—and of the receptivity of young artists living in that part of America to the ideas of Buddhism. The painter Mark Tobey returned from a visit to China and Japan, she has said, eager to share "his newly acquired knowledge of such things as *haiku* and Zen stories." Cage and Cunningham met Tobey and another local painter, Morris Graves, at this time. At the invitation of Bird and Cage, Nancy Wilson Ross gave a lecture at Cornish on the symbols used in modern art, in connection with an exhibition of the work of Paul Klee that they had organized. In this lecture Mrs. Ross made a specific connection between Zen and dadaism.

Cunningham danced in performances arranged by Bonnie Bird for her students; for one concert she produced a version of Jean Cocteau's *Les Mariés de la Tour-Eiffel,* with music by John Cage and Henry Cowell, in which Cunningham played the General. Cunningham also began to choreograph small works of his own that were sometimes included in these programs.

One of his great friends at Cornish, Joyce Wike, was an anthropologist who was studying the Indians of the Northwest, and both Cunningham and Morris Graves accompanied her into the Indian Reservations to observe their dances. (The title of one of Cunningham's earliest solos, *Totem Ancestor,* seems to refer to these experiences.) Later, his first major ballet, *The Seasons,* commissioned from Cunningham and Cage by Lincoln Kirstein for Ballet Society, a forerunner of the New York City Ballet, in 1947, similarly derived much of its imagery from Cunningham's memories of the landscape and legends of the Northwest, and he wanted Morris Graves to design it. In the event this proved to be impossible and the ballet was designed by the American-Japanese sculptor Isamu Noguchi, which meant that the ballet finally looked more Japanese than Indian, though it retained the cyclical structure of the original conception, inspired by the Indian view of life. Thirty years later, Cunningham realized his plan for a collaboration with John Cage and Morris Graves in *Inlets,* which in its music and design evokes the climate and geography of the Northwest.)

In the summer of 1939 Cunningham and others of Bird's students attended the Bennington Summer School of Dance, held that year at Mills College, in Oakland California, to open it up to students on the West Coast of the United States. Martha Graham saw him in class there and told him that if he went to New York she would use him in her company. Cunningham did not return to complete his three-year course at Cornish but instead accepted Graham's offer. As soon as he arrived in New York Graham began to choreograph a role for him in *Every Soul is a Circus,* and he continued to dance in her company until 1945.

In the meantime, Cunningham began to choreograph independently. In the summer of 1942, he and two other members of the Graham company, Jean Erdman and Nina Fonaroff, presented a joint concert at Bennington College, Vermont, where the company was in residence. They repeated it in New York the following October. One of the works choreographed together by Erdman and Cunningham, *Credo in Us,* had music by Cage, who had recently arrived in New York after teaching in Chicago. For the New York performance Cunningham added a new solo, *Totem Ancestor,* to the program, also with music by Cage.

Cunningham's first solo concert took place one-and-a-half years later, in April 1944, at which he performed six solos, all with music by Cage. At this time their method was to base both music and choreography on a common rhythmic structure, rather than fitting the steps exactly to the musical beat, coming together at certain points but at other times pursuing an independent course.

Cunningham was leading the typical life of a young dancer in New York, rehearsing and going to class (unlike most modern dancers at that time, he was studying ballet, at the School of American Ballet), and struggling to make ends meet. He and Cage paid all the expenses of their concerts themselves; Cunningham designed most of his costumes and Cage designed the announcements and programs. Cunningham began to go to art galleries and exhibitions and to become familiar with the work not only of the many European artists who lived in New York during the Second World War, such as Max Ernst and Yves Tanguy, but also of young American painters like Willem de Kooning and Jackson Pollock.

He was also reading James Joyce, and some of his early dance titles were derived from his writings such as *Tossed As It Is Untroubled, The Unavailable Memory of,* and *In the Name of the Holocaust.* In the summer of 1944 Cunningham both wrote and choreographed an ambitious "dance-play," *Four Walls,* presented at the Perry-Mansfield Workshop at Steamboat Springs, Colorado, where he had a summer teaching job. The text, densely textured, full of Joycean imagery, deals with darkly neurotic family relationships.

But Cunningham was becoming less and less interested in the dramatic or psychological subject-matter that was present in such early solos as *Roots of an Unfocus* and *Orestes,* and more concerned with movement for its own sake, partly in reaction to the kind of dancing he was required to perform in Martha Graham's ballets. He was also undoubtedly influenced by the work of George Balanchine at this time, at least by his tireless exploration of dance movement, and especially the sculptural aspect of the arrangements of dancers' bodies and limbs in space that preoccupied Balanchine.

In the mid-forties John Cage began to study Indian philosophy and music with Gita Sarabhai, and also to attend the lectures on Zen Buddhism given by Daisetz Suzuki at Columbia University, which Cunningham also went to when rehearsals permitted. The concept of space that Cunningham's choreography began to embody reflected an awareness of Buddhism—the concept of decentralization implicit in the principle that every creature is the Buddha—but also was analogous to the "field" approach to composition of the New York school of "abstract expressionist" painters, whose canvases resembled an arbitrary segment of what could theoretically be an infinite space.

Cunningham's use of space runs directly counter to the kind of rules of composition proposed by Doris Humphrey in her book *The Art of Making Dances,* according to which, for instance, certain areas of the stage are held to be "stronger" than others, which are therefore to be avoided. In general Cunningham was regarded by the dance "establishment" of the time as an enfant terrible whose disregard of such "rules" was willful and frivolous. He was accused of being dadaist—by definition anathema to the establishment—but in so far as Cunningham's dances had such an aspect, they may be said to be related to certain avant-garde ballets presented by the Diaghilev Ballets Russes and Rolf de Maré's Ballets Suédois, such as *Parade, Relâche, Mercure,* and *Jack-in-the-Box* (all of which, by no means coincidentally, had music by Erik Satie), rather than to any previous works of the American modern dance.

In the early fifties John Cage began to use chance operations in his musical composition. The composer Christian Wolff had recently introduced him to the *I Ching*, the ancient Chinese Book of Changes, which Cage used as a tool in his first chance pieces, *Music of Changes* and *Imaginary Landscape No. 4*. He drew up charts for such elements as tempo, duration, the kind of sound, and dynamics, choice of which was made by tossing coins, as when obtaining oracles from the *I Ching*. Cunningham began to think of ways in which he could apply similar methods to choreography, which he used for the first time in a large work, *Sixteen Dances for Soloist and Company of Three* (1951), with music by Cage, also composed by chance. Cunningham used chance operations chiefly to determine the order of dances, but one quartet used chance in the actual choreography: he drew up a gamut of movements, a different one for each dancer, and then determined the sequence of movements, their duration and direction, by tossing coins. Thereafter Cunningham habitually made use of such methods when making dances.

The following year, 1952, was a crucial one in the development of the Cage-Cunningham aesthetic. Cunningham had been invited by Leonard Bernstein to choreograph two works for a festival of contemporary music at Brandeis University in Massachusetts: a new version of Stravinsky's *Les Noces* and some excerpts from Pierre Schaeffer's *Symphonie pour un homme seul,* the first time musique concrète would be heard in America. Cunningham's choreography for *Les Noces* was made in the conventional way, following the music; the *Symphonie* was done by chance. It was clearly impossible for the dancers to count the latter piece in the normal way, so Cunningham decided simply to make a dance of the same duration, the sound and the movement to proceed independently of one another. (The music was to be played twice, with two different choreographic realizations, one a solo for Cunningham himself, one a group dance). This simultaneity—in itself a logical development from the way in which he and Cage had been working all along—became a fundamental principle in his work. Composers who collaborate with Cunningham are usually told only the proposed duration of a piece, and the dancers are accustomed to hearing music for the first time when they perform choreography that they have rehearsed in silence.

The dancers in the Brandeis performance included some experienced professionals, some who had been working with Cunningham in New York, and several students from the university with very little training.

The problem was to find a way of putting all of them on the stage together. It occurred to Cunningham that they could be given not only simple steps that he had devised but also ballroom dances and even everyday, non-dance gestures and movements. Accordingly, he made three charts from which the movements were to be selected, each comprising material from one of these categories. (The dance was later renamed *Collage.*)

Later in the same summer Cunningham and Cage were in residence at Black Mountain College, the progressive liberal arts school in North Carolina (where in 1948 they had taken part in a production of Erik Satie's play *Le piège de Méduse*). Robert Rauschenberg, whom they had met in New York the previous winter, was also there. "There was from the beginning," John Cage has said, "a sense of absolute identification, or utter agreement, between us." At Black Mountain they saw Rauschenberg's all-white paintings for the first time, which encouraged Cage to write his famous silent piece, *4'33"*.

Cunningham and Cage were friendly with painters of the abstract-expressionist school, who made up an important part of the audience for their concerts, but there was one very important difference in their approach: the work of these painters had as its subject "the heroically suffering artist" (in Calvin Tomkins's phrase). This was precisely what Cunningham wished to eliminate from his choreography, and Cage from his music. Like Marcel Duchamp, they wished to make works that were not reflections of their personal feelings. Rauschenberg and Jasper Johns took a similar approach.

During the summer Cage devised the famous untitled theater piece, generally regarded as the prototype of the Happenings of the sixties, in which Cunningham danced, Cage read a lecture, David Tudor played the piano, Rauschenberg projected slides of his paintings and played old phonograph records, M. C. Richards and Charles Olsen read their poetry. The performance was unstructured except for rough time-brackets, drawn up by chance methods, in which the participants were free to perform their activities. It lasted forty-five minutes. In planning this event Cage was influenced not only by his study of Zen but also by his reading of Antonin Artaud's *The Theatre and Its Double.*

These performances in the summer of 1952—the *Symphonie pour un homme seul* and the Black Mountain theater event—were crucial in the development of the post-modern aesthetic and decisively established Cunningham and Cage in their positions as the leaders of the avant-garde in the United States, with an influence both wide and deep not only in dance and music but also in painting and the theater. The following summer they were again in residence at Black Mountain. Cunningham brought with him a number of dancers who had been working and studying with him in New York. During the summer they rehearsed a repertory of dances that were performed at the end of the summer and again in New York the following winter. The Merce Cunningham Dance Company as a permanent entity dates from this time, but the foundation for Cunningham's work with his company in the next thirty years had been laid during this first decade of independent activity.

Cage and Modern Dance (1965)

Jill Johnston

Cunningham's first point of departure from all these concepts was to make an arbitrary time structure for his dances. The time was not determined by a piece of music selected in advance to accompany the dance, nor by the dance itself as he was making it. Rather, he would sit down beforehand and say the dance would consist of five parts and each part would be three minutes long. Deciding on such a structure, he and his composer, John Cage, would work independently to fill in the structure with sound and movement. This was the first example in dance of putting things together, or letting things go together, that are not logically thought to have any business being together. Actually, it was the logic of a simultaneous vision, and it seemed only necessary to recall a theater ticket and a landscape postcard appearing side by side in a collage by Kurt Schwitters to get the logic of it straight, or to watch your hand move from stove to sink and hear the children screaming in the other room at the same time. Similarly, Cunningham's art is actually a complex mixture of personal adjustments and random inclusions.

His adventures with chance began in 1951 with *16 Dances*. When he had made the dance he saw no reason why the parts should occur in any particular order, so he tossed coins to determine the sequence. This piece also included a small section in which the sequence of the movement itself was determined by chance. The following year, in 1952, he made several dances entirely by chance. *Variation* became a collage of ballet movement as the movements were broken down into a gamut of possibilities and put together again by tossing coins. The procedure began to involve time, space and movement charts. Each chart contained a number of predetermined possibilities, and the coin then decided what the movement would be, at what time and in what space it would occur. The method became more elaborate when it was applied to each dancer in a group piece. The resulting dispersion of the dancers projected a new kind of open space that is characteristic of Cunningham's work.

Since the sound and the movement were independent of each other there seemed no reason why the dancers themselves could not move independently. When the dancers are moving thus around the stage the effect is something like what you might see in a train terminal where the people are rushing, walking, waiting or sitting as they are, isolated in their own destinations. The result is also analogous to a Pollock painting where the colors are dripped independently on the canvas and converge and disperse in their own rhythms.

In the simultaneous vision there is no central focus, except where the observer, if not basking in the total effect, concentrates at any moment. The values become equalized; there are no climaxes or resolutions, which means that there is no necessary beginning or ending. It has often been remarked that Pollock's paintings suggest an infinite extension beyond the picture plane. Cunningham's dances suggest the same extension; and since he often juggles the order of the parts by chance, it is clear that he considers one beginning as good as another.

The containment of a picture within its frame, or the dance within the proscenium stage, is a practical expediency. But since that is, at the same time, all we see, that is all there is. We sense the boundless and see the limits. The facts are essential. The point is to accept what the immediate presence offers us and not judge that presence by the consideration of possibilities other than what we see in the presence. The judgment which applies to traditional forms, where the progression of one step to the next is understood as inevitable, must be suspended, since there are only facts, no inevitabilities. The facts are interchangeable. There are no laws governing the sequences or juxtapositions. The dances are lawless.

Cunningham's fourth step in liberating movement from conventional logic was to apply the simultaneity of action to a single body. He did this with *Untitled Solo* in 1953. By tossing coins to establish a movement of the head, then the arms, the torso, etc., he made a superimposition of motion which was a more concentrated fragmentation of elements. The resulting coordinations were so unusual as to render the performances of them extremely difficult.

The idea was not to make things impossible, but to find new ways of moving. Devising a certain gamut for each part of the body (i.e., the head twists, or rolls, or snaps in staccato from right to left, etc.), then putting the several parts together in simultaneous action, provided the possibility of movement beyond the habitual preferences of personal taste.

There is some analogy in Cunningham's method to the cubist analytical breakdown and reorganization of images. But a better relation is to the chance methods of the dadaists. Hans Arp composed collages by picking up scraps of paper, shuffling them, and gluing them down just as they fell. The chance methods of the dada painters and poets were primitive devices compared to the refined, elaborate chance methodology evolved by John Cage, Cunningham, and a number of avant-garde composers here and abroad. The devices then were usually as simple as pulling words out of a hat to make a poem (Tristan Tzara); and if one reads Jackson Mac Low's essay (printed in La Monte Young's *Anthology*) on the involved procedures he employs to make poetry now, one can see the difference. The complexity of present methods is the result of analyzing the various components of a medium and applying the devices, which may be various in themselves, to the different components. The attitude behind the method in either case is the same, but what has happened in the past fifteen years, which accounts for the complexity, is the programmatic extension of those early ideas.

The attitude is really the central issue. John Cage picked up where the dadaists left off. His inventive experiments with sound, and his studies in Zen, led him to the philosophy of indifference that Duchamp has so beautifully exemplified for many years. Dada wished to recover the natural, unreasonable order in the world, to restore man to his humble place in nature. The chance gesture became a spiritual insight into the condition of chaos, which is the natural order of the world. Cage has said that, "Form is what interests everyone and fortunately it is wherever you are and there is no place where it is not." Chance was a gesture of affirmation and acceptance; for to remove oneself, to whatever degree, from the means and ends of a composition, meant to identify oneself with the ground of existence. The heresy of dada and Cage is the abdication of the will. In a culture brought up on the pride of accomplishment in subduing the brute forces of nature, the admission of chaos seemed like madness from the beginning. But the philosophy has persisted and Cage has had an enormous influence on contemporary artists. The madness has become a new kind of order, and the possibilities extend in every conceivable direction.

Through chance Cage arrived at his position of "letting sounds be themselves rather than vehicles for emotions and ideas." Sounds, for Cage, are not structurally connected as in the melodic and harmonic designs of the past. Each sound is heard for itself and does not depend for its value on its place within a system of sounds. Similarly, Cunningham's movement is a series of isolated actions, and the connection is simply that of sequence or juxtaposition or whatever the observer wishes to make out of it. The emphasis is on movement as movement. "I don't look in a book," he says, "I make a step."

Music and Dance (1982)

Merce Cunningham

My first awareness of John Cage's relationship with the dance was at the Cornish School in Seattle, where he came to play the piano for Bonnie Bird's dance classes. I was a student, taking both technique classes and composition classes. John was involved in the composition classes at one point, writing or arranging music for some of the dances that the students were doing.

The first time I remember working with John was, I believe, in 1942. I had come to New York and was making a piece with another dancer, Jean Erdman. I suggested we try to get John to write the music, even though he was not in New York yet. (He had moved to Chicago, by this time.) We could send him the structure and all the counts, because we were still working that way. Jean thought that was a good idea, and we commissioned John to do it. We didn't hear from him for a long time, though, and Jean got nervous; but eventually he sent the music (or came with it—I don't remember which), and we performed it. The music is called *Credo in Us,* scored for radios and percussion and records.

When we began working together, we started with the idea that what was common between music and dance was time. Music and dance both took place in the same length of time, but they didn't have to carve it up in the same way. Jumping off from that premise, we were at first much stricter about structure than we are now. The pieces were much shorter, and there was a much more defined rhythmic structure. John would ask questions; he would want to know how many people were in it and what the structure was. Then gradually we became able to work in such a way that we almost didn't need to say anything to each other. It became more like a process than a fixed object. Practically speaking, it was an enormous advantage in one way because there was no need for a rehearsal pianist!

There were certain structured points at which we would meet in the dances; in between them we were free. But then we gradually elongated the time between the structured points: You start at precisely the same moment here, and you get there at precisely the same minute, but there is a great deal of freedom in between. That is roughly what happens now. I find that if a piece as long as *Locale* (which is 28 minutes and 45 seconds long) has been rehearsed clearly, the dancers come out within 10 or 15 seconds of the original length—and very often on the nose.

We do our own rehearsing; we almost never hear the music until the performance, as it often has to do with the composers making electronic sounds and devising the means by which to make these particular sounds. They can't just pick up conventional instruments to make them; they have certain sounds in mind, and they have to devise the way to produce them. So they are really working not only up to the last minute, but all the time, so that the music changes even after the dance has been performed for the first time. Therefore, where once I had heard a kind of sound in one area of the dance, sometimes the next time I would notice it coming in another.

The movements vary almost not at all from performance to performance, particularly in the pieces I make now, simply because of the complexity. If the dancers had to think about varying, they would run into each other. In earlier pieces there were variables. I would set the movements, but the dancers could make them slower or faster, or repeat them or change the direction of the movement, which would elongate a section or shorten it in terms of performance. However, as my movements got more involved, it became too complicated to do that on stage.

The whole dance scene was different when John and I were still doing our joint programs. Most modern dancers whom I knew were giving one performance here in New York and then spending the rest of the year trying to pay it off. And I thought, there must be another way. So I wrote long letters to colleges all over the country, to try to get anything. I would write 50 letters and get one or two dates, and we would borrow a car and drive out and do them.

We made one or two cross-country tours, including one during the worst winter in the history of the United States. The cows and the Indians were starving, the snow was piling up in the West, and we were driving from Chicago to Portland, Oregon! We went to a truck stop very early in the morning that first day to get some coffee. A truck driver sitting next to John asked, "Where're you going?" "Portland, Oregon," we told him. "My advice to you," he said, "is to go through Arizona." So, we did, all the way down through Arizona and back up. We got to California—after having slid off the road twice!—and were again in a coffee shop in a little town some place north of San Francisco, and we asked the waitress if she had heard anything about driving conditions. She said, "Well, my sister from Portland phoned up three days ago and said she was coming down right away, and I haven't heard from her since." So we left the car and took the train to Portland. Then we had to go back again to pick up the car and drive all the way back. But I thought it was better than staying in New York and pretending to be a dancer!

[*16 Dances*] (1984)

William Brooks

In the early 1950s John Cage began to turn his attention toward a new compositional domain. Previously, writing music for percussion and for prepared piano, Cage had concentrated on devising an aesthetic which would accommodate noises and silences as well as pitches. He had divided composition into four components: "structure," which concerned "the division of a whole into parts"; "materials," which were "the sounds and silences" of a composition; "method," which regulated the note-by-note choice of sounds; and "form," which reflected the underlying conception of a work, its overall morphology.[1]

At first Cage was much preoccupied with "structure" and "materials." He used a "square-root" principle to regulate "structure": a piece was divided into a number of units which were grouped into sections, and then each unit was divided into the same number of subunits grouped the same way. The "materials" of a piece were similarly limited—to a collection of percussion instruments, for example, or a group of preselected piano preparations. But although "materials" and "structure" were rather tightly controlled, "method" and "form" were essentially intuitive; they were guided not by a discipline but by Cage's personality.

At the same time Cage was composing for dance, and when he and Merce Cunningham began collaborating regularly in the mid-1940s, they agreed to structure the dance and music together, in advance. Cunningham later recalled that "this use of a time structure allowed us to work separately, Cage not having to be with the dance except at structural points, and I was free to make the phrases and movements within the phrases vary their speeds and accents without reference to a musical beat, again only using the structural points as identification between us."[2]

The *16 Dances,* first performed on 21 January 1951, were the most ambitious choreographic work to use this structural technique. In scope and content they recalled Cage's musical *Sonatas and Interludes* (1946–48): but the *16 Dances* also anticipated techniques to come, as Cunningham has explained:

> The *16 Dances* . . . was a long piece intended to fill an evening. It was also the first time the use of chance operations entered into the compositional method. The choreography was concerned with expressive behavior, in this case the nine permanent emotions of Indian classical aesthetics, four light and four dark with tranquillity the ninth and pervading one. The structure for the piece was to have each of the dances involved with a specific emotion followed by an interlude. Although the order was to alternate light and dark, it didn't seem to matter whether Sorrow or Fear came first, so I tossed a coin. And also in the interlude after Fear, number XIV, I used charts of separate movements for material for each of the four dancers, and let chance operations decide the continuity.[3]

Cunningham's choices yielded the following form for the *Dances*:

I.	*Solo:*	*Anger*
II.	*Trio:*	*Interlude*
III.	*Solo:*	*Humor*
IV.	*Duet:*	*Interlude*
- - -		
V.	*Solo:*	*Sorrow*
VI.	*Quartet:*	*Interlude*
VII.	*Solo:*	*Heroic*
VIII.	*Quartet:*	*Interlude*
- - -		
IX.	*Solo:*	*Odious*
X.	*Duet:*	*Interlude*
XI.	*Solo:*	*Wondrous*
XII.	*Trio:*	*Interlude*
- - -		
XIII.	*Solo:*	*Fear*
XIV.	*Quartet:*	*Interlude*
XV.	*Duet:*	*Erotic*
XVI.	*Quartet:*	*Tranquility*

Except for the penultimate interlude (no. XII), which is somewhat eccentric, the structure of each movement is straightforward: the first contains 7 sections of 7 measures each; the second, 10 sections of 10 measures each; the third, 9 of 9; and so forth. These sections, however, can be clearly discerned only in movements IV, VIII, XII, and XVI. In these, as in Cage's earlier compositions, the "method" was largely intuitive and expressive, with motivic repetition and variation used to mark structural units.

In the other movements, however, Cage used a different "method," which in its effects anticipated chance techniques. Before beginning, Cage chose a gamut of 64 sounds and short gestures, which he arranged in an 8 × 8 chart, with each square containing a single event. To increase diversity, Cage altered his "materials" as he worked; after each pair of dances he replaced eight elements on his chart with new ones.

These gamuts served somewhat like a prepared piano; but instead of composing with them intuitively, Cage used systematic moves on the chart akin to the moves of pieces on a chessboard. Thus the overall sequence would be unpredictable, although events located near each other on the chart would tend to occur together, producing some recurring patterns. And because the "method" would be applied consistently throughout each movement, the sections would no longer be differentiated; the movements composed this way would be heard as a single continuity.

However, the *Dances* contained two sorts of choreography; and although Cage's new "method" suited the abstract interludes, the expressionistic solos required something different. For these Cage limited his "material" to the sounds which he judged best suited the subject; in addition, he altered density, dynamics, and other details as needed. Thus movement III, for example, expresses "humor" by means of extreme dynamic and timbral contrasts; while movement IX, the "odious," is pervaded by finicky ostinati.

The structure of the *16 Dances* also reflects Cage's increasing concern with social issues: the individualistic expressionism of the solos is contrasted with the collective consistency of the ensembles. And just as the individual and the collective are reconciled in the dance's closing quartet, in which an emotion ("Tranquillity") is, for the only time, expressed by the full ensemble, so too are the compositional techniques ultimately integrated: in the final movement a tranquil ostinato, composed intuitively, is overlaid with an everchanging sequence of sounds derived from the charts.

Together with the *Concerto for Prepared Piano and Orchestra,* the *16 Dances* mark the beginning of both Cage's exploration of social questions in music and his use of chance techniques. Shortly after their completion, Cage explained privately that "by making moves on the charts I freed myself from what I had thought to be freedom, [but] which was only [the] accretion of habits and taste."[4] The paradox at the heart of this sentence—that in discipline alone is there freedom—has remained the core of Cage's practice ever since.

NOTES

1. John Cage, "Composition as Process," in *Silence* (Middletown, Conn.: Wesleyan University Press, 1961), 18.
2. Merce Cunningham, "A Collaborative Process Between Music and Dance," in *A John Cage Reader,* ed. Peter Gena and Jonathan Brent (New York: C. F. Peters, 1982), 108.
3. Cunningham, "Collaborative Process," 109–10.
4. John Cage, letter to Pierre Boulez, 1952.

Other Sources of Cage Criticism in English

This listing acknowledges as it supplements the most complete bibliography to date of Cage criticism, in all languages—Martin Erdmann's in *Musik-Konzepte Sonderband: John Cage,* edited by Heinz-Klaus Metzger and Rainer Riehn (Munich: Text + Kritik, 1990). A chronological list of articles about Cage appears in *Neuland* 5 (1984–85).

Several major essays on Cage, by various authors, appear in anthologies that will be identified through the following abbreviations.

JCR Brent, Jonathan, and Peter Gena, eds. *A John Cage Reader in Celebration of his Seventieth Birthday.* New York: C. F. Peters, 1982.

JC75 Fleming, Richard, and William Duckworth, eds. *John Cage at Seventy-Five.* Lewisburg, Pa.: Bucknell University Press, 1989.

JC Kostelanetz, Richard, ed. *John Cage.* 1970. Rev. ed. New York: Da Capo, 1991.

OIM Kostelanetz, Richard. *On Innovative Music(ian)s.* New York: Limelight, 1989.

Note that much of the most insightful criticism of Cage's art appears in Cage's own writings, collected in *JC* and in his own books, and in such interviews as those with Daniel Charles (published in his *For the Birds* [London: Boyars, 1981]), that about theater (in Kostelanetz, *The Theatre of Mixed Means* [1968; rpt., New York: RK Editions, 1981]), that with Kostelanetz about matters in general (in *JC*), that about radio with Kostelanetz (in *JC75*), and those recomposed in Kostelanetz, *Conversing with Cage* (New York: Limelight, 1988), which includes a nearly complete list of previous interviews with Cage.

Alpert, Barry. "Post-Modern Oral Poetry: Buckminster Fuller, John Cage, and David Antin." *Boundary 2* 3, no. 3 (1975).

Ashton, Dore. "Cage, Composer, Shows Calligraphy of Note." *New York Times,* 6 May 1958. Reprinted in *JC.*

Barker, David. "Untitled: Art, Music, and Nothing." *Exploratorium Quarterly* 13, no. 4 (Winter 1989).

Bell, Jane. "John Cage." *Art News* 23, no. 3 (1979).

Bowles, Paul. "Percussionists in Concert Led by John Cage." *New York Herald Tribune*, 8 February 1943.

Bresnick, Martin. "Cage's Unexpected Offspring." *Mosaic* 8, no. 1 (1974).

Brooks, William. "About Cage About Thoreau." In *JC75*.

———. "Choice and Change in Cage's Music." *Tri-Quarterly* 54 (1982). Reprinted in *JCR*.

———. "Instrumental and Vocal Resources." In *Dictionary of Contemporary Music*, ed. John Vinton. New York: Dutton, 1974.

Brown, Carolyn. "On Chance." *Ballet Review* (1968).

Brown, Norman O. "John Cage." In *JC75*.

Bunger (Evans), Richard. *The Well-Prepared Piano*. Colorado Springs, Colo.: Colorado College Music Press, 1973.

Campana, Deborah. "Sound, Rhythm, and Structure: John Cage's Compositional Process Before Chance." *Interface* 18 (1989).

Cardew, Cornelius. "Notation—Interpretation." *Tempo* (Summer 1961).

Charles, Daniel. "Entr'acte: 'Formal' or 'Informal' Music." *Musical Quarterly* 51 (January 1965). Excerpted in *JC*.

———. "Interpretation Without Obstruction: Senselessness Beyond Nonsense." *Inunija* 7 (1990).

———. "Music Beyond Narcissism." *The World & I* 1, no. 11 (1986).

Chase, Gilbert. "John Cage." In *International Cyclopedia of Music and Musicians*. New York, 1975.

Childs, Barney. "Indeterminacy." In *Dictionary of Contemporary Music,* ed. John Vinton. New York: Dutton, 1974.

Chou Wen-Chung. "Asian Concepts and Twentieth-Century Western Composers." *Musical Quarterly* 57, no. 2 (April 1971).

Clark, Robert Charles. "Total Control and Chance in Musics: A Philosophical Analysis." *Journal of Aesthetics and Art Criticism* 28 (Spring 1970).

Copland, Aaron. "The New 'School' of American Composers." *New York Times Magazine,* 14 March 1948.

Cowell, Henry. "Current Chronicle." *Musical Quarterly* 38, no. 1 (January 1952). Reprinted in *JC*.

———. "Drums along the Pacific." *Modern Music* 18 (November–December 1940).

Croce, Arlene. "The Mercists." *New Yorker,* 3 April 1978.

Cunningham, Merce. *Changes: Notes on Choreography.* New York: Something Else Press, 1968.

David, Beverly R. "Cage's *Mureau:* Another Revolution." *American Poetry Review* 6, no. 4 (July–August 1977).

Davidson, Audrey. "The Game John Cage Plays." *Michigan Academician* 4, no. 3 (Winter 1972). Reprinted in Davidson, *Substance and Manner: Studies in Music and the Other Arts* (St. Paul, Minn.: 1977).

DeLio, Thomas. "John Cage's *Variations II,* The Morphology of Global Structures." *Perspectives of New Music* 19 (1980–81). Reprinted in DeLio, *Circumscribing the Open Universe* (Lanham, Md.: University Press of America, 1984).

Dickinson, Peter. "Stein Satie Cummings Thomson Berners Cage: Toward

a Context for the Music of Virgil Thomson." *Musical Quarterly* 72, no. 3 (1986).
———. "Way Out with John Cage." *Music and Musicians* (November 1965).
Dinwiddie, John. "MEWANTEMOOSEICDAY: John Cage in Davis, 1969." *Source* 4, no. 1 (January 1970).
Erdman, Jean. "The Dance as Non-Verbal Poetic Image." In *The Dance Has Many Faces,* ed. Walter Sorrel. New York: World, 1951.
Etrog, Sorel. *Dream Chamber.* Toronto: Black Brick Press, 1982.
Ewen, David. "John Cage." In *The World of Twentieth-Century Music.* Englewood Cliffs, N.J.: Prentice-Hall, 1968.
Feldman, Morton. *Essays,* ed. Walter Zimmerman. Kerpen, Germany, 1985.
François, Jean-Charles. "Percussion Sound Sculpture." *Percussionist* 18, no. 3 (Summer 1981).
Griffiths, Paul. *Cage.* London: Oxford University Press, 1981.
Hamm, Charles. "The American Avant-Garde." In *Music in the New World.* New York: Norton, 1983.
———. "John Cage." In *New Grove Dictionary of American Music,* ed. H. Wylie Hitchcock and Stanley Sadie. London: Macmillan, 1986.
———. "Sound Forms for Piano." Liner notes to New World Records no. 203. 1976.
Hansen, Al. *A Primer of Happenings and Time-Space Art.* New York: Something Else Press, 1968.
Herwitz, Daniel A. "The Security of the Obvious: On John Cage's Musical Radicalism." *Critical Inquiry* 4 (Summer 1988).
Hicks, Michael. "John Cage's Studies with Schoenberg." *American Music* 8, no. 2 (Summer 1990).
Higgins, Dick. "On Cage's Classes." Reprinted in *JC.*
———. *Postface.* New York: Something Else Press, 1964.
Hiller, Lejaren. "Programming the *I-Ching* Oracle." *Computer Studies in the Humanities and Verbal Behavior* 3, no. 3 (October 1970).
Hitchcock, H. Wiley. *Music in the United States.* 3d ed. Englewood Cliffs, N.J.: Prentice-Hall, 1988.
Hobbs, R. C. "Possibilities." *Art Criticism* 1, no. 2 (1979).
Husarik, Stephen. "John Cage and Lejaren Hiller, HPSCHD." *American Music* 1, no. 2 (Summer 1983).
Johnson, Ben. "Harry Partch–John Cage." Liner notes to New World Records no. 214. 1978.
Johnson, Tom. "Intentionality and Nonintentionality in the Performance of Music by John Cage." In *JC75.*
———. *The Voice of New Music.* Eindhoven, Netherlands: Apollo Art About, 1989.
Johnston, Jill. "There Is No Silence Now." *Village Voice,* 8 November 1962. Reprinted in *JC.*
Klein, Lothar. "Twentieth-Century Analysis: Essays in Miniature, John Cage." *Music Educators Journal* 54, no. 9 (May 1968).
Kobrin, Ed. "I-Ching." *Source* 4, no. 2 (July 1970).

Kostelanetz, Richard. "The American Avant-Garde, Part II: John Cage." *Stereo Review* 22, no. 5 (May 1969). Repinted in Kostelanetz, *Master Minds* (New York: Macmillan, 1969).

———. "The Anarchist Art: The Example of John Cage." *City Lights Journal* 3 (1990). Reprinted in Kostelanetz, *On Innovative Art(ist)s* (Jefferson, N.C.: McFarland, 1992).

———. "Bigger Is Better, Longer Is Greater: The Keystone of the Cagean Canon." Liner notes to Wergo Edition John Cage 60156-50. 1989. Reprinted in *OIM*.

———. "Cunningham/Cage." In *Next Wave Festival.* New York: Brooklyn Academy of Music, 1986. Reprinted in *OIM*.

———. "Inferential Art." *Columbia University Forum* 12, no. 2 (Summer 1969). Reprinted in Kostelanetz, *Metamorphosis in the Arts* (New York: Assembling, 1981).

———. "John Cage, 75, Writes First, 'Great American' Opera." *New York Times,* 10 July 1988. Reprinted in *OIM*.

———. "John Cage: Some Random Remarks." *Denver Quarterly* 3, no. 4 (Winter 1968). Reprinted in *JC* and *OIM*.

———. "Master of Several Arts." *New York Times Book Review,* December 1979. Reprinted as "John Cage (1979)," in Kostelanetz, *The Old Poetries and the New* (Ann Arbor: University of Michigan Press, 1981).

———. "Milton Babbitt and John Cage Are the Two Extremes of Avant-Garde Music." *New York Times Magazine,* 15 January 1967. Reprinted in *OIM*.

Kubota, Shigeko. *Marcel Duchamp and John Cage.* Japan: n.p., n.d.

Landy, Leigh. "John Cage: Anarchist Musician." *Avant Garde* 3 (1989).

Lederman, Minna. "John Cage: A View of My Own." *Tri-Quarterly* 54 (1982). Reprinted in *JCR*.

Lee, Jonathan Scott. "From Emerson's *Nature:* An Essay." *Revue d'Esthetique* 13–15 (1987–88).

Lo Bue, Eberto. "John Cage's Writings." *Precisely: 13 14 15 16* (1983).

McGary, Keith. "I Have Nothing." *Antioch Review,* Summer 1962.

Markgraf, Bruce. "John Cage: Ideas and Practices of a Contemporary Speaker." *Quarterly Journal of Speech* 48, no. 2 (April 1962).

Mellers, Wilfrid. "From Noise to Silence." In *Music in a New Found Land.* New York: Knopf, 1965.

Meyer, Leonard B. "The End of the Renaissance?" *Hudson Review* 6, no. 2 (Summer 1963). Reprinted in Meyer, *Music, the Arts, and Ideas* (Chicago: University of Chicago Press, 1967).

Middleton, Richard. "Cage and the Meta-Freudians." *British Journal of Aesthetics* 12, no. 3 (Summer 1972).

Montague, Stephen. "Significant Silences of a Musical Anarchist." *Classical Music,* 22 May 1982.

Nyman, Michael. *Experimental Music: Cage and Beyond.* New York: Universe, 1974.

Oliveros, Pauline. *Software for People: Collected Writings, 1963–80.* Barrytown, N.Y.: Printed Editions, 1984.
Perloff, Marjorie. *Dance of the Intellect.* New York: Cambridge University Press, 1985.
———. *Poetic License.* Evanston, Ill.: Northwestern University Press, 1990.
———. *The Poetics of Indeterminacy: Rimbaud to Cage.* Princeton, N.J.: Princeton University Press, 1980.
———. "The Portrait of the Artist as a Collage-Text: Pound's *Gaudier-Brzeska* and the 'Italic' Texts of John Cage." *American Poetry Review* 11, No. 3 (May–June 1982).
———. *Radical Artifice.* Chicago: University of Chicago Press, 1991.
Peyser, Joan. *The New Music.* New York: Dell, 1971.
Pritchett, James. "From Choice to Chance: John Cage's Concerto for Prepared Piano." *Perspectives of New Music* 26, no. 1 (Winter 1988).
———. "Understanding John Cage's Chance Music: An Analytical Approach." In *JC75.*
Radano, Ronald M. "Themes and Variations." *Perspectives of New Music* 21, nos. 1–2 (1982–83).
Reynolds, Roger. "Indeterminacy: Some Considerations." *Perspectives of New Music* 4, no. 1 (Fall-Winter 1965).
Rockwell, John. "The American Experimental Tradition and Its Godfather." In *All-American Music.* New York: Knopf, 1983.
Rose, Barbara. "Not Wanting to Say Anything About Marcel." *Source* 4, no. 1 (1970). Reprinted in *JC.*
Roth, Moira. "The Aesthetics of Indifference." *Artforum* 16, no. 3 (November 1977).
Roy, Klaus George. "The Strange and Wonderful World of John Cage." *HiFi/Stereo Review* 5, no. 5 (1960).
Russell, John. "Seated One Day at the I-Ching." *ARTnews* 68, no. 9 (January 1970).
Rzewski, Frederic. "Performance: Indeterminate Performance." In *Dictionary of Contemporary Music,* ed. John Vinton. New York: Dutton, 1974.
Sabatini, Arthur J. "Silent Performances: On Reading John Cage." In *JC75.*
Salzman, Eric. Liner notes to *Four Walls.* Tomato Records 2696592. 1989.
———. Liner notes to *Three Constructions.* Tomato Records 2696172, 1989.
———. Liner notes to Wergo Edition John Cage 60157-50. 1988.
———. Liner notes to Wergo Edition John Cage 6158-2. 1991.
———. "Parallels and Paradoxes." *Stereo Review* 22 (April 1969).
———. *Twentieth-Century Music.* 3d ed. Englewood Cliffs, N.J.: Prentice-Hall, 1988.
Sandow, Gregory. Liner notes to Edition John Cage. Wergo 60151-50. 1988.
Schmitt, Natalie Crohn. *Actors and Onlookers.* Evanston, Ill.: Northwestern University Press, 1990.
Scholes, Percy. "John Cage." In *The Oxford Companion to Music.* London: Oxford University Press, 1955.

Schöning, Klaus. "Nichi-nichi kore ko-nichi." In *Roaratorio,* by Klaus Schöning and John Cage. Königstein, Germany: Athenaum, 1983.

Slonimsky, Nicolas. "John Cage." In *Baker's Biographical Dictionary of Musicians.* 5th ed. New York: Macmillan, 1971.

Smith, D. Newton. "The Influence of Music on the Black Mountain Poets: II." *St. Andrews Review* 3, no. 3 (1975).

Sutherland, Roger. "John Cage and Indeterminacy." *London Magazine* 11, no. 3 (August–September 1971).

Tan, Margaret Leng. "'Taking a Nap, I Pound the Rice': Eastern Influences on John Cage." In *JC75.*

Thomson, Virgil. "Cage and the Collage of Noises." *New York Review of Books,* 23 April 1970. Reprinted in Thomson, *American Music Since 1910* (New York: Holt, 1971); *A Virgil Thomson Reader* (New York: Dutton, 1984).

———. "How Modern Can You Be?" *New York Herald Tribune,* 10 February 1952.

Toland, Lilah. "Changes and Disappearances, 1979–82. *Tri-Quarterly* 54 (1982). Reprinted in *JCR.*

Tomkins, Calvin. "Figure in an Imaginary Landscape." *New Yorker* 28 November 1964. Reprinted in Tomkins, *The Bride and the Bachelors* (New York: Viking, 1965).

Tucker, Todd. "Jackson Pollock and John Cage." *Indiana Theory Review* 2, no. 3 (1979).

Vaughan, David. "Duet." *Ballet News* 4, no. 9 (March 1983).

Winslow, Richard. "Lecture." *Joglars* 1, no. 2 (Winter 1964).

Wolff, Christian. "Cage, John." In *Dictionary of Contemporary Music,* ed. John Vinton. New York: Dutton, 1974.

Yates, Peter, et al. "Excerpts from Reviews and Critical Articles." In *John Cage.* New York: C. F. Peters, 1962.

———. "An Introduction to John Cage." In *Twentieth Century Music.* New York: Pantheon, 1967.

———. "John Cage, Builder of New Music." *Vogue,* October 1964.

Zinnes, Harriet. "John Cage: Writer." *Hollins Critic* 17, no. 6 (February 1981).

Zukofsky, Paul. "John Cage's Recent Violin Music." *Tri-Quarterly* 54 (1982). Reprinted in *JCR.*

Contributors

Paul Bowles is a celebrated American novelist who was not only a composer but a music reviewer for the *New York Herald Tribune* before he began publishing fiction.

William Brooks, professor of music at the University of Illinois, has performed Cage's music, as well as written extensively about it, for over two decades.

Joseph Byrd was a post-Cagean composer who became a rock musician releasing two albums, *The United States of America* and *The American Metaphysical Circus,* for Columbia Records in the late 1960s. He currently lives in McKinleyville, Calif.

Deborah Campana is a Music Public Services Librarian at the Northwestern University Music Library, where she curates the John Cage Archive. The title of her doctoral dissertation was "Form and Structure in the Music of John Cage."

Daniel Charles holds a chair in philosophy and aesthetics at the University of Nice. Formerly a professor of musicology at the University of Paris, he has written several books with and about John Cage. Recent essays were written originally in English as well as his native French.

Henry Cowell (1897–1965) was the dean of American avant-garde composers, as well as a generous writer and lecturer on new music.

Merce Cunningham, the eminent choreographer, has been publishing occasional essays since the 1950s. His visual art is exhibited from time to time.

Eric De Visscher is a composer/musicologist currently living in Brussels. He took his M.A. under James Tenney at York University in Toronto and his doctorate under Daniel Charles at the University of Paris.

Thomas DeLio is a composer and theorist teaching at the University of Maryland in College Park. He has written three books on contemporary music: *Circumscribing the Open Universe* (1984), *Contiguous Lines* (1985), and *The Music of Morton Feldman* (1991).

Anne d'Harnoncourt is the director of the Philadelphia Museum of Art. She has written frequently on both Cage and Marcel Duchamp.

Peter Dickinson is a composer living in London. He was formerly Professor of Music at Keele University, where he started the Centre for American Music.

Henry Flynt is a composer/conceptual artist/economist living in New York. His early essays were collected in *Blueprint for a Higher Civilization* (1975).

Peggy Glanville-Hicks (1912–90) was a distinguished Australian composer who worked in America as both a writer and composer before returning to Australia.

Lou Harrison is a distinguished American composer who has known Cage since the late 1930s. He succeeded Paul Bowles as a music critic at the *New York Herald Tribune* in the mid-1940s.

Hans. G. Helms wrote *Fa:m' Ahniesgwow* (1958), a multilingual text, and other books of social criticism. Also the producer of a 1971 Westdeutscher Rundfunk documentary film about Cage, he lives in Köln.

John Hollander, professor of English at Yale University, has published several books of poetry in addition to criticism about literature and the relationships between literature and music.

Jill Johnston was the dance critic at the *Village Voice* in the 1960s; some of these reviews were collected as *Marmalade Me* (1971). She has recently been writing a multivolume autobiography that includes *Mother Bound* (1983).

Petr Kotik was born in Prague and came to the United States in 1969. Shortly afterward, he founded the S.E.M. Ensemble. Kotik has collaborated with John Cage since 1964. Presently he works and lives in New York City.

Jonathan Scott Lee is a professor of philosophy at Knox College in Galesburg, Ill.

Jackson Mac Low studied with John Cage in New York in the late 1950s and subsequently published books of poetry, plays, and experimental texts.

Roger Maren, a pianist and music writer, was until recently by trade a cabinetmaker in Hopewell, N.J.

Heinz-Klaus Metzger has, since the 1960s, been the most prolific German commentator on Cage's activities.

Michael Nyman is the composer of the opera *The Man Who Mistook His Wife for a Hat,* numerous soundtracks for Peter Greenway films, and *Six Celan Songs.* A sometime music critic, he wrote *Experimental Music: Cage and Beyond* (1974).

Manfredi Piccolomini teaches Italian at Lehman College of CUNY. He has written books of criticism in both English and Italian, the most recent being *The Brutus Revival* (1991).

Edward Rothstein, long the music critic of the *New Republic,* has recently become chief music critic of the *New York Times.* He is completing a book on music and mathematics.

Eric Salzman is a versatile composer and writer working particularly in musical theater. His books include several editions of *Twentieth-Century Music* (1967, 1974, 1988).

Natalie Crohn Schmidt is professor of theater at the Chicago campus of the University of Illinois. Her books include *Actors and Onlookers* (1990).

Stuart Saunders Smith is a composer/percussionist teaching at the University of Maryland in Baltimore County.

Ellsworth Snyder, formerly a professor of music at Milton College (now defunct), is an independent musician living in Madison, Wis.

James Tenney, an American composer teaching in Toronto, has been the subject of several retrospective concerts recently.

Virgil Thomson was a distinguished American composer and music critic.

Calvin Tomkins is a staff writer at the *New Yorker.* His classic 1964 profile of Cage was reprinted in his book, *The Bride and the Bachelors* (1965).

David Vaughan, born in London, England, residing in New York since 1950, has been associated with the Merce Cunningham Company in various capacities since the 1960s, presently as its archivist. He has written *Frederick Ashton and His Ballets* (1976).

Christian Wolff, a composer close to Cage for forty years, is also a professor of classics at Dartmouth College.

Peter Yates (1910–76) was the most persistent early critic of Cage's work, with reviews mostly published in California magazines. His *Twentieth-Century Music* appeared in 1967.

Paul Zukofsky, long a distinguished violinist, has recently been a conductor and music director in addition to producing records for his own label, CP 2.

Richard Kostelanetz (b. 1940) has written and edited scores of books of and about contemporary literature and art, including *Conversing with Cage* (Limelight, 1988) and *On Innovative Music(ian)s* (Limelight, 1989). As a composer he has been awarded annual Standards Awards from ASCAP; as a media artist he has received many grants and residencies for his work in radio, video, holography, and film. His visual art has been exhibited around the world. He lives in New York City.